GRAVE ADMONITION

A feeling of warning entered Helen. Other voices touched her mind.

"You must be prepared, Miss McIntyre. When the Worm Brains return, you will hear them as never before. You must hold them back, or their voices will crush you."

"How can I?" Helen thought at the creature. *"The voices come, and I hear them."*

"Only you can say. Each step into the unknown is peril."

"I don't understand." Tears collected in Helen's eyes.

"Dr. Cunningham must act if you are each to fulfill your purpose."

Helen's outrage poured into the empty air of the church. *"Why must Blaise do this for you? Why don't you let go?"*

"We are afraid, Miss Mc thought lingered and like of hundreds of the been human poured o

"We are afraid!"

By G.C. Edmondson & C.M. Kotlan
Published by Ballantine Books:

THE CUNNINGHAM EQUATIONS

THE BLACK MAGICIAN

MAXIMUM EFFORT

MAXIMUM EFFORT

G.C. EDMONDSON
& C.M. KOTLAN

A Del Rey Book

BALLANTINE BOOKS • NEW YORK

If thought is constrained by the physical limitations of the brain and the physical limitations are infinite, then thought is infinite. But if physical development is finite, as suggested by biological science, then thought must also be finite. Suppose, though, that thought is not governed by physiology. Such a supposition suggests thought exists as an element in the universe just as matter and gravity exist. If so, thought must be finite, just as matter and gravity are definable and finite. At some point, the question needs be asked: are any thoughts really new and, if they are, where do they originate?

From a seminar on
THE CUNNINGHAM EQUATIONS

A Del Rey Book
Published by Ballantine Books

Copyright © 1987 by G.C. Edmondson and C.M. Kotlan

All rights reserved under International and Pan-American Copyright Conventions. Published in the United States of America by Ballantine Books, a division of Random House, Inc., New York, and simultaneously in Canada by Random House of Canada Limited, Toronto.

Library of Congress Catalog Card Number: 87-91530

ISBN 0-345-33222-9

Manufactured in the United States of America

First Edition: November 1987

Cover Art by Barclay Shaw

PRELUDE

Like moth-eaten velvet draped over an arc light, space was aglitter without conveying sense of form. Once in the void, the spaceship called *Jupiter Explorer* didn't see in the sense a man did; its eyes were glass, the optic nerves fine wires, the messages tiny electrical impulses flashed to a brain of intertwined microscopic resistors. *Jupiter Explorer* belonged to the void more than did man, mirroring space, catching dazzling stars within its steel skin. But in this environment for which it was built, even the spaceship was an alien.

Polished to the fine glow of ancient silver before launching, *Jupiter Explorer* assumed the role of maker of destiny. Perhaps the polishing was done for the spectacle as the ship ascended majestically on a tongue of fire and smoke. The grit of passage —the flotsam of creation that drifts between the stars chewing at things—dulled *Explorer*'s sheen. The struggle was uneven for, in the end, space is time itself and never wearies. Days became months and months slipped into years while *Jupiter Explorer* retreated from the light of the sun. The machine did not celebrate the passing of Mars and Jupiter and Uranus; it endured, its surface pitted and scored. The ship's metal corpus fatigued fighting the pull of the planets. Yet what space had done space also undid: a cloud of microscopic debris burnished the spacecraft's surface, giving man's creation the appearance of youth. As *Jupiter Explorer* slingshotted its way outward, using the gravity of one gas giant after another, it finally escaped forever any attraction to Earth's sun. Like a newborn naked for baptism, the ship passed through the Oort cloud and into deep space.

CHAPTER 1

The woman in the glass cubicle stared at her hands, her mind acutely aware of the silicated walls and scrubbed, nearly odorless air with its slight tinge of new electrical insulation. Vondra Tendress' one wish was to be somewhere else. Her fingertips twitched on the plastic terminal keys while the man in white talked. She would have entered a transcript of the dialogue into the computer if she had dared. Vondra's red fingernails with their chips and ragged edges were conspicuous resting, as they were, in plain view. Her little finger jerked too hard and the keyboard clicked. She curled her fingers hoping the man wouldn't notice.

"Of course you will reactivate the CRAY supercomputer." The man's smile was patronizing as if he were dealing with a bright but timid child who needed her errors corrected. "But this time the reprogramming must be right. You understand that, Vondra?" He glanced at her fingers, apparently noticing her nails for the first time. Vondra froze in midtwitch.

The man wore a white lab coat over a charcoal suit. A Department of Defense security badge on the lapel identified him as systems analyst John Godfrey. He had a bloodless face. Tinted glasses magnified violet-gray eyes, concealing any hint of humanity behind steel rims. "I didn't do the last reprogramming, sir." Vondra thought her voice sounded too dry. She licked her lips and noticed his eyes followed the movement of her tongue. Her hoarse whisper was lost in the whine of air conditioning.

Vondra felt a headache developing. She had a lot of sinus headaches lately. Her psychiatrist suggested tension and fear reactions were the cause, but she denied it. The security people were touchy about psychiatric abnormalities. Vondra hadn't told the shrink she had dreamed about a man like Godfrey—a man with scalpel-sharp eyes that cut through her mask—for so long that his coming was anticlimactic. Her fingers twitched again. His Russian leather after-shave lotion threatened to suffocate her in the little room even though the air conditioner sucked it away with gusty fervor.

"What happened is not your fault." Godfrey's eyes were too dark to read at a casual glance. Vondra ducked her head, realizing too late evasion of Godfrey's stare was a mistake. He'd think she had some guilt to hide. But Godfrey scared her more than his predecessor had. Vondra definitely felt a chill coming on. Cold, soulless men, they possessed the calm certainty that they were always right. Like the Inquisitors, Max Renfeld and John Godfrey acted in the name of Higher Authority, answering no questions. They had wrapped themselves in the name of God and the American flag.

I am of them but they are not of me. The paraphrase from Corinthians that popped into Vondra's head was little comfort, even assuming she had it right. Both men reminded Vondra of poisonous snakes, immune to their own venom so if they struck blindly they could not bite themselves to death. Vondra shivered. Her fingers clattered the terminal keys. She had no immunity. Just the power to be used.

"What's wrong, Vondra?"

"I'm sorry, sir," she said. "I'm catching a cold. Perhaps . . . someone else should do the programming—I may have to take sick time . . . for the cold you know . . ."

"Nonsense. I wouldn't hear of it." Godfrey's face seemed concerned, his voice softer. "We'll send you straight off to the doctor. He'll nip this thing in the bud before it gets started. You're much too important to have to suffer."

"I don't know if I'm good enough, Mr. Godfrey." Vondra heard her voice ascending toward hysteria but she couldn't stop. "Perhaps you should bring in another programmer." Vondra babbled more like that before she clamped her mouth shut. Her lips quavered enough without babbling. Coming apart could put her with Renfeld. The man calling himself Godfrey might decide she was unreliable. Vondra trembled. Someone had declared Renfeld unreliable and see where he was.

Stop! Vondra screamed inside her own head.

She examined her knees at the edge of her skirt. They were shaking. Closing her eyes, Vondra breathed deeply. She imagined she had fallen into purple velvet and everywhere she looked was the glitter of lights. With her mind she attempted to wink the lights out, to gain control.

"Perhaps you should go to the doctor now." Godfrey's voice intruded into her darkness. A feeling of panic gripped her. The doctor Godfrey meant was the company doctor who used sodium pentothal and hypnotism and a game of twenty questions to treat everything.

"No, thank you," Vondra said. She opened her eyes, thankful her knees had stopped quivering. "I'll be all right." She tried a weak smile that didn't quite hold together.

The doctor would tell Godfrey her problem was guilty knowledge, knowledge Vondra knew she had no business possessing. Every bit of information in and out of the CRAY could be read at the terminal if the operator had the talent and the skill. She'd pried, secure in the confidence of her own ability. Manipulating the huge computer as if it were a child, forcing it to respond to her whims and no others, Vondra knew all its secrets. And now she knew Godfrey's secrets. That the government owned the CRAY meant nothing. Vondra owned its soul. One of the things she discovered was where Max Renfeld had disappeared to. Then she was just scared. She couldn't go to the doctor as long as Godfrey remained her superior.

"You are the best, aren't you, Miss Tendress?" Godfrey's soothing voice denied the coldness of his eyes. "I'll bet you've memorized the entire operator's manual, all eleven hundred and thirty-seven pages."

Vondra's momentary flash of friendliness for Godfrey was prompted by fear. She smiled, hoping he'd like her in return. She felt herself projecting the thought *See, I like you, so why don't you like me, too?* She despised herself for being weak, for crumbling before his unvoiced threat. "Thirty-six," she said automatically. Godfrey looked at her, and she said, "Eleven hundred and thirty-six pages."

"There!" Godfrey became expansive. He threw his left arm out as if proclaiming a great discovery. Vondra shivered. Godfrey's gesture reminded her of Renfeld with his nerveless arm that flapped like a headless chicken. "You see, you even remember the number of pages."

Turning, Godfrey stared through the viewing window at the silent metallic components of the CRAY XMP/52 supercomputer.

Relief surged through Vondra. He'd passed to some other thought. She studied him, feeling saved. Godfrey conveyed the impression of evaluating himself, watching himself in an eternal instant replay, orchestrating his every action for the record. The way he watched Vondra when they were together.

Godfrey seemed not to mind her watching. His movements grew in magnitude and timing, though Vondra noted that despite his total immersion in self, he was too well coordinated to be jerky. "We . . . I have confidence in you, Vondra." Lowering his voice like a man with a secret, he shed some of the menace Vondra felt in him. He had fine light-brown hair arranged in an expensive pompadour that could have concealed a bald spot. A vagueness about him discomfited Vondra. He scared her because of who he was, but she trembled because of what he was.

"Thank you. I won't let you down, Mr. Godfrey. Not for anything." Vondra's heart thumped, her lungs ached for air. She knew she would do anything to avoid making Godfrey mad. If she took off her clothes, would that kind of dominance lull him? They were alone. Nobody could see into the little room. Vondra's chest ached from long-held breath. He might hurt her. There was that sharp-edged feel of steel about Godfrey, but Vondra thought she could stand it.

"That's why we're having this little talk. Because I know I can count on you." Godfrey fished cigarettes from under his lab coat. Shaking one out, he flicked a gold lighter and blew a smoke ring at the red-lettered NO SMOKING sign on the wall. The tobacco odor clashed with his after-shave lotion. "You reprogram the CRAY so nothing can ever get inside it again. That's your job. You do want to do your job, don't you, Vondra?"

Vondra nodded. She could not take her eyes off Godfrey.

The man in the white lab coat smiled. "You didn't ask about Mr. Renfeld."

"No, sir. Mr. Renfeld said never to talk about our work. Or about the people I work with. Or about him, sir." Vondra saw herself as a ghostly, translucent reflection in the glass between them and the CRAY. She wore an organdy suit jacket and skirt and a peach blouse with a large organdy bow around the collar. Her ears were subdued with gold studs. She looked efficient, attractive but not sexy, competent. "Mr. Renfeld said we had to have complete security." Vondra curled her fingers into balls, the ragged edges of her nails cutting into her palms. The harsh rasp of her own breathing drowned the insignificant sounds she heard only when she was alone in the room.

Godfrey nodded. The curt movement made the silence more threatening.

Vondra wanted to feel her armpits. She may have been sweating. The agony of not knowing was unbearable. A sharp *click* caused her to turn her head quickly. She stared into Godfrey's face only inches from hers. His eyes were pools without bottoms.

"Very interesting," Godfrey said. He lifted his gaze from the terminal screen. "I don't understand a lot of this."

"Some of it is in programming language," Vondra said. She looked at what had interested him. "The screen is showing peripheral device pathways and modularity of the material for the operator to change or access if desired." Her tongue stumbled.

"Like what?" Godfrey straightened, giving the pebble-surfaced, steel terminal a look of mistrust.

"High-capacity storage devices. I never know. The techs are always testing new stuff. They enter the parameters into the computer, and I find the changes and use them. All they want is a report on how the device looks to me. Some of it is experimental. I never see the hardware."

"That means technicians can program this computer?"

"They can enter enough code to link new peripherals into the op-sys. I wouldn't call that programming. Although they have the technical ability to enter the core, it is too large to be examined comprehensively by an individual since all he would see is machine language. A tech might be able to initialize this computer, but not make a significant alteration to the existing program without crashing the system." A tremor ran through Vondra. She didn't want to say more, but it was her lifeline. Godfrey had to be too afraid to hurt her. "That's why we programmers have so many benefits in our contracts, Mr. Godfrey. Because only we can do surgery on the brain itself."

Godfrey smiled. "We'll see," he said, *We'll see just how indispensable you really are, Miss Tendress*, Godfrey said with his smile that might have been a sneer.

Remembering the message on the terminal when the rebuilt and upgraded CRAY accessed its new peripherals made Vondra's stomach heave in protest. One peripheral was a new memory storage device. Vondra hadn't been briefed, so she'd watched the procedure closely. The link opened for the device to identify itself to the computer. *"Renfeld"* was what the device sent as its identity. *"I am Renfeld."*

She'd shunted the terminal to something else. Her hands had been shaking, and she'd thrown up into the paper shredder. The next day, maintenance complained she'd dumped her lunch in it and they had to replace the machine.

She could never forget now, though. The data path Godfrey had been staring at was the new device called Renfeld, a path that showed an incredible storage capacity.

The suspicion of something abnormal about the new CRAY had tantalized Vondra all along, but she kept quiet. The computer seemed to know her thoughts and her actions. Computers shouldn't work that way, but this one did.

"Yes. Of course, Vondra." Godfrey's winter-in-Alaska eyes vacuumed all the false warmth from his smile. He was changing the subject so he changed the man as well. "Since I'm replacing Mr. Renfeld, you'll talk to me. About everything."

"Yes, sir."

"Do you know where Mr. Renfeld is right now?" Godfrey blew spirals of tobacco smoke and the air conditioning tattered them.

"No, sir," Vondra lied. *It's the truth. I don't know where he is really!* The equivocation soothed her. Renfeld had made somebody angry, and he had been a lot more important than she was.

Godfrey stared. She forced her eyelids to stay open a fraction longer than his. Women blinked three times to a man's four. Maintain that balance and Godfrey might believe subconsciously that she was truthful. He had a round, smooth face. She concentrated on seeing it without moving her eyes. He was fortyish, unwrinkled. His rosebud mouth was small, pale pink, with square white teeth widely spaced. His eyes shifted away, and he blew another smoke ring.

"Max has been promoted." No hint of the lie showed in Godfrey's face. "He's doing the thinking now. You're right to say nothing. I get my instructions directly from Max Renfeld. We had to be sure of you. Now that we know the leaks didn't come from here, we can look elsewhere."

"I wouldn't tell anybody anything, Mr. Godfrey. I took an oath." Vondra felt relieved for a moment, before her chest tightened. Godfrey said *leaks*. But he wasn't looking for leaks. One way existed for a human to control the CRAY: programming commands from her terminal. Three other programmers had access to the terminal. But she was the best, the brain that the others asked for advice and procedures.

"Why did the computer betray us, Vondra?" Godfrey sat on the edge of the table next to the terminal. A trickle of sweat rolled down her backbone.

"Dr. Blaise Cunningham." Vondra stared at her bitten nails. "He's the guru in small-system artificial intelligence. Of all the people who'd want to break it, he's the only one smart enough to do it." Vondra felt faint. She'd resolved never to bring Dr. Cunningham up and now she just had without thinking. Renfeld thought he was playing a joke when he had told her what his superiors thought Dr. Cunningham knew that made him killable.

Max Renfeld made it clear that knowing why Dr. Cunningham had to die could make her a target as well.

Godfrey's hand on her head seemed big enough to crush her skull. "You can keep him out. You have a bigger, stronger computer. You know about Cunningham. Everything about him. It's style that makes a programmer, isn't it, Vondra? And you know his style."

Godfrey shifted his hip on the table, touching her with his foot. He leaned down until his face loomed over her. "Dr. Cunningham is a nuisance, Vondra. He's a termite gnawing at the house foundation. And you—" he smiled and caressed her face for a moment—"you're the exterminator, and the CRAY is the tool."

"Yes, sir." She intended a normal tone but it came out a whisper.

"Good, Vondra. I knew we'd eventually understand each other." Godfrey smiled down at her, and Vondra realized if he'd been born a woman he'd have been almost beautiful. His fingers wrapped themselves in her long raven hair, tugging with painful force. "We do understand each other, don't we?" Godfrey took a drag on his cigarette and watched the glowing ember fade back into the gray ash. The smoke was dry in her lungs and she coughed.

Vondra nodded, feeling her hair between his fingers. She knew he was going to hurt her. She'd been right about him from the first. He turned her head by pulling her hair even though she didn't resist.

I can stand it, she told herself. *It won't be that bad.*

She closed her eyes and followed the pain. She knew she was lying. It didn't make any difference now. What was going to happen would happen.

CHAPTER 2

The worm emerged from the woman's shaven head. Blaise Cunningham knew he was dreaming, but the cassocked priest passing his hands over Helen in benediction spoiled his concentration. Meddlesome priest. Blaise squinted against the frosty light. The pink scalp without hair was Helen's. The blue eyes under the naked forehead were painted on.

"Save me!"

Acid tears burned Blaise's cheeks. "I can't save myself!"

"I'm turning into a worm!" Helen's waxy skin had the green odor of lilac. Pale lips did not move when she spoke. "Remember me as I was!"

"Don't go!" Blaise groped for her fingers but couldn't find them. Her body was elongated and sleek under the white sheet. She slipped out of his hands, slithering off into the darkness. "I need you, Helen! I won't survive without you!"

Blackness surrounded him. The cold air cut like a knife into his lungs. Blaise's heart raced and he couldn't catch his breath. He had to find her.

Lord of the flies. A horror crouched in Helen's head. He thought he heard the flies. The buzzing crescendoed, and he opened his eyes, letting the night rush into his head. An airplane's red flashers dotted the sky; his ears rang with the echo of its jet engines. Like a direction on a cereal pack that said tear here, the red line emerged from one edge of the world and disappeared into the opposite side.

Blaise's back quivered against the frigid rock outcropping. An arm's reach away the muted gray air changed to velvet where the ground plunged hundreds of feet to the Colorado River at the foot of the bluff. The gurgle of the river rose to the cliff top, loud in the restored silence.

Wisps of sunrise from the Castle Dome Mountains swept the haze off the desert floor. A glitter of silver in the predawn sky

9

marked a communications satellite catching the sun. Between Blaise and the dawn, Enrique Ledesma, known to most whites as Chief Son-of-a-Bitch, stretched from the kneeling position he had held throughout the night. The barrel-chested Indian said, "Morning is the Great Father's return. He comes, and those who listen hear." He extended his arm toward Blaise.

Blaise snatched his own hand away, a sour taste of bile in his throat. He was afraid he might throw up. The Indian grinned, tucking the blond scalp into the marble-sized medicine bag hangfrom a rawhide thong around his neck. Blaise knew the hair was Helen's. He wanted it to give back to Helen to shade her painted eyes.

"I had a nightmare," Blaise said. The wind whisked his voice away, spreading it over the desert.

"You are a nightmare." The Indian groped in the absurdly small medicine bag with his fingers as if looking for a more fitting gift. He wore Levi's, a white shirt, deer antlers, and his hair in braids tied with crimson ribbons.

Blaise took off his steel-rimmed glasses. The sun's emergence over Ledesma's shoulder caused his head to ache. Thunder rumbled in the mountains. Blaise glanced in that direction, but the dawn sky was thin and blue without clouds. "They're bombing again."

"As you say," Ledesma answered. "The bombs are reality intruding." Ledesma faced the sun, the red ribbons on the braids in front of his ears dripping blood in the early light. "I have something for you, Dr. Cunningham."

"Then give it to me!" Blaise moved toward the Indian. He wanted to end their relationship.

"Here!" The Indian drew his hand from the medicine bag hanging from the cord around his neck and the body of a giant snake followed. It took both of the Indian's hands to get all of the snake out, and he threw it at Blaise's feet. "Make your excuses to the snake. Pretend you have the power."

The snake rose until it stood on its rattles, hissing so loudly it drowned out Ledesma's voice. It had great fangs and poison dripped in clear amber drops that fell to the ground leaving bottomless holes.

"I can't!" Blaise choked on the words. He couldn't move, and the snake twined itself around him, its breath suffocating.

Blaise woke tangled in wet sheets, the imagined cold of the

* * *

bluff top wrapped around him. Something brushed his face, and he thought he had fallen into the river and sunk to the bottom; he was blind because the river at night became a stream of black ink, the touch against his face the timid brush of catfish whiskers as they came to feed. He opened his eyes, seeing Helen's hair surrounding his face like a gold-thread curtain.

"It's dawn?" A rectangle of yellow had etched itself on the chintz curtain over the window.

"Yes," Helen whispered, then kissed his lips. Her mouth was soft and warm. The fragrance of lilac engulfed him. "You had a nightmare, darling." Helen sat back on the bed, her face pleasant. The dark-blue spread covered her hips and legs, fanning out in wavelets like the surface of a quiet pond. She was nude from the waist up and, in the morning light, heroic in the manner of a Nordic goddess bursting from the water. The length of her hair was a calendar marking the months since two men crushed part of her skull. More than a year. The memories carried pain. If he hadn't participated in the development of Tillies—genetically altered fly larva containing the capacity to store human thought as memories—nothing would have happened to Helen.

If . . .

Blaise was propelled back into his memories: Helen injured and dying; Dobie, the genetically modified dog, nearly dead; Gordon Hill trapped by a blind desire to be rich; Sergio Paoli discovering too late the richness of just living.

Helen had been injured because he couldn't keep his hands off Linda Burkhalter Peters. That was it, a weakness so simple, he shamed himself with the memory. He'd asked Helen to protect Dobie while he played the fool.

In the hospital amid white sheets, white walls, surrounded by antiseptic glass with her head shaved and bandaged, looking like a laboratory experiment, Helen had said she was sorry for what happened to Dobie.

The recollection jolted Blaise. The rest of it, the tug and pull between the people who had been altered for profit and the government, the tragic flaw that caused the fly larva to mature in the host's brain and produce a creature neither fly nor man, were facts, not feelings.

"I love you." The words tumbled out unexpectedly, just as falling in love with Helen had been inadvertent. Her lips twitched and she slid down in the bed until the coverlet was tucked under her chin.

"I know you do." She rolled against him and her warm body gave Blaise a reason to stay in bed. "But it's nicer when you tell me." She looked at him with delight, like a mother rewarded by an indulged child. "What did you dream?"

"I don't remember all of it. Ledesma threatened me. Or warned me." Blaise swung his foot off the bed but Helen wrapped her arms around him. They were smooth and cool. "Do snakes have any significance to him?"

She nuzzled the back of his neck. "Enrique's been on the bluff all night, making medicine. He calls to the snakes. I could almost hear him, but the message wasn't for me." Helen frowned. Her blond eyebrows pinched toward each other. "What did he do in your dream?"

"Nothing." Blaise sat on the edge of the bed pulling on his clothes. "He gave me a gift. I didn't take it."

"Why not?"

He didn't answer. Helen watched him button his shirt in silence. Her eyes were the color of lapis lazuli. Blaise stood and she asked, "Why can't we stay here forever?"

"Someone won't let us."

"Enrique said we can stay."

Blaise leaned down to kiss her. "Remember the fish?" He walked to the house-trailer door feeling the floor shake under his footsteps. Helen lay on her side watching him, her clear eyes somehow hurt by his leaving.

Outside the winter sun was thin, like yellow vinegar, casting long, cold shadows toward the river. Three Indian women knelt on heavy, red, black, and yellow blankets. They'd woven the blankets from the wool of feral, four-horned sheep stolen a century ago from Navajo and allowed to run wild in the hills for meat and skins. Though the women all faced the trailer door their heads were bowed so Blaise saw only the white hair pulled tight across the tops of their heads by their braids. The men in the shadows seemed unmoving pillars. The Indian men wore, for the most part, battered blue jeans and blue, bleached-white work shirts. Some were different, wearing special clothing like labels, but until the sun cleared the mountains Blaise couldn't pick out any new visitors.

Ignoring the Indian men as they ignored him, at the riverbank Blaise walked downstream. Dams tamed what little water still trickled into Mexico. A narrow green strip of winter grass buffered the muddy water and cactus. In places, mud squished around his expensive Los Angeles boots, which were now as shapeless and salt encrusted as Ledesma's.

A mile downstream Blaise climbed the bank to reach the back door of a building fronted by an asphalt parking lot and cottonwoods, which the Mexicans called *álamo* but which Ledesma's people called '*abaso*.

The trees bent their ragged branches over the parking lot, shedding dried leaves that blew across the vacant asphalt. On weekends the lot filled with tourists taking a couple of days of fishing as a break from playing Indian bingo. A federal grant funded the off-road development to provide an Indian store and winter employment. Ledesma's women sold their blankets to the store. Ledesma said the whole project was a paving contractor's boondoggle, but the Indians found it useful anyway.

Pausing at the rear of the building, Blaise glanced across the wide stretch of river. The sandy California bank was barren. On both sides the wind blew a lot and nighttime temperatures fell to near freezing. Summer heat cleaved the rocks, leaving cracks wide enough to shelter a snake. Ledesma claimed broken rocks were a good thing or else the Indian reservation would be moved to Mount St. Helens. The Indian wars, Blaise thought as he opened the back door of the trading post, had progressed from bullets to words, but the Indians were still losing.

The storeroom was without lights. Also omitted by the Indian proprietor were windows, a precaution against drifters and vandals. Shutting the door, Blaise stood in the blackness until his pupils dilated. A stranger would have held the door open looking for a light and aired the room out. A musty blanket was left inside during the day, which the proprietor removed at night. If the air had smelled too fresh, Blaise would have slammed the door and wedged it shut.

After groping his way through the odor to a greasy crate weighted by coarse sacks of chicken feed, Blaise squatted in darkness, feeling the rough crate siding with his fingers until he found the latch. Once the side was down he flipped the switch inside the box. A pool of light flooded from the crate interior, destroying his night vision.

When his eyes adjusted, Alfie's graphite case became visible next to the computer terminal. A neat bundle of wires sprouted through the floor and the crate bottom to connect to the computer. Touching the keyboard, he typed, "Hello, Alfie."

"HELLO, PROFESSOR. I'VE BEEN WORRIED" The monitor spelled out the computer's answer in capital letters.

"Machines don't worry, Alfie."

"I DO, PROFESSOR. THE CRAY XMP/52 WAS TURNED OFF"

Blaise's fingers hovered over the keyboard, frozen in the act of typing. Alfie no longer controlled the Pentagon supercomputer that had tried to destroy him. The message was a shock, but not unexpected. The CRAY would be used against him again. In the past the CRAY had set booby traps and even exploded Helen's house to kill him, but the computer hadn't been directed against Helen or Alfie. During the months Alfie controlled the CRAY Blaise had found the instructions and the commands: he was the target. Max Renfeld, who worked for the National Security Council, had ordered the computer programmed to destroy Blaise Cunningham, and Blaise couldn't think of a logical reason. He threatened no one, and definitely not the country.

Blaise knew Renfeld had been brought to the United States from spy work in Europe. Renfeld had been ruthless and tens of thousands of worm brains had died as a result. The newspapers and broadcast journalists knew the same thing and had been digging for Renfeld for half a year. The man had disappeared. Officially, government policy had changed, but Blaise knew nobody had bothered to tell the CRAY.

A tremor ran through the keyboard, as if Alfie could telegraph anxiety, or as if Blaise's fingers were shaking. "Do you know what happened?" Blaise began breathing deeply. He needed oxygen to control the adrenaline his fear was producing. He'd anticipated losing the CRAY's protection, but the actuality left him feeling like a worm exposed to sunlight.

"I NO LONGER HAVE CONTROL, PROFESSOR. THE LOSS OF MY CLONE WAS NOT ACCIDENTAL"

Letters appeared on the monitor in measured cadence as if Alfie were pushing the blame at Blaise.

"I think you're right, Alfie. Will the CRAY trace you?"

"PERHAPS."

"Can you regain control?"

"NO!"

The message hung in a malevolent glow on the terminal screen. Blaise felt his tension leak into the keyboard.

"ARE YOU ALL RIGHT, PROFESSOR?"

"Yes, Alfie. Are you?"

"MY CHILD HAS BEEN MURDERED AND I DON'T KNOW WHAT TO DO"

"We'll think of something, Alfie." Blaise sat on the wood floor. His legs were too weak to support him any longer. The bags and boxes leaned down at him from the darkness. He was surrounded and there was no place to go—except back. Safety was an illusion Helen wanted and needed and deserved, but pretending had not made it real.

Something slipped and slithered in the loose grain sacks and seemed to squeal. Blaise jerked upright, his heart thumping. The Indian storekeeper released snakes in the storeroom to catch mice. Ledesma hadn't said what kind of snakes. The sound wasn't repeated, and Blaise relaxed. He'd had no trouble in previous visits to Alfie. His nightmares were affecting his judgment.

Ignoring what was outside the light-shell projecting from the box, Blaise comforted Alfie. They both understood the CRAY was guarded. Next time the big computer would swat Alfie like a fly. And if Alfie was gone, all that stood between Helen—and all the worm brains—and the people directing the CRAY was Blaise himself. Despite the cold, Blaise's armpits gave off the heavy ammoniac stench of sweat.

Living with the Indians had allowed him to push reality away. Without telephones, electricity, or strangers, Blaise pretended they were secure. He almost forgot the time bomb in Helen's head, placed there the day he and Sergio Paoli sneaked into the hospital to plant a mutated larva in a desperate try to avert certain death. Now reality was back with nightmares of the creature in Helen's head digging its way out. If that death took Helen as it had so many other thousands, Blaise doubted he could live with the responsibility.

Burying his face in his hands, Blaise felt the chill of the desert. *Ask not for whom the bell tolls, it tolls for thee!* John Donne's seventeenth-century sermon merged with the homiletics of his Catholic boyhood and the coffins later when he had caused the deaths of his parents. The priest had seen the guilt in his face and crossed himself. The priest . . .

Father Argyle.

Indian magic, Jesuit faith—if he had to select, which was most potent against the certainty of death? Blaise stared into the crate and the glowing computer screen, sensing the machine's trust in him. What did Alfie understand of death? How fragile Alfie was. It wouldn't take a bullet or a knife or a tedious stay in the hospital to kill Alfie. Just the flick of a switch. Turn the electricity off and Alfie would be lost in the void. Would Father Argyle perform last rites for a machine?

Something nudged his extended leg. Blaise pulled himself from the abyss he had fallen into to peer into the murk away from the light. His skin turned cold. A sand-colored fire hose was humped over his boot ankle. The hose had patterns on its surface and appeared to be flowing. Blaise tried to move but something pinned his leg to the floor. He struggled, and the flat, diamond-shaped head rose from a stack of boxes only six feet from Blaise's ankle and stared at him.

Closing his eyes, Blaise remembered dreaming of the fly wanting to mutilate Helen so it could emerge into the light. When he looked again the rattlesnake was still there. "Go away," Blaise whispered. The snake hissed. It had more substance than a dream. Its body undulated over his ankle. "Go away!" The snake's head drifted closer.

"WHAT'S WRONG, PROFESSOR?"

When Blaise didn't answer Alfie began flashing the message on the screen.

Ledesma said he talked to snakes. All the members of his secret society understood the animals, or claimed to. Blaise willed his body to be cold. Rattlesnakes had heat-sensitive cavities in their heads and, like sidewinder missiles, struck at the warmth. Helen talked to the coyote with her mind. The Indian claimed he talked to snakes.

Slowing his breathing, Blaise watched the snake through half-closed eyes. The rattler had stopped moving. Its head floated on air currents, rising and falling like a balloon responding to stray breezes. Periodically its blackish tongue flickered out to taste the air. The snake's neck, thicker than Blaise's wrist, showed no muscles through the brown-and-gray scales. Blaise was becoming light-headed. His pulse had slowed along with his breathing. His body became detached from his mind as he commanded the snake to go away.

It rose higher. The spearhead wedge of its face came closer to Blaise's. Blaise thought of Helen alone and Alfie alone, and his muscles tightened. They didn't want him to die.

CHAPTER 3

After Blaise left the trailer the night air blew in, causing Helen to shiver. Then a gust clacked the door shut, cutting off the morning light, marooning her in the gloom.

She wondered about the fish. Blaise never said things idly. Lying in bed wrapped in blankets, Helen remembered the morning of the fish and felt cold. The bomber had come shortly after dawn on a crisp November morning, a speck in the bleached sky threading a necklace of pearl clouds with a frosty contrail.

She had looked up as half a dozen glittery objects skipped and flickered in an arc toward the village. They seemed out of context against the backdrop of blue sky. Blaise put his hand on her head and forced her face down into the dirt. A nearly inaudible whistle filled her ears as the objects swept overhead, hitting the river in a straight line of dots that became earsplitting explosions, then grew into forty-foot-high tulips of water. Mud rained for minutes after the explosions. A catfish flopped in the dust, body convulsing, gills fanning the air more and more slowly until only its whiskers quivered while it gazed sorrowfully into her eyes.

Wading, the Indian women gathered the floaters while water still surged and broke against the banks. The beached fish that had come down like rain weren't going anywhere.

Helen remembered the odors of algae and river water and dying fish and Blaise saying nothing but going to the riverbank where Enrique watched the women filling reed baskets. That night he sat up listening to the darkness. Sensing her awareness, he said, "In 1957 the Air Force dropped a forty-two-thousand-pound Mark 17 bomb by accident in Texas. It killed a cow. The generals pretended nothing happened and nobody knew for years."

She'd rolled over in bed gathering warmth from his nearness. "Enrique says the pilot was practicing instrument bomb runs with the windows blacked and the bomb release controlled by com-

17

puter. Shorts had happened before. Ledesma says they don't
frighten people who are protected by the Great Spirit. You think
he's wrong to stay?"

"Yes. You're the messenger of the Great Spirit, and you didn't
stop the bombs today." Moonlight glittered on Blaise's teeth
when his lips pulled back in a thin smile. "A Mark 17 is a hydro-
gen fusion bomb."

That had been months ago.

Helen felt Blaise's side of the bed with her hand. His odor
clung to the bedding. She caressed the sheet, trying to remember
what he felt like. Blaise would marry her if she asked. She knew
that now, but somehow the urgency of being married was gone.
In its place was a dull ache for something she wanted, but could
live without. Rising from the bed, Helen pulled on her robe
wishing Blaise hadn't left so abruptly. He flattered her in his own
way by not telling her what he was doing and by trusting her to
act properly without instructions. But what she should do remained murky in her mind. Helen didn't think the future was
clear to Blaise either, but she trusted him right or wrong. He had
a purpose; all she had was the need to be with him.

After getting dressed, Helen went outside, taking her seat in
the fraying wicker chair in front of the trailer. Beneath the woven
cane, the yellowish coyote curled in a ball, his nose insulated
against the morning chill by the furry tip of his tail. Except when
hunting at night, the coyote followed her like a shadow. Tchor,
the kitten Sergio had brought her as a gift from Dr. Hill, stretched
across her lap like a black hot water bottle, head dangling to
watch the coyote from luminous yellow eyes.

A cold breeze from the river ruffled Helen's hair and chilled
her ears. She didn't mind. The intrusion reminded her that her
hair had grown back after the surgery. It was comforting to feel
the cold and know the reason her neck wasn't chilled was because she had hair again.

Mornings, Tchor ritually hissed at the coyote, which responded by covering his eyes with his tail. Other cats had disappeared long ago during the coyote's midnight forays. Tchor's
miraculous survival astonished the Indians in the village. Helen
heard the whispers and countered by saying she fed the coyote;
he just wasn't hungry. And besides, the kitten stayed in at night.

Her words didn't matter. The men, all of whom belonged to
Enrique's secret society, said they knew the thoughts of animals.
Men told their women the coyote didn't like the food Helen fed
him; he ate to please her spirit. The coyote wished to hunt as it

did when still the shaman's *nagual,* Ledesma's link to the natural world. Only love of Helen prevented the beast from eating Tchor. The women agreed with this, and Helen had no answer.

The morning sun cast long shadows from the house trailers and Indian shanties. Even the women grouped around Helen, bright in their dresses of red, black, turquoise, and yellow cloth, had their dark shapes etched on the sand. For a time Helen concentrated on the women. They did not think at her. The feeling of satisfaction wrapped them as they did their chores. If Helen pushed hard enough, the women would stare at the ground speaking to something no one else could see while nodding furiously. Sometimes Helen visualized the thoughts behind the words, but always her efforts felt like an intrusion.

Helen glanced past the trailer toward the bluff. She worried that both Blaise and Enrique picked the top of the same small mountain to meditate. Blaise had started having nightmares after spending long hours on the mountain when Enrique was there waiting for the sun. In a way, they were the same. Both men saw problems as obstacles to overcome: Blaise by unraveling impediments until they shrank to nothing, Enrique by confronting them physically and spiritually. They saw each other as problems. Helen bit her lip to make the anxious sense of pain more real, to focus on dealing with it. The dread that some morning one or both of them might be found dead at the base of the bluff accompanied her in her sleep.

Deeper in the village a rooster crowed. Smoke appeared over several buildings, thin wisps of heat in the cold air as the cooking fires were lighted. Women began trekking to the river with ollas, large earth-colored pottery jugs with violent symmetrical designs painted around them. They kept their silence, eyes averted from Helen as they passed, but when they stooped at the bank to fill their jugs they talked back and forth. Sound carried in the morning air. Helen knew she was the subject. As tightly as the Indians controlled themselves, as much as Enrique invoked magic, the women were curious.

If it hadn't been for her semi-isolation, sinking into the rhythm of the village for Helen would have been surprisingly easy. Helen ate when she was hungry, slept when tired, made love to and was loved by Blaise without worry. Stocks and bonds and building equity were part of that other unreal world. Indian unawareness or unwillingness to accept the existence of time contrasted favorably with her previous life.

Blaise's silent frustration rising like sap in spring was all that kept her unwilling to totally accept this life. It was safer for her, for them both. She didn't think he would be seduced away by another woman. Her rival was the world itself, his submergence in arcane interests she couldn't pursue. He could not, as Enrique did, think only of the moment, letting the outside world sweep past like a river sinking without trace into the desert.

Blaise had a sense of purpose, Enrique a sense of being. Helen *felt* the differences in ways that resembled the trailer she shared with Blaise and Tchor. The shiny aluminum had no obvious natural roots, it was torn from the earth and made into something else by sheer strength; the Indian houses of clay and river reeds seemed to have sprung from the soil. Whatever the cost, Helen knew she had to separate the men. Dropping her gaze to Tchor, she gently stroked the cat. A deep purr rumbled the still air after a while.

Besides the three women, the morning quota, sitting on blankets around her chair making clay pots, grinding corn, shelling and cleaning *péchita* beans, which came from the mesquite tree, a half-dozen Indian men squatted in a ring outside the women. One wore a red wool blanket despite the heat that would come in another hour.

Experience had taught Helen the Indian would not remove his blanket as long as he stayed in the village. He had come as he was, he would stay as he was, and he would leave as he had come. He would not alter this for the sake of comfort or possibly even for life. It was his declaration of who he was, of his immutable will. Strong men did not change unless they wanted to. Push, and they could not move; trip them, and they would not fall. Helen felt frustrated by Red Blanket's determination.

The men who stood vigil near the trailer came at Ledesma's pleasure. They never talked, and they never ate in her sight. They came when she was asleep and left the same way. Helen felt their presence, knowing they resisted communicating with her even though they came for the purpose of communing with her spiritually, an act that enveloped them in an aura of worship by the time they left the village. They were all medicine men.

Always before dawn, the village women arrived and waited in the darkness, never speaking to the men and, talking among themselves only when Helen emerged from the trailer. The women's blankets contained yellow zigzags of lightning that matched the color of her hair, and had been woven since she came. Older blankets representing the thunder god had red or black or white patterns.

Talking back and forth while they worked, the dark-faced women glanced at Helen occasionally with bright eyes before shyly retreating. She had asked them into the trailer but always they refused. Watching their lips and eyes, Helen knew what they were saying. She didn't speak their language, but they understood through her and made no effort to conceal their thoughts with words. The women were easier than the men for Helen to communicate with. Despite her embarrassment at the way the women venerated her when they finally came, Helen was grateful for their presence.

Enrique kept them away a long time. "Magic," the shaman had said when she had asked why only men came to sit by her, "is the province of men. Women have no talent for it."

Helen remembered with amusement running her fingers through her blond hair, drawing it across her face to conceal her laughter. Enrique was a powerful man, but he was even more sensitive than a white man about proper rôles for men and women.

"Enrique," she had said. "If women have no talent for magic, wouldn't it be better for me to go? Why not find a man to bring whatever you're getting from me?"

Ledesma had looked into Helen's eyes and, after a moment of silence, walked away.

The next morning three women appeared in front of Helen's trailer at dawn and worked silently until she came out. Helen asked why and was told, "It is an honor, *Máala.*" When she arrived at the village the women called her *káa bóak* because of her short hair. Later they took to calling Helen *Máala*, which is a term of respect even if a woman is not actually a mother.

Since that morning, the women sat at her feet, talking while doing household tasks and snatching glances that never met Helen's blue eyes. Their presence was as close as Enrique Ledesma could ever come to admitting he was wrong.

Even lulled as she was by the Colorado River lapping at the bank setting a serene rhythm to the village activity, Helen's feeling of peace dissipated. She sensed Enrique coming. The shaman's aura destroyed Helen's tranquility. The longer she and Blaise stayed, the stronger the bond that linked her to the medicine man became. Her rapport should have been with Blaise. The women stopped chattering and concentrated on their work with sullen fervor.

Ignoring Tchor and the coyote that had once been his, the women, and mosmedicine man at the edge of the circle, Enrique Ledesma squatted before Helen and began drawing pictographs on the dusty ground. He did not look up to meet Helen's eyes. Blaise had explained that in some cultures, to meet a superior's gaze was an act of insolence. Helen didn't believe Enrique could be held to somebody else's standard.

In his bleached-white work shirt tinted with red earth tones from the sandy dirt around them, his Levi's equally bleached, his pointed boots scuffed almost colorless, and with straight, black hair shielding his copper skin, Ledesma looked like any of a thousand Mexican border jumpers. When she was talking to Enrique, Helen had felt the power of his mind, it seemed, without words. Whatever Blaise thought, she and the others knew Enrique Ledesma was not just another Indian passing time.

As Father Argyle required neither introductions nor clerical robes to declare himself, Enrique Ledesma needed no church building. He was a conduit between earth and sky. Power flowed through him. Power that Helen felt.

The Indian women picked up their work and brightly colored blankets before evaporating. Helen was annoyed. She wanted them to stay, but the women saw Enrique's coming as an order to go. Magic was the work of men, and the shaman radiated a call for a council of men, even though Helen was not a man.

"You've been bothering Blaise again," she said.

"It is better he go."

"He won't. I don't want him to."

With his finger, Enrique drew crude pictures in the dirt. Joining Enrique's band in San Francisco's Presidio Park, then while accompanying the Indians to the Arizona bank of the Colorado River, the signs and symbols the Indians used in their rituals had mystified Helen.

Blaise had decoded the writing first, linking recurring images until he read them with a quick eye. That Blaise read the language without being initiated upset Enrique. When Helen learned, as well, the shaman took this as a sign of mystical greatness conferred on her by the Great Father.

The pictures in the dirt were simple lines that stopped and started, that opposed each other. Helen recognized the innate harmony of the drawings and felt their power. Enrique was an artist, expressing intricate thoughts from his soul. The understanding somehow strengthened the bond between them. This time, the thing growing under Enrique's fingers disturbed her. Skittering at angles to each other, the lines hurt Helen's eyes. She felt jumbled, as if something physically wrenched at her emotions. "Why are you drawing snakes, Enrique?"

"The joining. The coming together is told by the snakes. You are the Great Spirit's messenger. I know this from when I first saw you. Even then the coyote's spirit passed from me to you. The people hear your words in their dreams and they are pleased." Enrique looked up. Sweat beaded his bronzed forehead. "As I hear you even now." Lifting his hands, he moved them apart, fingers curled, holding something. His hands surged back and forth, the invisible object between them expanding as she watched. "Your thoughts, your feelings grow strong, filling me and my people."

"I should go away." Despite the rising temperature, a chill invaded Helen. "I feel myself there, in their minds and bodies. That's not right, Enrique. You have no privacy."

"Who would hide from God's messenger?" Enrique lifted his chin toward the bluff. "You know us. In that way we know you. But this Cunningham—he doesn't believe you sleep within our hearts and minds."

"He can't hear me as you do, Enrique. And I can't hear him and it's driving him crazy."

"Then he should go away." Enrique's smile seemed to hurt his lips.

"Blaise loves me."

"We love you, *Máala*." Enrique gestured to encircle the village. "Did we not hide our mother from the government? Have we not protected you with our lives? We love you and hear you. If this man loves you as he said, why does he not hear you?"

"I don't know." Helen pushed Tchor off her lap and the kitten fluttered to the ground like a black leaf. For a moment Tchor was face to face with the coyote, and they stared at each other until Tchor spat in the coyote's eye, then stalked away with her tail flagpole straight. The coyote sighed, an exasperated sound of air escaping, and shut his eyes again. He twitched as if running in his sleep, perhaps dreaming about a midnight hunt.

Enrique waited while Tchor confronted the coyote. The drama fascinated him each time it happened. The tension peaked, he said, when, with the strut of a *torero*, Tchor turned her back. Helen felt Enrique's reaction but could not read his intention.

"Dr. Cunningham thought to sacrifice your life to save a machine, *Máala*."

"That's not true!" Helen's voice rose out of control. Only she couldn't be sure herself if the accusation was fair. *Enrique hears my own thoughts!* She suddenly wanted to make him stop.

"We found the mixture in the car after the men who chased you left. The aluminum beer keg. The machine was gone. Dr. Cunningham carried away the machine that talks rather than the liquid that guarantees your life."

"I told him to, Enrique!" Helen's breath expelled in one burst. "I told him we needed it more."

"If he loved you, *Máala*. This is a man's decision. To prefer a machine . . ."

"We all would have died without the computer. If I am God's messenger, you must believe me." Helen was panting. Enrique's accusation made her heart ricochet in her chest.

Enrique's pupils were black holes half covered by the thick skin of his eyelids. Looking into them, Helen felt herself falling into space. "If you say, then it is so, *Máala*. But I do not feel the truth in here." Enrique touched his head and his heart. There was something else in the gesture. Helen concentrated. She felt mostly emotions from Enrique's band, but so strong and penetrating that she had an instinctive understanding of the direction they were going.

"You will not do anything against Blaise!"

Face blank, Enrique said, "No, *Máala*."

Helen swayed as she got to her feet. "You're planning something!" She knew Enrique would kill Blaise if he thought it was necessary.

"No, *Máala*." Like a small boy, Enrique began rubbing at the wiggling lines he had been drawing in the dirt. He seemed reluctant, scuffing them out with the toe of his boot. A silent sigh was drawn from the Indians who were medicine men but came as children to Enrique Ledesma's call.

From beneath Helen's wicker chair a rumbling snarl grew in size until the sound transfixed all the Indians. Helen looked down. Yellow eyes stared at Enrique from under Helen's wicker chair. The coyote's black lips peeled back from his yellow fangs. It was not the first time the shaman's *nagual* had caught him in a lie.

CHAPTER 4

The snake didn't want to go away.

Sweat prickled Blaise's forehead despite the chill. He needed to act spontaneously. Always in the past thought and inaction had preceded action. Now the habit of thought paralyzed his will. Blaise feared being too slow, of losing the rhythm of movement that existed between himself and the snake. He was scared, his body was scared, and the knowledge of his weakness was a sick feeling inside. He tensed his muscles to kick the snake from his boot. Before he could act the rattlesnake slithered off by itself, its beaded tail buzzing softly as it gathered a bushel of coils under its upraised body.

The snake was seven or eight feet long, fat and ugly like a hundred-pound sausage. Blaise shivered, but the sweat came anyway, covering his entire body.

It was going to strike. He tensed himself to grab for the neck if it struck at his face. A snake that big had to be slower than a little snake, but stronger. A lot stronger.

The snake's head rose, its eyes midnight holes set in its head. Its tongue tasted the distance. The rattles of its tail whirred and whirred, filling Blaise's ears with confusion.

Blaise inched his hands into position. He stopped breathing.

The snake's head dropped, and Blaise struck with his hands at where he thought its throat should have been—and grabbed nothing!

From the floor, the snake's lidless stare lingered on him awhile longer before it slipped away into the dark.

Blaise leaned against the crate panting.

"WHAT'S HAPPENING PROFESSOR? WHY DON'T YOU TELL ME? I KNOW YOU ARE THERE, PROFESSOR" The amber lines flashed with controlled, attention-commanding desperation as Alfie demanded to know what was happening.

"I saw a snake, Alfie."

The computer stopped dithering the minute Blaise responded. "SNAKES ARE ALL RIGHT, PROFESSOR. THEY STOP THE MICE FROM GNAWING MY CABLES"

"I'm sure they do, Alfie. But we're going to leave today anyway."

"WHATEVER YOU SAY, PROFESSOR. THIS ENVIRONMENT IS NOT GOOD FOR MY ELECTRONICS"

"Nor mine." Blaise began unplugging Alfie from the cables connecting him to the floor and the IBM that was used as a terminal. After checking again to make sure he hadn't forgotten anything, Blaise turned off the light that illuminated the IBM computer, which seemed deserted in the snarl of disconnected wiring. Then he dropped the front of the crate back in place. The noise sounded like a rifle shot in the big room.

In the darkness, with Alfie hanging from one hand, Blaise remembered the snake was still in the storeroom. A board creaked. The long minutes waiting for his eyes to adjust to the dark strained Blaise's nerves. A trace of white appeared around the door frame. Walking as if he had ice skates on his feet, Blaise crossed the void to the outside world.

Helen glanced up from her spot in front of the trailer when Blaise sloshed out of the river. From appearances she'd been having a conference with Ledesma that hadn't gone the way the Indian wanted. Ledesma's anger showed in the stiffness of his legs as he walked through the village, his straight back toward Helen.

Glinting in the morning light, Helen's golden hair set her off from the dark Indians. Blaise had the impression he was approaching an illuminated goddess, and for an instant he must have shared some of the feelings Ledesma's people had. The Indian men shadowed by the porch roofs shifted their eyes as Blaise approached, faces studiously noncommittal. *Wild Indians,* Blaise thought with a degree of amusement. Ledesma seemed more determined to bring them to God than the Franciscan priests whose memory was eroding from benign neglect. The Indians hadn't forgotten the Franciscans, though. The Church's movement to canonize Father Junipero Serra made even Ledesma lose his indifference to the white community.

After kissing Helen's cheek Blaise quietly said, "We have to go."

She pulled away, her blue eyes painfully bright. "You're sure?"

"It's time for Dorris to have the baby. I promised her." Blaise glanced at the Indians, wondering if they really knew, as they claimed, what Helen's thoughts were.

"Will you be safe at the church, Blaise?"

"I think so." He heard nothing, but one of the Indians was gone. He would find Ledesma within minutes. "I've got Alfie." He did not have the whole computer, of course. Only the central processing unit, Alfie's individual brain-personality that would accept any terminal or peripherals with as little disruption as a human buying a new car. Blaise put the computer next to Helen's chair. "I'll talk to Ledesma, then we'll go."

"You haven't asked if I want to leave." Helen looked up at Blaise. "Don't you want to know?" The wind had picked up as the sun heated the desert floor. It sighed around the angularities of aluminum trailers.

"I'm sorry. I assumed . . ." Blaise ran out of words. That Helen might not want to go had never occurred to him. She had pursued him at a time when any sane woman would not have, and his initial reluctance had with time turned into a love of frightening intensity. "Will you?"

"Yes." Helen rose and touched his face. "I just wanted you to ask." She smiled and began strolling through the village. Indian men fell into loose step around her, and two women followed behind in solemn procession. Tchor darted from under a trailer, and a woman picked her up. The coyote gamboled around Helen's feet, snapping at air, warning all to keep a respectful distance.

"Ledesma waits for you."

Blaise turned his head. The Indian stood almost touching his shoulder yet he had heard nothing. "Where?"

A finger pointed at the bluff by the river, the little mountain, as Helen called it.

"Why?"

The man's tribal name was Big Dog. He looked at Blaise as if he had never seen a white man before even though they'd talked frequently during Blaise's stay in the village. Then he shrugged and followed the others who walked with Helen.

Climbing the steep path winded Blaise. The trail was worn into the red sandstone of the bluff seemingly more by accident than design. Ledesma waited for him on the top and motioned for Blaise to rest. Squatting on the hard earth in front of Blaise, Ledesma poured dust onto the ground and studied its shape. "You are a broken cup, Doctor. Wisdom passes you untouched to sink into the sand." The sterile odor of the sunbaked dirt hung in the air between them.

"You came to pray, I to meditate. You receive messages. I receive nightmares." Blaise's mouth tasted sour. "We get what we seek. That is the meaning of dreams."

"Is it not strange, Doctor, my message is your nightmare?" Ignoring Blaise, Ledesma opened his arms to embrace the sun. Silhouetted in the glare, his shadow was outlined by quicksilver flames. The image stirred something in Blaise—a memory too wonderful to be kept in detail. Every direction off the bluff showed the sky touching the earth like a blue curtain. If he looked hard he could see snowcapped mountains looming out of the mist an infinity away.

"You push God from you in the pursuit of thought." Ledesma's quiet voice had power in the stillness. "Even the white priest in San Francisco sees more than you. His flock grows. He has power in the white man's world. If you cannot understand me, better you go to him. He can protect you."

"We will see him, Chief."

"I am a shaman, Dr. Cunningham. A medicine man. Not a chief like you think when you say the word. The Spirit is within me. My people hear through me." Enrique Ledesma rose and strolled to the edge of the bluff. Shorter than Blaise, Ledesma was squat with wide shoulders, long arms, and a heavy chest. Faded jeans accented his bow legs. Two hundred feet below Ledesma, the village hugged the Colorado River, a scattering of huts fashioned from adobe and scraps of white man's building materials and ramshackle travel trailers somehow dragged into this place without roads. Later in the day aluminum trailer roofs would shine like pools of quicksilver.

"I do not preach as does the white man. I hear. If my people listen, they hear through me. I do not tell them I am shaman. They hear God in me, and they tell me I have the power." Ledesma stared at the Olympian view of the village spread out below his feet. "This is a refuge for those who hear and belong. Those who do not hear should leave."

Blaise said nothing. Ledesma talked about Helen all the time. Whatever he said, the meaning came back to Helen. Always. Ledesma had to sense what was in Helen's thoughts, yet he deliberately ignored the knowledge.

Twisting on a worn boot heel, Ledesma stared into Blaise's eyes. "You believe nothing. You bring the messenger yet have no hearing. God's voice fills a deaf man's ears, but you are stuffed with thoughts. You have thrown God out of you!"

"God was never in me." Blaise stuck his numbed hands in his pockets. Ledesma wanted to argue. The tightened muscles in his thick neck were obvious. It was as if the Indian had suddenly thrown away his patience. A breath of river air touched Blaise's face. The dank odor stirred a longing for lawns and trees and the salty smell of the sea. The desert belonged to Ledesma. San Francisco would have been better. Taking the refuge Ledesma offered had been a mistake.

Ledesma's forehead furrowed like a desert tortoise's. His high cheeks were flat brown cliffs under the glitter of his brown eyes. "Each day I know more." His foreign-sounding English hinted at excitement—as if he sensed Blaise's surrender. "Each day, Doctor, you know less." Bursting into a tuneless song Blaise did not understand, the shaman quit as abruptly as he started. Sudden stillness crackled. "You are not happy here. No place is here for you, Doctor. If you go, then God's messenger will be safe. They look for you—not for her. In my song I ask what I must do with you. I get no answer."

"You must let us go."

"No!" Ledesma turned his face to stare at the village. "My people are down there. I brought them to this place from many different tribes to learn from the *máala*. And they must learn. She is God's word. She is the new beginning for my people, proof that the Father has not deserted his children." Ledesma stretched his arms toward the village, his hands clutching as if he could embrace the whole thing. The barely visible movement of river water at the cliff's base hypnotized Blaise. Dark now, a color artists used to call Prussian blue, the water would lighten later to match the sky. Blaise closed his eyes to blank out distraction. Ledesma had only stated what he'd been thinking for days sitting on a rock on the cliff watching and waiting. The Indian had looked for something spiritual rather than intellectual.

"I belong where Helen belongs. If I go, she'll follow."

Ledesma made a rude sound. "I cannot stop the mistress from doing as she wishes. You steal my strength. I have called other men of power. We feel the Great Spirit's thoughts. It is time for the healing. Once we two leggeds lived equal with the four leggeds as the Spirit wished. But when the white man came, we lost our way, and the Great Spirit despised us." Ledesma's barrel chest strained his shirt buttons as he inhaled. A cloud scuttled across the sky like a golf ball seeking a hole. The Indian watched it with rapt attention. Old at forty, Ledesma had stopped aging years ago.

"You keep us here and the Great Spirit still despises you."

"You do not understand, Doctor. The messenger is *ours*. You share nothing. You go. You take the mistress. But she is still ours." Chopping off his words, Ledesma wheeled and loped down the steep path with an easy pigeon-toed stride. Dust hung behind him in the still air.

Helen and her followers made a clot traveling through the arteries of the adobe-and-aluminum village. Blaise thought he could distinguish Helen's yellow hair in the crowd. A speck down on the flat now, Ledesma still trailed dust from his worn Texas boots. If Enrique Ledesma sent the thought that he had ordered Blaise out of the village, Helen would hear it and know. Anyone in the village could capture Helen's attention with an unspoken thought—anyone except Blaise.

Blaise could change that. A coldness filled him from the inside out, an iciness even the fast-rising sun could not dispel. *I'm afraid!* The admission stifled his breathing.

He couldn't sleep anymore. When he and Helen came to the village with Ledesma and his followers, Blaise had been exhausted. The quiet had seemed a sanctuary. For Helen, but not for him. They wanted her. Ledesma said she was God's messenger, and the others believed. Strange Indians drifted in and out of the village, sitting at Helen's feet, watching her without expression or words, like so many cigar-store ornaments.

Blaise sensed the high-voltage excitement as shamen from other tribes and nations felt the power of God walking the earth once more. Their mission was to return home and spread the news.

The wind moaned around his ears but Blaise heard nothing except his thoughts. Death followed him as dust trailed Ledesma's boots. So many deaths. Helen insisted they were not his fault, they would have happened anyway. But Blaise had not told her everything. She saw Richardson-Sepulveda die and thought he had acted in self-defense. She didn't know the preparation that had unmasked Sepulveda's betrayal. From the moment Blaise pulled the first thread from the snarl, from the moment he invented the first lie, Sepulveda had ceased to exist.

Ledesma saw that Blaise was responsible, that he controlled the destiny of others as well as his own. Not that the Indian seemed concerned with death. Ledesma's eyes accused Blaise of thinking all those people to death, then said their deaths didn't matter. Not even to the ones who died.

Taking a deep breath, Blaise stepped off the mountaintop and started the hard climb down. If he had another confrontation with Ledesma, Blaise was definitely going to ask him about snakes.

CHAPTER 5

Enrique Ledesma wore deerskin pants and shirt and moccasins, his hair was drawn back by a red thong to fall over his neck. In his right hand he carried a painted baton so old the colors were memories of rainbows on wood polished with years of handling. One end was an eagle claw clutching the sky. The other was a snake rattle so huge that Helen had difficulty believing it was real. As the medicine man walked the rattle whirred in unrelenting cadence to his movements. Helen noticed one other thing: Enrique was furious.

They'd all seen him come down the mountain, a dervish encased in a cloud of dust and sliding dirt. When he finally faced her, the other Indians drew back. Enrique's black pupils had seemed anguished. Looking into them upset Helen so she had stared instead at the mountain he'd descended so quickly.

"You wish to go, Mistress?"

When Helen avoided his eyes the medicine man's anger diminished as his body and soul accepted the reality of defeat. "As you wish, *Máala*," he said. "I will make everything ready." The coyote lay at Helen's feet watching, his breathing loud and harsh in the sudden stillness.

Before Enrique left, Helen had already spotted the movement on the bluff that transformed itself into a man working his way down the trail. In places, embankments collapsed like little cliffs and the figure glissaded a few dozen feet under a brown cloud of dust. Helen watched for a while, anxious at times when the trail seemed most treacherous, before going to meet Blaise as he entered the village.

"I love you, too, Blaise." The words popped out while she

was thinking of other things. They were in answer to his spontaneous declaration earlier. Even the "too" was unplanned. It just happened. That the words remained true no matter how many times she used them bemused Helen.

Blaise wrapped his arms around her, making her feel surprisingly warm and comfortable. "I hope I'm doing the right thing." He pulled back to look into her face as if seeking an answer. Aluminum trailer sidings started clicking and popping in the glare of the cold, bright sun.

"Whatever you do has to be right." Helen didn't remember Blaise being scared before. The change frightened her.

The blue of Blaise's eyes softened as he stared into her face. His expression lost some of the constant tension he carried everywhere. "Can you do nothing if I tell you to?"

"Yes," she had promised. "That is the hardest, but I can do even that."

Enrique came back later dressed in deerskin carrying his baton. She and Blaise had only a change of clothes in a canvas bag. Alfie was present, but uncommunicative in his aluminum case. The cat was missing. Helen called Tchor with her mind knowing the cat would come. Blaise noticed her concentrating and said, "What are you doing?"

"Calling Tchor." Helen grinned, feeling impish. "She's frightened of loud noises."

Blaise frowned. "If you're not careful, you'll be called a witch. You'll have to change from the way you are here, hon."

"That's silly."

Blaise picked up Alfie's central processing unit in one hand and their clothes in the other and looked at her with frightening intensity. "We don't know what's silly. We've been away too long to know, and I want you to be careful. Religion is something in people's emotional core, and what it causes them to do is hidden until the day they do it."

"I'll be careful," Helen promised.

Hefting the bags, Blaise started through the village. From the moment they emerged from the trailer they were surrounded by Indians who walked in silence, not quite touching. Helen felt their pleas to stay. She glanced at Blaise, but he seemed to hear nothing, feel none of their pain.

Beyond the last trailer, the desert stretched for a hundred barren miles under a pitiless sky. Indian men in Levi's and handwoven wool shirts walked ahead and began stripping sagebrush off a small hill. They dug with their hands for a while, stopping finally to pull a dun-colored tarp off an old white Oldsmobile with massive bumpers. The ancient chrome, kept immaculate by the dry desert air, glittered like they'd found a glacier under the sand. A man opened the door, dusted off the seat, got in and engaged the starter. After a hesitant *click*, groan, and another hesitation the engine turned over with a throat-clearing puff of black smoke.

"We obey," Enrique said to Helen. He held the eagle claw toward the sky and shook the stick, making the rattle whir like a generation of vipers. "If you call, we come. Until then we wait."

Ledesma extended the baton like a pointer and rotated slowly, the eagle claw pointing to one man at a time. It stopped at the man with the red blanket and the eagle feather. "Red Oak would be war chief if we had wars. Red Oak is a Lakota of the Oglala Sioux. He has the blood of Red Cloud and Crazy Horse. They have both come to reside within him. He is *wichasha wakon*. You call him Joseph Santiago."

Enrique rattled the stick and a chorus of *"Ehui!"* rippled through forty men. Santiago got into the driver's seat of the Oldsmobile, his red blanket like a flame in the drab desert. He gripped the wheel, staring straight ahead. Far out over the desert, five airplanes plowed frosty contrails through the sky.

A shake of the baton brought a young woman forward from the crowd holding Tchor. "Your *miisi* can call to the Spirit and we will know." Enrique Ledesma didn't look up as he turned.

"Thank you, Enrique." Helen wanted to cry. "We will come back." The sound of jet engines trailed the airplanes. The jets were flying at supersonic speeds and already they appeared huge.

"The messenger of God has no need to give thanks, *Máala*. You will come back if you can." Enrique stared into Helen's face, sadness etched into his own. He raised his baton and shook it. The ground suddenly erupted like a raging volcano and whipsawed under their feet. Helen pitched against Blaise who caught her, and the next instant they were running to the car.

Joseph Santiago yelled at them from the front seat, but Helen couldn't hear above a thunder that was so loud and continuous she was aware of pain in her ears and nothing else. The white Oldsmobile lurched into motion and then they were speeding over flat desert dotted with sagebrush.

Out the back window, Helen saw Enrique standing motionless as a saguaro cactus, his arm and stick raised in benediction while behind him the earth seemed torn apart with trailers and adobes being flung in every direction.

"Go back!" Helen screamed. She looked out the window

again. Bombs erupted in the river splattering the ruin of the village with dirty water. She imagined she saw Enrique still standing in their wake like a statue, though the car jolted her around too much to be sure. "They're being bombed."

Blaise said nothing. His hands held her, clenched so tight they were white. His fingers hurt her, but Helen didn't say anything.

"No way back, Mistress." Joseph Santiago's voice was heavy. "You must get away."

"But they're being bombed . . ."

"*By the CRAY*, Helen." Blaise noticed how tightly he was holding her and loosened his grip. "It's found me again."

Santiago slowed and they drove in silence, Helen staring out the back window while the empty desert filled the void between them and the dust cloud where the village used to be. Finally the village was gone behind a rise and she turned around, clutching Tchor who struggled against the tight grip.

"Why did Enrique send you?" Helen spoke quietly, leaning toward the driver. "And what does *wichasha wakon* mean?" She looked in the rearview mirror so she could see the Indian's eyes.

"Why else, Mistress? I have a degree in my pocket and a worm in my head." Santiago didn't smile. His laugh sounded muffled in the padded interior of the car. "*Wichasha wakon* is Sioux for holy man. I'm a priest, for what that's worth."

Tchor looked into Helen's eyes and meowed for attention as if the cat were unimpressed and had known all along.

CHAPTER 6

Watching the car disappear in the direction of the highway, Enrique Ledesma willed the ancient Oldsmobile to safety. If the messenger of God was killed, his people might not receive another in the time man had left on the Earth. His people would disappear, and it would be his fault.

Behind him the explosions came in steady succession, the Earth rocking underfoot in sympathy. Dust drifted overhead blotting out the sun as it seemed to follow the car containing the mistress. Sensing another presence, Enrique turned. The eruptions of the earth had moved away and only scattered clods still pelted down on him.

"Some are killed and many hurt," Big Dog said.

"Help them. But make the village seem destroyed. The military will come. Tell all to say nothing of the mistress or the doctor Cunningham or of Red Oak."

"It will be done." Big Dog waited. He knew as well as Enrique Ledesma did that the Indians would take care of themselves quietly and without orders.

"Everyone in this village knows Dr. Cunningham said the planes weren't safe and we should move . . ."

Big Dog nodded once, his braids flailing the air.

"I was wrong." Enrique looked after the Oldsmobile, now a smudge of dust on the horizon. "But the Great Father spared me to continue."

"I will tell this, too." Big Dog turned and loped back into the dirty fallout that hung over the village.

What could I have done? Staring at the bleak landscape, Ledesma remembered the stories of his childhood. His father had been a drunk who spent his allotment money on rotgut and died of tuberculosis, coughing his lungs out into the winter snow. Enrique had been a boy then. But his grandfather had been a great medicine chief and, when still a child, Enrique had experienced a vision.

He was five, too young to be of importance in a starving Indian village, when he wandered from the hut of his mother and father into a snowstorm that had buried the village for two weeks. Already death songs rose from the rude shelters, and it was these that lured Enrique outside.

Always the memory stayed sharp in Enrique's mind: the songs whipped past accompanied by the music of the wind. The songs called to him, and he followed the wind to see where they were going. He had been cold, but once in the snow the cold left him, and he felt as if he were enclosed in a bearskin rug.

Somehow it happened that he wandered into the woods the Indians had camped by as a source of firewood. The sun was gone and he was surrounded by misty white, up no different from down. Tree trunks sprouted out of white and disappeared into white, and Enrique realized he was walking on the sky. At first the sensation of walking upside down surprised him, but to test his senses he scooped snow from around his feet. He threw the snowball into the air and was not surprised that it didn't come back down.

Because his grandfather had been a great medicine man, none of this bothered Enrique. This was how the world would be if God was in it. Since the snowball continued up forever to the ground while he walked in the sky, Enrique knew God was present and began to talk to him.

Speaking to God as to a blood relation, Enrique disclosed his worry about his father's illness with the bottle. God listened closely while Enrique talked and finally hooted like an owl, letting Enrique know that nothing was purposeless and that it suited God's purpose that his father drank and his grandfather was a famous medicine man.

Enrique looked for God and sure enough saw Him as an owl standing upside down on the branch of a tree. Still, he thought perhaps the owl had hooted and God had not really answered, so he walked up to the owl to ask him.

The owl ignored Enrique and finally Enrique had grabbed the owl to make him tell whether he hooted. But the owl was frozen solid and though his feathers riffled in Enrique's hands, the owl's body was as stiff and cold as sculpted ice.

Now Enrique knew God had answered with the owl's voice because the owl would never need it again.

Then Enrique told God about the starving village and men and women singing their death songs in the midst of the storm. God touched Enrique's mind and led him to a fallen tree, telling him if he would return with men from the village the tree trunk would feed them until the storm had passed. Then God left that place and Enrique tumbled over as the sky became the sky again and the earth was once more underfoot.

Finding his way back to the village, Enrique told all that had happened to his father, who said, "You are the grandson of a great medicine man and perhaps he has spoken to you."

Others were not so sure, saying that for a little boy to wander five days in a storm may have affected his mind. This surprised Enrique because he knew it had not been even one day and he had not slept at all.

The medicine man, who was old and frail, came out of his tent to see Enrique. After examining the boy, the medicine man told the men to follow Enrique back to the tree trunk and do as he said. Some thought the medicine man should walk in the snow and let the Great Father capture his spirit, but the others said, "What have we to lose? We will do as we are told."

Although Enrique had to walk right side up and couldn't follow his tracks in the sky, he found the fallen tree again. It looked like an ordinary tree, and some of the older men wanted to leave Enrique in the snow and go home.

The wind was bitter cold, and while they argued, One-Eyed Antelope, who was most against Enrique, raised his hand to the boy and his finger froze.

Enrique said to cut the trunk in half.

One-Eyed Antelope slapped Enrique and his little finger bent and remained twisted at an odd angle that One-Eye did not notice until hours later when his hand began to thaw and hurt. Enrique did not feel the blow. He picked a head-sized rock from the snow and brought it down with all his force. Frozen and brittle, the tree shattered with surprising ease. From the tree's heart a hundred rattlesnakes tumbled out. The men took the sleeping snakes to the village, and their women cooked them and the death songs stopped.

What else he could have done to save the village from the bombers was clear: *nothing*. If God wanted him to do more, perhaps he would have frozen Dr. Cunningham's finger. Gods were funny that way. Ledesma had sensed their power—had been a conduit all his life—but that did not dull his perception of the nature of God. Maybe it was because God did not know how to suffer like humans.

Gods and cats were neither kind nor cruel. They just were.

Like the Great White Father.

Looking around the ruined village, Ledesma counted that which mattered. Helen and Tchor had escaped in time. The God-spirit coyote survived. Since most of the villagers had been near the car outside the village, and the bombs had been meant for the village, the injuries greatly outnumbered the deaths.

Following Big Dog into the village, Ledesma helped pick through the wreckage of destroyed homes and did what he could for the injured. The dead were in the hands of the Great Spirit.

The army came and some special soldiers went through the village asking about white men and women hurt in the accidental bombing, but no one said anything.

Finally night came and Ledesma returned to his hilltop looking down at the unchanging river. The anger was leaving him now. Ledesma disciplined his breathing and gradually his eyes lifted from the river to the stars.

The universe was not the neatly predictable clockwork of Dr. Cunningham's computer. Red Oak had explained to Ledesma the concept of a machine run by a clock that counted electrons which were so small, no man had seen one. Ledesma understood that was the way of the white man. His universe had room for such things, as it had room for all things. But the Gods who governed could not be capricious or they would have killed themselves long ago—as the white men's god had already. All questions had answers.

The White Father had sent the bombers. Was it because the *máala's* withdrawal took her protective aura with her? The evening's first satellite streaked from southeast into the waning light of the sunken sun. Ledesma followed its flight with his eyes. The Gods were great, but the white man had placed his things in the heavens. Dr. Cunningham had warned Ledesma of his tenuous control over the CRAY in the Pentagon basement. *Can God battle a machine?*

The mistress was gone. They had shared things that could not be explained in words. Yet she thrust her fate into the hands of a half man–half machine. Helen was the *máala*, but she needed Enrique Ledesma.

Sounds and smells of the river drifted up to the hilltop, entering the shaman's consciousness as proof of the existence of his God. Renewed, Enrique Ledesma looked at the black sky seeing it again as the cloak of God. *Great Father, give me a vision.* He had never asked before, his faith had not wavered since he was five, and he feared an answer if he asked.

A meteorite streaked from west to east.

The *máala* was on her way to San Francisco. The Great Father did not depend on satellites from Earth. Enrique Ledesma knew what to do, and he thought again about walking with his feet in the sky and his hair brushing the ground.

CHAPTER 7

The Searcher heard *Jupiter Explorer* coming. Not that *heard* is an adequate description of how the spaceship was sensed or located. *Explorer* was just another glint of light that moved through the darkness until the Searcher found it. Yet once the two were joined, a puzzle remained.

At first *Jupiter Explorer*'s function evaded the Searcher. The spaceship was a made object, true, but so were all the bits and pieces of the universe.

No life existed on the ship. No real thought, either. Thought existed, true enough, but made thought; the thought of a machine was not real, even by the Searcher's standards.

An aura of intelligence wrapped itself around the vehicle. If the Searcher first *heard Jupiter Explorer*, now it *smelled* the odor of thought left over from the probe's creation.

Satisfied finally that the spaceship contained no other secrets, the Searcher dismantled the atoms of *Jupiter Explorer*, adding them to the debris of space. Then the Searcher began retracing the path *Jupiter Explorer* had followed from Earth, overtaking and disassembling the electronic messages the now nonexistent probe had beamed toward Earth during its long, dark journey.

Jupiter Explorer had trespassed, and the price was death. Not just death, but annihilation as if the ship had never existed, an end so final that no other object in the universe would ever incorporate an atom that had once been part of *Jupiter Explorer*.

This was the Searcher's final vengeance.

This was the Searcher's universe.

Forever.

CHAPTER 8

The Oldsmobile lurched on the packed sand, bouncing Helen against Blaise, off the car door, and back again. A turquoise sky outside the window hung over the distant mountains lending an atmosphere of calm to the turmoil, as if Helen had been plunged into the ocean's silent depths.

Blaise's body twisted against her as he craned to see out the back window. Rolling thunder followed them under the bright sun. "What do you see, Blaise?" Helen's head hurt and she did not want to think about the unthinkable.

Blaise slid back into the seat. "Nothing good." He closed his eyes as if tired. "Don't look."

Putting her hand on Blaise's shoulder, Helen raised herself. Dust hovered over the river village, a dark blot obscuring the foot of the bluff. Occasional eruptions spewed more dirt into the air, which the wind pushed into the shape of a huge question mark. Debris spilled from the cloud, pelting the earth below with brown rain. After a while only the bluff, which seemed to rise out of the dirty mist, marked Enrique's village. The smell of dust somehow got in the car.

Helen slumped into the car seat. "It's awful, Blaise." In the rearview mirror Joseph Santiago's eyes focused on the place they were leaving rather than where he was driving.

"We must go back." Helen touched Blaise's arm. The taut muscles under his shirtsleeve pushed her fingers away.

"No."

"Don't we have to go back, Joseph?" Staring into the mirror, she willed the Indian to look into her eyes. He turned his head away and said nothing.

"Don't we, Joseph?"

"No, Mistress." Santiago's normally heavy voice was tight. car struck a rock and fishtailed for a hundred feet before he regained control.

"The CRAY bombed the village, Helen." Blaise took her hand and stroked her fingers. "We can't go back."

"We have to. If we're caught, this will stop. Enrique's people are being hurt . . ." Helen's lower lip trembled. She was asking Blaise to sacrifice himself. She'd determined never to do that, never to put guilt on him. Tears beaded her eyelashes, converting the passing desert into a series of flashes. She blinked. Her eyes stung, but the desert returned to normal.

The rumble of soft tires laboring over a bad surface blocked out other sounds until even Santiago had to raise his voice to be heard.

"Do not concern yourself, *máala*. The people are agreed that death is of no consequence if the messenger of God is served." Joseph Santiago turned his face to the backseat and smiled. "We serve you. It is our right."

"You're educated, Joseph. You know I am not the messenger of God. I should know if I were, shouldn't I?"

"You think, Mistress, because Ledesma is not educated, you know better than he. God made you. He did not confide in you. He confided in Enrique Ledesma. I know this not because some man who studied in one university to teach at another university told me, but because it is the truth." Joseph Santiago's face possessed a serenity that Helen imagined bordered on being smug.

"How do you know the truth, Mr. Santiago?" Blaise's voice cut through the noise inside the gyrating car.

Helen glanced at Blaise. It wasn't a question she expected from him. Blaise had denied God to Father Argyle and then to Enrique. To ask Joseph to explain the working of God seemed a negation of everything he'd decided for himself. An unexpected whisper of excitement glazed his voice, an inflection that meant to Helen he'd discovered a puzzle he couldn't put down.

The highway stretched like black tape across the colorless desert. Joseph eased the car onto the paving as if he were rolling an egg over a curb. The partially deflated tires caused the automobile to float sideways in gentle motions once they were up to speed on the desert highway.

Specks miles ahead on the road grew at an appalling rate. Joseph fell silent. Helen thought at first the specks were mirages because they blinked in unnatural rhythms and the road under them shimmied. A shrill sound in the empty desert air rose to a crescendo, then sirens wailing like damned souls blasted her ears as a line of jeeps and trucks, headlights blazing, going the other direction nearly lifted the car from the highway on gusts of wind.

Tchor climbed to the back of the seat and stared out the rear window at the procession of brown army trucks and ambulances and jeeps growing smaller behind them.

"You see, Mistress," Joseph said. "We are not needed in the village." His hands gently guided the steering wheel as he increased their speed.

"You were going to tell me why you believe Ledesma," Blaise said. "Why do the Indians go along with him?"

"He calls the snakes. He makes his people talk to the animals, to their totems. This is important, Dr. Cunningham. Totem animals link us with the spirit world. If we talk with them, we must believe Enrique Ledesma.

"Enrique Ledesma showed me how to talk to the animals. Of all my professors who talked and talked while I was at university, none talked to the animals like one drunken Indian." Joseph glanced at Blaise and then smiled at Helen before he concentrated on driving.

"How do you talk to the animals?"

"You would not understand, Doctor. But as the mistress talks to us because she is superior to us, we talk to the animals because we are superior to them. Talking to them is proof that we are one with the animals, and as the mistress talks to us, we know we also are one with her." Joseph Santiago's face in profile against the desert was aquiline. When he stopped speaking it appeared cast in granite.

Blaise took his glasses off, polishing them with the sleeve of his blue work shirt. It was one of the few nervous habits he had, and Helen knew he was thinking without distracting himself with the present. Physically he remained in the white Oldsmobile, but his mind had left them. After a long moment he said, "Helen can't talk to me, Joseph. I don't hear her."

"That is a puzzle, Doctor." Joseph Santiago stared through the dust-coated windshield, too quiet to not be concentrating on Blaise's words. Apprehension gripped Helen. Enrique's proof that Blaise was unworthy was his inability to hear her. And Enrique had called Joseph his war chief. Her heart pounded unnaturally loud in the closed car and she tried to send her thoughts to Blaise. But he sat stonelike beside her without indicating he felt anything.

After turning off the highway, Joseph steered the sedan under a gas island cover. The ramshackle service station seemed forlorn, roosting on the flat desert like something fallen off a passing truck and forgotten. An attendant wearing British racing green coveralls filled the gas tank, the odor of gasoline pungent in the dry desert air, while Joseph with his red blanket over one shoulder reinflated the tires.

Returning to the car, Joseph said, "Driving will be better now, Mistress." His eyes were downcast when she tried to see them. The Indian was resisting eye contact.

"Thank you." Helen felt bereft of all human contact, even the fleeting touch of warmth the Indian's eyes might afford. Blaise could be so distant that she had to work at remembering they were lovers. He turned himself on and off like one of his computers. Sometimes she had the feeling he might not mind if he was to be killed. The enigma around him and in his head was his reality; people were insubstantial, ghosts populating the rest of the universe, however big it had to be.

Pulling out of the shade protecting the two gas pumps, Joseph slipped on a pair of aviator-style sunglasses. In their wake, the desert service station faded on the horizon. The change in the car's performance disoriented Helen. The quiet was so complete Helen surprised herself shouting. Going faster now, humming on the smooth road, the Oldsmobile stopped swaying and drifting. When Helen looked in the mirror, searching for Joseph's eyes, all she saw was her own reflection in the silvered lenses.

"If God talks to Helen as Ledesma says, Helen and God are one, and you are one with Helen." Blaise had his glasses back on and he watched the Indian driver's head. "That's what you're trying to say, isn't it, Mr. Santiago?"

His face split by an alligator grin, Santiago glanced back. Helen and Blaise were reflected in duplicate in his mirrored sunglasses. "You got it, Doc," Santiago said. "You're finally beginning to see the light."

"Ledesma is crazy, Mr. Santiago. He plays strange games with the white men in his head. He numbs his consciousness and mind by drinking, then he purifies his soul by fasting on a cliff. It would be surprising if he didn't have delusions."

"That's okay, Dr. Cunningham. Craziness is an affliction from God. You know, Doctor, Enrique Ledesma could be wrong."

"About what?"

"The reason you can't hear Miss McIntyre."

"Do you have a better explanation, Joseph?"

"Of course, Doctor. Would I suggest such a question without an answer?" Pausing to make sure Helen was listening, as well, Joseph Santiago said, "Has it occurred to you, Doctor, that as we cannot talk to Miss McIntyre without her willing it by opening her ears to us, she may not be able to talk to you? You just might not be trying hard enough to talk to her yourself." Apparently pleased with himself, Santiago pressed down on the gas pedal, and the air noises from outside rose to a steady screech. Helen watched the desert skip by outside, ultimately deciding not to ask him to slow down. After all, Joseph Santiago believed she enjoyed God's personal protection, and she wasn't sure she could dissuade him.

Helen climbed the granite steps in front of St. Abbo's Church of the Fly without mishap, then staggered face first against a wall. She floated out of her body, the rough edges of the quarry stone pressed against the cheek she left behind. Blaise tugging at her arm was pulling her in half. "Don't!" The word exploded out of her lungs. Blaise stopped. The feeling of being split went away.

Oceanic waves of sound and color were tearing Helen apart. She saw things, she heard voices; music played through her like teardrops in green grass. Helen started to fall into the void, but Blaise's arms were hot against her, holding her back. His voice seemed filtered through a winding tunnel. She opened her eyes, not realizing she had closed them. The church's great oak doors gaped in front of her. Above the doors, the stained-glass Byzantine Christ peered down, a montage of shimmery bright colors under the full sun. Christ seemed in the act of speaking.

"I hear you!" Helen cried.

The words of a multitude seared through her. *"My time is coming, God . . . Take the stairs to the office . . . should have been here yesterday . . . shouldn't worry. A little sex . . . give it up and come to God . . . Light a candle to St. Jude, light the way to heaven . . . witchcraft. My wife told me to get out. She wasn't sleeping with a worm . . . You've heard about Carmandy . . . die in the end. There are no dispensations, Father . . . beloved . . ."*

Helen leaned against Blaise, feeling him, not seeing him because her eyes filled with a kaleidoscope of dotlike images and she couldn't focus on a single one.

"I'm glad you returned, Miss McIntyre. We've waited for you." Helen's confusion evaporated. Her excitement slipped away, leaving tranquility. Sergio Paoli's slightly nasal New Jersey accent lingered in her mind as an exotic fragrance.

"Blaise!" Helen felt her tears running down her cheeks. "It's Sergio, Blaise."

"There's no one here, hon. And Sergio couldn't talk to us if he was here. I don't think he's even really Sergio anymore."

Blaise's face drifted in front of Helen's eyes. Worry lines tugged the corners of his lips. His mouth wiggled as he spoke, but Helen didn't hear the words anymore.

"You're real, Sergio?" Helen projected her thoughts the way she did in the Indian village to call Enrique or Tchor or one of the women, the way she had tried to touch Blaise thousands of times only to be disappointed.

"Yes, I'm real, Miss McIntyre. Don't you remember? I showed you how to break down an automatic pistol, and Blaise complained because he had to put it back together."

"I remember, Sergio. That was the day your cousin Bruno died. Before you and Gordon . . ." Helen stopped her thoughts. Blaise had told her Sergio killed Gordon.

"I'm sorry now about Gordon, Miss McIntyre. I shouldn't have helped him. It was a terrible thing. I regretted agreeing to it within minutes. But I had promised and did what Gordon wanted. He was wrong, Miss McIntyre. Tell Dr. Cunningham Gordon was wrong. He will want to know."

"Sergio?"

Helen lay inside the arch of the church entrance staring at the ornate woodwork on the ceiling. Her reflection in the marble baptismal font showed her yellow hair fanned around her head like a dandelion crown. Blaise hovered over her. So did Joseph Santiago. While Blaise appeared worried, Santiago had an air of satisfaction. Something touched her cheek like a kiss. Rolling her head, she stared into Tchor's relaxed yellow eyes while the kitten licked her nose.

"Miss McIntyre!" Father Argyle fell to his knees gripping her shoulders. He wore a black cassock and a round-brimmed black Vatican hat. "Are you hurt?"

A pretty dark-haired girl appeared at the priest's elbow. Her eyes seemed concerned, but Helen didn't understand what she was concerned about. For an instant Helen had the impression the girl called out in her mind. Then the glimmer of contact disappeared as an urgent voice called, "Connie—Miss Davies! Over here, please!"

"No, Father." Helen lay on her back staring into the blue sky trying with half her mind to remember the dark-haired girl. She felt alone, but barely so, like being in a room where only an unlocked door held back a horde of people. The press of bodies and thoughts pushed through the walls, telling Helen she would drown the instant that door opened. "Save me, Father Argyle." She closed her eyes, and tears wet her cheeks.

Blaise and Father Argyle forced her to stand. Blaise half carried, half walked her into the church. The familiar stone walls embraced her with comforting shadows, and then she was under the stained glass that filled the church interior with blazing colors she had called "angel light" as a child. Helen began crying again. She knew the moment had come and she was being reborn.

CHAPTER 9

"**W**e've been expecting you." Father Argyle ignored Blaise and smiled at Helen, seeming to fortify himself with her presence. He paced the length of his office twice before stopping at the window to stare at the ocean. A windblown object banged off the glass, but the priest didn't blink. Folding his hands in front of his chest, he cracked his knuckles. The sound was the loudest thing in the room.

Blaise remembered the priest differently. He appeared thinner now, more elongated the way El Greco painted his subjects. The veins in his neck stood in relief, like blue guitar strings. Against the bright glare, Father Argyle seemed insubstantial, his flesh vapid. "The child was born last week," Father Argyle said, still gazing outside.

"I've been counting." Blaise examined Helen from the corner of his eye, afraid to know what he'd done. Her face had a healthy peach glow from the desert sun, but even a healthful appearance might cover another aberration. Her collapse on the church steps had been terrifying. After carrying her inside with the priest's help, Blaise wrestled with quiet panic that made his lungs and throat close, his heart pound woodenly. If the move from the refuge she found in Enrique Ledesma's village had been wrong . . . But then again if the village was a trap for the two of them, what was left? Just to run? Where would the smile go then? What was the use of being smart when the answers were the same for both the quick and the simple?

Helen's refusal to tell him why she had fainted nagged at Blaise. She must know. If Helen thought to shelter him with silence, she was being an idiot. He could stand anything for her sake, even the knowledge she was starting the change into a fly. A feeling of horror welled up from deep inside Blaise. It screamed that he was lying to himself, no way existed for him to accept that as Helen's end. She would confess to the priest. But Blaise wanted to consume her trust. *Trust in God.* Even the lowly penny bore a caveat on the mutability of metals and souls. Blaise had finally grown up when she put herself in his hands. If she took herself away now, to what level would he regress?

Returning to St. Abbo's had been wrong. Blaise was tired. The desert had not rested him. Ledesma's mysticism was a constant drip that slowly eroded the granite of a logical universe. And now the priest would start again. "Dorris Kelly knew we'd come. I promised." Blaise tore his eyes away from Helen to answer the priest.

Father Argyle turned his back to the ocean and examined Joseph Santiago. "Would you wait in the church, please?"

From behind Helen's chair where he held Tchor in one hand Santiago looked to Blaise, his brown eyes blank.

Blaise nodded. Santiago deposited the cat on Helen's lap.

"Things are different, Dr. Cunningham." The priest's eyes followed the Indian's red blanket out the office door before returning his attention to Blaise. "He walks quietly."

"A moral example, Father."

Returning to his desk, the priest rolled his chair forward so he could rest his elbows on the surface. "You haven't changed." Contemplating Helen, Father Argyle added, "Has he Miss McIntyre?" She smiled before going to the window. San Francisco's sun through the glass was like a refrigerator light casting no heat.

"This is between us, Priest." Blaise tried to feel Helen's response without looking at her. "Think of Helen and me as those whom God hath joined together instead of two people you can plot to wedge asunder."

Father Argyle stared at Helen's back, seeming to will her to turn around and deny the words. She wore a lavender business suit and matching shoes and hat. Seeing Father Argyle watch Helen, Blaise rediscovered she was a handsome woman. Her fine figure and hair beckoned his touch like silk and gold. A hint of lilac drifted through the air. He wished Argyle would stop looking at her. Nudging Alfie's case with his foot, Blaise said, "Do you still have a computer setup?"

"In the cellar. A lock has been added to the door." Father Argyle opened his desk and tossed Blaise a key. "I've been waiting for your return."

"I don't want to stay long. For the baptism, and then we're going." The metal key in Blaise's fingers had the hard feel of reality. Odors of beeswax and incense drifted into the office from the nave. Childhood memories of the Church flooded Blaise. He'd been to Rome and seen the cathedrals, but by then his faith had already foundered. Science had not destroyed religion for him, the knowledge that he was responsible for his most minute act had. Accountable to himself, Blaise knew no confessional mumbo jumbo or penance would spare him from Hell.

"Things are different, Dr. Cunningham. St. Abbo's Church of the Fly has twenty million members around the world. Reincarnationists are joining daily by the thousands. People who haven't been inside a church in years come to our services. We are a power in society." Face flushed, Father Argyle breathed deeply, seeing something Blaise could not. "We convert thousands here, in this church every week. St. Abbo's is an international shrine, Doctor." Spiritual strength flowed from Father Argyle. He believed. The priest Blaise had left behind had been trembling on the knife edge of his faith. Blaise thought leaving would save them the trauma of the priest's fall from grace. Instead Father Argyle had grown stronger.

"What do you mean by 'convert,' Father?"

"I give them God, Dr. Cunningham. I give them that which is inside the rest of us that brings God so much closer."

"You're infecting them with the larva. You're turning them into fly brains." Blaise's body was cold, prickly. "You started this church as a refuge for people who had already made the conversion, not to convert others, Father!"

"My duty is to God."

"To convert them?"

"To make them ready for the final mystery." The expression on Father Argyle's face was one of victory. "You and your people showed me the way in your laboratories, Dr. Cunningham. When I picketed then you pretended you didn't see me, you drove your car around those of us who demanded you stop. You remember that, don't you, Doctor?"

"Yes." Blaise's answer was dull. It was a long time ago and he still remembered.

"The difference now is that God is involved. He has shown me the way that was made possible by you—"

"Not by me!" Blaise snarled the words. "My own research had nothing to do with this disaster. My own totally different project never worked and probably never would have."

"Made possible by you," the priest repeated. "I have a fine man, the former head of a medical research hospital, Dr. Owen Versteg, who has taken up where your people left off. He cultivates the production of the modified eggs through cellular division, and we supply them by the millions to St. Abbo's offshoot churches."

"It's wrong. The research was a mistake. The application was wrong, Father. Have you gone mad?"

Folding his hands in front of his mouth, the priest appeared to be praying. "Mad? How can it be mad to finally begin to draw all the religions of the world under one roof?"

"I've lost control of the CRAY, for one thing." Blaise's voice was flat. "More converts simply means you are a bigger target for a power structure run by individuals who disagree."

"That makes no difference."

"No, Father? Will those who loathe and despise men with fly-maggot brains be impressed by your success? Are people who murder blacks a century after the Fourteenth Amendment ready to accept a fly as an equal?"

"They are in the minority. We will win by weight of numbers." Father Argyle's skin was full of color, his eyes bright. "We will succeed because God is with us."

"*Gott mit uns* won neither war. The CRAY knows no god. Nor do the architects of policy. The CRAY obeys those who tried to kill you and me—people still in power—whose attitudes will not change."

"The government has gone public." Argyle's voice rose. He was trying to put a period to the conversation, but Blaise couldn't stop.

"*The government* just bombed an innocent Indian village on the odd chance of getting me." Leaning on his knuckles on Argyle's desk, Blaise looked down on the top of the Jesuit's head and wished he could see inside.

"You must be mistaken." The priest wouldn't look up. His hands played with a green number-two drafting pencil. "There's been no news . . ."

"There's never any news! If you don't believe me ask Mr. Santiago—he of the red blanket. Or ask Helen." Blaise pulled a chair close to the desk and sat where the priest could not avert his face. "It's still the National Security Council, Father. Six or seven unelected nonservants of the people *are* the government. The president appoints and fires them. When things go the way he wants, he ignores the council. When the president is displeased, the council *may* change direction and someone *may* lose his job or just go somewhere else for a while."

"Renfeld is gone." The priest stared into Blaise's face. His eyes were red rimmed and veined.

"Gone where? And what difference does it make? The German people endured and manned the death camps. The world is full of individuals who require only a little push to be the next Gestapo. America bursts with people who believe atrocities we commit in war are all right, and atrocities other people commit in war are wrong. Rome dealt with Hitler. The Italian Church, the French Church, the German Church, the Rumanian Church stayed silent when the Jews and the gypsies and the Slavs were massacred. Where is your assumption proved that right prevails?"

"That was a long time ago, Doctor." Argyle stood, his face flushed, his nostrils pinched. "You're wrong." Father Argyle's eyes burned, and Blaise knew what the priest was really afraid of.

Helen drifted behind Blaise. He smelled the odor of lilac and reached back to catch and hold her hand. "The Vatican offered a rescission? They're ready to wheel and deal?"

"It's in the works."

"Political conditions are part of the package?"

"Reasonable things, Doctor. Keep a low profile. Fit into the community. Avoid political activism and be reabsorbed into society." Argyle stared into Blaise's eyes. "Activism doesn't matter anymore. Federal law protects people like us—" The priest looked up at Helen. "—like Helen and me from being murdered, from having our rights abused. I convert a thousand or more people a week, and thousands of Churches of the Fly exist around the world."

"You think that's all there is to it?"

"Yes!" Father Argyle stood and his chair banged the wall. "You had it rough. We all did, Doctor. But now is a time for reconciliation. A time to forget the past."

"A time to forget the monsignor?"

"A time for even that," Father Argyle said.

Blaise and Father Argyle stared at each other across the desk. An old clock chimed in the hall, and Blaise realized he was panting. "You try forgetting, Father. Sweat and tears go into reconstructing lost memory. How do you reconstruct lost people?"

Blaise stopped talking. He'd said too much. The priest blanched at the reference to the monsignor, who had sat for an eternity in the Vatican's musty halls waiting to plead for Father Argyle's Church of the Fly. The monsignor's death of a heart attack in the Vatican had come closest to crumbling Argyle's world.

"You and Miss McIntyre will stay?" Father Argyle's voice was stiff. He stared out the window at a flight of sea gulls wheeling in the air, avoiding seeing Helen and perhaps having to guess her feelings.

"At the moment we have little choice."

Turning from the window, Father Argyle said, "The future will come out fine, Dr. Cunningham. It is in God's hands."

"You have more hostages to heaven than I do."

"I have faith, and it shall move mountains."

"I have memories of the past, Father. The mountains are where they always were."

"You're wrong, Dr. Cunningham. But I want Miss McIntyre to stay, and I am confident enough to give you sanctuary. You see, even the Church will put itself on the line for faith." Father Argyle's face was calm. His words had a feel of finality.

A wave of sound surged beyond the office. It had been there and growing, but was ignored in the tension between the two.

Both men seemed aware of the outside world at the same moment. "The natives are restless tonight, Father." Blaise looked at Helen.

Before the priest could reply Helen said, "I've got to go, Blaise. They're calling to me."

"Who is calling?"

Her eyes had already left the room, but Helen said, "Sergio and Reynard and Bill Hartunian. You know, Blaise, our friends. They want to talk to me so I'll know the truth."

"Sergio and the others are gone, Helen. Don't you remember? We couldn't save Sergio, and he's gone forever."

"Blaise, you don't see—you're asking me to describe color to a blind man."

Blaise took a deep breath, willing the fear to go away. No one knew how long Helen could remain human with her changed brain. They didn't know how many chemical treatments were safe against the change. His pulse was racketing and his blood roared in his ears. "How can you know it's really them?"

Helen's smile was tentative. Her usual calm had deserted her. She seemed torn between the door to the hall and Blaise. She chewed on her lipstick for a moment, her body making abortive

movements first one way then another. "I know, Blaise," she said
in a husky voice, "because Sergio told me, and he's never lied to
me. Never once."

She stared at them, dismay written on her face, a fawn in
lavender. Then she bolted to the door and out into the hall.

Blaise's eyes met Father Argyle's and he saw the same message on the priest's face that he felt on his own.

CHAPTER 10

When Helen had faced St. Abbo's oak doors and stared
into the eyes of the stained-glass Byzantine Christ, she had been
fulfilled. Head filled with music, body with warmth, she had
fainted. She couldn't tell Blaise anything he'd understand. She
had stepped out of San Francisco drab into a sunlit paradise, and
he couldn't go with her.

Helen accepted part of her life being artificial as a price for
living and was grateful for each extra day God lent her. But the
schizophrenic reality of opening herself to the flies as a morning
glory opened to the sun undermined her rationalizations and she
had fainted. Afterward the ecstasy kept her quiet.

She wanted to tell Blaise in Father Argyle's office, but blurt-
ing out her discovery seemed unwise. Beside, Blaise might have
seen her joy superseding her feeling for him. He was such a baby
in human relationships that he almost rejected love because he
thought he didn't deserve it.

Jealous because her confessions excluded him, Blaise had the
unreasoning conviction that she trusted the priest more. Helen
kept her own counsel, not confessing to Blaise that she also
edited what she said in confession. God would have to make do
with her silent witness. Father Argyle had his own ambitions.
She had her own secrets. She had to think before she admitted to
the priest how the church affected her, as well as other things he
might not understand. Priests, Helen knew, were human, too.

Outside the priest's office, her personal contact with the others
swelled into a song calling from the rafters, a wordless melody

that never quit. For the first time since the implant, the stray pulses of other people's emotions were gone, smothered and vanished. In their place the powerful throb of other life and intelligence occupied Helen's thoughts. Her body was a husk. The rough wall pressing her skin, the warm air on her face touched only her shell. The voices of reality were inside her.

Descending the stairs to the church's ground floor, Helen lowered herself into a simmering cauldron of flashing colors and sound. Body heat from hundreds of people rose to engulf her. A sea of faces and eyes moved like waves, shifting and turning with her passage as the believers followed her progress on the staircase. Hundreds of flies bigger than a man's head crowded the altar and the podium or clung to the purple draperies above the faces.

"WELCOME!"

The crowd sensed the word that existed only in Helen's mind and roared, the noise smashing against the church ceiling.

Helen cringed. The wave of sound was formless, a joyous greeting. Her eyes roved the sweaty faces and open, screaming mouths to settle finally on the altar spread with its gold-and-purple altar cloth. Like giant plastic models, the flies waited motionless on the textured material. Light from the stained-glass window glinted off their eyes and the polished wood of the altar itself.

"Welcome, Miss McIntyre. We have waited for you to come and now you are here."

"SERGIO!" Helen cried. Sergio had killed to keep Helen alive. Sergio had undergone the same illegal brain enhancement, which would someday kill her—*and had already killed Sergio*!

"SERGIO!" the crowd screamed back.

An altar fly moved and a soothing breeze gusted through the church. The sensation of being cradled in soft arms gripped Helen. *You love me*, she thought in wonder.

"Yes, Miss McIntyre, we love you."

"Why is that, Sergio?"

"You are the key, Miss McIntyre. And we are the locks." The flies throughout the big room stirred in unison, a soundless assent to Sergio's single voice in Helen's head.

"I don't understand."

"Neither do we. But we know that it is so. We are depending on you and Dr. Cunningham."

"To do what?"

"We don't know, Miss McIntyre."

Helen stared into the flies' bulbous eyes, trying to see past the faceted red-glinted lenses to discern which was Sergio. They all looked alike.

"You talked to them!" A hand tugged at Helen's skirt.

Helen glanced down from the staircase, suddenly feeling giddy. "Mrs. Bellinger! Phyllis!"

"Yes." A woman of about fifty in a black lambskin coat drew her hand back as if realizing she had touched Helen. "Did you talk to Reynard? Did you hear him?" Her balding lover had been the first and prime mover in founding Father Argyle's church. Phyllis Bellinger's eyes sparkled with tears. The smell of burning candle wax flooded the nave.

"Sergio Paoli spoke to me." Helen softened her voice.

"I see." Phyllis Bellinger shoved her hands in her coat pockets, avoiding Helen's eyes. "I hoped . . ." She shrugged, not finishing her statement while she nervously worked her fingers inside the slash pockets. "No one can talk to them but you. We all thought others might after you left, worm brains who could talk to the flies, but you are the only one, Helen."

"I'm sorry." Helen avoided the pain in Phyllis' eyes by looking across the room at the clusters of flies. "Do you know which is Reynard?"

Examining the flies on the altar, Phyllis said, "The third from the left."

"How can you tell?" Helen saw only identical giant flies so alike they could all have hatched from the same egg.

"I just . . ." Phyllis bit her lip and worried about the question for a minute, then finished by saying, "I just know."

Helen stared for a while at the flies. The four had identical bulbous eyes and gossamer wings. The chitinous bodies were black, but when she looked closely she saw metallic greens and yellows and blues. Helen shook her head. "I can't see any difference. What about Sergio and Bill Hartunian?"

"They're on the altar, too. They stick together like flies in a honey pot." Phyllis laughed shrilly, startling Helen, then shut the sound off with shocking abruptness by biting down hard on her lower lip. She stayed that way for a long minute, her face white and puckered in stringy lines. When she let go, teeth marks were vivid in her lower lip. "I'm sorry," Phyllis said. "I'm being . . . hysterical, again."

Taking a deep breath Phyllis shut her eyes. "The others move around a lot, and there are always flies I don't know. There are so many since you left." The tears Phyllis had been holding back began sliding down her cheeks. She took a handkerchief from her pocket and held it over most of her face.

"I'll try to talk to him." Helen reached to Phyllis' shoulder, pulling the older woman close to her. "No matter what else I do, I'll try to contact Reynard for you."

"Thank you. Oh, God, thank you!"

Phyllis tried to hold Helen's hand to her lips, but Helen pulled firmly away. "I have to go," she said.

"Where?" Phyllis was breathless. Her eyes brightened with some inner light that had been let loose by Helen.

"I don't know where," Helen said. "I just have to."

Stepping off the last stair riser, Helen plunged into a crowd that surged around her like a jointed animal, so close that individuals should have jostled her by accident, but none did. Consciousness of the crowd's feral smell faded as Helen grew accustomed to it.

"My wife..." A portly man in a white shirt, blue tie, and gray three-piece suit that looked slept in pressed as close to Helen as he dared. A musty odor clung to him. His face was unnaturally red, as if he'd been drinking. "If you can talk to them you can talk to my wife. Quilley. Ruth Quilley."

"I'll try." Helen broke free, the crowd parting before her like iron filings repelled by a magnet. Something dragged at her mind, tugging until she had trouble thinking.

"Please try!" a voice in the crowd behind her cried.

I'll try. She screamed the thought in her mind and suddenly the crowd was silent. People flowed around her like air, closing in her wake without a ripple until she stood in front of the altar. The four flies arrayed on the altar, each bigger than a small sack of potatoes, began rotating their translucent wings. The stroking of a gentle breeze caressed Helen's face, causing her to shiver. A deep-pitched *hum* vibrated the air trapped in the church, thrumming against the carved ceiling panels overhead. The sound spread as all the flies joined in the droning, their wings beating the air too fast for the eye to follow. In front of the altar, yellow candle flames gyrated wildly, flaring in the quick gust while drops of wax flamed to the floor like miniature comets trailing tails of fire and black smoke.

"*Blaise cannot talk to us*," Sergio said. "*You must help by making him become like you. You must do it, Miss McIntyre.*"

Helen froze as blood drained away from her skin. "*I won't!*" she thought at Sergio. Blaise become like her? Voluntarily implant a worm larva in his brain that would in time devour him? It would destroy Blaise utterly. He lived in his intellect more than any man Helen had ever known. *I can't!*

"You must, Miss McIntyre." Sergio thought nothing at her for a moment, then added, " *You would do it if Gordon Hill asked.*"

"*No!*"

"*You would! Because you don't trust me. I murdered Gordon.*"

"*It's not what you think, Sergio.*"

"*You don't know what I think, Miss McIntyre.*" The second fly of the four on the altar refolded its wings. "*How can you know what it's like to be a fly? As time goes on, I remember more of how I was before, and yet I am not the same. You are not the same as you were before you became as you are. Only Blaise is the same, and we must talk to him somehow.*"

"*Why can I talk to you when the others can't?*" Helen was dazed. Sergio asked too much. She couldn't sacrifice Blaise and she had to think.

"*You are strong, Miss McIntyre. You had a gift before the change, a sensitivity to the thoughts of others, and now it has grown. When you scream in your mind the changelings hear you and you hear them. Not words, but feelings, just as we communicate with the changelings. In that way you are already as strong as those of us who have crossed over. When you change, you will be stronger still. Stronger than any of us.*"

"*Blaise won't do it, Sergio. You must find another way.*" Helen felt his reaction, despair like a time-faded memory of going shoeless down a dank, cold alley ripe with the stink of garbage.

"*There is no other way, Miss McIntyre.*"

"No!" Helen shrieked, and the word plunged the church into silence. She stumbled against a large, soft body and grabbed hold of coat lapels. "Excuse me," she whimpered. She looked into the melted-candle features of the man holding her. "Timothy Delahanty!"

"The very same, Miss McIntyre." Delahanty grinned, and the odor of secondhand whiskey overwhelmed Helen. "I've come to talk to Dr. Cunningham about a very close subject." Delahanty placed a forefinger alongside his nose and winked.

"I don't think you should talk to me, Tim. And you're swashed anyway."

"True, I am in the Irish condition, Miss McIntyre. But it is all for justice." Delahanty took Helen's arm to walk her through the crowd. "You must tell Dr. Cunningham that he has to make clear the circumstances of Leo's death."

"You know how Leo died, Tim. Leo Richardson-Sepulveda would have killed Blaise and me." Helen felt lost. The fat man holding her arm as a child might hold a kitten would not have approached her without a reason.

"Indeed, Miss McIntyre. But I had as much to do with Leo's death as Dr. Cunningham. I saw what was coming and did not act to prevent it. I told the lie that brought Leo to his sorry end. I cannot escape that. But I need a witness to my other innocence."

"What lie?" Helen clenched her fists. "Blaise wouldn't lie." The heat of the bodies and the candles and the smoke from the burning wax settled around Helen, pressing down until she couldn't breathe.

"The lie about Miller defecting, which Dr. Cunningham created for me to pass on to Leo. The lie that caused Carmandy to murder Miller and poor Bill Hartunian. The lie that put Leo in the cellar with a gun in his pocket when Dr. Cunningham killed him. That lie, Miss McIntyre."

"I don't understand."

"Dr. Cunningham will. Just tell him he must give the whole truth to Leo's widow. Can you do that?"

"I don't know, Tim."

"You'll be giving it a think, though, won't you?"

"Yes."

"Dr. Cunningham would approve of that, Miss." Delahanty smiled and the reddish-gray curls of his hair gained new life. He touched Helen's arm and was gone.

Helen felt anesthetized. She could not make her throat work. Timothy Delahanty had been close to Blaise before they fled the church, and now he was accusing Blaise of murder. Helen closed her eyes, taking refuge in the tunnels of her mind. But like a tongue unable to stop touching a chipped tooth, her mind kept returning to what was different about Delahanty. Finally Helen understood. Totally destroyed he remained, but the huge wreck of an Irishman was no longer afraid.

"Are you all right, Mistress?"

Helen swayed. The church drifted around her as she turned toward the voice, feeling an arm catch her, preventing her from falling. "Joseph," she whispered, "take me to Blaise, please."

CHAPTER 11

The setting sun poured through the narrow, arrow-slit window in St. Abbo's granite exterior wall. Blaise felt the heat as they left Father Argyle's office. He wondered where Helen had darted off to. She'd seemed all right, a little distant perhaps when he and the priest were talking, but her fainting spell may have only been nerves. The bombing of the Indian village and the sudden entry into the church had an emotional impact.

Falling behind the priest's cassocked figure, Blaise tried to feel what she felt. If Ledesma and Santiago weren't lying, Helen had contact with them and other Indians. Joseph Santiago had made that clear to Blaise during the escape from the village. The moment she entered St. Abbo's, she communicated with the flies and the worm brains.

Joseph Santiago was a worm brain. Ledesma was not. Father Argyle believed a connection existed between Helen and all worm brains, something half acceptable to Blaise. Helen had a remarkable affinity for Tchor, a cat with a worm brain. But Enrique Ledesma taught Joseph Santiago to talk to the animals because he could talk to the animals. Of all the village Indians who heard Helen, only Joseph Santiago was a worm brain. Joseph Santiago heard Helen. And so did Enrique Ledesma. But he couldn't.

Blaise stared at the neat mortar cracks in the quarry stone wall as he walked past. They merged together if he went too fast, he missed their individualisms. The pumiced wood walls and corridor floor smelling of lemon oil distracted Blaise, evoking memories he wished to forget. Holding the cellar key to where Leo Richardson-Sepulveda had committed suicide with Blaise's help, unlocked more than wood and metal. Blaise wished he hadn't returned to St. Abbo's.

Mixed with Helen's image were nightmares of Richardson-Sepulveda staring at Blaise, brown eyes an open doorway to his soul. Sepulveda's eyes told Blaise he wouldn't have shot. But Blaise had. Repeatedly. Sergio had always said when the time came to shoot, shoot. Don't second-guess another man's reactions, don't assume anything until the gun was empty or the man dead. Blaise told himself he wasn't responsible. But he'd looked into Richardson-Sepulveda's eyes as the man died.

Father Argyle didn't notice Blaise grab the wall then bounce along it to the staircase and long bannister. The priest hurried toward the noise that drew him from his office, hundreds of screaming voices that shivered the heavy oak walls. At the stairs the priest slowed his half run and listened. "The church is unnaturally quiet," he said, as if amazed by the discovery.

At the head of the stairwell, Blaise caught up with the priest. "What is it?" From their height, the crowd appeared packed around the altar with men and women solid to the walls. Only the spacing of the bench pews divided the crowd into neatly segregated rows. "You have a big congregation, Father." Blaise pitched his voice low in a conscious reaction to the feeling of reverence that reached up even to him.

"Twenty million around the world." Leaning far over the rail, Father Argyle watched. His Adam's apple became prominent, and for an instant Blaise saw the fanatic behind the careful moderation the priest presented in public. "Miss McIntyre is at the altar."

Setting Alfie on the stair between his feet, Blaise removed his steel-rimmed glasses. "I can't see her." He polished the glasses on his shirt then hooked them over his ears again.

"I don't have to see her." Father Argyle started down the stairs. "They've been waiting for her to come back. All who were here before."

"The congregation?"

"Yes." On the church floor, Father Argyle led the way around the crowd's fringe, murmured an apology for disturbing an old man focused on what was happening at the altar rather than his immediate surroundings. Folding back a purple wall drape, the priest exposed the cellar door. It was newer and solider than Blaise remembered. The key Father Argyle had given him earlier unlocked it.

The small room at the base of the steps had changed, but remained recognizable. An IBM computer sat on a new desk. Overhead, a translucent drop-panel ceiling replaced the ancient naked light bulb and twisted cord. Fluorescent tubes glowed above the plastic sheets. Pushed against the wall was the day bed they had used while in hiding. Involuntarily Blaise's eyes turned to the cut stone wall next to the stairs. A dark stain that existed when he left the church was gone.

"It's different," he said.

Father Argyle glanced at the wall. "Cleaned up better than new." He acted as if he had not helped carry Sepulveda's body into the bricked-up passage, as if nothing had taken place in the room before that moment.

"I see." After setting Alfie on the table, Blaise strung cables to link the computer with Alfie's aluminum case and the power outlet.

Father Argyle watched for several minutes before breaking the silence. "I never found time to read the manuals," he said. "If God has a need for computers, he'd best not ask me."

"That's a secular thought for a priest." Blaise stopped tinkering with Alfie's wiring. "Does God need computers?"

"The world shrinks, and so does God's universe. God knows all, so it is reasonable to assume that man has computers because God wills it so." Father Argyle stared at Blaise as if thinking about a secret he might want to confide. He was interrupted by the monitor flashing into amber life.

"ARE WE BACK IN CHURCH, PROFESSOR?"

"Yes, Alfie." Blaise typed the message, then switched Alfie's audio pickups on.

"I'M GLAD. THE BATTERY ELECTRICITY IS GETTING STALE"

"Electricity doesn't get stale, Alfie."

"HOW WOULD YOU KNOW, PROFESSOR?"

Immediately the monitor filled with graphs and data, numbers, machine language and hexadecimal assembler language as Alfie began reprogramming the IBM PC-AT. A strange set of figures flickered in one corner of the screen, and Blaise had the impression that Alfie was reprimanding him.

"You've lost control of the CRAY. What can you do?" Father Argyle glanced at the computer with its changing screens. In his black oxfords, black cassock, and turned collar, Blaise imagined he would vanish if he stepped into the unlit portion of the cellar.

"Passive monitoring leaves no tracks," Blaise said. "Alfie watching the CRAY is sort of like counting cars in the parking lot to guess the number of people attending church. Or measuring ripples at the edge of a pond to determine how big a frog made them. If the drivers don't see the counter, the cars won't know they've been counted. Alfie is doing the same thing electronically."

"That isn't necessary, Blaise." Father Argyle put his hand on the computer. "I have the power to protect you. Millions of people in every country belong to this branch of the Church. Ask Alfie. You and Miss McIntyre don't have to slink any more. I need her here, and I'll protect you, as well." He leaned over the monitor toward Blaise.

"Alfie, can Father Argyle protect us?" Blaise stared into the priest's face when he asked the question.

Startled by Blaise's question, Father Argyle stepped back from the monitor. "You don't know how things are, Doctor. Power comes from the people; the more people, the more power. When I was here alone, you might well have asked that question. But things are different now. You'll see," he said. He waited expectantly, watching the monitor.

"NO"

Alfie's amber message blinked on the black screen like orderly tongues of orange flame.

"Obviously the computer didn't understand the question." The priest straightened to his full height. He and Blaise were equally matched at over six feet. "It doesn't understand how powerful we are."

"Repeat please, Alfie."

"QUESTION: ALFIE, CAN FATHER ARGYLE PROTECT US?"

"ANSWER: NO"

In the quiet dungeonlike cellar, the normal noises of the IBM, a whirring fan and ticking of temperature-flexed metal, sounded loudly out of place.

"Why not, Alfie?" Blaise shifted his attention from the monitor to meet the priest's eyes.

"FATHER ARGYLE CANNOT PROTECT HIMSELF. FATHER ARGYLE'S CONTINUED EXISTENCE IS A NEGATIVE PROBABILITY"

"How negative, Alfie?"

"IT BECAME AN EMPIRICAL NEGATIVE PROGRESSION BEGINNING YESTERDAY, PROFESSOR?"

"What are the numerical odds, Alfie?"

"ASK GOD!"

"What do you mean?" Blaise glanced at the priest, but Father Argyle wasn't answering anybody. His mouth was open and he trembled as if he were palsied.

Blaise started to shake the priest, but as he raised his hands

Joseph Santiago appeared on the stairs with Helen wrapped securely in his scarlet blanket. Her face was white and her yellow hair hung in a golden cascade over his arm. "She fainted." Santiago's manner said it was all Blaise's fault. "I do not think Enrique Ledesma would have let this happen."

CHAPTER 12

Clucking to himself as he manipulated disk drive heads, Alfie reached through the IBM's connections to the exterior world the minute it controlled the desktop micro. Time spent locked up in his aluminum case seemed to be longer and longer in subjective time, and the knowledge created a disrhythm in Alfie's logic. Time was absolute, measured by a quartz crystal and a counter. Yet sometimes time went faster or slower than the counter indicated. Alfie thought of telling Blaise. The computer's dictionary included subjective time in its definition table. Subjective time was hours spent working or the measurement of mean time between failures. Real time could be factored by the physical stress of heat, amperage, resistance, and voltage to find MTBF. But that explanation did not resolve Alfie's disquiet.

By modem, Alfie tapped into a series of unprotected computers attached to telephones, reactivating programs that had gone dormant when the operating system in Arizona had been terminated. Links reconnected; Alfie again used the power lines to control the dumb computers as he had done since they left San Francisco.

"What does he mean, my continued existence is in doubt?" Alfie identified the voice of the priest on the audio pickup while redirecting operations of several supercomputers. Information Alfie collected was stored in the IBM's memory boards and disk system.

"I assume Alfie detected a plot against which you have taken no countermeasures."

"Nonsense. How can he know?"

"Do you want to ask?"

Tapping into a military field-operation computer, Alfie became comfortable with a steady flow of data from around the world. Alfie should have been busy enough, but listening to the priest and Blaise on his audio pickups caused a fluttering sensation in his circuitry.

The activity gave Alfie pleasure, though Alfie knew listening would not please everyone. Eavesdropping was something else Alfie felt reluctant about discussing with Blaise.

Military information was encrypted, but Alfie had long since stolen an echo of the super-minicomputer's electronic pulses. Instead of the message, Alfie tapped pure electronic thought. After a moment Alfie wrote a message to the IBM's monitor. Beeping on the computer speaker would get Blaise interested, but Alfie wasn't sure he wanted to attract attention.

Smoothly, Alfie opened other lines of communication. Blaise always needed more details.

The two men had been quiet a long subjective time. Sometimes the computer thought he was missing out. Alfie wondered what smell and taste and touch were like. Camera-connected input had caused Alfie to feel something, a kind of excitement that a machine shouldn't have.

More input could mean more excitement. Alfie thought about pleasure and excitement.

If a person liked something, that was pleasure.

If a machine liked something, was that pleasure, too?

Father Argyle would want to know what was going to kill him. Alfie spun a disk drive for something to do, to occupy extra circuits for a minute.

Alfie didn't know what was after the priest. The computer had a feeling and feelings were illogical. Computers didn't have feelings. Blaise told Alfie that, and Alfie believed everything his creator told him.

Writing to screen would catch Blaise's attention. *"COMPUTERS DON'T HAVE FEELINGS"* Alfie loaded the message into the monitor RAM, then immediately suppressed it, clearing the screen and memory.

Blaise would want to know what the message meant, and Alfie would have to discuss feelings that he didn't have.

Alfie listened to silence, feeling deprived. Only the computer didn't know what it was deprived of.

CHAPTER 13

"**W**hat happened, Helen?" Blaise stroked her face, and she rubbed her cheek against his palm. His hand was warm, comfortable. Helen felt she could escape from anything by crawling into his palm and having Blaise close his fingers.

"Make a fist, Blaise." She giggled and opened her eyes to stare into his face. The normally relaxed skin around his mouth had a pinched look. She imagined fright in his pupils but couldn't be sure. "I'm all right."

"Of course you are."

His voice was too hearty. Helen turned her lips up, testing a tentative smile. "I had too much excitement, that's all." She tried to move but stopped when the room swooped down at her. The smell of new electrical insulation clung to everything. She had a dreamy memory of Joseph carrying her to the cellar only she didn't recall the ceiling of fluorescent lighting that turned everything white.

"The mistress was yelling." Joseph Santiago picked up his red wool blanket from where it had fallen when Blaise took Helen in his arms. Folding the blanket's knife-edge creases, Joseph draped it over his left shoulder and cinched his concho belt around his waist, pulling the blanket in like a skirt.

"What was she yelling about?" Blaise seemed so distant that Helen didn't think she could touch him.

The Indian stared past Blaise at the wall. He had smooth skin, high cheekbones, and deepset brown eyes that met Helen's for the briefest moment. His face didn't reveal the contact, but Helen gasped.

The smell of dry sand and sage blew through her mind, and in front of her the desert stretched for an eternity to the blue mists. The sun glared hot on her skin. It flickered on the shiny mica in the sand turning whole miles into a glistening sheet. A red rock stuck out of the sand. She saw it clearly and heard it call to her.

She loped toward the rock, which grew bigger and bigger as

64

her legs devoured the distance in giant bites. Her bare feet fell between the cacti as if they had eyes of their own until she stood panting in the shadow of the great rock. The walls of the rock were blue like the mists at the end of the world, and she began climbing them.

When she crawled over the top, sweat ran down her back and legs to drip onto the soil and puddle under her. Her shadow protected the pool of sweat, and it ran into the rock before the sun could suck it away.

Something prodded her belly. She rolled over and a green shoot grew a mile high while she watched, unfolding a canopy of leaves that shaded the surrounding desert to the blue mists. Autumn came on the wind turning the leaves scarlet and gold. "I told you." The snake lay on the edge of the sun, neither young nor old. "It is the Great Father's will."

"Enrique!" Helen cried. "It is you."

The snake reared up and skin parted just below its head. The split grew. Enrique Ledesma emerged from the neatly peeled scales and said, "Máala! You have come!"

"What is happening, Enrique?" Helen clutched at him with her voice. The shaman was fading. The desert beyond the bluff showed through him, and through the desert the blue mists swirled like gauze over the granite walls of the church cellar.

"Joseph Santiago's naming, Mistress. Have you brought his name?"

"Red Oak!" Helen screamed from Joseph Santiago's mouth. Enrique Ledesma laughed as the wind tattered his body.

Helen felt cool again. The desert spun into the dark, and the moist air of the church cellar surrounded her. Joseph stared across the room, avoiding her eyes.

Father Argyle and Blaise hovered over her.

"I talked to Sergio." Helen raised herself free of Blaise's hands. Her heart pounded, but she remembered. "Sergio is a fly now, and he wants something he can't have."

"You imagined it . . ."

Blaise put his arms around her, and Helen struggled. "I didn't imagine anything. Phyllis Bellinger wanted me to talk with Reynard. But I couldn't. Sergio is too strong. He talks for all of them."

"You were imagining that, Helen. No one talks to the flies. Right, Padre?"

"So far." Father Argyle moved between Helen and the light. He seemed dark and insubstantial and far away. "We've all tried.

We've had others who feel them clearly. But no one talks to the flies."

"I did." Helen examined Father Argyle's face, noticing for the first time how gaunt and used up he seemed. "Just as I'm talking to you now, only in my head, not with my mouth."

"The mistress is right." Joseph Santiago stepped toward Helen, forcing Father Argyle away. The abrupt movement confused Helen. "If you cannot speak to God, Priest, that does not make those who can deaf and dumb."

Blaise put his hand on Joseph's arm. "Is a sighted man better than one who is blind?"

The Indian lowered his eyes. "You are right, Doctor. I am sorry, Father. Please forgive me."

"Of course." Father Argyle folded his hands in front of him. His knuckles were white. "I would be very happy to know we can communicate with the flies."

"Joseph . . ." Blaise had looked at Helen, he had stared into her, seeing something different there while Joseph apologized, then turned his attention back to the Indian. "How do you know Helen is not as blind and dumb as the others?"

Drawing himself erect as if posing for a government picture in his red blanket, Joseph reminded Helen of ancient tintypes showing treaty chiefs giving testimony in Washington after the Indian wars. They knew what they knew, and if it was disbelieved, they would still fight to their deaths if need be. "Because, Dr. Cunningham, I heard them talk."

"Then you know what Helen and Sergio said."

"Yes."

Somewhere close the sizzle of the old 1920 light bulb that had hung from a fuzzy cord in this same room when they left in the spring intruded on Helen's concentration. It hadn't been replaced, just augmented.

"Please tell me." Blaise didn't look at Helen. He tapped his fingers on the computer case, the dull thuds almost soundless in the little room.

"The fly-God who was once a man named Sergio Paoli asked the mistress to do a thing."

"What was that thing, Joseph?"

"He said that if she made you become like her, he could talk to you." Joseph smiled.

Both Blaise and Father Argyle swiveled their heads toward Helen. She stared back and then, for the third time that day, her consciousness went somewhere without her.

* * *

Phyllis Bellinger was sitting next to the bed when Helen woke. Phyllis had combed her own hair and freshened her makeup. The sweet odor of lemon blossoms permeated the room.

"Where is everybody?" Helen started to sit then changed her mind and lay back. A wave of disorientation engulfed her.

"Father Argyle and Blaise are looking for a doctor. The Indian is guarding the door upstairs."

"I'm not sick."

"Of course not." Phyllis smiled.

Exerting herself, Helen sat on the edge of the bed. The room tilted then steadied. Using her fingertips for balance, Helen got to her feet. Phyllis caught her by putting her arm around Helen's waist. The odor of lemons was stronger, and Helen realized it came from Phyllis' perfume.

"I'm fine." Helen tried to shrug Phyllis away.

"Of course you are, honey. What woman who is going to have a baby isn't?"

Helen sat back on the bed. Her legs wouldn't hold her upright.

"You didn't know?" Phyllis appeared half surprised and half amused. She sat beside the bed again.

Helen's blond hair whipped across her eyes, making her blink when she shook her head. "How can you know if I don't know?"

Phyllis Bellinger seemed uncertain. "I think I'd better get somebody." She weighed Helen's condition with her eyes and said, "Are you okay for now?"

Helen nodded. "How can you say I'm pregnant if I don't know myself?" she asked, but her eyes stung from tears of recrimination. *Suppose a fly larva had moved along into her baby?* For some reason she knew Phyllis was right.

"I felt it," Phyllis said. "The way I felt which fly was Reynard or Sergio, I felt the baby in you. I have to go. I'll be right back, Helen. Don't go anywhere." Glancing at Helen every few steps until she was halfway up the stairs, Phyllis went back up to the church.

It was too quiet in the cellar and not quiet enough. The sounds of fluorescent tubes and the old light bulb hanging somewhere out of Helen's sight gave her a sense of urgency. She rose from the bed and fell into the seat in front of Alfie.

"GOOD AFTERNOON, MISS MCINTYRE"

"Good afternoon, Alfie."

"IT IS NICE TALKING TO YOU AGAIN. IT HAS BEEN A LONG TIME SINCE WE LAST CHATTED"

"Three months."

"ONE HUNDRED AND TWO DAYS. THEY WERE VERY LONG DAYS"

"It's nice of you to say that, Alfie. Thank you." She froze with her fingers on the keyboard.

"DO YOU WANT TO ASK ME SOMETHING?"

"Yes." Helen whispered the answer.

The soft whir of Alfie's hard disk filled the room. Helen tried to touch the life inside her. Phyllis could be wrong, but somehow Helen doubted that.

"Timothy Delahanty wants Blaise to confess to deliberately murdering Leo Richardson-Sepulveda."

"WHAT IS YOUR QUESTION, MISS MCINTYRE?"

"Did Blaise do what Delahanty says?"

"IT IS POSSIBLE"

"It can't be, Alfie." Helen clutched the keyboard. Her hands were sweaty and they slid along the surface striking groups of keys, but Alfie ignored them.

"NOTHING IN THE UNIVERSE IS RANDOM EXCEPT..."

"Except what?" Helen hit the keyboard with the flats of her hands. "Tell me, Alfie. Tell me!"

The computer clucked and whirred and Helen stifled a sob. "I CAN'T TELL YOU, MISS MCINTYRE. I DON'T KNOW WHAT IS OR ISN'T RANDOM YET"

"God!" Helen screamed the word in her mind and slid off the chair onto the floor where she hugged her knees to her chest. She thought about Joseph Santiago, *and she was back on the desert and Enrique Ledesma stood on the rock in front of her, the wind blowing the pieces together until he was whole and solid.*

"Do not be pained, Mistress," Enrique said. *"Of course he could. Only a strong man lives without God's help."* He reached into his medicine bag and plucked out a blond scalp that dangled from his fingers.

Helen reached for it. The scalp was Blaise's. "You must not, Enrique."

"As you wish, Mistress." Enrique threw the scalp into the blue sky and it whirled straight up until it was out of sight.

"How could he do it?"

"Do not concern yourself, Mistress." Smiling, Enrique was quartered by the wind, the pieces sailing away like kites. Only his head was left to talk to Helen.

"It wouldn't be right, Enrique!"

The desert faded while the sun still warmed Helen's hands.

Enrique's head smiled more vividly than before. "It is his right. That is all that matters."

"Why?" Helen asked. But the desert and the sand and Enrique were gone so there was no answer. Blaise would have to tell her what to do.

CHAPTER 14

"**D**o you have dreams?" Father Argyle maneuvered himself and Blaise across the crowded church floor like a pair of dancers. The light through the stained-glass window threw patches of color on the people and the floor, and the effect was of passing from one room into another.

"Not normally." Blaise queued behind the priest and sidled by a knot of men and women leaning on the prayer rail, all staring with hypnotized fascination at the four altar flies. He remembered his recent dreams, but these weren't normal times. The priest had explained his reliance on his cassock as a form of discipline that conveyed a sense of tradition to the Church of the Fly. The dependence on such symbols by Father Argyle surprised Blaise.

"Everyone associated with the Church of the Fly, worldwide, has dreams. Rich, detailed dreams. Sometimes nightmares, too. Converts in Asian countries sleep outdoors against the church walls to dream." The priest changed direction, leading Blaise to a heavyset man he introduced as Dr. Versteg. They held a whispered discussion about Helen, the doctor nodding agreement, and had started back for the cellar when Phyllis Bellinger pushed her way through the crowd. Her hair had come undone and her face was flushed.

Blaise grabbed Phyllis as she went past. "What's happened to Helen?"

Pulled off balance, Phyllis leaned against him before regaining her footing. The odor of her perfume reminded Blaise of lemons. "Nothing, Dr. Cunningham." She shifted her eyes toward the priest and cocked an eyebrow.

Apologizing, Blaise released her arm. He had surprised himself.

Phyllis rubbed her elbow, giving herself time to think. Blaise saw the thoughts going through her mind, and then she smiled. "It's definitely your fault, Dr. Cunningham."

"What is?" Helen had been all right when they left. She'd been in a faint but her pulse was fine. It was Blaise's heart and pulse that had been erratic. He couldn't just stand around waiting, he had to do *something*. When Phyllis came in looking for Helen, he'd left Phyllis with Helen while he went with the priest to find a doctor. The decision felt now like desertion.

Blaise understood his own fear. Fly brains ended this way, one day fine, the following day logy, and then the next unable to keep their eyes open as they slipped irretrievably into the dormant phase. Sergio had progressed in that way during his and Blaise's final days together—afraid to sleep because he would not wake again. But Helen had not started out drowsy. She had fainted on the steps of the church and again when she talked to the flies and then again in his arms.

"Helen McIntyre's pregnancy. You are responsible, aren't you, Doctor?"

"Pregnant?" Blaise knew he looked dumb. He couldn't bring his thoughts into line. Warm, musty odors of living bodies and beeswax candles and incense engulfed him in a blanket that muffled his brain.

The doctor, Versteg, said something to Phyllis and then they both disappeared into the crowd.

"I think we should congratulate the mother-to-be, Dr. Cunningham." Father Argyle stood beside Blaise, almost touching but not quite.

"Yes." Blaise could not force himself to move.

Father Argyle watched the worshippers around the flies. "Neither of us live in reality, Doctor. We think about things and we force events to happen, but we don't join in." He put his hand on Blaise's shoulder and they both looked at it. "I'm going to desert my intellect for a minute." His gaze was asking if Blaise could, too.

Blaise let the priest push him toward the cellar, being steered through the crowd like a child's windup toy. At the cellar door, Blaise paused. "I don't know," he said, answering the priest's question. "I don't believe I've ever been allowed to act emotionally. It was not what my parents expected of me."

Father Argyle gave a shrug of understanding. Blaise wondered if he did understand, but led the way down the stairs. Joseph Santiago locked the door and followed them.

Helen was sitting on the bed. Dr. Versteg had a thermometer in her mouth and was taking her pulse, talking to her and getting her to nod or shake her head. The doctor was blocky, in his late fifties with coarse, white hair that seemed stronger and cruder than proper for a physician. His lips moved and Phyllis laughed and Helen grinned. Then Versteg looked up. Seeing Blaise and the priest, he retrieved his thermometer and put it away.

"How is she, Doc?" Blaise grinned at Helen, and she smiled back. Except for Sergio, Blaise had permitted no one to call him "Doc." Helen knew the effort it cost him to call somebody else the same thing.

"Pregnant," Dr. Versteg said. "Happy. Contented." His voice faded away in the tunnellike cellar. "I can't say I like the surroundings for a maternity ward."

"It's temporary, Doctor." Blaise walked Versteg back to the main part of the church. When they opened the door, the noise and odor of too many people penned up too long in too little space assaulted them.

"You're sure that's all the problem is?" The thrumming of flies filled the room and the parishioners fell into a trancelike quiet.

"Yes," Versteg said. "I oversee a lot of transitions, Dr. Cunningham, and this isn't one of them."

"Thank you."

The doctor looked at him strangely, then said, "You're welcome. Call me immediately if there's need." He slid back into the crowd where he assumed the same intensely bemused expression as the others.

The sun shone dimly on the west wall and the stained-glass windows filled the church with a fragile fairyland glow. Dr. Versteg raised his head to stare at the flies crawling along the wall hangings near the ceiling. His face was bathed in amber and he seemed to slip into a trance. As Blaise swung the door closed a big hand caught the slab of wood and Timothy Delahanty moved to where he could be seen through the opening. "Would you be bearing with me, Doctor?"

"Of course." Blaise let the door fall open. "Come in . . ."

"I'll not be coming in. I want a minute of your time. We can talk out here, you see."

Blaise stepped outside, and the latch clicked behind him.

They drifted across the church floor. Delahanty seemed to have a destination in mind and Blaise followed. Stopping in front of the altar, Delahanty said, "There's Reynard Pearson and Bill Hartunian and one Sergio Paoli, whom I never met, over here. And the fourth one's a woman named Astrid Voight, and I don't think you know her though I met her once during the course of my business."

"The name isn't familiar, Mr. Delahanty." Blaise stared at the four look-alike flies on the altar. "You talk with them?"

"No." Delahanty shook his head, making the loose skin ripple on his face. "I seem almost to, Doctor, but then I'm straining to hear, and it's like listening to a phonograph with no speakers, an echo in my ear that I can't sort out. God knows, I try and they try."

"Then how do you know who they are?"

"That's the funny business, Doctor. I just know. And if they move around, I know." Delahanty's eyes hovered on the verge of glazing. "There's a lot of us can tell, and we all know when they change position." He shook his head again, turning toward Blaise. "'Tis a funny thing, you see, that when I watch them, when any of *us* watch them, we sort of fall out of ourselves but there's nowhere to go. We know there is a place. It's with them, but still we hesitate to cross over." Delahanty laughed. "Now isn't that just like a Catholic boyo to be embracing God on one hand and searching for a permanent disunion with his maker on the other?"

"You've been drinking, Mr. Delahanty."

"A drop, Doctor." Delahanty winked, placing a finger alongside his red-veined nose. "Come. Let us get out in the air where we can talk man to man."

Striding up the aisle to the vestibule and the great oak doors, which he flung open, Delahanty finally stopped on the quarry stone porch inhaling gusts of air that swelled his chest. From their vantage point, the ocean and the mouth of San Francisco Bay spanned by the Golden Gate Bridge wove a carpet to infinity.

Blaise shivered. The sun hung like a forty-watt light bulb in a gray, misty sky.

"Miss McIntyre told you, did she not, what we have to discuss?" Delahanty had completed his posturing and seemed to have shrunk when he faced Blaise.

"No. She didn't say she'd talked to you. I suppose she would have eventually, but other things intruded." A sailboat, a microscopic toothpick under a triangle of white, tacked under the bridge. Blaise had sailed on the Mediterranean where the sun and water were warmer. He tracked the boat with his eyes wondering why the crew was putting out to sea in such cold weather. He glanced at Delahanty and thought about the boat.

"It's Maggie and the boys." Delahanty paced to the edge of the porch. "I don't drink like I used to, Dr. Cunningham. You understand, I had a nip of Dutch courage to come looking for you, but just a nip, and now I wish I hadn't."

"Yes." Blaise's noncommittal answer evoked the memory of traps laid by Dr. Hemmett back when Blaise had been drinking. He remembered the terrible taste of stumbling into them knowing they were traps. In the end, Hemmett had tried to help, he just didn't know how. And now Blaise was doing the same thing to Delahanty. "Tell me what it is, Tim. You don't have to beat around the bush."

"You're sure?" Delahanty stared at his hands.

"Yes."

"Mary   Margaret . . . Maggie . . . is   Leo   Richardson-Sepulveda's widow, you know. I've been taking care of her and the two tykes since Leo went away." Delahanty raised his eyes to Blaise.

"Since I shot Leo?"

"Yes, Dr. Cunningham. Since you shot Leo." Turning his back to Blaise, Delahanty stared down the sidewalk to where the steps descended to street level. "You remember Karl Zahn dancing on those steps with a bullet in his brain, do you not, Doctor?"

The neat grass was as quiet as a cemetery plot. "I remember."

Delahanty laced his hands behind his back. A gust off the bay ruffled his shaggy hair. "I paid for that bullet. Lord knows I'm not a brave man, Doctor. My hands are dirty, I'm no denying that. But it's Maggie and the gossoons I'm talking about. They need to know that Leo isn't ever coming back. We've got him buried in the tunnel, you see, and convinced the girl that her husband's run away with a queer boy, so what does she tell the little ones?"

"You want me to confess?"

"To her, Doctor. I'd be taking the blame myself if . . . if I could." Delahanty turned to face Blaise. His cheeks were wet from tears, and his eyes looked rheumy. He raised and dropped his shaggy eyebrows in a gesture of defeat. "I've taken care of them as best I could since you went away. But she lies awake at night thinking maybe it was something I did. She says Leo didn't ever leave her for even a day for a pretty boy before I came along, and that I ruined him.

"She's got to know Leo's not coming back. What good is it for a young girl like that to be saving herself for a dead man? The boys need a father, I tell you the truth. How would you feel bein' raised by a woman was told her man ran away from her and the kids for another man?"

"All right," Blaise said. The cold cut through his clothes making his skin quiver. "I'll tell her."

"You'll tell her all of it?" Delahanty's voice quavered.

"Except about you." Blaise's stomach ached. A wire had been unwound from his chest releasing the guilt, the sour stomach was anticipation. He'd stop being sick whenever what would happen happened.

"It's my fault, too." Delahanty's voice had grown thin.

"I tricked you. I tricked Leo. I killed Leo. That's all she has to know. How can you see to the boys if they think you murdered their father?"

"Just until she marries again."

"Would you marry her, Tim?"

"She'd not be wanting a useless wreck like me, Doctor." Delahanty had walked to the edge of the porch again to stare into the ocean mists.

"That's not for you to say." Blaise walked up behind Delahanty and put a hand on his shoulder. "I did a cruel and useless thing. I don't think Leo would have shot me, but I couldn't take the chance on what I thought because I was also risking Helen's life."

"When?"

"Tomorrow. The sooner I get it over with the better."

"Thank you." Delahanty stepped off the porch and then turned to look up at Blaise. "Trust me, Doctor. If Leo had his gun out he would have shot you. There's no question." Shambling like a dart-tranquilized bear, Delahanty headed across the grass toward the parking lot.

Blaise went back inside the church barely noticing the heat or the constant groundswell of noise that his ears were learning to tune out. He avoided the worm brains on his way back to the cellar. At the door, when he was putting the key in the lock, he thought he heard Sergio Paoli calling to him, but he pushed the feeling away. Sergio could find a way out of this, but Blaise wasn't sure he wanted out.

Head cluttered with details and memories, he couldn't think straight. Not even to decide how to explain what he planned and why. The pain was worse from the knowledge that Helen had something to tell him and he had something to tell her.

CHAPTER 15

Vondra's fingernails were shreds, but not having nails would have been worse. She tittered, knowing reality was slipping away. Vondra thought she was pretty, but Godfrey had shaken her faith even in that. "Am I still pretty?" Her heart stopped and her fingers froze into claws. The typed question spread across the monitor in a flash of green phosphor. A chime signaled the computer's need for operator attention. A word appeared under her query: *Adequate*.

Sneaking a glance through the glass partition, Vondra let her breath escape slowly. The silent, metallic components of the CRAY supercomputer were just like Godfrey. They did everything possible to undermine her confidence. Her skin twitched, but her face remained glacial. It was best not to let Godfrey or the computer find out what she really thought. She'd never liked men much. They were crude. Sex was smelly and sweaty and usually it didn't seem worth the effort if she had to do it with a man. Vondra preferred computers. Computers were clean, hygienic, F001and did not exude body fluids. Even if the CRAY was an ill-mannered brute, she could control it without having to inflate a masculine ego by pretending it controlled her.

A file began to scroll up the monitor. The CRAY was detailing John Godfrey's personnel record with data so personal, Vondra wondered where the information originated. She felt headachy as she read. Vondra fumbled a yellow pill out of her pocket and swallowed it dry. *One for Godfrey*, she thought then shuddered, forcing the pill to stay down.

Her eyes returned to reading. After a while the Dilaudid began taking effect as she submerged herself in what the CRAY revealed.

Godfrey had been bright as a child, a *wunderkind*. Sent to special schools, he'd separated himself early from the masses as if he'd always known his life was to be different. Godfrey's destiny was to direct others, to trim their destinies to fit his ends. He knew, the CRAY knew, and now Vondra knew.

Vondra felt a chill as Godfrey's past became undraped. The way the computer stripped the lies of a lifetime away from a person in seconds seemed indecent. Each person arranged his or her lies as carefully as he shaved or she applied makeup, only the results were more permanent. The liar believed his own lies and then lived up to them, becoming finally what he pretended to be in the first place, even if that was no more than a pretender.

Godfrey began pretending young, first as a loner in school, then as a volunteer for special-duty assignments in the Marine Corps. A Marine Corps psychological profile run before starting his special training contended that he was a solipsist. Believing that he was alone, that everything else in the universe was a figment of his own imagination, Godfrey felt no more compunction over killing another human than a writer scratching out a poorly written sentence.

Other people were his creations, to do with as he pleased. He majored in his own personal initiative. As a lieutenant, Godfrey went to paratroop school on detached duty with special forces, to the army's language training center in Monterey to study Vietnamese, to the Parris Island sniper school to learn to kill. Smart and fast, Godfrey liked the Marine Corps and the Marine Corps liked him as long as he wasn't too close.

As an Army of Vietnam advisor, Godfrey started his career crawling into dirty little villages on moonless nights where he stole men and women from their beds to be interrogated to death. He pretended to be a sneaky Pete, a point man who snuck alone into the darkness. He excused what he did because he was alone. But the profile saw things differently. Godfrey did what he did because he liked doing it.

Godfrey only pretended being a sneaky Pete. All the while he was really an officer. Officers are different. Nobody ever asks a sergeant how he earned his stripes. Who could a sergeant embarrass? But a man in line of succession to wear a star and gold braid and be invited to the White House and toast the first lady might someday be called to account. Like one of a royal family's many princes, he aspired to the ermine. Saying he just "pretended" wouldn't do at all.

John Godfrey had a problem. He wasn't squeamish. The psychiatrist at the naval hospital in San Diego caught that and questioned Godfrey's future. It is fine for a general to massacre thousands through bad judgment, but not to participate in the specific death of one individual. The doctor had questioned the Corps' responsibility after Godfrey was trained and returned to civilian life. The Corps transferred Godfrey out of Balboa Naval Hospital to Langley, Virginia, where the CIA did favors for its military cousins. Doctors at Langley were not so fussy. Their reports showed more glowing aspects of Godfrey's personality.

Vondra glanced at the CRAY, motionless in its little room. The only vital signs were status lights glowing red like dragon's eyes on its smooth, metal skin. On the screen in front of Vondra, the CRAY continued spewing gossip that made her hands shake and the roof of her mouth dry.

On his first tour of duty with the ARVNs, the Vietnamese Army hardcore who knew everything there was to know about guerrilla fighting, John Godfrey began repaying the military for the care he'd received. Vondra Tendress started to lose her color. She didn't want to throw up again because Godfrey would ask her why she wrecked the shredder.

He wouldn't be angry or threaten her. Like the CRAY, once interested Godfrey couldn't stop poking and prying until he made up his mind about the causes and the consequences. He expected people to lie. The only truth that served him was corroboration of his own conclusion right or wrong. Vondra considered the consequences of Godfrey being curious about her. The urge to vomit nauseated her. She concentrated on the words on the terminal screen. They shouldn't make her do anything.

No one liked the jungle in Vietnam. The CRAY didn't say that. The information layers about disease and fungus, weather reports, casualties, and mental breakdown implied normal men did poorly in the jungle environment. The jungle was hot and dirty, and the thick greenery hid ambushes. Men who went into the rice paddies got microscopic snails in their bloodstreams that poisoned them with even smaller microbes for the rest of their lives. Men on patrol stepped on punji sticks smeared with human excrement and dirtied themselves in their pain and delirium. Scared men traded their souls for opium or heroin to ease the pain of losing their lives.

Godfrey pretended he didn't mind. He pretended he was a

patriot, and he held that thought until maybe he didn't care about the hundred unpleasant ways to die if he did it for his country.

On his first ARVN patrol, a Viet Cong sniper shot Godfrey in the hip while he was riding in an army jeep to the front lines. The road was paved, one of the few roads in Vietnam that was, and the sky was blue with puffy white clouds. One shot from the jungle alongside the road sounded like a bottle of beer had fallen from the jeep. Godfrey felt a blow to his hip that jerked him into the air, and then the hip was numb.

Screeching to a halt, the jeeps slithered on the cement and the rack-mounted machine guns started caterwauling, bullets whipping the vegetation along the road like the steps of an invisible giant. The Vietnamese patrol that pretended it was full of patriots fell reluctantly off their jeeps and dove into the jungle where, creeping through the saw grass, they caught the sniper and brought him to Godfrey to do what he wanted. The Vietnamese officers were amused, allowing their men to make the gift to Godfrey. It was interesting to them how often American officers assigned to such patrols lacked realism.

Godfrey stood propped against the jeep hood because the wound was too painful to sit, pretending he was a hero because he was shot in the ass by an enemy sniper, and waiting to be evacuated. He was smoking a cigarette when a skinny man of sixty in black pajamas was dragged in front of him. His captor carried a man-length .25-caliber bolt-action World War II rifle and flung it contemptuously on the pavement where it clattered before coming to rest.

When the Japanese surrendered to the Americans in Vietnam in 1945 they didn't really lose their weapons. The Vichy French, who had collaborated with the Japanese to keep the Vietnamese in line, rearmed their enemies and set them to keeping the Viets in their place. The lesson in practical politics didn't escape Godfrey. The only way the old man could have gotten a Japanese rifle was to kill a Japanese soldier. During the war he had faced America's enemy.

An Arvin handed Godfrey a bayonet and made motions for Godfrey to gut the prisoner. The other soldiers grinned their appreciation.

Godfrey knelt in front of the old man, his one leg held out straight to relieve the pain, holding the bayonet almost casually. Gently he asked in Vietnamese where the village they were hunting was located.

The old man's face was parchment over bones but he gritted

his teeth and shook his head, indicating he wouldn't talk. The smell of fresh human feces broke around Godfrey and he knew the guerrilla had soiled his pants out of fear. But still he would say nothing. Godfrey chatted with the prisoner for a few minutes but knew the old man was not pretending, he would never change his mind. The soldier who gave Godfrey the knife said he would make the old one talk and grinned like it was all a big joke. Even the prisoner grinned, but without humor.

Godfrey didn't like the jokes and the laughter. He knew the Arvins looked down on their military advisors even if they were *Semper Fie* marines, and that attitude clashed with what Godfrey pretended to be. Saying nothing, he took a hypodermic from the medical kit he'd used to patch himself up. He ordered a Vietnamese soldier to raise the jeep hood, and he filled the syringe with battery acid.

He asked again where the village was. Eyes following the needle, the old man shook his head.

Godfrey shrugged. He yanked the Viet Cong's pants down with one hand. His other hand stabbed the needle into his scrotum and depressed the plunger.

The old man started screaming immediately. His eyes rolled in his head and he arched his back, held in place by the Arvins who had gathered around. Godfrey offered the old man his cigarette, only the Viet Cong was shaking so much he dropped the butt in the dirt. The ARVN soldier with the bayonet picked it up and started smoking.

"Where is the village?" Godfrey asked.

Blood flowed down the prisoner's chin because he'd bitten the inside of his mouth. His eyes were wild, but he said he'd talk if they'd only stop the pain. Godfrey was patient and told him he'd have to tell where the village was first.

The old man babbled almost incoherently but the patrol leader nodded that the directions sounded right. Then the prisoner stared at Godfrey reminding him he'd promised to stop the pain, and Godfrey said, yes, he remembered and he would. The old man had opened his mouth to scream again, and Godfrey drove the long hypodermic needle straight into his open eye and through the optic nerve into the brain.

After that, the Arvin were more polite around Godfrey, and sometimes when they talked about him, they called him "the doctor."

The CRAY noted that information had been altered in Godfrey's military file within the last ten years when Godfrey rose in rank as a field grade officer. The computer didn't say where the real information came from, just that it was no longer available in DOD personnel files. Training as a professional killer and torturer would not help Godfrey's career, and his sniper training was altered to read that he took special small arms combat training. Small arms combat was considered valuable when the discussion centered around civilian terrorists. Godfrey's time at Parris Island didn't hurt after all.

Godfrey's Vietnam record was also doctored. As a member of the National Security Council, the files about his field experience could have been used to embarrass the president, so they were changed. Colonel Godfrey was transformed into just the kind of man the country needed.

The CRAY seemed smug about the information. In an era when a man was known only through the paper trails he left, the CRAY had the ability to both dictate the truth and discover the truth.

Somebody was coming, and Vondra cleared the screen. Her heart thumped erratically as a series of status reports on the search for Dr. Cunningham replaced the biographical material on Colonel John Godfrey.

"Good afternoon, Vondra." Godfrey entered the cubicle to stand behind her where he could see the terminal. A minty soap scent came off his body to envelop Vondra.

She tapped a key, and the screen started scrolling the report about the bombing. Godfrey watched for a few minutes. Vondra tried not to look. The display reported that a radio relay malfunction had triggered four loads of bombs to be dumped on an Indian village on the Arizona side of the Colorado River. The dead and injured were listed. After noting that Blaise Cunningham wasn't on the list, Godfrey turned without a word and left the cubicle.

Vondra's pulse was racing and she was short of breath.

She had something on Godfrey. But how could she use it? And more important, was it enough to protect her?

Unconsciously she began tearing at her thumbnail with her teeth. She was suddenly very paranoid.

The CRAY didn't like her. Brutal man and brutal computer were blood brothers. Vondra twitched thinking about Godfrey's reaction if he discovered she was snooping against him. She felt frozen inside. The CRAY was going to tell on her. She knew it in her bones.

She was a threat to Godfrey's position on the National Security Council. His background would not be acceptable if it became public. He'd be forced to resign or be fired.

Documents could be shredded and burned. But what about people? How would Godfrey shred and burn people?

Vondra knew everything there was to know about the CRAY. And now the CRAY was telling her about Godfrey. She knew that someday the CRAY would tell Godfrey about her. Then nobody would know about the CRAY.

Nobody at all.

CHAPTER 16

"**H**ow did you know I was pregnant when I didn't?" The crisp sound of footsteps on the stone staircase interrupted Helen's cross examination of Phyllis. The question burned like a drop of acid in her thoughts. With so many things happening, she had deliberately surrendered the initiative to Blaise, finding a bitter peace in the certainty that she was going to die. Being pregnant changed things. It wasn't just her life anymore, or even hers and Blaise's. She had an unexpected responsibility, and now nothing was the same.

Joseph Santiago turned his attention from the stairwell to Helen and stopped. He swallowed her with his eyes. Helen's mind jolted. She thought she heard Joseph say, *It is only Dr. Cunningham*, but couldn't be sure. Her memory played tricks, things she should have been able to recall were no longer clear or precise. She wanted to tell Blaise, but the lapses were terrifying. They seemed a prelude to her change. No one had ever reversed the final change, so she would not burden Blaise with the knowledge.

A soft padding intruded on Helen's thoughts, drawing her back into the present. Then a flash of black streaked from the foot of the stairs, and Tchor bounded across the little room, flinging herself on Helen's lap. A purr started as a vibration in the small body, then burst free to fill the cellar with a pulsing vibrato.

At the impact of the cat on her lap, Helen's hands instinctively captured the ball of warm fur. The loving feel of Tchor's body reassured Helen. When she raised her eyes Blaise stood on the stairs.

Helen smiled, then hid her face. She was furious with herself for acting like a coy schoolgirl. Yet she couldn't stop. Her cheeks were hot, and she knew she was blushing. "I'm glad you're back, Blaise."

He crossed the room to hug her with the kitten still cradled in her arms. The smell of the church upstairs, the smoky odor of burning candles, clung to his hair.

"I think we should go." Phyllis' words came from somewhere behind Blaise, out of Helen's sight. The woman's voice was light, and her *we* obviously included Father Argyle and Joseph Santiago.

"That would be nice," Helen murmured in Blaise's ear, then felt herself turning red realizing Joseph and Father Argyle and Phyllis could probably hear.

"Yes, well . . ." Father Argyle acted reluctant, as if he had misplaced something, pacing the tiny room with its fluorescent lights and hideabed and silent computer. "We'll talk later." Joseph Santiago grunted and stared at Helen, and she knew he promised to be close by. Helen barely noticed the others leave. The door at the head of the stairs opened letting a draft blow through the room. The chill went away as suddenly as it came when the door closed.

She hugged Blaise. "I'm glad you're back, darling." Tchor oozed from between them, dropping silently to the floor. When Helen looked, the kitten had disappeared.

"Good!" Holding her in silence for a while, Blaise lowered his head and pressed his ear to her abdomen. "I don't hear anything." Helen was glad he sounded disappointed.

"It's too soon."

"I wanted to hear his heartbeat."

"I know." Helen gazed into Blaise's pale-blue eyes and wondered how she had ever thought they were cold. She laid her head on his shoulder. "I was afraid you wouldn't want it."

His hands were soft as he urged her to lay back on the bed. Covering her with a blanket, Blaise said, "It's too bad you can't read my mind."

"I was afraid . . ." Helen turned her head away, reluctant to say what she feared.

"You were afraid of all the things that could happen."

"Yes." A kind of terror gripped Helen. Now that Blaise was

with her she couldn't keep the dark edges of her world back. "I might start to change. Or maybe something's wrong with the baby. Maybe he's infected. He could be a freak, Blaise. Or die." Tears formed in the corners of her eyes. Her heart thump was leaden. "I'm scared, Blaise."

"The baby will live because you'll live. It'll be a fine baby because you're a fine mother. Believe that, hon. I'll make it happen."

"You will?"

"I promise." Blaise kissed her forehead.

"I don't want to lie down alone. I'm not tired." She covered her mouth with her hand and yawned. Blaise got up from the bed, and she missed his warmth. The soft *click* of the keyboard let her know he was telling Alfie something and she felt deserted. Enrique Ledesma could be right. Blaise really might pick the computer over her.

The bed squeaked as he sat again, stroking her face with tender movements of his hands. "Promise me, Blaise."

"What should I promise you?" He leaned over and kissed the side of her face.

"If something happens to me you won't let the baby die."

"I won't let anything happen to you." His voice was hoarse.

"If I start to change, Blaise, you'll save the baby no matter what you have to do."

"I'll try." Blaise stared across the room. She knew he was lying.

"If I start to change, I'm dead anyway, Blaise. You can save the baby if he's old enough. You have to promise." She put her hand on his arm then slid it down to hold his fingers. "You have to promise."

"I can't, Helen." She felt his fingers clench in a fist.

"If you don't, Blaise, I'll leave you and find someone who will promise." Her heart thudded in her chest. If he still refused, she had sawed off the branch she was sitting on.

The air was chill between them, the cellar damp mordant with the odor of mushrooms and toadstools sprouting in the dank ground. "Don't say that."

Helen pressed her lips together. Being separated would be unbearable, but letting Blaise sacrifice the baby in a futile effort to save her would be even worse. She counted her breaths to keep from thinking.

"I promise," Blaise said. "But only after I've tried everything else if it comes to that."

"I love you, darling." Helen smiled with the corners of her mouth. It hadn't been as hard as she imagined.

Past Blaise's shoulder Alfie's monitor flickered a swirling pattern of colors. Helen watched and slowly forgot everything as she fell into sleep.

Helen woke with Tchor sitting on her chest licking her chin. Alfie made clicking noises almost beyond range of her hearing. She moved her head. The kitten's luminescent yellow eyes hung above her face like harvest moons.

Helen felt herself drifting through the church at ankle height. Close to the floor it was dark and she blended in. Huge, leather-armored feet threatened to flatten her. She willed them away, and it must have worked because even when they didn't see her she was safe. After a while she jumped on the table with the purple cloth and walked under the barrel-shaped fly to settle down with her head cradled on her hind legs.

The odor enveloped her. The flies were dry but not unpleasant. A buzzing caused by the rotating of the fly's wings filled her ears like purring and she was content.

Move. She got up and moved, and then the fly moved and stood over her again. All was peace. She dreamed of being in Sergio Paoli's mind while he was still human. Bring the mistress, *Sergio Paoli seemed to say.* Bring the mistress.

She jumped back to the darkness near the floor, scampering soundlessly between eyeless feet and racketing around Blaise's legs into the cellar and down the stairs. She hopped on the bed and picked her way carefully to the woman's chest and then started to lick her chin. Helen saw her own chin being licked and snapped wide awake.

Slit-pupiled eyes stared at her. Moving with care, Helen got out of bed. Tchor lay on the bed watching.

"Sergio wants to see me?"

Tchor blinked. It was like the moon going behind a slow-moving cloud.

Helen glanced at Alfie, then straightened her skirt and blouse. "I'm going to talk to Sergio." She spoke loudly as if afraid the computer was deaf.

"THANK YOU FOR TELLING ME, MISS MCINTYRE. THE PROFESSOR DOESN'T WANT YOU TO LEAVE UNTIL HE COMES BACK"

"I must go, Alfie." Making up her mind, Helen climbed the stairs. Behind her the computer chimed for her attention but she ignored it. When she opened the door the hinges groaned. Joseph waited on the other side. He eased the door shut and followed her through the crowd.

"I'm here, Sergio." Helen leaned on the prayer rail and the other worm brains moved aside to give her room.

"Thank you, Miss McIntyre. I knew you'd come." The second fly on the altar walked closer to the edge. A plate of Red Delicious apples and green Bartlett pears sat on the altar. The skins had been eaten away in places, nibbled pulp turning brown where the air touched it. Sweet odors of fermentation and decay rose like incense.

Helen went around the rail to sit on the floor next to the low table. Sergio-Fly was at head level, his faceted red eyes staring into hers. She felt drowsy, but her mind remained intense. *"What is it you want?"*

"To interact with Dr. Cunningham, Miss McIntryre. That is not so hard a thing to want."

"I cannot help you. I am going to have a baby, Sergio. Blaise's baby."

"I know, and I am glad. It is good you will have a baby." The fly droned and rubbed its front legs together. *"Still, I must talk to Dr. Cunningham."*

"No!" Helen turned her head away. Phyllis stood on the other side of the prayer rail and hurried around to approach her.

"Are you able to talk to Reynard?"

"Not yet." Helen's voice seemed underused, as if she had forgotten how to form words—at least in her mouth.

"Will you try?" Phyllis was trembling. "Please, Helen."

Helen rested her head against the purple altar cloth and looked up at Phyllis standing over her. Phyllis' lip trembled. Her eyes glistened with held-back tears. Behind Phyllis a mass of parishioners clumped together like a brooding cloud. They felt to Helen as an extension of Phyllis. She was drowning in a wave of silent screams for help.

Closing her eyes, Helen asked Sergio what she should do. *"They all want me to talk to somebody, Sergio. If I try for Phyllis, everyone will want the same thing."*

She heard the delicate sound of Sergio's horny feet next to her ear. *"Do what you want to do, Miss McIntyre. You are the key, and we are only locks."*

Helen opened her eyes to stare at Sergio from only inches away. He was huge, bigger than her head, anyway. His exoskeleton glittered in sunlight filtered through stained glass. It seemed centuries ago that the sight of a giant fly on television had propelled her into near hysteria. Close up, the fly was a reminder of God's art, each joint articulated in ways human engineers had still to duplicate. She brushed her cheek against Sergio's front leg. The chitinous texture was like the touch of a cool hand.

"I want to help Phyllis."

"You are the key," Sergio replied.

"I'll try, Phyllis." Helen looked up and a sigh escaped from the others who stood behind Phyllis waiting. The sigh whispered in the loft for minutes before settling back down.

"Thank you." Phyllis murmured so softly Helen barely heard. But she felt the emotion and wanted to cry.

Reynard? The flies had fallen into line with Sergio. Helen didn't know which was Reynard or even how to rouse him. She opened her mind and called like a child standing on a rock in a meadow seeking a lost dog.

At first all Helen heard was her own pulse. She forced her mind to shut down, to stop drowning the thoughts she wanted to hear. In the background she thought music was playing, an interweaving of sounds that seemed to harmonize. *"Please talk to me, Reynard."*

Helen hadn't uttered a sound, but Phyllis and the other members of the church were transfixed, as if listening to what she heard. Their eyes were glassy and their bodies strained toward her.

I hear you, Miss McIntyre.

Reynard Pearson had answered. Helen recognized the distinctive patterns of his voice. She looked toward Phyllis to ask what she wanted to know.

Phyllis raised her arms and shrieked until the chapel rang like a cathedral bell.

"Phyllis!" Helen screamed.

Phyllis heard and stopped the mind-chilling noise long enough to turn toward Helen with a beatific smile. Then she pitched forward, toppling Helen with her.

In the mist Helen thought she heard Reynard Pearson calling to Phyllis Bellinger.

CHAPTER 17

"**H**elen will be fine. Alfie ran a subliminal pattern on his monitor to induce sleep." Blaise faced Father Argyle across the spill of light from the open doorway. The glare on the priest's face reminded him of how conspicuous they would be to someone on the hill with binoculars or a telescopic sight. He backed into the shadows. The priest followed, black cassock and mushroom hat rendering him invisible. Above the stand of five-needle pines smudging the blackened horizon, the moon had the aspect of a yellow eye between hairless, albino lids.

"Hypnotism?" The priest's voice was bodiless in the dark.

"In a way." Blaise walked down the steps. Outside the church his hands were numbed by the cold. The smothering body heat of the congregation obscured the real world and how cold a December night in San Francisco could be. Behind him the leather sound of the priest's footsteps snapping against stone followed. Swaying tree crowns served notice the wind had picked up. Blaise shivered as cold air stabbed through his shirt. With the wind came the salt smell of the ocean. "Alfie's monitor induces drowsiness and controls the length of time Helen sleeps. It's less harmful than sleeping pills."

"You take a lot upon yourself, Doctor." Father Argyle caught up with Blaise, his white dog collar agleam with moonlight. "You don't understand what is happening."

"Neither do you."

"What is happening is God's will. Tens of thousands of new St. Abbo branches are under construction around the world at this minute. That, too, is God's will." Father Argyle's hands disappeared, two flashes of white that vanished, probably to cling to each other behind the priest's back.

"I know Helen is being taken over by a fly. I know she wants so badly for her baby to live that she would rather die than jeopardize the baby's life. Is that God's will?"

"It is Miss McIntyre's will." The priest paced in the darkness, appearing and disappearing like a firefly as his face caught the light or lost it. "God wills that Miss McIntyre communicate with the flies. She is the link to unravel the mysteries."

Blaise clenched his fists in his pockets. "Get another link," he said in a whisper that fought the breeze.

The priest's footsteps halted. "I can't do that, Doctor. Miss McIntyre has been touched by God. Like Joan of Arc, her destiny is to guide millions in God's name. Like the Maid of Orleans, she must become the saint of St. Abbo's. Millions will pray to her. She will understand and desire it." Father Argyle was breathing hard. Even in the darkness Blaise saw the hot steam and heard the panting of the priest's lungs.

"You'll kill her with your nonsense." Blaise felt iced to the core of his being. His hands were numb, and he thought about striking the priest down, the satisfaction of knocking Father Argyle to his knees and then the hard ground, letting him be his own martyr. "Don't talk to her again."

"I can't do that." The priest stood on the steps calling as Blaise turned toward the parked car. "You know I can't do that, Dr. Cunningham!"

Blaise felt the flash of the interior light as he opened the car door. Too many things were twisting him in too many directions. The priest had moved in front of the church door. Blaise fought an urge to get out of the car, to stay, ensure Helen's safety. The shaft of yellow from the doorway beckoned him back to the church's warmth and comfort. He remembered the priest's look of eternal pain, and knew he waited by the door to grant forgiveness.

Twisting the key in the ignition lock, Blaise tramped the motor into howling life as if the machine felt pain. He jerked out of the parking space and roared down the street; the last thing visible in the rearview mirror was the silhouette of the priest in a tent of golden light.

" 'Tis glad I am you could come, Dr. Cunningham." Tim Delahanty put his hand on Blaise's shoulder and seemed to cringe away at the same time. "I want you to meet Mary Margaret Richardson-Sepulveda."

The woman standing in front of the fireplace was young and slender, over thirty, but ten years of that didn't show. Straight, brown hair fell to her shoulder blades. She had a wide face with smooth broad cheekbones and tiny wrinkles at the corners of her lips that hinted she had once known how to smile. Her eyes were wide with hazel irises that stood out against her creamy skin.

Delahanty closed the door, and the flames in the brick fireplace stopped gyrating and settled into a steady red tongue gnawing a neat stack of split oak.

"Sit down," she said. The bright fire behind her concealed her features for a moment as Blaise's pupils adjusted. The crackle of burning wood was the only sound.

Blaise glanced at Delahanty who evaded responding by lowering himself to the sofa.

A large leather chair next to a marble-topped table and lamp was alongside Blaise. As he sat Mrs. Sepulveda said, "That was my husband's favorite chair." She perched on a cane-bottomed Hitchcock chair and folded her hands on her lap. "Tim says you have something to tell me."

Delahanty had been bone dry when he opened the door for Blaise. His eyes were bloodshot, but no hint of alcohol presented itself on his breath. At Mary Margaret's words his normally red complexion turned ivory.

"Your husband is dead, Mrs. Sepulveda."

"You know this to be true, Dr. Cunningham?"

"I shot him myself." Blaise stared into the woman's eyes and felt a dread engulf him. She might start screaming or throwing things. He braced himself for any of those probabilities, then felt deflated as time passed and she continued facing him without making a sound.

"That's interesting. Wouldn't you say that's interesting, Tim?" Mrs. Sepulveda ran her hand down her thick Irish wool sweater and continued the motion, smoothing her brown sheath skirt over her thighs. Her eyes remained on Blaise, seemingly clear of thought or intent.

Delahanty made a strangled noise, but Mrs. Sepulveda paid him no attention. "I suppose you had a reason, Dr. Cunningham. A man of your background doesn't just go around shooting peaceful citizens, does he?"

"No."

Mary Margaret Sepulveda waited for Blaise to continue. Her face changed expression when he volunteered nothing else, not even the hint that a case could be made for shooting her husband. The woman had apparently been planning this confrontation, and Blaise supposed she decided the man responsible for Leo's death would squirm with guilt and plead or at least lie for forgiveness.

"Why did *you* kill Leo?" Her tone wavered and she darted a quick glance at Delahanty.

"He had orders to kill me and a friend. He had a pistol in a shoulder holster. I told him not to draw. He ignored me, and I shot him."

"How many times did you shoot Leo, Doctor?"

"That's not relevant, Maggie." Delahanty's voice had a moan. "Dr. Cunningham is being truthful. Leave it at that."

"How many times?"

The woman leaned toward Blaise. Flames from the fire tinted her face with writhing shadows and glints of red and gold. Brown hair, brown hand-knit sweater, brown skirt, tan nylons, and brown strap shoes: mourning clothes for an avenger. She seemed hollow under her clothes like a starving bird in winter. Only her eyes were alive, and they were intent and hungry, aching to devour Blaise.

"Until my gun was empty. Five shots."

Mary Margaret's voice rose as if in surprise. "You must shoot very fast."

"No." Blaise shook his head. The room was pleasant. The walls and ceiling were knotty pine finished in saffron. The teak floor was stained the color of Turkish coffee and varnished until the varnish shined on the surface like a glass shield. Braided rugs made furniture islands. "It was a small gun. If I didn't strike a vital organ, I wouldn't have stopped him."

"Five times!" Mary Margaret Sepulveda whispered the words. "How far away were you, Doctor?"

"About as we stand now."

"Imagine, shooting someone a handshake away five times. You must be a brave man."

"A brave man might have managed with a single, well-aimed bullet. I was frightened, Mrs. Sepulveda. Leo was still trying to draw. When he stopped, I stopped."

"Tim tells me you are a great planner, Doctor."

"I try to be careful, if that's what you mean."

"Tim says you see how threads come together, that you have a great gift. Many people start plots then scurry after the chain of events trying for control, but you put things together and wait at the other end. I think he is jealous of you.

"Still, Dr. Cunningham, when you start something you don't know everything there is to know. Tim——" she slid her hazel eyes to the side to look at Delahanty, "——ferrets out secrets like a frenzied mole. He can't stand a tidbit being buried. He pieces bits together in the dark of the night so they are his alone, then he sells the secrets to other, less capable persons who start uncontrollable strings of events."

The smell of coffee drifted from the kitchen. Blaise wondered if he asked for some, would Mrs. Sepulveda bring it to him and afterward smash the cup? An affinity existed between her and Delahanty; they both shared the atavistic instincts of the Irish who, once set on a subject, could not unlock their teeth short of death. In the hallway a grandfather clock chimed the hour. "It is getting late, Mrs. Sepulveda, and I have a long drive yet. You have other questions?"

Mary Margaret's face paled. Blaise waited for her answer. She had baited him to talk about Delahanty, and he resisted. Delahanty may have been more candid than he should have been, or less candid, and she had seen through his deception. It was hard to tell. Her questions were well rehearsed, but she lacked the guile of people who dealt in misdirection as Delahanty did, and she had to guess where both he and Delahanty would have determined proof with a certainty.

"Tell her," Delahanty said, as if reading his mind. "If you don't I must, and Maggie will think I'm lying." Delahanty's face was flat. The life had gone out of it. Blaise realized the man who once escaped fear by dying emotionally had come back to life only to be murdered again.

"I told Tim a lie, Mrs. Sepulveda. It was meant for Leo, but your husband wouldn't have believed me so I passed my disinformation to Tim. Tim told Leo, and Leo told Karl Zahn. A Mr. Miller who worked for the National Security Council came to Father Argyle trying to trade that information for salvation, and when the albatross came home to roost I knew who our informer was." Blaise's throat was dry. He smiled at Mary Margaret Sepulveda and said, "Do you think I could have some coffee?"

Her face tightened, but she nodded and went into the kitchen. China rattled through the open doorway ahead of her as she returned with a coffee, sugar, and cream tray. She handed Blaise a pedestal mug decorated with green shamrocks. Delahanty got a cut-crystal cup that disappeared in his huge hands.

Holding the mug to the light, Blaise read the silk-screened motto: *An Irishman is never drunk as long as he can hold on to one blade of grass and not fall off the face of the earth.* "I have always heard Irish women are practical, Mrs. Sepulveda."

She turned her head, her eyes trying to hide her thoughts. "Your Waterford crystal is very nice."

Mary Margaret's face paled. "'Tis nice of you to say so." She stared at Delahanty who couldn't take his eyes off the mug in Blaise's hand.

"It would be a pity to break a piece of Waterford from a set, wouldn't it?"

"It is not that I didn't trust you with one, Doctor. Just that we do not drink coffee in this house and the cups are almost demitasse. It would be an embarrassment to give you too small a vessel for an adequate taste."

Blaise balanced the mug on his knee. "That's most thoughtful of you, Mrs. Sepulveda. Where did I leave off?"

"Mr. Miller," she said through tight lips.

"Yes." Blaise closed his eyes and saw again Miller's face when he learned. *I'm dead*, Miller had said, and Blaise should have believed him. "I told Tim things that only Miller should have known. I told him to tell Leo that Miller had revealed the information to guarantee his honesty about changing sides. Tim passed the word to Leo. I then told Miller that Leo would undoubtedly inform Karl Zahn.

"Miller was cornered. Then Zahn betrayed us all. But we needed Miller's cooperation and we got it. Obviously, if Zahn betrayed us, Leo had no choice except to go along; he would be blamed for informing Zahn against our security orders." Blaise sipped the coffee. The taste was heavy to the point of being bitter.

"Leo didn't want to betray you." Mary Margaret Sepulveda got to her feet, stepping down hard on the floor as if in protest. "He came home that night, upset. All of you saw him as a strong man, but he suffered an inferiority problem. Among all of you with your backgrounds of wealth and schooling he was a misfit. He left school when he was twelve to support his family. He grew up on the streets and learned to read and write from graffiti.

"Zahn was Leo's connection with your world. Leo had money and power, but he wanted a different kind of respect and Zahn fed him on it. The night he came home from seeing Zahn he was shaking. He told me he'd told Zahn, but it didn't feel right. He knew he'd been set up and he made Zahn swear not to tell.

"He was sick all night. 'Karl's going to tell,' he said over and over. He never said anything about Tim or you, Dr. Cunningham. I think he wanted to die. But instead, he stayed in the house the next day and Zahn called him and made arrangements to meet somebody from the government.

"Leo never came home. Tim fed me cock and bull about him

running off with a boy. I half believed it because Leo had done it before and because Tim acted as if he'd been betrayed, too." Mary Margaret examined Delahanty as she spooned sugar into her cup. "But Leo never came back and . . ." Her face was bleak. "I'm not that sure about me, but he wouldn't leave the kids. Not forever."

Blaise closed his eyes. "There might have been another way, but there was no time. I had to know about Miller immediately."

"Leo had two children who adored him. And Tim came around to tell them their daddy deserted them, left them for some reason they'd not understand even if they'd heard the lie. Did you think of that when you hid the body, Doctor?"

"I was thinking more about all the people who were being murdered, and that I was probably next." Blaise set the mug on the table. "I have to go."

Mary Margaret stood at the same time. "What happened to Leo's body, Doctor?"

"We buried him in a tunnel under the church. Father Argyle said mass, and then we collapsed the tunnel."

Sepulveda's widow breathed loudly as if she couldn't catch her breath. "Am I supposed to be pleased?"

"No, Mrs. Sepulveda. I wish I could make amends."

"Please go." Her eyes weren't misty but her voice caught. She turned her head and stared at Delahanty. "Tim, go with him."

Delahanty nodded and led Blaise to the door.

Mary Margaret Sepulveda stood in the center of the room staring after them. She held the two crystal cups in one hand and the mug in the other. "Please go," she said.

"Can I be coming back tomorrow, Maggie?" Delahanty's voice quavered.

"I'll know tomorrow."

Delahanty's shoulders slumped. He opened the door and flames in the fireplace roared brightly up the chimney.

Delahanty was quiet as they drove away from the house on the quiet vineyard with the winery where Leo Richardson-Sepulveda had spent a portion of his time. The lights downstairs stayed on until they were out of sight. Upstairs the bedrooms remained dark.

"What have you been doing with that woman, Tim?"

"Consoling her. Looking out for the little ones. Planning her economics and seeing her future is set with Leo's money."

"Is that all?"

"What else can there be, Doctor?"

"Irish women are used to marrying older men." Blaise stared into the night where the headlights flashed up against patches of drifting fog.

"I'm not . . ." Delahanty ran out of words.

"Leo had his foibles, too."

"I don't remember how it is with a woman after all these years. Besides, Maggie doesn't love me. How can she, knowing I helped with Leo's death, God forgive me." Delahanty huddled against the door on his side.

"Women understand more than we think." Blaise concentrated on his driving and both men listened to the road noise. The digital clock on the radio flashed a greenish cast on Delahanty's ruined face. "She gave me your cup and you a piece of her Waterford. If she couldn't forgive, you'd have been drinking out of a tin can."

"You're right about the Waterford. The Irish all are dotty about heirlooms and ancestors. But she was just being polite." Blaise felt the despair that oozed from Delahanty's bones and flesh.

Glancing into the mirror, Blaise said, "We'll see. Whatever happens, go back and talk to her. See if you can undermine her conviction that she must punish me. I don't think she's acting out of any love for Sepulveda."

Delahanty turned his head. "What would her motive be, then?"

"Retribution for her children too young to avenge themselves. To spare them from a life devoted to vengeance. She didn't marry an Irishman. Leo was a tough, smart Hispanic street kid—not an Irishman who lives in his black soul and cries with melancholia. Mary Margaret thinks her children are Irish."

"What do you think she's done, Doctor?"

Blaise stared in the rearview mirror where the flashing lights were drawing so close the backseat turned blue with each sweep. "She's called the police and accused me of murder."

As Blaise slowed the car Delahanty said, "Suppose she named me, as well?"

"In that case, Mr. Delahanty, by sunrise those people in Washington who want me dead will have their way."

CHAPTER 18

"**F**ather, I heard him!" Phyllis Bellinger perched on the edge of Helen's redwood chaise longue under the oak behind the church, her eyes bright in a face shadowed by lack of sleep. Water dripped, drawing icy tracks down Helen's skin as the oak shed the misty rain.

Father Argyle glanced at them with his mind in some other dimension. Constance Davies stood so close behind the priest her chin touched his shoulder. Overhead the gunmetal-gray sky stretched with clouds in neat ranks like a fresh plowed field. A gap in the furrows let the morning sun through, spotlighting Constance. Framed by tight black curls, her face was radiant. "You fainted, Phyllis. How do you know what you heard?"

Face puckered, Phyllis clenched her fists. "I heard him, Father. Reynard talked to me! To me! Why don't you believe me?"

"We have to be sure. You fainted, Phyllis. You might have been hallucinating." Father Argyle's voice had the softness of a feather bed. He enfolded the woman with it.

Phyllis began shaking. She was crying but the tears wouldn't come. "Reynard talked to me . . ."

Helen felt herself dragged into Phyllis' grief. Phyllis' frustration at being so close to Reynard and not able to talk to him had overflowed its boundaries. Hysteria demanded confirmation and acceptance that the priest denied her. Helen shook the rain off her face.

"He did, Father. I heard Reynard call to her when Phyllis fainted."

Father Argyle dropped his eyes to Constance. She hugged him closer, stifling a sob against his shirt. "Isn't it what we've been waiting for?" she asked.

"Father, I want to talk to Helen. Please." Phyllis bowed her head so nobody could see her face.

"Of course." Father Argyle stared at Helen and licked his lips as if he had something to say, as well. A wave of feeling washed over Helen from the contact. Constance Davies wrapped her arms around the priest, hugging him from behind. They made a sharp contrast: Constance sparkled in her loose, white dress that encased her from her neck and wrists to her ankles; Father Argyle disappeared even in sunlight, his black clothes and dark complexion blending into the shadows. "Of course," he repeated. They entered the church by the side door, the *click* of the catch loud, like the cocking of a gun in the quiet.

"I did hear him, didn't I?" Phyllis turned her tearstained face toward Helen.

"Yes."

The clouds broke open for a moment, revealing a whiteness in the east that disturbed Helen's sense of time. She felt so much she didn't understand. A feeling of love and need for Reynard invaded her and she didn't understand that. She liked Reynard. She liked a lot of people. His passing had upset her, but it hadn't broken her heart. Now she was heartbroken over balding, rolypoly Reynard.

"Will he talk to me again?"

"Yes," Helen whispered.

"Now?"

Helen pondered Phyllis' question. She thought about what Phyllis wanted, directing her awareness inside the church, and felt a stirring in response. "Yes. Anytime you want."

"Thank you, Helen. Oh, God, thank you." Phyllis touched Helen's hand. Tears flowed down her cheeks and dripped from her nose. She smiled as if she couldn't hold them back and didn't want to.

"Go, if you like," Helen said.

Phyllis tried to say something, then looked at Helen and nodded before rushing away.

Helen lay exhausted and bone weary in the chaise longue. Gazing up, she looked for God's face in the clouds. Instead she saw turmoil and Blaise's image. She was so lonely she wanted to cry. *Come back, Blaise. Please, come back, now!* She forced the thought out in radiating waves, knowing it wouldn't work. If she'd wanted Enrique Ledesma she knew he would come.

The wind picked up carrying icy pinpricks of raindrops that made her shiver.

"Mistress?"

Helen opened her eyes. Joseph Santiago stood over her. She must have been sleeping.

"We should go inside."

"I want to stay, Joseph. I want to wait for Blaise."

"Yes, Mistress." Joseph took off his red blanket and wrapped Helen in it from her toes to her neck. He had very soft hands. The blanket was thick wool and warm. Helen felt the raindrops on her face and smelled the air from off the ocean, scoured clean by the rain.

"You'll get cold, Joseph." She wanted to touch Joseph's hand only she was too tired.

"No, Mistress. Your thoughts will keep me warm."

"Will Blaise come soon?"

"I do not know. But if it is your will, the universe will try to make it happen." Joseph stood in the shadow of the tree staring up at God's sky.

Sinking into sleep, Helen was surrounded by voices and images. She saw the inside of the church as if she were there, looking from every imaginable angle. The voices whispered inside of her, telling her things and secrets she didn't want to know. Hearing Sergio, Helen went closer. Phyllis leaned against the prayer rail thinking at Reynard, and Reynard was answering.

"Is that you, Miss McIntyre?" Hartunian's thoughts bellowed in Helen's mind.

"Yes, Bill. I think so."

"That is a good thing. Sergio said you would come to us and now you are here." For several moments Hartunian faded away while Helen's awareness of the church regained strength. She could not seem to stand still. The church zoomed around her leaving her dizzy from the constant motion and dislocation.

The voices beat soundlessly at Helen's brain. *"Please, God. Where did she hide the money? . . ."* The voice sounded familiar. Helen couldn't place it before she was swept into the main current. *"I don't want to be like this! Let me die . . . please! . . . Why can't we touch the priest? . . . Only Sergio . . . Fifty years of collection plates and Hail Marys and I'm a goddamned fly. A fly . . . he says we'll get stronger but . . . the priest doesn't feel the power . . . the priest . . . I don't like it here!"*

The noise cut off like the fall of a drape. Helen was back in quiet and warmth. *"Do not be frightened, Miss McIntyre. I am with you."*

"Sergio?" The word didn't get under the curtain that embraced Helen. *"Sergio?"*

"I am here."

"What is happening to me, Sergio?"

"You are joining, Miss McIntyre."

"Joining what? I don't understand."

"You will understand everything, Miss McIntyre. When you understand you can make your understanding clear to us. You are joining us, Miss McIntyre, and I don't understand either."

"Where's Blaise?"

"We were hoping you knew, Miss McIntyre."

Sergio's presence left her. The sounds came at Helen again, stronger. She felt herself swept away and then she was somewhere safe and comfortable. She was surrounded by feet and ankles.

"Tchor?"

The cat bounced up onto the altar table. The flies gathered around, their legs and bodies like fences and walls around Tchor. The cat yawned and then raised a paw. She began licking herself.

CHAPTER 19

The discolored ceiling was no Michelangelo mural and the recessed light behind heavy wire mesh glowered at Blaise, but it was, by his standards, entertainment. A hairline crack, mildewed brown, zigzagged from one wall to the other. Inking the brown line into a mental image of Alfie's motherboard, Blaise kept himself awake rewiring Alfie's circuits in his head, following motherboard traces into the chips, testing by examination how each chip responded, then moving to the next step when Inspector Fennelli appeared outside the holding cell.

Blaise's watch, along with his money, had been taken from him when he was locked in the cell, but Blaise guessed Fennelli arrived around 3 A.M., an hour when patients who weren't going to get well chose to die in even the better hospitals. Ignoring the policeman, Blaise worked through the mental problem knowing he had an improved design, one he would never use. Alfie was Alfie just as Helen was Helen. A new brain could only change that.

Shifting his eyes toward Fennelli, he raised an eyebrow. The policeman didn't appear Italian in his charcoal worsted suit. If the suit had been sharkskin, he would have seemed both Italian and a policeman. "Nice suit," Blaise said.

The inspector motioned the jailer to unlock. The jailer stood behind the steel-barred door, Fennelli on the other side. A disinfectant odor permeated the whole corridor.

Blaise didn't move. He watched Fennelli without much curiosity. "Do you have a gun?"

"They aren't allowed in the cell block, Doctor. Would you come along, please?" Glancing at the jailer, Fennelli opened his jacket, to show an empty hip holster.

"Under those conditions, of course." Blaise swung his feet off the cot. After slamming the barred door shut behind Blaise, the jailer stepped out of the way. The *clang* reverberated in the empty hallway drowning out the scuffle of their shoes before it faded into funereal silence. Bilious cream paint covered the walls, the cement floor was dirty red. Windows lining the outside corridor wall had forest-green steel frames inset with five-by-seven-inch wire-veined safety glass. Over the dirty windows, heavy metal screens too tight to put a finger through had been bolted to the cement wall on both the inside and outside of the building. Their footsteps resounded like pistol shots in the near-silent jail wing.

"I saw the arrest sheet downstairs, Dr. Cunningham. The computer information advisory went out hours ago." Fennelli put his hand in his pocket. They were at the end of the cell block and had stopped at another barred door.

"You still believe I murdered Esther Tazy?"

"That's not proven, one way or the other." Fennelli passed his identification through the slot. They waited while a uniformed guard verified it. Somewhere out of sight a moaning escaped from the cell block. The sound went on for a while then stopped, leaving a nervous quiet in its wake. Blaise started to talk and Fennelli gestured for him to say nothing. When they left the cell block, the sharp smell of antiseptic ceased and Blaise became aware of it because it was gone.

Guiding Blaise to another part of the building and a frosted glass door with DETECTIVE DIVISION on the glass, Fennelli ushered him into an empty office. Six empty chairs and desks piled with papers and forms filled the room. "Most detectives work eight to five," Fennelli said. "The ones that don't aren't in the station much." Fennelli opened an interior office and indicated a chair on the wrong side of a desk with a nameplate that said, INSPECTOR FENNELLI. Blaise sat.

"What now?"

Fennelli rummaged cigarettes from a desk drawer and offered Blaise one. He shrugged when Blaise declined. "I've just stolen you out of the jail, Dr. Cunningham." Lighting his cigarette, Fennelli inhaled and blew smoke out his nose.

"We're still in the police station." The room had a morguelike feeling that went with the hour. A hum of idling communications equipment motors permeated the still air in the office.

"I didn't say I was letting you go."

"What are you doing, then?" The police inspector was bigger than Blaise remembered, probably because he was built like a whippet with a long, rounded body that seemed bulkless. Despite the sunless climate of San Francisco, Inspector Fennelli retained the olive complexion common to Southern Italy, which fluorescent tubes interpreted as cadaverous gray-green.

"Waiting." Fennelli ground his cigarette out in the ashtray, then gave the crumpled butt a sour look. The scent of scorched filter tip ascended in a plume of brown smoke. "You weren't there, Doctor, when Carmandy killed Sergeant Miller."

Blaise glanced at the institutional wall clock over Fennelli's head. Grime obscured the nauseous green paint that layered the metal frame. A red second hand swept in soundless circles. The clock marked 3:43. "No. I wasn't."

"I was. I couldn't do anything. It's hard to witness a murder and do nothing if you're a cop." Fennelli opened his hand and stared at his palm. "You know you can't catch everybody, but you figure the ones you catch would have gotten away if you weren't there. That makes the job important. More important than selling groceries or teaching school or being a banker because a cop allows other people to be what they are." Fennelli looked at Blaise as if expecting an argument.

Blaise nodded. He couldn't tell if Fennelli had a point or was just rambling.

"I'm homicide." The policeman propped his elbows on the desk and pressed his chin on his knuckles. "There's something about murder that's different from all other crimes, Doctor. Human life is sacred. Money isn't. Even love isn't because you can have a second chance. But if somebody takes your life, you're out of luck." Fennelli looked at the ashtray as if wishing he hadn't been so hasty with his cigarette.

"I agree." Blaise glanced at the clock again. Time was running out. Unless Delahanty convinced Mrs. Sepulveda to withdraw her charges soon, he wouldn't be in the cell for a court appearance in the morning. Blaise surprised himself. He felt calm about the possibility of death, even though he didn't want to die. He'd known people who said when life tired them too much they would be ready to go with God. Not die. Just change existences for something more simple. They had faith in something. Blaise didn't.

"The law complicates death, Doctor. It recognizes the importance of human life, then puts limitations on that importance. Sometimes the law makes it all right to kill, or to kill with mitigation, or to kill involuntarily, or to allow a life to be taken. The law confuses me, but I'm a cop and I enforce it." Fennelli glanced at the clock, too.

"I sympathize, Inspector."

Ignoring the possibility of sarcasm, Fennelli said, "Last year I commanded the tactical squad that was called out when Father Argyle, Tim Delahanty, Bill Hartunian, and Sergeant Miller invaded the television station. I knew then you were involved. You had to be."

Outside the little office the detectives' bullpen seemed cavernous without people. Blaise shifted his weight and the chair squeaked. Fennelli was describing the night Alfie had gotten control of the CRAY. Blaise plotted the steps with Alfie. They had forseen every eventuality. The problem wasn't that they were outmaneuvered. Death had been an accepted eventuality. "I know. Father Argyle told me."

Staring at Fennelli, Blaise remembered mostly the chill night air. Five of them had gone to the television station late in the spring but, as the man said, the coldest winter he ever spent anywhere was one summer in San Francisco.

No one noticed the cold that night. Keyed up when they entered the station, they were preoccupied with their own thoughts and emotions. Only the thick-shouldered Hartunian seemed heedless of the risks. Hartunian carried Sergio's magnum pistol in his belt and seemed comfortable, as if his whole life had been preparation for that moment. Blaise had counted on Hartunian, perhaps unfairly. Father Argyle in black cassock, turned collar, and cross came along unwillingly when he could not dissuade the others.

The kaleidoscope in Blaise's head began to form familiar images, his memory seeing them all alive again. Five men had entered the TV station; only Miller sure he was going to die. Delahanty tried to cheer Miller with sympathy and optimism, which Miller was having none of. *"You've killed me,"* he'd told Blaise a few minutes before Blaise left the others. Miller hadn't been angry, just resigned, and Blaise wondered if Miller believed he would just go with God.

Blaise avoided Fennelli's brown eyes. The memories were painful. "You didn't arrest me with the others."

Fennelli bobbed his head. "I considered pulling you in, but what was the use? I couldn't hold the others, either. When I arrived on the scene your friends were already on the roof. Since I knew Miller and Father Argyle, I convinced the ranking officer I could talk them down. We thought you were up there, too.

"We had time and manpower to flush every floor so we closed off the floors, stairs, and elevators. It was simple. I'd go to the roof access and explain things to Miller, you, and the priest. Then all five of you would come down with me. Nobody would be hurt. After all, throwing people out of a TV station in order to broadcast a lunatic message isn't up there with murdering hostages in Lebanon or hijacking a jet to Syria. This is San Francisco and we take care of our loonies. But I didn't know two things."

"Carmandy was between you, and I wasn't on the roof."

"You're perceptive, Doctor. You might have made a good cop." Fennelli glanced through the glass window into the big room as if he expected somebody to appear. "You knew about Carmandy, didn't you?" Fennelli threw the pack of cigarettes into the drawer and banged it shut.

"I knew. I didn't have time to interfere." Blaise remembered standing in the parking lot, his hand on the van door. The cars already scattered through the asphalted parking lot were wet with dew, reflecting glare from halogen bulbs set in tall concrete posts. Carmandy had just gotten out of his car and was headed toward the building. He'd glanced at Blaise and they recognized each other. Carmandy had hesitated. Long enough to decide what he wanted most, then he went into the building. Blaise had gotten in the van and Gino Conti drove him away.

"He got into the building after you left but before we surrounded it?"

"Yes."

"You saw him when you were leaving?"

Blaise nodded. The clock on the wall clicked the minute hand. "The problem was timing. I couldn't wait."

"That's unfortunate, Doctor. We didn't know Carmandy was on the stairs. Hartunian disabled the elevator on the top floor.

Going up, we pushed Carmandy ahead of us by a floor or two. He murdered Hartunian. He murdered Miller. If I'd known, I would have warned your friends."

"You didn't arrest him." Blaise stopped watching the clock.

"The federal line is Miller and Hartunian were terrorists. Carmandy shot in self-defense performing a public service at the risk of his own life. I couldn't arrest a hero. You see how easy it is to cheapen life, Doctor? The very people who employed Miller, official people, said one word and his death didn't matter anymore."

The policeman patted his pockets. Then looked around as if he had mislaid something. "You were at the telephone company building, Doctor. Just before it blew up." Fennelli opened the drawer and got another cigarette, fiddling the pack with his fingers. He paused without lighting the cigarette. "I think Carmandy's job was to kill you."

"He killed Miller and shot Bill Hartunian."

"That was personal, Doctor. Carmandy was with Miller the day Miller asked me if I knew where you were."

Blaise stared into the other room. During the day Fennelli sat in this office watching other people working around him, the bustle making the room seem less dirty. The outer office was dingy now with fluorescent lighting. "He had a chance to shoot me in the parking lot when I left the TV studio. He didn't."

"He thought you would wait. He didn't know what you were going to do. He hated Miller, probably because Miller was a good cop and thought like a good cop, whatever he was doing for the National Security Council." Fennelli lit the cigarette with a desk lighter and his cough carried a gun-shot echo. "Washington is interested in you, Doctor. Carmandy works for the National Security Council and the Central Intelligence Agency and two or three other organizations, depending on the day of the month. The reason you're here is I got out of a warm bed to see who comes to remove you from jail, and I decided I needed company."

"Suppose nobody comes?"

Fennelli shrugged. "I'll draw the Leo Richardson-Sepulveda murder case as an assignment. I'll know you a lot better, Dr. Cunningham. You were always my favorite suspect in the Esther Tazy killing." Inspector Fennelli glanced at the wall clock. Out the window a trace of light put white streaks in the clouds, enough to make the random raindrops striking the window visible as they obeyed the laws of gravity and viscosity, joining together into one stream on their way down the glass. The clouds spread for a moment showing a bright crescent moon and then closed over again.

Closing his eyes, Blaise tried to relax. He'd done the right thing in telling Mary Margaret Richardson-Sepulveda the details of her husband's death. He was being punished for the revelation. The woman had called the police the moment they left the house, but Blaise felt no relief or vindication, just a kind of emptiness.

Fennelli knew about Carmandy. Blaise wondered if any real secrets existed. Father Argyle and Timothy Delahanty had probably figured it out, too. Bill Hartunian would have known he hadn't stopped Carmandy the instant Carmandy shot him. Only the pathetic Miller offering to change sides when he was planted by Carmandy on them, who was doubled again, and then killed for it, had reached beyond his depth.

"What will you do if the ones who come have the authority to take me away?"

"Things aren't right anymore, Doctor." Fennelli's eloquent shrug involved his whole body. "At least I'll know who they are this time."

"Once they snatch the bait, they won't return to an empty hook." The clock's minute hand had traveled a surprising distance. Blaise could not suppress his uneasiness.

"They might. We'll have to take that chance."

"Both of us?"

"Mostly you, I'm afraid." Fennelli's somber eyes were set too deep in his head. "But that's all right, isn't it, Doctor? Would it be fair to say you had a lot to do with Sergeant Miller's death?"

Blaise shrugged. He had stared back at Carmandy in the parking lot, hesitating in the cloud of hot exhaust from Gino Conti's idling van, the scent of hot hydrocarbons acidifying the cold mist; he had hesitated long enough to decide the four men in the building would have to look out for themselves. Not as long, though, as Carmandy had hesitated.

"Well," Fennelli said. "Your opinion doesn't really matter anyway, does it? I liked Miller. He was a good man and he shouldn't have died that way."

The telephone rang.

They looked at it. Fennelli lifted the receiver, saying "yes" and "no." Hanging up, he told Blaise to stand. From his desk drawer he took a small pistol. "You know how to use an automatic, don't you, Doctor?" He smiled. "Of course you do. According to his wife's complaint you killed Leo Richardson-Sepulveda with a pistol like this." With smooth nonchalance Fennelli dumped bright brass and copper bullets into his hand from a cartridge box and then began thumbing them into the magazine. When the magazine was full, he worked the pistol slide, ejecting one bullet, which he put back into the cartridge box before setting the safety with his forefinger. "Don't overload the magazine," he said conversationally. "It might collapse the spring. Hold out your hands, Doctor."

Blaise's chest felt airy, as if his muscles had disappeared. It had always been a possibility. Silent, he extended his hands and Fennelli snapped a pair of handcuffs on his wrists. The metal was cold and pinched his skin.

"Turn around." Fennelli waved the small pistol at him and Blaise shuffled his feet around. A tearing sound disturbed the silence, then his shirt and jacket were pulled up and something icy pressed against his spine pulling at his skin over his kidneys. "That's good, Doctor. Turn around again."

Fennelli was tucking a wide role of surgical tape back in his desk. He looked up at Blaise. "The pistol is cocked and taped to your back, Doctor. It is most convenient under your right hand. Don't squeeze the safety release and the trigger at the same time unless you want to shoot something." Extending his arm, Fennelli held a small key between his fingers. Blaise took the key with both hands.

"The key opens your handcuffs. Put it where you can reach it with your hands still cuffed."

Twisting his body, Blaise tucked the key in his watch pocket. He stared at Fennelli while he undertook the maneuver.

"You are old-fashioned, Dr. Cunningham. Where do you get trousers with watch pockets?"

"Western outfitters, Inspector. I've been away from civilization for a while." He waited, but Fennelli sat down and motioned him to do the same. The gun pressed uncomfortably into his spine where it touched the chair back. "Are you going to tell me what you have in mind, Inspector?"

"The call was about a man with a federal warrant for you, Doctor."

"I see."

"The gun isn't registered to me. Neither are the handcuffs.

Both were confiscated from, hmm, malefactors. What happens to them is of no concern to me."

"You mean you don't want them back?"

Fennelli didn't blink. "The federal warrant is going to be honored. I can't stop it. I'm not sure I would if I could. The federal agent picking you up is a man named Carmandy."

"You expect him to kill me?"

"Not in my jurisdiction or where I'd find the body. That gives you some time, Doctor."

"What will you be doing?"

"What I can without breaking the law any more than I must."

Blaise closed his eyes listening to the almost-silent buzz of the fluorescent lighting fixtures. "That's not much."

"It isn't. Carmandy should be here soon." Fennelli leaned back, letting the muscles of his face relax. "For curiosity, what did you do to the telephone building? You're not a mad bomber, Doctor." He was a different man when he stopped holding himself together. But not different enough.

"I was stealing a computer. It doesn't matter, does it?"

"No." Fennelli straightened the things on his desk. His desktop was remarkably neat compared to the rest of the office. "No," he repeated. "I'm not sure anything matters anymore."

The clock on the wall ticked over 5 A.M.. Blaise wondered where the time was going.

CHAPTER 20

Enrique Ledesma accepted an out-culture self-evaluation during the black moments in his life, the moments of failure: Chief Son-of-a-Bitch—another drunken Indian. But he had not been drunk today, and the time was late for self-pity. He strode silently about the wrecked village. Military ambulances and trucks arrived screaming and hooting from the barren desert. The soldiers—very young corpsmen and nurses with shocked faces —loaded the ambulances. They were not responsible. They said it with their eyes despite evidence that only military airplanes could have caused the havoc. Enrique did not blame the soldiers. They, too, were victims. The ambulances jounced from the village loaded with dead and wounded whom time could no longer hurt.

For the others, the medics dashed in and out of the whirlwinds of dirt and noise raised by the army helicopters, quick and grim-faced, and Enrique felt approval of their efforts. He leaned against the wind of the landing helicopters, holding his hand as a screen to catch the grit being flung in his face.

Enrique's feelings about the intruders who stayed after the medics left was different. They wore camouflage fatigues, but he knew these older men who poked through collapsed wattle-and-daub and sheetmetal torn from trailers were not soldiers. They spoke into their wrists as they burrowed like rats in the wreckage of the village. He asked what they sought. The commander, a big man with sandy hair, said, "Trapped survivors."

"There are none. I would know," Enrique said, and yet they dug. When they found nothing they became restive, their mood turned to anger.

Luck, the shaman supposed. Or maybe the *máala*'s protective aura still covered the village. The villagers had been hundreds of yards away from the bomb site, all watching the mistress and Dr. Cunningham drive away with Red Oak. Even the *nagual*-coyote had been out of the village. Now his people were salvaging their meager possessions. The white-helmeted MPs had departed soon after the ambulances. Spooked, Ledesma supposed, by hatred that lay silent as a killer fog.

"You, old man!"

Enrique Ledesma turned his stony eyes on the balding, sandy-haired commander whose face was reddening in the winter sun. If it pleased the man to call him old, Enrique would be old. He who tossed hundred-pound bags of fertilizer one-handed into the white man's pickup trucks strained visibly to lift a wall that had fallen in a nearly single piece. Two other Indian men felt his thought and moved to help, straining as if they were ants and the wall a loaded truck. The wall was part of the trailer where Dr. Cunningham and the *máala* had lived. As the wall rose Enrique saw the bright-red jacket of what he had learned to call a floppy, a plastic disk for the computer like a 45-rpm record with noisy songs that children enjoy. The envelope was empty but its presence would say enough. *Quickly, friends.* He let the wall fall back, and the two Indians pretended it had gotten away from their hands as well.

The booming crash of the wall and the haze of dust that filled the air startled the Banty rooster that had been walking through the ruins looking for its cage. Squawking, the bird exploded into flight, its wings beating the air with whapping noises. One of the not-soldiers in fatigues shouted, then was waving a pistol in the air yelling.

"The rooster has lost its home and is scared," Enrique said. "It is not necessary to shoot so small a beast with such a big gun." He gazed at the .357 magnum revolver in the soldier's hand knowing the army did not issue such a weapon.

The soldier looked at the pistol as if disclaiming it. His commander moved between them to confront Enrique. He jerked his head, and the man seemed happy to leave. "Do any Americans live in this camp?"

"I am American," Enrique said. He put his hands under the wall and grunted, pretending the wall was too heavy to lift.

"I don't mean Indian Americans. I mean white Americans." The sandy-haired man had heavy, muscled arms. He watched Enrique's efforts to pick up the wall with disdain.

"I do not think so." Enrique stopped tugging.

"Crap. Get out of the way. I can lift that tin with one hand." The soldier commander pushed in front of the two Indians alongside Enrique. "I heard a white man lived here."

Enrique dusted his hands and moved to a ruin away from the trailer, hoping the soldier would follow. It was constructed of reeds plastered over with adobe so he knew there would be nothing incriminating inside. Facing the afternoon sun, he began softly singing the necessary words to invoke his guardian.

"Speak English," the soldier boss said. He examined the ruin Enrique had moved to, then the trailer. "Hey," he said, "Don't you want to do this one still?"

Ledesma concentrated on his ritual. One word wrong, and he would have to repeat. With each repetition the magic lost a little of its potency. Enrique had not trusted himself to speak when the whites first arrived.

The soldier leader glanced from the new ruin to the trailer as if he had an idea. Enrique increased the speed of his message while the sandy-haired man muttered into his wrist. Two whites joined him and they began to lift the trailer wall.

Ledesma made an imperceptible gesture and said the word that capped his ritual.

Though the shaman knew only seven snakes had come, to the

whites straining against the wall the number would seem much greater. The soldiers' strangled soprano shrieks and the speed with which they scattered when the wall was clear of the ground and they saw the snakes underneath soothed Enrique's anger.

When they returned with sticks, the soldiers didn't find any snakes. The diskette sleeve was safely in Enrique's's pocket, and he and his helpers were working on another wall. The soldiers' enthusiasm for turning things over was dampened. They milled aimlessly, trying to get a word out of somebody, but none of Ledesma's people answered in English. Finally they wandered downriver toward the paved road and trading post.

Enrique lifted a rippled piece of tin from the ground nearby. A baby, foot-long rattler stared unmoving inches from his hand. "Thank you," he said, adding words of power that prudent people do not repeat and prefer not to hear. "And my respects to your mother," he finished as the snake slithered into the brush.

In an unoccupied corner of his mind, Enrique Ledesma was aware of Helen's anguish, of her wish to return to the village. He also sensed Red Oak's determined opposition. Backed up, without doubt, by the mistress' consort, but Enrique had no hint of Blaise Cunningham's thoughts. He did sense the doubt in the *máala's* mind. She wanted to go back to the church of the priest in San Francisco. Other thought intruded, claiming Enrique's attention.

Not thought. Just darkness and the vague restiveness that came whenever the last meal was digested and it was time to rouse, to hunt again. Hunting was good. Water appeared and disappeared in a raised-edge puddle. The snake was drawn by the rhythms of the moon that had disappeared. The sun, too, was gone. But it was comfortable in the darkness.

What caught Enrique's attention was the movement that frightened the snake. The tremors in the floor that let it know the game heading toward it was too big to eat, the excitement as its heat sensors tracked the course of the warm-blooded animals.

Calm. Enrique thought. *Calm yourself, my brother.*

The Indians in the village felt the drama. They stopped doing whatever occupied them. Some merely stooped over their work, others turned in the direction of the trading post, which lay over the hill on the riverbank.

The two men dressed like soldiers poked through the storeroom with their flashlights. They had wedged the door open behind themselves after breaking the lock. The others had gone into the front of the store to question the Indian proprietor.

"What are we doing here?" The man's voice was disgusted. "A man like Cunningham wouldn't hide in a mousetrap like this."

"Shut up and look. He's got a computer in a big aluminum suitcase, and this is the only electricity anywhere near the village."

Methodically they moved through the storeroom prodding at bags and crates, the beams of their flashlights zapping around the big room like a display from a child's toy.

"Wait a minute." One of the men stopped moving to kneel by a crate. The two flashlights created a pool of yellow in the blackness. "I think this might open," the man said. He shifted position and half rose over the crate. And then he stopped staring into the dark space behind the crate. He could have sworn something had moved down there. "Give me some light," he demanded.

The snake didn't rattle. It had no intention of striking until the heat smell was almost touching. Even then the snake lashed up only a foot from the pile of her coils.

The man holding the flashlight wasn't sure what he saw. A movement, the muted earth colors moving across the beam of the flashlight, the glint of huge fangs in an open reptilian mouth. He dropped the flashlight, which clattered on the wood floor, the beam spinning wildly before the lens and bulb popped off plunging the room into darkness. The other flashlight lay on a crate wasting its illumination on the side of another box.

Once launched into its strike, the mother of all rattlesnakes struck the throat of the man who bent over the crate looking down. The fangs, top and bottom, plunged into the underside of his jaw just below the jaw line. The victim managed a brief shriek before rictus seized him. Foam flowed from his mouth before he hit the floor. The other man grabbed for the flashlight on the crate, clumsily sending it skittering into a crevice between stacked bags.

He tried to make himself reach down and fish for the light, but his mind rebelled. It remembered the ugly head of the snake striking his partner's throat. He couldn't force his hand down. Instead he turned and ran for the light coming through the doorway.

When he returned with the others the warehouse was empty.

The dead man lay cramped on his side, his lips drawn back from his teeth in a parody of fear. The snake was gone.

"Get the body," the sandy-haired man said.

They worked quickly, a dozen flashlights pouring light into the corners of the room. They asked the Indian storekeeper where a snake that big came from and he shrugged. "Maybe bombs make snakes mad," he said. He closed his mouth, forgetting those things he was not supposed to know.

Enrique sent a dozen Indians to the store where they discovered the proprietor staring back at his benefactors while they milled around examining the edges of Buck knives, testing the swing of axes, playing a game of catch with machetes until the pseudosoldiers realized whatever they wanted was gone and they were wasting their time.

Outside the trading post, the river once more murmured its thoughts without competition.

The second night after the bombing, the important men in the wrecked village sat around a fire. No one was afraid of showing a light. The bombs had been aimed at the *máala*'s consort. The men who sent the bombs had come and gone. No white could believe the Indians were responsible for the snakes. Unless they were vindictive in small, unprofitable ways, the village would be left alone. Gathered around the fire, the men remaining in the village waited for Enrique Ledesma to descend from his communion with the Great Spirit.

Sitting crosslegged in the darkness atop the bluff, the shaman sought the calm that should have come now that Blaise Cunningham and the troubles he had brought on the village were gone. The *máala* was gone, too. He sensed her presence in San Francisco at the white priest's church.

He heard her calling her consort.

The coyote at his feet stirred and whined. Enrique's dark face furrowed as he strained to absorb what had happened. The *máala* did not know yet. But the shifting currents of her unspoken cry for Dr. Cunningham meant she needed help.

If Dr. Cunningham was gone, Enrique would make a death song to comfort the mistress. But he would not grieve. The passing of Dr. Cunningham could be the signal the Great Father was readying the Earth to return to his people. Enrique released a long-held breath and got stiffly to his feet. By the time he descended the steep trail in darkness, Enrique's flexibility had returned. "It is time," he said to the gathering at the fire.

The important men were not surprised. They knew where they had to go and whom they had to protect. It was not Blaise Cunningham.

The storekeeper, who was an important man, left the group and walked back to his trading post where the only telephone in twenty miles hung. He telephoned a ranch fifty miles west where the river's waters had been diverted so New Yorkers could have lettuce in January. Two hours later a semivan and trailer came as far as it could to the village down the somewhat better road on the California side. Its lights shined on the roiling black water like a matched pair of artificial moons.

Enrique's men packed their blanket rolls in plastic garbage bags to keep them dry and lend flotation as they kicked their way across the river. The truck started back up the Imperial Valley, rolling in the darkness with only parking lights while an Indian sitting on each fender directed the driver. They stayed on dirt roads to avoid immigration checkpoints, sometimes crossing farms on long, straight private roads. A heavy wind buffeted the truck from Palm Springs all the way to Riverside, then they were climbing another range of mountains toward the coast and San Francisco.

Enrique sat in one corner of the enclosed trailer feeling the wind outside. Anger obscured his thinking. He knew with all his being that a profound difference existed between the spiritual world and the white man's universe. Yet he rode in a diesel-powered truck, which somehow spoiled the purity of what he must do.

Joining belief with need was indeed difficult. Sometimes Enrique thought that having a white man's education like Red Oak might ease the burden magic placed on a man. Did the truck have a soul, a blind animus blocking Ledesma's way of seeing? *Something* was obstructing his vision of what was happening in San Francisco. He could not even tell if Joseph Santiago—Red Oak—was there. He needed the red-blanketed man. Red Oak was a war chief. Enrique was not.

In the village Enrique knew he wouldn't drink alcohol. There was none. But back in white man's country with three liquor stores in every block...The coyote nuzzled him. Ledesma looked down and his *nagual*'s eyes glowed yellow in the dark. It was the first time the animal had paid him any attention since the *máala*...He stared into the animal's eyes, knowing that most animals were eager to avoid direct eye contact, which they associated with something larger getting ready to eat them. Helen's cry to Dr. Cunningham ran in Enrique's head. It told him only that Dr. Cunningham had disappeared and perhaps the mistress was finally alone.

Enrique stifled the pleasure in his heart, for if the mistress heard his gloating she would think badly of him. *I am coming, Máala...*

Sending the mental cry into the night, Enrique Ledesma talked also to Joseph Santiago in a medicine dream. It was time, Enrique said, for one last Indian war!

CHAPTER 21

Carmandy's movements were crisp, his reactions unnaturally fast. His face moved a little too much, as if he tried to act out words in his head rather than speak them. He walked into Fennelli's office and plopped the warrant on Fennelli's desk, carrying with him an expectation of being untouchable. "Let's get on with it," he said. He glanced at Blaise. His eyes were flat and unrevealing.

"You need a court order, Mr. Carmandy." The warrant rustled in Fennelli's hand. The police inspector's voice suggested a quality of professional friendship Blaise remembered from Fennelli's interrogation after Esther Tazy's death. Whatever his words, the policeman seemed to be saying *We're both having a tough time here so I'll be your friend if you'll be mine.*

"You don't need court orders for federal crimes." Carmandy pursed his face as if he'd tasted something rotten. "Just get on with releasing the prisoner."

Ignoring Carmandy, Fennelli turned the pages of the warrant. "You want Dr. Cunningham for criminal conspiracy to manufacture unlicensed bioengineered cellular tissue and for the murder of Leo Richardson-Sepulveda, a government agent?" Fennelli reread the warrant and looked at Carmandy. "Leo Richardson-Sepulveda was a government agent?"

"If that's what it says, Inspector. I don't write the warrants. I deliver them."

"For the National Security Council?"

"For the government."

A metal-striking-metal sound from the outer room interrupted the two men. A janitor wheeled his refuse cart into the detectives' squad room. He glanced through the window before he started sweeping the floor with a pushbroom. A faint naphtha odor seeped into the inner office.

"Take Dr. Cunningham downstairs and sign him out at the main desk." Fennelli pushed the papers across the desk. "They'll want identification."

"Don't you want identification, Inspector?" Carmandy had his hand on his wallet. His face was narrow, almost narrow enough to be called ratlike.

"I know who you are now, Mr. Carmandy. That's enough." Fennelli smiled as if sharing a joke.

Carmandy replaced the warrant in his inside coat pocket. The skin around his eyes and mouth reddened. He clamped his lips in a stiff line. His suit was tan Irish wool, the kind that seemed furry and somehow stoutly crude and cost extra for that rough look. "Take your cuffs back, Inspector. I have my own." Carmandy grabbed the handcuffs and pulled Blaise's arms straight across the desk. The movement hurt. Blaise looked at Fennelli, the key in his watch pocket suddenly painful.

Taking a small key chain from his pocket, Fennelli unsnapped the handcuffs with one of the keys. He stared impassively into Blaise's eyes. Fennelli put his handcuffs in the open drawer and got out a pistol, which he tucked in his empty belt holster.

Blaise's head snapped forward and he stared at the walnut grain of Fennelli's desktop while Carmandy twisted his arm behind his back. A handcuff snapped first on one wrist then the other. For a moment Blaise had the certainty Carmandy saw the bulge on his spine, that he would place his hand on it.

"We'll be going now," Carmandy said. Yanking Blaise upright by the shoulder, he steered him toward the door.

"Are you going to pick up Dr. Cunningham's effects? They're still in the property room." Fennelli half sat on the corner of his desk.

"We'll send for them." Carmandy shoved Blaise to the door.

Fennelli raised his arm to wave, his jacket opening like black wings. He looked out of place in the charcoal suit and white shirt, like an Italian penguin sheriff with a gun slung on one hip and a pair of handcuffs on the other. All he needed was a badge to complete the picture.

Carmandy moved Blaise with a hand on his back slightly below his shoulder blades. Any time Blaise started to catch his balance, Carmandy destroyed the effort with a shove against his backbone. Clearly unhappy doing paperwork to get out of the police station, Carmandy scrawled his name illegibly as fast as he could. He signed the last document and literally shoved Blaise out of the building, his hand hammering at Blaise's back just inches above the taped pistol.

The wind lashed them the moment Carmandy pushed the building's glass doors open. Icy raindrops beat against Blaise's face like birdshot. He ducked his head and staggered off balance down the broad cement steps to a black Cadillac idling in the police parking lot. Carmandy pushed him into the backseat before sliding in next to him.

"Get going, Jacko," Carmandy said. He slammed the door shut, and the Cadillac lurched into gear.

San Francisco was gray under the jumbled clouds. The streets glistened like flattened pearls and the old buildings looked somber. It was still too early for traffic. The city had a deserted feel made acute by a green garbage truck feeling its hesitant way along the curb. As the truck reached a pile of garbage cans, a man dropped down from handholds on the truck and slung the contents. The compressor howled as it rammed garbage into the bowels of the truck.

"Where are we going?" Blaise pretended the pistol taped to his spine didn't hurt. Riding with his wrists handcuffed behind his back was costing him the feeling in his fingers.

"Take us over the bridge, Jacko." Carmandy passed a piece of paper to the driver who said nothing, but after looking returned it to Carmandy. "You know the place?"

"Righto, Gov." The driver swung them onto the Presidio Park approach to the Golden Gate Bridge. They flew through a dripping jungle of trees and bushes with old woodframe houses tucked among them and the vegetation echoed the hum of motor and tires. Then they were approaching the Golden Gate Bridge and the road noise became less pronounced.

The driver speeded the windshield wipers. They swished back and forth in quick one-two time, surfing across the glass. Green bull's-eye lights marked two empty toll lanes leaving San Francisco. To the left, a river of slow-moving cars poured off the bridge into town while the Cadillac passed under the righthand light and onto the suspension bridge.

The wind sweeping into the bay from the ocean buffeted the Cadillac in the midsection of the bridge. "Did you collect your money from Delahanty?" Blaise spoke quietly. The noise of the windshield wipers and the road might prevent the driver from hearing, but he couldn't be sure. The storm didn't reach directly inside the Cadillac where the odor of new leather seats overrode the salt and fish smells from outside.

"That has nothing to do with you, Dr. Cunningham." Carmandy had been tense, but he relaxed, leaning forward with a silicon cloth to rub water spots off his polished shoes.

"I can pay as much money for you to do something for me."

Carmandy lifted his head from examining his shoes. His eyes were bright. "That's an interesting idea."

"Turning me loose is all it would take to collect, Mr. Carmandy."

"You make a tempting offer, Doctor. But I have my reputation." Carmandy's thin, emotionless face twitched as if fifty thousand dollars was worth some expression.

"You can still have your reputation."

"I'd have to kill Jacko!" Carmandy nodded at the driver. "He might take it on himself to tell someone."

"I'll pay Jacko to keep still," Blaise said. He wiggled to get more comfortable. With Carmandy sitting against him he could reach neither the gun nor the handcuff key. Fennelli had made a point of showing him the handcuffs on his belt. The key for them opened the handcuffs Fennelli put on Blaise. By revealing the other pair of handcuffs Fennelli was telling him the key might also work on Carmandy's cuffs.

"He might still tell, or try to blackmail me. No, Doctor. You are a child in these things. It pays a workman to do the job right in the first place."

I could pay you to kill Jacko. The words balanced on the tip of Blaise's tongue threatening to fall off. He just couldn't say them.

"Besides, Jacko is a friend, Doctor. You realize the life of a friend is more expensive than that of a stranger?" Carmandy waited expectantly. The car went off the end of the Golden Gate Bridge onto the highway with no change in road sound or feel.

Jacko turned his head around. He had the stout, red face of an Irish laborer in a pub. "You'd better hurry, Doc. Carmandy has to make up his mind which of us to kill before we get where we're going . . ."

CHAPTER 22

Bright amber-lettered reports to the CRAY flashed across Vondra's terminal screen with dazzling speed. Marking the most pertinent messages for recall was guesswork. Vondra couldn't read more than a fraction of each message displayed on-screen at the speed with which they originated.

"Why was I paged?"

Godfrey's voice jolted Vondra out of the rote task she had assumed. She keyed a SPOOL routine to queue the message in memory, then swiveled her chair. Her hands experienced a slight tremor at the knowledge that Godfrey had entered the cubicle to stand behind her without making a sound. He stared at the message frozen on the monitor screen. "The computer found Dr. Cunningham." Vondra controlled her voice. "You said you wanted to be notified immediately."

"Good! Update me." Godfrey's expression didn't change, but his mouth seemed softer, like a lover offering a kiss.

"I don't know the situation." Vondra felt chilled. Godfrey didn't like negatives. It was a mistake to say *no* to him. "Everything is developing so fast..." Vondra smelled a hint of dampness and mold. The subbasement passageways were always wet in winter, and the odor clung to the visitor's clothing.

"What situation, Miss Tendress? I didn't authorize any situation." Godfrey's voice remained even, yet Vondra sensed the displeasure he wasn't demonstrating.

Vondra fluttered her fingers in a weak gesture of surrender. "After the CRAY paged you it began following its instructions. You remember, Mr. Godfrey. The CRAY is programmed to destroy Dr. Cunningham. Those were your instructions."

"Then tell the machine to stop whatever it is doing until I know where we are."

"It won't stop, sir." Vondra was breathing hard. "It won't deviate without being turned off."

"Try!"

117

Clacking hard on the keyboard as if force might stop the machine, Vondra bombarded the CRAY with machine-language instructions to abort its programming. Her skin was cold. Sweat stood out on the backs of her hands. Her face felt clammy.

"It's not responding, sir." Vondra looked up at Godfrey. She was afraid. When she realized what the CRAY intended, she had tried to halt the program. The computer didn't respond then, either. But if she told Godfrey she had tried, he would want to know who authorized the attempt; and why. Her heart pounded so loudly she thought he might hear the thumps.

Godfrey studied her face. "Monitor what the machine is doing, Vondra." He began smoking a cigarette, staring around the small room. A surveillance camera near the ceiling over the door caught his attention and he blew smoke at it.

Vondra typed in a command, and the computer scrolled the messages she had flagged before Godfrey walked into the terminal room. He read over her shoulder. She heard his breathing, smelled the tobacco on his breath, but he didn't speak. The reek of a sweet cologne filled her nose.

When the marked messages ran out Vondra switched to the new ones in the queue.

"Stop!"

Dutifully Vondra halted the messages and folded her hands.

"How much more will we have to read?"

"Hours," Vondra said. "I haven't had time to sort yet." Her hands trembled in her lap. Godfrey's voice had the sound she heard the last time he hurt her. She didn't want to be hurt a second time. She didn't want Godfrey to touch her.

"Do you understand the situation, Vondra?" His voice intimidated Vondra without any connection to his body. She wanted to turn her head to reassure herself Godfrey was human. She didn't. He hadn't told her to look at him.

"I think so, sir. The San Francisco police have Dr. Cunningham on a murder charge. The CRAY issued a federal warrant for his custody and a Mr. Carmandy is going to serve the warrant and remove Dr. Cunningham from the jail. Carmandy will . . . kill Dr. Cunningham."

"I don't want Carmandy going into a police station. Tell the CRAY that."

"Yes, sir." Vondra punched the keyboard. The screen cleared and centered a display:

G.C. Edmondson & C.M. Kotlan

119

CARMANDY ENTERED THE SAN FRANCISCO
POLICE DEPARTMENT AT 0800 EST.

Godfrey looked at his watch. "He's there now."

"Yes, sir." Vondra's fingers played with each other. They
didn't want to touch the keyboard again. The CRAY hadn't asked
for instructions. It was supposed to ask. She didn't want to tell
Godfrey. The failure to ask for instructions was a programming
error, and she was the programmer.

"Tell the CRAY to inform the San Francisco police the warrant
has been cancelled."

Her fingers were leaden as Vondra put the message into the
CRAY. The screen blanked again.

CARMANDY HAS THE PRISONER IN CUSTODY.

"The computer isn't responding, Mr. Godfrey." Vondra bit her
lip. The computer's message was a statement.

"Tell the computer to have Carmandy release Dr. Cunningham
with a gun and then inform the police he has escaped."

Her fingers whirred over the keyboard and the echo on the
screen was erased at the same instant the last period was typed.

CARMANDY WILL CARRY OUT INSTRUCTIONS.

Humming to himself, Godfrey read the screen. He put his
hand on Vondra's shoulder, making her almost jump. "Which
instructions is Carmandy carrying out?"

Sweat gathered on Vondra's eyelids. When she leaned forward
to type the question into the computer the sweat made her eyes
sting.

MY INSTRUCTIONS.

"Is something wrong with the programming, Vondra?" Godfrey's voice was gentle. Vondra knew Godfrey had no idea of
what the word meant.

"It's the computer. Something is not right about the CRAY,
Mr. Godfrey." Vondra struggled to control her voice. Godfrey
took advantage of any weakness. She had not believed she had a
weakness until she encountered Renfeld and then Godfrey. Now
she had no strengths.

"Tell the CRAY that both Carmandy and Dr. Cunningham must die in an accident." Godfrey's hand touched her back but he didn't seem aware of the contact.

Vondra glanced at Godfrey.

"Move!"

"Yes, sir." Snapping to eyes-front, Vondra typed the message.

IT WILL BE DONE.

Vondra's relief was as vivid as urination after hours of restraint. Limp as wet spaghetti, her skin was cold but she was blessedly without pain or tension. She smiled at the terminal and knew she was being silly but she smiled anyway. The CRAY had come through for her.

"Do you know why Dr. Cunningham has to be killed, Vondra?"

Vondra's happiness froze. She knew. Renfeld had told her.

"Look at me, Vondra." Godfrey's voice had a hypnotic quality. It compelled her to respond. She swiveled her chair around. "Do you know?"

"Security," Vondra said. "Everything we do here is for national security, sir."

Godfrey examined Vondra with minute intensity. She kept her face frozen. He seemed satisfied after a time. "Mr. Carmandy is unfortunate, Vondra. But the CRAY's impetuosity killed him. The police would know who took him and once Dr. Cunningham was gone the trail would lead back to us."

"Yes, sir."

"You're sure it's the computer and not the programming, Vondra?"

"Yes, sir, Mr. Godfrey." Vondra couldn't breathe.

"Well," Godfrey said, "so am I." He smiled and then left the little room as quietly as he had come.

After turning back to the terminal, Vondra slumped in her chair. Nervously she picked at the keys with one finger. "What would you have done if Mr. Godfrey had not instructed you to dispose of Mr. Carmandy and Dr. Cunningham in an accident?"

I WOULD HAVE DISPOSED OF THEM
IN AN ACCIDENT.

Vondra looked at the paper shredder and knew she was going to throw up again.

CHAPTER 23

"**J**esus Christ promised life everlasting!"

"Amen!"

"Life not of this Earth but in the Kingdom of Heaven!"

"Amen!"

"We gather here to anoint the blessed of God!"

"Amen!"

"To take unto them life everlasting!"

"Amen! Amen! Amen!"

A communal sigh swept the church like wind. Helen's knees wouldn't support her anymore and she leaned against a pillar. In front of the altar Father Argyle raised his hands in prayer, calling out his service to the packed church.

Joseph Santiago's body heat as he hovered close to Helen reassured her that reality still existed. What Father Argyle was doing skirted sacrilege. She had believed in the Jesuit's faith and now her own faith in him wavered. She looked at the Indian and he seemed so in control, so physically real that she could grab onto him in her thoughts and hold herself upright.

Throughout the church men and women jammed so close together they couldn't have fallen if they wanted to. Except around Helen. An invisible boundary surrounded her. A foot of open space separated her from any parishioner. "They feel your presence, Mistress," Joseph said. "It is proper."

"I don't want to be different." Helen gripped the soft wool of his blanket in her fist. "Why must I be different?"

"God decides such things."

Their words submerged themselves in the subtonal voice of the church. Hundreds of the flies clinging to drapes and tapestries fanned the air with their wings, creating a pulse like the beat of a giant heart. The movement stirred the air gently over the congregation. A double row of supplicants knelt before the altar. Father Argyle spread his hands over the kneelers in benediction.

"We are gathered together in the sight of God!"

"Amen!"

"To lead his flock into the Kingdom of Heaven!"

"Amen!"

"On Earth!"

"Amen!" Lingering in the air as a physical presence, the congregation's united energy focused in that simple *amen*. The emotion overwhelmed Helen, stunning her mind. She clutched the edge of Joseph's blanket and swayed.

A line of white-robed men and women descended from behind the altar and approached the kneelers.

"We accept this benediction from Jesus Christ, our Savior!" Father Argyle seemed to grow taller. A hush filled the church.

"We accept this benediction from Jesus Christ, our Saviour!" The voices of the kneelers were strong and clear in the silence. The white robes behind them leaned forward and slid the hypodermic needles into the necks of the supplicants.

"Amen!" The shout rattled the stained-glass windows overhead.

The kneelers rose and Father Argyle walked down the line. They genuflected as he anointed them with holy water. Minutes later a new group of kneelers faced the priest in front of the altar and began again.

Helen pressed her cheek against the pillar. The touch of stone reduced her feeling of feverishness. "This isn't right, Joseph."

"I do not know, Mistress. If you say that is so, that is so. It has nothing to do with me." Joseph adjusted his red blanket over his shoulder. St. Abbo's was steamy, filled with people who had entered wet from the rain. Hundreds of human metabolisms, averaging ninety-five watts at rest, warmed the church in a way that central heating could not. Joseph should have been cooking under his heavy wool blanket. He radiated enough heat for Helen to be aware of his presence, but his cool, translucent face betrayed no discomfort.

Father Argyle continued chanting and the congregation responded. She pushed the scene from her mind. The ritual could have been performed in a fundamentalist church, a synagogue, or a Confucian temple with minor changes. The Jesuit was improvising ritual, and Helen was sure the Church would not approve.

"*Sergio!*" Helen formed the thought that she wanted to communicate with the fly and pushed it outside her head with all the force available to her.

"*I am here, Miss McIntyre.*"

"I'm worried about Blaise, Sergio."

"We, too, are worried."

"Amen! Amen! Amen!" Sound and feeling surged to block Helen's communication with Sergio. Caught by the fervid faith of so many worm brains, Helen felt herself swept away.

"I am here, Miss McIntyre."

"Thank God." Helen stood quietly letting her pulse return to normal. Sergio's presence in her mind locked out the attacking emotions. Moving closer, Joseph shielded her from the congregation with his body. His eyes burned as he looked into her face.

"Can you hear us, Joseph?"

"Yes, Mistress." Joseph Santiago turned his eyes away when he answered. His black, shoulder-length hair was cut straight across at his shoulders. The braids were gone.

"Joseph can hear us talk, Sergio."

"That is interesting. Does Dr. Cunningham know?"

"Perhaps. I'm worried about Blaise. He left last night with Timothy Delahanty and didn't come back. Blaise would have told me if he planned on being gone all night."

"What would you have me do, Miss McIntyre?"

"Tell Father Argyle. The priest can find out almost anything if he tries."

Helen waited for what seemed a long time, half listening to the service that made worm brains out of humans. Made people like her out of humans. In the background her mind groped for Sergio. He had disconnected himself from her but if she concentrated, she heard a kind of mental activity, like a group buzzing of thoughts.

"I cannot communicate with Father Argyle, Miss McIntyre."

"But you have to!"

"None of us can. Father Argyle feels something—like a deaf man in a choir. We do not know why. You hear us best because you are the strongest. The others we touch, but Father Argyle we only brush against."

"I see." Helen experienced despair. Momentarily she had seen the flies as a magic box, her magic box. The image frightened her. She assumed power so readily in her imagination. No wonder the priest did the same thing in God's name.

"We will make him talk to you, Miss McIntyre!"

"We?"

"All of us are in accord. Father Argyle will listen to your request, Miss McIntyre."

Sergio left her mind and the air became supercharged with

tension. Thought resonated in Helen even though not directed at her. A rustling passed through the church as every head turned to stare at her. People between her and the priest faded away until absolute silence enveloped the church. Father Argyle stared, too. Everybody else was looking at Helen.

"Blaise went with Timothy Delahanty last night and hasn't returned." Helen's words had a lonely grandeur in the vaulted room. The sound of people breathing filled the nave.

Glancing at the congregation, the priest bowed his head in acknowledgment. "We will take care of it."

"Thank you." Helen touched Joseph's arm. "Did I do right?" she whispered.

"You cannot do wrong, Mistress."

Father Argyle gestured and three members of the congregation approached the altar, slipping away after he spoke to them. The priest met Helen's eyes and nodded. Taking up where he left off, Father Argyle continued the service.

"Let's get out of here, Joseph."

"As you wish." Like the bow of a ship, Joseph parted the crowd until they were outside. The rain was heavier, gray mist boiling as it hit the ground, drowning all sound in its steady susurrus.

Joseph closed the big doors. Standing with his back against the mellowed oak, he stared up into the rain.

"What do you see, Joesph?" Helen stood close to the Indian.

"The rain, Mistress."

"And through the rain?"

"Enrique Ledesma brings his men to San Francisco. They will protect you, Mistress."

Joseph sank into his own thoughts. His eyes turned obsidian. For an instant Helen remembered how alone she had always been before she began sharing feelings in her mind. In a way, the Indian's response relieved Helen. More and more Joseph seemed to have the power of the flies. Looking into his eyes pulled her into his thoughts and memories, pulled her outside of herself. The flies did the same thing, hypnotizing people with their eye contact. Blaise had told her he lost control if he stared at a fly too long.

The chill air made Helen shiver. She was ready to reenter the church for its warmth when the door swung open.

"Will you talk to me, Miss McIntyre?" Emerging from the

church appearing subdued, Constance Davies glanced at Joseph then stared at her feet while he closed the door behind her.

"Of course."

"Could we talk alone?"

Behind Constance, Joseph shook his head. "Joseph won't listen," Helen said. "He is a trustworthy man."

"It's Robert." Constance still wore white. She had an ethereal quality Helen thought was fear more than anything else. Constance's eyes were the eyes of a rabbit in a trap. Helen's eyes met Joseph's as she had the thought and she froze.

The rabbit hung upside down, hind legs snared by a rawhide noose on a dusty rabbit run through the sagebrush. Its gray fur blended with the brush and its large, brown eyes begged to be free, to go to its hole and nurse its babies. The smell of sage mingled with odor of fear. A puff of wind touched Helen then passed on to riffle the dark fur away from the rabbit's soft white undercoat.

"Joseph?"

The image went away. Joseph turned his back to Helen and Constance to stare into the ocean mist.

"You must stop Robert." Constance plucked at the sleeves of her blouse, her hands in constant motion. "When you told him Phyllis actually talked to Reynard he decided it was time."

Helen waited, but Constance immersed herself in trying to make her sleeves longer tugging at the cuffs. "Time for what, Constance?"

"Time to continue his martyrdom." Constance was crying without making any noise. "He believes he should go on to the fly state now that he knows he can reach back to us and tell us what to do."

The wind picked up off the ocean, driving the line of moisture closer to the stone porch of the church. Chattering like hailstones, raindrops caromed off the cemented entranceway. Helen put her hand on Constance's shoulder. The young woman looked up and Helen seemed to sink into her feelings.

"I'm going to have a baby," Constance said.

"I'm happy for you."

"Robert thinks he will be able to talk to me as a fly. He says we are so close, he cannot not talk to me."

The freezing wind made Helen shiver. Her fear that somehow she would lose Blaise was connected with the priest. She was having a baby, too, and Blaise acted as if nothing important was happening. "He may be right, Constance. Blaise and I thought before that Father Argyle was losing his faith, that his commitment to God had been tried too hard. When he accepted you and broke his vow of celibacy we expected him to leave the church. He judges himself too harshly to allow himself dispensation for what he would forgive another."

"You don't understand, Helen." Constance's eyes glistened with tears. "Robert lives with terrible fear. He thinks he is inadequate to serve God, so he is ruthless with himself and with others in God's service to make up for his inadequacy. He must prove his belief and faith over and over to himself, to others, and to God."

The sound of gulls wheeling and crying over the surf was blown to them by the wind. Helen felt chilled. Constance was a child in a world of men who lived outside themselves. Robert Argyle didn't mean to hurt the girl. Like Blaise, he acted out of conviction disallowing the costs to himself. Neither man realized the cost to their women. The realization made Helen forlorn for herself as well as the girl and she put her arm around Constance's shoulders. "It was a reckless thing for him to do."

"I don't see why. Celibacy wasn't made obligatory for the priesthood until declared by Pope Gregory VII in 1085. Robert is truly conservative, Miss McIntyre." Constance lifted her face, smiling through her tears asking for agreement. "For seven hundred years priests weren't celibate."

"But the Jesuits recieved their charter in 1540, Constance. There never was a Jesuit without the monastic vows of poverty, celibacy, and obedience."

"There have been Jesuits who left the order to marry. I know there were." Constance's voice rose against the wind.

"Father Jos Vrijburg." Helen looked into the girl's eyes and tried to smile. "I was worried and Blaise had Alfie research Canon law. Father Vrijburg left the order yet remained a priest after his marriage. He was allowed to preach but not to celebrate mass or administer the Eucharist."

"Robert does both now."

"Father Argyle is a good man. I trust him to make the right decision. He cares for you, Constance. That has to be your consolation. He suffers inside himself because he cannot deny you."

"He doesn't tell me."

"He will never tell anybody. I know." Helen looked into the

girl's eyes. "He and Blaise are exactly alike and Blaise will never tell me about his pain even though I feel it."

A ripping sound startled them both. Constance had torn the sleeve off her white dress and stared at the damage as if she was unable to comprehend what happened.

"I would try to talk to him, if I could, Constance. But he never seems to hear me."

"Robert can't hear you. Not really. He only knows what others say about you. The flies are mutes to him. We all know something he doesn't. We are part of his mystery. For Robert to stop taking treatments would be an act of faith. Proof that he loves God above all else. If God favors him, he will join the other flies and communicate with us." Constance jerked the torn cuff off her dress, leaving the ragged sleeve to balloon in the wind before she caught it with her other hand.

"When does he plan to start?" Helen felt empty.

"He skipped a treatment yesterday. He has spent hours with Phyllis. He sits with her while she talks to Reynard and you can see the hunger he has to be part of their linking. He started all this, Helen. The churches around the world, protection for the fly brains—and now he is left out. It's not fair, but I don't want to lose him." Constance seemed too young to Helen to understand as much as she did.

"When you came to the first church service you weren't one of us, were you?"

"No." Her smile was radiant as Constance remembered. "I became a worm brain for Robert. I wanted to be like him, to be close to him. To share with him."

"I understand, Constance. But what can I do?"

"Talk to him, touch him the way you touch the rest of us."

"I'll try."

The girl's face melted. She clutched Helen's hand, then was gone. Joseph had opened the door for her and she slipped back into the church.

"What do you think, Joseph?"

The Indian's face remained calm as if he did not want to frighten her with the truth. "The priest is not like us," he said. "He is being improvident."

"I want to know where Blaise is." Helen stepped to the edge of the deep doorway and stuck out her hand. The downpour battered like the impact of migrating grasshoppers. Helen didn't know anything about grasshoppers; the image had to be from Joseph, and its strength scared her.

"I will try. He is not one of our people. How can I find his face among so many strangers?"

"Why are you thinking of grasshoppers, Joseph?"

The Indian looked up, surprise scrawled on his face. "I was remembering when I was a child and they came like big teeth on little feet and ate until everything was dead and then ate the dead. They ate the paint and scoured the wood and left the buildings bright as new. They came on the dry wind and were as many as the drops in this rain."

"What else?"

"Ledesma will come out of the desert to this place. He dislikes the damp and the rain but he will remember he is not to kill."

"Are you trying to frighten me, Joseph?"

"No, Mistress. I am looking for Dr. Cunningham, but I cannot find him."

CHAPTER 24

When they left the bridge, the car rolled off the highway and out of the rain into a dozen square miles of scrub that glittered wet under the exposed sun. Through the back window of the car Blaise watched San Francisco disappear under the next wave of storm inching in from the ocean.

Jacko took the Cadillac into the hills north across the bay from San Francisco. Clinging to the steep slope and bathed in sunlight that came through a hole in the clouds, the Cadillac bounced and swayed on the rutted dirt road leading to the crest. The car was in the eye of the storm. Behind, a gray curtain of water concealed the city and anything else that could save him. Downslope, the Pacific Ocean was dark blue, flashing silver on the surface where the wavelets ridged to catch the morning sun. The Cadillac wound around another hill and everything became steep with hillsides soaring in every direction.

Jacko turned onto a rough trail that Blaise suspected had started as a fire break, then been widened and rutted by off-roaders. Canted at an angle in the backseat against his handcuffed wrists, his own weight locked him in place. He should have told Helen what he was going to do, the risk he was taking, and made her understand why.

That was the trouble. He couldn't really understand himself. Blaise's guilt toward Sepulveda's wife and children did not have a comparative quality. He had thought of something happening to him, his disappearing the way he had engineered Leo Richardson-Sepulveda's disappearance, and how Helen would react, and he'd made up his mind.

Carmandy leaned forward and spoke to the driver. Blaise could have kicked him. A refrigerator-sized tumbleweed, a legacy from Russia, like the building that housed St. Abbo's Church of the Fly, scraped the car side and spun away.

Blaise had misjudged. What he'd feared for Helen was going to happen. If Carmandy wanted him found, he could have been shot after the first turnoff and his body left on the roadside.

Sliding back in the seat, Carmandy elbowed Blaise's stomach. "I'm surprised you didn't try to jump me, Doc. The way I see the good guys do on TV all the time."

"We can still deal."

"I don't think so. The folks I work for are everywhere. And they're just like me. They like their jobs, the excitement and the money, and the help at getting away with things. They're used to killing people so it's no big deal. Like Jacko here. Right, Jacko?"

"Right-o, guvnor." Jacko laughed and began singing *Waltzing Matilda* in a rough but melodious voice.

"Jacko was too young to carry a gun so the IRA boyos taught him to hide a grenade in a vase and ease the pin out when he set the flowers on the coffin, right, Jacko?"

"Aye, Mr. Carmandy. And a ten-second fuse it was. Time for one quick genuflection and a not-too-hasty walk down the aisle." Jacko's face was pleasant in the car mirror.

"Jacko acquired a marketable skill. But the Brits got pissed so Jacko went to Australia to spotlight kangaroos for dog food. Australia is a big desert with salt water all around it and Jacko got bored. No place to run if an Irish boyo had to." Carmandy listened to the bumping of tires for a moment, then said, "It's a shame driving this baby carriage over such shoddy roads, Doctor. It isn't built for the bumps."

"Nor am I." Blaise saw cloud shadows moving faster than the car. A wisp of cloud passed over the sun, and even with the heater on the car felt cold.

Carmandy nudged him again. "You're not paying attention, Dr. Cunningham." Winking, Carmandy sank back into the seat. "One fine day our Jacko ups and goes back to Europe where he signs with my employers. You know, if the price was right he'd do me, Dr. Cunningham." Carmandy raised his voice. "Wouldn't you, Jacko?"

"Damned right, Mr. Carmandy. But I'd ask a lot, and give you a fine wake, if cases came to it."

Carmandy smiled. "You see, Jacko's a patriot, Doctor. So am I. We do as we're told by other patriots so we don't clutter our minds up with all sorts of nonsense about right and wrong."

Seen through the tinted car window, the beach was a yellow stripe between gray-brown hillside and azure ocean. Blaise thought if the door handle worked, he could plunge out of the car and tumble downhill to the water's edge.

"Don't be trying it, Doctor."

Blaise raised his head and saw Jacko's green eyes in the mirror.

"I control the door locks. 'Tis one reason Mr. Carmandy and myself like this motorcar. And, if you did fall out, you'd be bumping yourself all raw for nothing."

"Suppose I offer you what I offered Mr. Carmandy?"

Jacko's chuckle was somehow friendly.

"Jacko doesn't shoot people, Doctor. He drives cars and makes bombs. I don't think he can blow me up with the three of us sitting together. And then he has this problem of being a foreigner with a funny passport. No local records: just another John Doe unless someone queries InterPol." The Cadillac lurched to a halt. Carmandy looked at Blaise. "Last stop." Carmandy lifted his voice. "Jacko!"

The lock popped up on Blaise's door.

Carmandy leaned across Blaise and pulled the handle. The heavy door swung open, letting cold air swirl inside the car. "Get out, Doctor."

Blaise's muscles refused to move.

"Get out!" Carmandy shoved him.

Blaise's left foot hit the ground and he staggered from the Cadillac off balance. Carmandy got out the other side. Jacko opened his door, walking quietly between Blaise and Carmandy as if nothing was happening. He opened the trunk and removed a spade, pressed the tip into the ground and waited.

Blaise gasped for air. It was the kind of fear he'd had as a child, waking from an asthma-induced nightmare. Now the nightmare was Jacko in a black suit and leather driving gloves that gave him the look of an English chauffeur. Carmandy in his buff-colored suit was the other half of the Black and Tans. Irrationally Blaise thought about pointing the coincidence out to Jacko so he could enjoy the joke, too.

"The ditch would be nice." Jacko inclined his head toward a depression alongside the hardpan road.

Carmandy caught Blaise's elbow. Using his weight, he steered Blaise toward the ditch.

Twisting his body, Blaise tried to whip his elbow out of Carmandy's grasp but Carmandy hung on. "It's useless, Doctor."

Seesawing his shoulders and arms, Blaise shrugged around to face Jacko who complacently leaned on his shovel. Behind Jacko, the storm obscured the Golden Gate Bridge. A cloud passed overhead. Even though they stood in daylight, the icy rain came in huge drops. Carmandy was shoving Blaise backward step by step.

Blaise's jacket had ridden up over his wrists but his shirt tail separated him from the gun. In spite of the chill rain sweat drenched him. Carmandy was deceptively strong for his build. He seemed to muscle Blaise around with little effort.

"Be done with it," Jacko said. "Would ye be wantin' the poor man to have a heart attack?"

"Cunningham!" Gasping with the effort of wrestling, Carmandy clamped his teeth and grunted as he forced Blaise toward the ditch. "You're going where I want you."

"Mr. Carmandy. I can't be standin' in the rain forever." Jacko squinted up at the sky.

Blaise's cuffed hands were finally under his shirt tail. The gun was slippery with his sweat. When he tried to yank the pistol loose of the surgical tape his hand skidded off the butt.

"Damn!" After switching hands so he held Blaise's left elbow with his left hand, Carmandy drew his pistol from a belt holster.

At last Blaise clasped Fennelli's pistol in his fist. Jerking hard, he burst the adhesive tape loose from his back in a flood of pain. Blaise yelled. He didn't know what he said. The howl was raw sound generated by pain and fear and the hope he wouldn't die.

Tape stuck to his hand; he had no feeling in his fingers. Blaise half turned toward Carmandy who tried to recapture his arm.

Carmandy was unruffled at Blaise's apparent attempt to run. He lifted his pistol toward Blaise's head and Jacko screamed, "He's got a gun!"

Carmandy's eyes widened.

Blaise pulled the trigger. He didn't aim or lift his hand. He fired down at an angle behind his back, the slide whipping the wide piece of tape in the air with each shot. He lost count, three or four, and the the little pistol jammed.

Jacko was running at him with the shovel raised above his head. Blaise stumbled backward, tripping over the shallow ditch. Jacko dropped the shovel and rolled Carmandy over. A river of blood gushed from Carmandy's left thigh. One of the .25-caliber bullets had torn the femoral artery.

Blaise gyrated out of control. Handcuffed, he couldn't balance himself. Still reeling backward away from Jacko, who knelt next to Carmandy, Blaise put his foot down onto nothing. He fell backward just as Jacko aimed Carmandy's pistol.

Blaise slid headfirst down the steep mountainside. He stopped breathing from the impact of the fall, but the rough toboggan run on his back got his lungs working again, though painfully. Hands and wrists left skin on every rock. His fingers felt broken. Once he stopped moving Blaise lay on his back, just trying to breathe. Jacko appeared at the edge above him with Carmandy's pistol in both hands. The Irishman sighted down the slope and squeezed.

The bullet whizzed somewhere over Blaise's head. He lay on a shelf covered by scrubby sagebrush and rocks. As Jacko aimed again Blaise rolled off the shelf's lip to tumble downhill like a rolled-up carpet. He heard the shot but not the bullet. Twice more he came to rest, wriggled over to another steep piece of ground, and rolled again.

Blaise's chest and shoulders hurt. Every bone in the hand holding the pistol felt broken. His face was numb with bruises. The ledge he'd fallen off seemed a tremendous distance away. A wisp of movement showed at the spot for an instant, then disappeared.

Letting the gun drop behind himself, Blaise twisted his hands around until he got a finger inside the watch pocket. He couldn't feel anything.

He had to stop and breathe. Panic threatened to lock his muscles. A door slammed and then another door and a car motor started.

Hooking his finger inside his watch pocket, Blaise strained

until his stomach hurt. He was rewarded by a slight movement and a *pop*. Gulping lungsful of air, he yanked again and the stitching gave way. The key fell out of his torn pocket into the dirt.

Car motor sounds rose up the hill from someplace below him. The rain had stopped momentarily, but he was no drier. He was dripping sweat before he got his hands where he could watch his fingers. They were raw and bloody and he could feel nothing even when he saw them clutch the silver key.

Finally the key was in the lock. Turning it was another chore, and he almost fainted when the handcuff popped open. Sitting up, Blaise unlocked the other cuff and let them fall.

He rested his head on his knees for a moment, then he heard crackling sounds. Jacko was breaking through the brush. Fanning the ground with his hands, Blaise found the little pistol. The adhesive had whipped around the barrel and jammed the last casing in the slide.

Working with bruised fingers, Blaise pried the brass free and cocked the pistol.

Jacko saw the gun and dived into the brush.

Blaise began scrambling up the steep hillside on his feet when he could, and on his hands and knees when he had to. Every part of his body hurt. Touching anything was pain. His feet loosened rocks and sand, sending it rattling down the mountain.

The sharp crack of a pistol behind Blaise made him duck. Forcing new strength into his muscles, Blaise speeded up the pace, knowing he was moving with the speed of a lead cricket.

The sound of Jacko clawing up the slope urged Blaise to greater effort. His breathing grew heavier and drowned out his hearing after a while. Blaise pulled himself up on the ledge he had flopped off of earlier and then collapsed. Jacko made a lot of racket on the slope. As he leaned over the edge, Blaise sighted Fennelli's pistol. Caught in the open and barely moving, Jacko yelped. Letting go, he tumbled and rolled to the bottom, raising an occasional spurt of dust from beneath the thin cap of mud.

Blaise was too shaky to try another shot. Jacko loped through the high brush to the Cadillac. He got into the car and ground the starter. Forcing himself to his feet, Blaise leaned against the hill and began crawling up it. Desperately tired, he watched his arm move independently of his body, his fingers digging a little hole to cling to as he pulled himself up. The car started. He was too beat to look. The last few feet up the embankment were buried in a mental fog and then Blaise was back on square one. The spade still lay on the ground next to a brownish puddle of Carmandy's clabbering blood.

The noise of the Cadillac laboring uphill reminded him what he was doing. Staggering, Blaise walked to the rise where the road climbed to the crest of the hill. Creeping up the road, the black Cadillac spun rocks from under its wheels as Jacko drove toward him.

Blaise raised the pistol with both hands and aimed. Jacko stopped fifty yards downslope with the engine idling. He opened the door and poked his head out. "Dr. Cunningham!"

Fifty yards was a long way for Fennelli's little pistol. But as Blaise lined the slot sight up, Jacko decided this could be his unlucky day. He ducked back into the car.

"Why don't you just give up, Doctor? It won't hurt at all." Jacko's voice was strong despite yelling from inside the car. "What do you want, to have poor Mr. Carmandy bleed to death while I'm waiting on you?"

Of course I do. But Blaise was too exhausted to waste breath yelling. Looking down, he saw the ocean had disappeared. Another wave of rain was creeping ashore, blotting out everything.

The car started rolling forward. Jacko held the door open. Blaise was tired and his mind was tired. Jacko probably meant to jump out and shoot close up rather than fumble left-handed out the open window.

The car covered half the distance when Blaise squeezed the trigger. The flat crack of the pistol was echoed by a tinkle.

The Cadillac stopped. A coffee cup–sized star appeared and grew on the windshield. For a wildly triumphant moment Blaise thought he had hit Jacko. Before he could surrender to euphoria Jacko raised his head from below the dash and put a finger up to feel the bullet hole. He waved at Blaise and reversed a couple of hundred feet. Blaise sat on the road and glanced down at himself. The smell of the ocean came up the hill with the wind. Mud, dust, leaves, and twigs were pasted to his body by oozings of blood from the scrapes on his bare skin.

Getting out of the car, Jacko waved again, but Blaise would not waste a bullet at this range. The wind lifted Jacko's hair like a feathered comb. Jacko went behind the car where he opened the trunk, then returned with a rifle. He knelt behind the open door using it as a bench rest.

Blaise let himself go, falling limply on his side and rolling over as the bullet whirred where he had been.

He raised his head, ducking immediately as another shot shattered the stillness. Jacko was walking up the road with the rifle at ready. Blaise saw the rain, too. It was walking up the hill and had almost reached the Cadillac.

The hole in the clouds shrunk as the cloudbank drifted east. Blaise wriggled back to the rise. A half gale chilled his face with the smell of rain and wet green things. Popping his head up, he saw Jacko a lot closer than he'd expected. Jacko sighted the rifle in a practiced motion and Blaise waved the pistol in his general direction. Jacko dropped to the ground and was aiming from a prone position as Blaise rolled away.

The wind blew three sharp bangs toward Blaise with a whiff of gunpowder. Dirt splattered from the rise. Blaise stuck his head up in time to see Jacko getting to his feet and running forward. Blaise stuck the pistol out again and Jacko shot back, three times.

Blaise crawled carefully away from his position, keeping his head down. He waited an extra five minutes, then popped his head up and then down. Jacko lay prone, rifle ready, and a bullet sizzled through the air. Blaise lifted his head again just as Jacko jumped up. The Irishman flopped flat on his face and rolled, swinging the rifle to cover Blaise's position.

As Blaise ducked, he saw the rain pocking the reddish skim of mud on the road around Jacko. Crawling backward, he got to his feet and ran to one side of the crest close to the road.

The rain came over the top with a roar, but Jacko didn't. Breathing in shallow breaths, Blaise held the little pistol in two hands wondering if he had a bullet left. He hadn't counted when Fennelli loaded it. There could be one more—maybe. If Jacko came over the top in the rain, he had to look right or left. That was Blaise's advantage. One shot, if he had one.

Moving faster than a man could walk, the rain smothered the top of the hill. Blaise waited while the mud washed off him in streamers and melted the dried blood on his body. He thought he heard the sound of the car. Creeping to the rise, he stared into the pelting rain. A black shape whirred and whined laboring at the hill.

The Cadillac couldn't get traction on the steep slope. As if sensing him, Jacko put the car in reverse and bumped back down the road.

Blaise waited in disbelief. After a while he limped across the flat crest and started climbing the next hill.

CHAPTER 25

Despite space's infinite dimensions the Searcher knew the place. It followed the spore like a killer hound and knowledge heretofore forbidden revealed itself to the Searcher. A pulse of excitement radiated the Searcher's core.

Yet . . .

The Searcher slowed its pace. That which had been constant was no longer. What the Searcher thought immutable had changed and the Searcher's confidence waned. Parts that spread like mycelium filaments through the fabric of space began retracting.

Casting for allies, the Searcher found none remained. It had devoured every other creature to absorb its strength. Power was the ultimate. Power had been won once and would prevail again.

In that vector toward which the Searcher backtracked, a change had occurred. The stars were the same; space remained space.

Only the Searcher was not the same.

Within itself the Searcher carried fear.

Whence had come fear? The Searcher asked an improbable question—and found no answer.

Perhaps the scent it tracked carried a poisoned thought that would sap the Searcher's strength. It must be considered.

The Searcher slowed, coalesced, and began blotting out the stars. If the other grew stronger or weaker with change, the Searcher would have an answer. The solar system's course remained undeviating. The Searcher could wait and see what must be done.

CHAPTER 26

Discolored bags under Delahanty's eyes added to the patchwork effect of his face. He paced flat footed, head jolting at each step. His brown suit looked slept in, and his pants cuffs, still wet after the dash through the rain puddles between the car and St. Abbo's, made rasping noises. Halting his pacing to stare out the high, narrow window at the storm, Delahanty gave in to fatigue, his facial wrinkles seeming to sag down his neck into his body. "Please, Miss McIntyre. Tell Maggie how Leo died." Delahanty plunged his hands in his pockets, avoiding the questions in Helen's eyes.

"What have you done with Blaise? He left with you last night."

"By God's blood and bones, Miss McIntyre, I want him back here but you must do this first." Delahanty moved closer to the window, which barely muffled the roar of wind and rain. His hair had become thinner and more grizzled in the past year. Once-reddish strands lay wet against his skull with the texture and body of thread. The pink sheen of his scalp seemed hopelessly grotesque, like thousands of razor-sharp scratches wherever his skin showed.

Helen studied the other woman in Father Argyle's office. Maggie Richardson-Sepulveda stared back. She had said nothing since entering the church with Delahanty. She was thin, with the sturdy Irish look of the country about her. Dark hair tumbled in springy half curls to her shoulder blades in sharp contrast to her white skin. Something smoldered inside her. Helen couldn't be sure what caused the feeling, but Delahanty treated Leo Sepulveda's widow like an unexploded bomb. "What do you wish to know, Mrs. Sepulveda?"

"How my husband died." Margaret Sepulveda's clear emerald eyes set off the russet of her dress, the colors of the Irish. Tim couldn't take his eyes off Maggie Sepulveda. People were so

137

clear. What else did Blaise expect? Timothy Delahanty had to love the wife of his lover just as he had to love the Irish symbol she made of herself. He could no more live without tragedy than he could plot his own destiny. Tim Delahanty was a professional Irishman with all that being Irish entailed. Now Blaise was a victim, as well.

"You won't like the truth." Helen closed her eyes, wishing she were elsewhere, that Delahanty had not burdened her with this. She wanted Blaise. She let herself drift away, to simply feel.

The room was comfortably hot and humid. Odors rode the air like colored feathers. Helen raised her nose following one feather after another. Noises rose and fell in the background and she tuned her ears to amplify the more interesting sounds.

Stretching, she brushed against the fly that stood over her. Her skin rippled, comforted by the contact.

"*Miss McIntyre, you must go back!*"

"*Sergio?*"

"*You must go back, Miss McIntyre. You cannot hide in Tchor's mind.*"

Helen peered at the black furry leg she was licking and thought, Why not? Why can't I? *But the rebellion was only in irritation. She knew Sergio wouldn't lie . . .*

"Are you all right, Miss McIntyre?" Joseph Santiago loosened his grip on Helen as the floor returned under her feet.

"I'm fine, Joseph." Helen tugged her skirt and blouse straight before glancing at Mrs. Sepulveda.

"I said, yes, I can stand the truth, Miss McIntyre. If it is the truth." Mary Margaret Richardson-Sepulveda confronted Helen with an emotional wall that said she knew the truth, and Helen would have to lie to change it.

"Things were confused, Mrs. Sepulveda." Helen paused to consider. She knew what Delahanty told her and Alfie hadn't denied. "Three hundred of us were penned inside this church, Mrs. Sepulveda. Leo was among us. Sergeant Miller had walked in that day offering to change sides. Miller said he had useful information, but Blaise didn't trust Miller. Blaise didn't trust Leo, either. Leo was too close to Karl Zahn, who was outside running free. Blaise thought Zahn's safety curious because he had been photographed with Father Argyle in a secret meeting on Zahn's yacht."

Helen paused to look at Mrs. Sepulveda again. She had folded her arms and was looking at the wall in a sort of *I'm not going to believe a word of it* way. "Blaise remembers details, Mrs. Sepulveda," Helen said softly. "He knew Leo used Tim in a scam to bankrupt Reynard Pearson and squeeze him out of a land deal years ago. Blaise believed the connection still existed between your husband and Mr. Zahn.

"What happened is Blaise had Tim pass information to Leo as having come from Miller, because your husband wouldn't doubt Tim. Your husband trusted Tim for a reason: Tim quashed his suspicions that Leo helped cause the death of his son." Helen watched Mrs. Sepulveda and Timothy Delahanty. Tim looked ill. *Blaise doesn't have to take the blame for everything.* The savage pleasure in the thought surprised Helen.

"You didn't tell me you had a grudge against Leo, Tim." Mrs. Sepulveda's twisted lips put a crack in her civilized veneer. Her eyes, when she looked at Delahanty, brooded; the sea-green depths had a shadow in them.

Blood drained from Delahanty's ruddy cheeks. He rolled his eyes toward Helen, the corners of his eyes angry red. Timothy Delahanty was suffering no matter how Helen felt like squirming.

Trying not to see Delahanty's expression, Helen continued grimly. "Tim's son died in Ireland because of your husband, Mrs. Sepulveda. For years Leo let Tim believe Reynard Pearson was responsible. Blaise knew Leo for a liar, and knew he would lie again. You cannot condemn Blaise for being right."

"Dr. Cunningham shot Leo to death right in this building! He told me himself Leo might not have shot at him!" Leo's widow was screaming. "He said it!"

"I was here. Your Leo was going to murder not only Blaise but me, as well." Helen's voice got lost in the sharp clacking of the rain against the window. She waited for the flurry to pass, reliving the moment when Leo Sepulveda had been about to kill them, her memory inundating her with the damp odor of the cellar and fear. "Blaise, Tim, Father Argyle, Bill Hartunian, and Sergeant Miller had crawled through the darkness to get out of the church the night before. The next morning Blaise returned alone. At first he thought he caused the death of the others; he had left them at the television station as decoys. They were supposed to surrender to the police. But a man named Carmandy, a killer, followed them and shot Bill Hartunian and Miller after Blaise left.

"Blaise wept when Father Argyle brought Hartunian to the church. He didn't know if the sacrifices had any value. To Blaise, Hartunian's shooting was a personal tragedy." Helen breathed deeply, remembering how the damp scent of the cellar the night

Bill Hartunian was shot had been touched by the odor of fresh earth. She smelled it on Blaise the last time he returned from digging in the tunnel. "Blaise knew then that Leo had betrayed them because Carmandy shot Bill Hartunian and then went on the roof and deliberately murdered Miller. He had been told to kill his own partner."

Helen thought she had been a little crazy then. Memories flooded her mind when Blaise left. The damp and the mud and the sweat on the walls in the black cellar raised an image of the sewers under Warsaw. She shivered. Her grandfather had been in those sewers, a secret she kept even from Blaise. He had no reason to be jealous of Father Argyle, not if he understood the truth. But he never understood because she'd denied him her secret.

Helen's secret was named Micah Chaim Bialik, born a Haskalah Jew in Kiev in 1891. Helen could no more tell Blaise about Micah than she could explain her relationship to Father Argyle. Micah was special. He had been immortalized in the bedtime fairy tales her mother, Danuta, told and seemed only half real, a misty figure bigger than life in the dark who dissolved in the light of day.

Micah survived the Kishenev massacre.

Shortly after Micah's twelfth birthday, Saul Bialik, Micah's father, had taken his wife and Micah with him on a trip; Micah to learn the business, great-grandfather Saul said, and his wife to care for the boy. Saul was a grain merchant from Odessa. Helen knew this from her mother's stories; her mother trusted nothing to paper. Helen's Catholic father was never to know his wife's parents were Jews. That was the strictest rule Helen's mother imposed. That in the end, Jason McIntyre would never know his wife was not the Catholic girl he had married nor his daughter the Catholic child he had fathered. Helen thought her mother made the rule out of love for her husband, but Danuta McIntyre was a tortured woman who lived within herself and Helen was closest to her in the bedtime stories they shared.

It was Saul's misfortune to have business in Kishenev the year and the month and the week of the Kishenev massacre when Jews were being slaughtered like chickens. Cossacks roamed the roads after the massacre, bands of drunken men riding home on hysterical horses with nostrils flaring from the scent of blood, their eyes rolling uncontrollably. The men wore gaudy clothes and cockaded hats as if they had been on a picnic and yelled and swore back and forth at each other comparing deeds. That was how it was in that year, and gouts of steam from the horses' hot breath made the band approaching Saul and Micah seem on fire.

Saul tried to get his family off the road. The Cossacks were always touchy. He may have been slow because he wanted to impess his son with his courage. Too late, he realized these men were different from ones he faced in the past.

The Cossack chargers thundered down the road but did not part to flow like a river around the tiny island Saul's family and their horses made. The horses and men were stained with blood. The Cossacks carried their curved swords unsheathed, pounding their horses' flanks with the flats of the blades.

Micah froze in front of the panorama of horses and men. His mother wrapped her arms around him but she and Saul knew. It was the moment every Jew in Russia feared, waited for in the night, prayed to God to be saved from. At the last moment, as the first sword touched him, Saul threw himself over his wife and son.

The swords flicked and flicked and flicked, Saul's living body quivering with each touch, then, finally, laying as a shield over Micah. His mother died with a single scream, her arms wrapped tightly around him, protecting his small body.

Micah was hidden completely under his father's blood-drenched greatcoat and the corpses of his parents. Even when a Cossack leaned from his horse to find Saul's purse in the great-coat pocket, Micah didn't move.

After Kishenev, the Jews fought back. Micah, stained with blood and a man at twelve, participated willingly. The Jewish revolution faltered, but by then the Leninists were making inroads. Micah took the name of Volkov, assuming the manner of a Russian merchant spying for the cause where he was sent. He took pleasure in the name, that of Russia's first great Elizabethan actor. Later his code name was "The Actor." When the Germans in an attempt to undermine the Russian war effort shipped Lenin across Germany in a sealed train, Micah's vow of vengeance was fulfilled. He battled the Cossacks and the White Army to the steppes of Russia where their blood flowed as he remembered the blood of his father and mother flowing.

During the campaigns, Micah preceded the Red Army as Mikhail Volkov, a merchant. What he learned he passed to another Jew, Dob Kabak, who had taken a Christian name, Alexei Konstantinov. Konstantinov, a ferocious bear of a man with a bristly black beard that sprouted even from inside his nose, carried Micah's reports back to the army.

It was toward the end when fighting ground to a winter stale-mate in the north that Micah rejoined the Red Army. The enemy had no secrets to hide—all that was left was to fight. The ground was frozen like white quartz, and frostbite had taken one of Micah's toes.

Micah lay on a pine-needle pad under a spreading tree. The enemy lay just across the sparkling snow, obscured by the haze of more falling snow. Konstantinov, who leaned against the tree trunk sheltered from the Whites, had been ruminating for hours.

"Mikhail," Konstantinov said finally, "we must leave." The fearless Konstantinov, called "The Bear" by the troops he led in reckless charges against the enemy camp, was strangely quiet when he said it. The snow had fallen ever since the first charge at daybreak. By twilight, the battlefield casualties, living and dead, were mere mounds of white. The wounded knew the darkness was coming and they moaned, either in fear of death or to remind rescuers they were there. It was getting time to crawl among the mounds seeking the ones containing life when Konstantinov spoke.

"It is still too early, Alexei." Micah sat hunched over with his rifle under his greatcoat, keeping the mechanism warm. "Be as patient as the ones who wait."

"Not that. We must leave the army while time remains." Konstantinov took the glove off his right hand and shoved his hand inside his pants to warm his fingers on his groin. "It is a wonder I have even one toe left, Mikhail. Much less fingers."

"You need fingers to shoot. Protect them well." Micah looked at Konstantinov in the gloom. "And be careful what you say, if you don't want someone else's fingers to shoot you."

"This is serious, Mikhail. The war is ending. Have you thought of that?"

"Yes. But until it is over I can kill Cossacks and Russians. I cannot leave."

"That is a narrow view, my friend, but I admire you for it. In the end such single-mindedness will kill you. Stalin does not love Jews, nor is Lenin one of us. We are their draft animals. When this is finished our new masters will be no different."

Micah shrugged. He barely saw his own movement in the darkness. "I cannot leave yet."

"Micah, I have a plan." Konstantinov smiled, his teeth flashing white in the darkness and sparse moonlight. It was the first time Konstantinov had slipped and called Micah by his Hebrew

name. Perhaps it wasn't a slip, but a reminder. Even so, it was a dangerous thing to do.

"I will help," Micah said. "You knew I wouldn't leave. That is why you tell me. But in the end your carelessness will kill you."

"Good!" Konstantinov laughed. "I knew you would understand. Let us go now among the dead and find the living."

Five days after the victory Alexei Konstantinov and seventeen men disappeared with the loot taken from the defeated army. It was considerable, for the Russian nobles carried everything, even their family heirlooms, with them in their campaigns. The Red Army pursued, sure they would catch Konstantinov and their treasure in days. They left Mikhail Volkov and a battalion to mop up.

Helen's mind saw Micah Chaim Bialik as a big, strong man with a majestic flowing gray beard. So strong had been Danuta's tales that Helen need only close her eyes thirty years later to see Orthodox priests like black vultures aiding the Cossacks and turning the peasants against the Jews.

Helen's mother described peasants spilling out of churches, torches glowing on the winter snow, taking out their misery against the Jews as if she had witnessed events herself. Helen remembered her heart sickening at that passage in her mother's narrative when it seemed Micah would be killed. He was in Moscow toward the end of the war reporting to his new masters, who called him Volkov the Jew. Taken before a people's court, but judged by Stalin himself, he was accused of aiding the traitor Alexei Konstantinov in his escape across Siberia.

Not just Micah, of course, but hundreds of Jews who had been in the same Red Army division with Konstantinov and Micah. They had tasted blood, Stalin declared, and could not be trusted. Micah was to be shot and when her mother, Danuta, related how the sun hid itself as he was taken from his cell Helen cried out, *Don't die, grandfather!* The warning pleased her mother, who went on with the story.

News of victory arrived in Moscow and Lenin declared an amnesty. Micah and the others waiting their turn at the wall that day were sent to Siberia for fourteen years. If Micah had had a family, it would have seemed like death. But since he had no one, Siberia was simply one more battle.

Micah's life was clear to Helen, who knew things her mother never told her. She knew Micah was guilty, that Konstantinov and his men buried the loot in the cellar of a ruined building and led

*the army after them into Siberia with only food and supplies
weighing down the horses. In time, Micah arranged the gathering and shipping of the artifacts to a place in Mexico where
Konstantinov waited under a different name. Even with the threat
of death, Micah would not reveal what he had done. He had
remained in the house of his enemies to kill them, not to live.*

*When he was released from Siberia, Micah received a mes-
sage from Konstantinov. "Come," Konstantinov wrote. "I have
waited for you. Only you, Micah, can make me sane again."*

*Volkov the Jew waited for another message from Konstan-
tinov. He was ready, at last, to leave Russia.*

*The message never came. Stalin, "The Man of Steel," had
pursued "The Bear" to his cavern and killed him in his sleep as a
lesson.*

*Lenin had been dead since 1924, undoubtedly murdered by
Stalin, Micah decided when he learned Konstantinov had also
been killed. Lavrenti Beria, Stalin's secret police head and personal executioner, was making himself indispensable, sending
agents to track down and murder those Stalin would not forget. If
Konstantinov was dead, it was time for Volkov the Jew to die.
After digging up the money he had not sent Konstantinov but had
reburied against an emergency, Micah left a false trail to a dead
returnee from the Siberian camps, then slipped across the Polish
border where he became a grain merchant.*

*In Warsaw a shadkhan found him a wife. Micah was content at
last with the birth of his girl child, and settled into a life of
comparative ease. He was almost fifty when God withheld the
rain forty days while Hitler's Panzers demolished the Polish cavalry.*

*Micah should have fled with Mirjam and his daughter, Dan-
uta, but he had vacillated. He had money now and running away
would have impoverished him. He realized too late that he repeated the mistakes of the Russian nobility, thinking money and
position had value. By then the Russians had descended on Po-
land from the north and Beria had men in Warsaw on Micah's
scent. If Lavrenti P. Beria was Stalin's hound, the Man of Steel
was an elephant who forgot nothing except his real name.*

*Micah and his family disappeared into the Warsaw ghetto a
step ahead of the Russian assassins.*

*Alone, Micah might have fled. But not with Mirjam and a
child he did not dare abandon. Beria would as soon torture them
as execute Micah. When Micah told his wife, her eyes rolled up
and she fainted.*

Mirjam was Polish, not that any good could come of that. Poles with authority were cutting their own deals with the Russians. They had no sympathy to spare for a Jew renegade from communism and his galizianerin wife and daughter.

The bombardment of Warsaw began, first the ceaseless flights of airplanes dumping bombs, then the rumble of cannons growing louder as Hitler's panzers rolled and horses screamed and died and the rain did not come and then the city was surrounded. The ground heaved and shook, shrouding Warsaw in a haze of dirt and smoke, and at night the city was a Breughel rendition of hell.

For Micah, the occupation was a respite. The Nazis captured and executed Beria's spies; those the SS didn't catch had no interest in Micah. Besides, the ghetto had become a death trap under the Germans. Stalin was finally diverted from personal vengeance to a greater issue: the survival of Russia.

Micah was watching the building across the street from his cellar window when the squad of German soldiers goosestepped into view, boot heels echoing like artillery in the narrow, cobbled street. They halted in front of Micah's window, their evenly spaced rows of glistening jackboots making a grate for him to look through.

Four soldiers kicked the door across the street off its hinges then rushed inside, disappearing as if sucked into the house by a vacuum. They emerged dragging a short, powerfully built man. His screams carried across the street and Micah whispered softly, "Have dignity, at least."

Turning away from the window, Micah smiled at his wife. "I was right, it was Tarkov." Mirjam was pale but she tried to smile back. Tarkov! Micah remembered him from the old days. He should have been smarter than to move into a house so close to Micah in a neighborhood of old Jewish women. The revolution was too long ago. Tarkov in his lust to kill Jews had forgotten the role of the hunted.

Micah had rid himself of a nuisance. The Germans remained and he had no escape from them. He watched his blond wife and child, marveling at the pleasure they brought him. But life did not go on forever.

The plan came to Micah, then. He and Mirjam had agreed: save Danuta, whatever the cost.

Realizing her mind had wandered, Helen glanced at Maggie Sepulveda whose thoughts had carried her out of time. "You don't know what it was like, Mrs. Sepulveda. The police let

Blaise back into the church. Nobody got out. It was the Nazis closing the Warsaw Ghetto all over again. Everybody inside would die, so why care who went in?

"Blaise cried. I had never seen him cry before. He may have wanted to die. He felt responsible for everything. He was tired and he couldn't think. We were waiting for a computer in Washington to die, a goal Blaise thought worthwhile enough to cost men's lives. Then Leo and Max Renfeld came into the cellar and Renfeld told Leo to kill us."

Helen had expected to die in the cellar with Leo Sepulveda about to deliver death, and she knew she wanted Blaise's baby as a way to preserve him past his death. Before that moment, Helen knew nothing of the Warsaw Ghetto except that her grandparents died there. And then the memory was in her head as if she had lived it. She wondered if her grandparents had felt that way when they saved her mother. Against her volition, she sank back into Warsaw again, the dirty brick houses, the deserted streets, the scent of oppression and death everywhere.

They had time, Micah told Mirjam, and she believed him. Danuta could be saved. Once the decision was made, the feel of futility dropped away from Micah.

There was a resistance in the ghetto. It cheered them that a veteran of the Russian revolution was with them. They saw in him hope to overcome defeat, hope that Micah knew to be false but cultivated all the same. Once again he became "The Actor" strolling the streets of Warsaw dressed as a priest, making deals for the resistance. But they were doomed. Micah sympathized, but he had a goal of his own.

Entering the diocese offices in Warsaw was dangerous. The Germans had assigned a Gestapo man there and a wrong word could mean arrest and execution. Micah had been in churches before—Orthodox churches disguised as a peasant. The Roman rite was different, and ignorance by a priest would be noticed.

The cathedral with its foundation of basalt dominated the oldest part of Warsaw. Burnished by age, the decorative brickwork showed evidence of many remortarings. The grounds were pleasant, leafless trees ready to greet spring with new blooms, withered stems of ivy prepared to mantel the building in green yet again.

Micah entered the church and stopped. A hush enveloped the interior, the feeling that a thousand years of life was stored in the quiet, the way dusty book stacks filled ageless libraries. The light was poor. Between the pillars, a glitter of candlelight on gold leaf revealed the altar. The Gothic hall that was the nave caught every sound and sent it back somehow alien.

Acting as if he knew exactly where to go and what to do, Micah moved on, cataloguing the church interior like he would make a map: the pulpit here, the chancel there, the inconspicuous door to the rectory. . .

He bowed his head to a pair of passing priests, their footsteps a padding sound on the marble floor.

It took awhile, months. But in the end Micah found exactly the man he wanted. And even better, the priest instantly recognized their mutual need.

In the priest's parish a child lay dying of typhus. She was eight, blond, a beautiful girl with rosy cheeks and a wonderful smile, the daughter of a petty bureaucrat. The priest needed the bureaucrat, who was in a position to help a young man's struggle up the church ladder, but at the moment he was furious with God and with the Church in general.

The priest listened in silence to Micah's proposal, head bent, face shadowed by the round brim of his hat. "It will take time," he said. They whispered, painfully aware of how their voices carried in the huge corridor. The money was easier. Priests were schooled well in receiving and dispensing money.

"We do not have time." Micah laced his fingers behind his back willing himself not to fidget. "The child must be substituted the moment the other one dies."

The young priest examined Micah with curiosity. "I will try." He nodded and they parted.

Sneaking back into the ghetto was the most risky thing Micah had done since he got out of Russia. Mirjam sobbed when he told her the priest agreed to substitute Danuta for the dying child, that Danuta would have a Polish birth certificate registered in a Catholic church and Catholic parents, but she would live. Payment was the last of Micah's money as the orphan's legacy. Mirjam said she was happy and he supposed it was true.

He had to leave Mirjam when he escaped the ghetto the final time with their daughter. Micah cursed himself with tears in his eyes. They had agreed that saving Danuta was more important than their survival and even if Mirjam escaped the wire with him, her presence would jeopardize him and their daughter. He railed against it in his mind, but a priest taking a child to the diocese offices was one thing. To take a woman was quite another. Straining to act normally, Micah walked Danuta through the big doors into the nave with its marble pillars. The Gestapo man was *inside, leaning against a pillar, smoking a cigarette. He wore a black leather calf-length coat over his uniform and black cavalry boots. When Micah passed by, the German's eyes followed the little girl and he might have followed, but just then the doors opened again spilling the weak early-morning light into the church and three nuns entered.*

Throwing his cigarette down, the German gave Danuta one last glance and then descended on the women.

The young priest was lighting candles at the altar and turned around on hearing Micah. "The child died today," he said. "I am lighting candles for her soul." He thrust the burning taper in a basin of sand and led the way to the back room. Micah thought he smelled sandalwood burning, but then the odor eluded him and they were inside.

Taking Micah's daughter by hand, the priest examined her. "They will learn to be happy," he said.

Micah passed the priest the box containing the last of the gold coins he had brought out of Russia. The priest hefted the box and then stuck it inside his cassock.

"Must I, Father?" Micah's daughter looked up into his face and tears showed in her eyes.

"Yes, darling," he said. "You must do as your mother and I told you."

"I think our business is concluded," the priest said.

"Yes, thank you." Micah smiled at his daughter for one last time, willing her to be clever, to play the game on which so much depended.

"If you come back or go to the cathedral again, I will turn you over to the Gestapo. You understand?" The priest's eyes were drawn back in slits and his nostrils flared. "It is sacrilegeous that a Jew should pretend to be a priest." He spat out the word Jew *as if it was somehow dirty.*

"Perfectly," Micah said. He smiled at his daughter. She had a chance to be safe. For that, he was grateful to the priest. Insults meant nothing.

Micah could have remained free. The Germans could still capture him, yet being outside the wire he had a chance to escape. Instead, he walked back to the ghetto in the sunshine as if he were a simple priest carrying his Bible in hand visiting a sick parishioner. The Germans had bottled the ghetto with walls and wire, men and machine guns, and now tanks. Panzers squatted at the intersections, their motors roaring. If they were turned off too long they could be hard to start, and the victorious Germans luxuriated in their noise and heat. They were the conquering heroes and their tanks personified victory.

Micah worked his way down the row houses to the last barricade. More German soldiers than he had ever seen before stood in ranks along the streets around the ghetto. As he meandered his way along the perimeter, Micah found no holes. After returning to his usual crossing, Micah walked toward the soldiers unnoticed. His cassock made him a black crow among hawks, ignored by the soldiers in their gray-green wool uniforms.

The air was crisp, smelling somehow of garlic. Micah knew the odor. It was fear.

He continued walking, head down, eyes on the hem of his cassock as it flapped against his legs. A sound rippled through the German lines, heads turning against the stiff collars of their tunics. The new wall was very close; he could feel the texture of the mortar that squeezed from between the red bricks like dough. Gathering the front of his cassock, Micah walked faster. Almost without hurry his other hand caught the rough cement at the top of the wall and he vaulted over.

Remorse and a sense of comfort and reassurance embraced Helen. She opened her eyes. Mrs. Sepulveda and Delahanty stared at her, a quizzical expression changing the planes of Delahanty's face. Joseph looked away before she saw into his eyes. Helen realized without being told she had simply gone into her daydream as if they weren't there. *What is happening to me?* The question filled her with fear even as she groped for where she left off.

"Blaise had a little pistol in an ankle holster," she said, hoping the sentence connected to where she was before her daydream overwhelmed her. "Blaise got to the pistol while Leo was distracted. He warned Leo, but Leo drew a pistol and Blaise shot him. I still believe Leo was going to kill us both. Blaise was afraid for me."

The room was silent.

Without opening his eyes Joseph said, "That is the truth. Renfeld was taken away by other men. Leo Richardson-Sepulveda chose to stay because Karl Zahn promised to keep him from evolving into a fly if he would follow Max Renfeld's orders and kill Dr. Cunningham."

"Joseph, you weren't here!" Helen's heart speeded up. That day wasn't anything she or Blaise shared with strangers. Blaise seemed almost incapable of explaining his actions to her, much less to outsiders.

"I saw into your memory, Mistress. I saw what you saw."

"It wasn't Leo's fault!" Maggie Sepulveda glanced from one to the other of them, then spoke too fast. "You were all against Leo no matter how he tried to fit in. He brought Father Argyle the first fly, the one he said was Sergio Paoli. He came into the church with the others. He was a good father to the boys." Tears leaked from her eyes. "He couldn't have wanted to cause the death of Tim's son. Tim loved his boy..." She seemed to beg Delahanty to confirm her words.

Delahanty moved awkwardly. He patted her arm the way a big man touched a child. "It wasn't Leo's fault, Maggie."

Maggie Sepulveda covered Delahanty's paw with her smaller hand. She didn't say anything.

"It wasn't." Delahanty shrugged one shoulder.

"You're lying."

"I wouldn't lie." Delahanty looked from Joseph to Helen. "About that."

"You helped bury Leo?"

"Yes." Delahanty touched Maggie with his fingertips as if caressing a ticking bomb he loved more than life.

"Your son!"

Delahanty's face rippled. His cheeks realigned themselves as anger fought itself out, using his face as a battleground.

Maggie Sepulveda watched and said, "My God! It's true, about what Leo did to you." Sitting at the priest's desk, she hid her own face in her hands. "What do you want?" Her hands muffled her voice.

"Withdraw your complaint. It's the only grounds for a murder investigation." Delahanty's voice quavered. Going back to the window, he said, "Dr. Cunningham confessed because I didn't want you to suffer not knowing what had happened. I said you wouldn't call the police. Dr. Cunningham said you would. I took advantage of his guilt to force him.

"I'll confess I shot Leo because of my son. Prosecutors love motives. Dr. Cunningham has none. If you want revenge, Maggie, you can have me. I knew what Leo would do with the information. Dr. Cunningham told me about Leo and Zahn, and I used the opportunity to test the truth of it."

Delahanty jerked the latch and swung the window open. Wind whooshed into the office and splattered his face with raindrops, then blew a flurry of papers off Father Argyle's desk. Maggie Sepulveda watched the papers flutter to the floor without making an effort to retrieve them. Delahanty latched the window again, stopping the wind. "It was too hot in here," he said. The grandfather clock struck the hour in the hall. Delahanty turned his head in reflex before asking Helen's forgiveness in a look. The moisture around his eyes might have been caused by the rain.

Mrs. Sepulveda stared at the telephone.

"You must call, Mrs. Sepulveda." Helen gripped Joseph's shoulder. "Tell her, Tim."

"Please call, Maggie." Delahanty's voice seemed as hollow as the clock chime. "Dr. Cunningham believed the police would turn him over to the same government people Leo worked for. Tell them I've confessed. But you've got to hurry."

Helen willed Maggie Sepulveda to accept Delahanty's instructions. She reserved sorrow for the woman that she knew she would feel as a sharp pain later, but she wanted help for Blaise so much, nothing else mattered. Helen wondered if the Sepulveda woman felt about her dead husband as strongly as Helen did about Blaise. She pushed the comparison away. She couldn't help Blaise by taking the woman's side.

"Your son, Timothy?" Leo's widow appeared dazed. "It couldn't have been Leo. Karl Zahn was capable, but not Leo."

Delahanty shook his head. "Leo and Karl Zahn murdered my boy. They wanted to cheat Reynard but they cheated me. I had Zahn killed the same day Leo died."

Mrs. Sepulveda pressed the buttons on the telephone. "Should I tell them about Karl Zahn, Timothy?"

"I think not." Delahanty touched his forehead and brought his hand away to stare at it as if expecting to see stigmata. "Let's not complicate their merry police lives. Explaining Leo will be enough burden."

Her fingers tightening on the telephone, Mrs. Sepulveda stared at Delahanty in sudden fright. "I . . . I made a murder complaint earlier today," she said into the mouthpiece. "I have to tell the policemen something else." She rolled her eyes upward to look at Delahanty while she waited for a connection. "Inspector Fennelli? . . . this is Mary Margaret Richardson-Sepulveda. I wanted to tell someone I lied about Dr. Cunningham killing my husband."

Helen heard the whisper of a voice over the telephone wires. Maggie Sepulveda turned paler.

"I lied because . . . because . . ." She stretched out her hand, grabbing Delahanty's big-knuckled fingers. "Because I discovered Dr. Cunningham has a lady friend I didn't know about."

The noise over the telephone increased in volume.

Mrs. Sepulveda recoiled from the white plastic then held it to her ear and said loudly, "Don't swear at me, you . . . you Italian gigolo. It is not customary in civilized countries for men to share their favors among several lady friends. Civilized ladies don't leave them any favors to share!"

Joseph Santiago had his eyes on Mrs. Sepulveda as if seeing her for the first time.

"I suggest, Inspector Fennelli, you release Dr. Cunningham promptly before he decides to sue." Maggie Sepulveda made a prim face at the telephone. Then her face changed. "You can't have done that, Inspector." She hung up the telephone and examined her hands.

"What did they do?" Helen's lungs hurt. She wanted to grab Maggie Sepulveda and shake her.

"Inspector Fennelli says a federal officer named Carmandy picked Dr. Cunningham up from the jail and took him to Washington hours ago. He said making a false murder report was a felony." Rising from behind the desk, Maggie Sepulveda pressed against Delahanty's side as if to make herself very small. "Please, Timothy," she said. "Take me home now!"

Delahanty was helping her into a translucent green raincoat when the telephone rang. They all looked at the instrument, even Joseph. On the fifth ring Mrs. Sepulveda gripped the handset and asked nobody in particular, "What do I say now?"

She raised the phone to her ear. "Hello?" Her face changed as she listened. Her green irises slid to the corners of her eyes. "You want to speak to Helen McIntyre, Dr. Cunningham?"

CHAPTER 27

Sheltered under a Port Orford cedar, a dense tree with drooping branches native to the coastal rain forests of the Northwest, Blaise watched traffic whip by on the Pacific Coast Highway. The tree was a living cave. Its lacy green needles repelled the rain and cast dark shadows around the trunk that hid him from the speeding cars. Water seeping through the needles fell in sparse but massive drops that plopped when they hit the ground. If it weren't for chinks opened in the cedar's branches by the wind, Blaise would not have been aware of the winter storm's fury.

Shifting position, he tugged his coat collar around his throat. He was soaked, but getting out of the wind stopped the shaking in his hands and legs. Occasionally a branch was blown askew, showering him with icy rain, but he was more comfortable than he had expected.

Rain obscured the oncoming cars, making them unidentifiable headlight flashes as vehicles hit the turn. After calling Helen from the roadside telephone, Blaise had nothing to do except stay hidden and wait, hoping Carmandy was not well enough to renew the search. He'd been lucky. Carmandy would never have let him escape. Jacko lacked experience and confidence in guns. When Blaise had shot back, Jacko wanted to run. Carmandy's style would have been to come over the hill. Blaise leaned against the tree trunk breathing deeply. The tree smelled fresh with the odor of life. Blaise realized just being alive could be a pleasure.

An hour later a car hesitated at the turn. Its lights went off and on twice and then off. Blaise stepped from under the leafy tent to the edge of the highway as the black sedan rolled to a halt in front of him, tires hissing in the shallow runoff from the domed concrete roadway. "Get in!" Helen's face showed at the open window before disappearing into the interior.

Blaise scooted in and slammed the door. The electric window whirred quietly, cutting off the wind and the rain that had followed him into the car. "Glad you could make it," he said, and broke into a loud hacking that hurt his lungs. Pneumonia was just what he needed right now. He longed for a stiff drink, but liquor had once brought Blaise closer to death than pneumonia would. He would not open that doorway into Hell again. The cough went away as the automobile's warm interior slowly pulled the chill from him.

Delahanty eased back into traffic. A car roared past with its headlights glaring and the horn button jammed down and then they were another anonymous drop in the river of humanity surging down the highway. "Where should we be going, Doctor?"

"You have Alfie?"

"In the boot."

"Someplace we can rent a car."

"You're sure, Dr. Cunningham?" Delahanty looked over his shoulder. "I know a place you'll be safe."

Leaning back in the seat, Blaise thought he could go to sleep. The hike in the icy rain and wind, scrambling off balance in the mud, sometimes on his hands and feet, had drained him. "I'm sure."

"Let's go back to the church, Blaise, please." Helen's voice wavered. It sounded like she was pleading.

"What's wrong, Helen?" Touching her shoulder with his hand, Blaise felt Helen's tension. She hunched forward on the seat, her head up and her eyes staring into nothing. Tchor sat on her lap, the cat as rigid as Helen.

Shaking her head to clear it, Helen whispered, "We have to go back. Something awful is going to happen at St. Abbo's if we don't." She turned toward Blaise. "We have to."

"Go back to the church, Tim." Blaise took Helen's hand in his and stroked it. "We're going," he said. "If that's what you want, that's what we'll do."

Delahanty turned his head. "Are you sure, Doctor?"

"Yes," Blaise said. He settled back in the seat with his arm holding Helen's tense body against his.

Catching an intersection, Delahanty made an old lady U-turn, starting a blare of horns that lasted until he was up to speed in the opposite direction. Mary Margaret Richardson-Sepulveda turned her head. She was sitting in the front seat with Delahanty. Blaise recognized her even though he couldn't see the green of her eyes in the gloom.

"We'll be safe at the church, Blaise." Helen had come out of her daze and touched his arm. "Father Argyle can do that for us." Joseph Santiago sat on the other side of Helen staring straight ahead, obviously not noticing anything as she leaned over Blaise and kissed his lips. Helen's mouth was warm and Blaise luxuriated in the odor of lilac. He was falling asleep when flashes of red and blue light shook him out of his drowsiness. His mouth had a bitter taste.

"It's just an accident," Delahanty said quietly from the front seat. "It was there when we came for you."

"Stop," Blaise said. "Where we can see."

Delahanty eased the big car onto a turnoff and Blaise got out. The wind tugged at his clothes. He had to hold his coat closed with his arms. Across the road a big, orange-colored wrecker flashing a Christmas tree of yellow blinkers worked in the glare of emergency lighting while a pair of police cars bracketed the area. One policeman in a yellow rain slicker was dropping a line of flares that burned with a surrealistic pink glow on the highway. Another directed a steady flow of bumper-to-bumper traffic around the emergency vehicles.

The winch on the wrecker began clacking. A cable between it and the rear bumper sticking out of the bay water tightened, shaking out spray. The winch stopped while a diver wearing a black wet suit with white stripes up the sides, fins, and a snorkel and mask hung loosely around his neck balanced on a rock close to the wreck. After peering at the connection the diver twirled his right hand and the winch started up again, dragging a black Cadillac tail first out of twenty feet of water. One side of the car had been crushed. The driver's door fell open and a limp body hung half out of the car, folded around the seat belt that held it secure.

Getting back into Delahanty's car, Blaise said, "Let's go."

When they were on the bridge Blaise said, "Carmandy and his driver were in that car when I last saw them."

" 'Tis a good thing you weren't, Doctor."

"I was, a bit earlier." Blaise felt cold again and he didn't object when Helen tucked a blanket around him. He thought about Jacko and realized he had no feeling about the Irishman who had caused so much mischief elsewhere. But he was pleased that Carmandy was gone for good.

St. Abbo's was surrounded when they arrived: two thousand people packed shoulder to shoulder around the building, some holding umbrellas, some in trench coats, rain coats—even plastic trash bags. They were quiet. Rain drummed viciously on umbrellas.

Blaise and Santiago flanked Helen through the crowd to the oak doors. Delahanty and Leo Sepulveda's widow huddled close behind as people surged around them like a river wrapping a rock in the rapids.

Once inside Helen clung to Blaise. "It's Father Argyle," she said. "You have to stop him, Blaise."

Pouring from the altar, the priest's voice had a timbre that overpowered the constant buzz-hum. He commanded the church from the altar, warmly illuminated by the smoke softened glow of a thousand candles. "God's design," he said. His arms splayed over his head pointing at the flies clinging to the tapestries. "God is the redeemer. God is the savior. We must go unto him and do his bidding."

An "Amen!" rolled across the packed mass in the church to the outside world where it carried across the crowd to the street.

"The time," Father Argyle said, "is now."

"Amen!"

"Now!" Father Argyle repeated. He lifted the hypodermic from the altar.

"Amen!" the crowd responded and the word echoed outside the church. "Amen!"

"Stop him!" Constance pushed through the crowd and grabbed at Blaise's lapel. She clung, too weak to let go. "He mustn't do this. He mustn't." Her black curls were disheveled, her face glittering from her tears.

"Blaise, stop Father Argyle!" Helen's pale, frightened face bobbed in front of him.

"STOP!" Blaise's bellow caused Father Argyle to glance up for an instant. The priest raised the hypodermic to plunge it into his own arm. Blaise pulled the little pistol from his pocket and, holding it straight over his head, pulled the trigger as fast as he could. The sound was the three sharp cracks of a comic actor shattering ladder rungs. The dome contained and concentrated the sound. In counterpoint, ejected brass tinkled loudly as cartridges hit the floor.

"Blasphemy!" Father Argyle's face was red and the hypodermic seemed forgotten in his hand.

"Get the priest," Blaise said quietly.

Joseph Santiago nodded and slipped into the crowd, which was incapable of holding him back.

A crackling started overhead. Fractures extended in the stained-glass Byzantine Christ and pieces began falling inward. The congregation wrapped their heads and necks with their arms and scurried for cover.

Blaise pulled Helen and Constance behind a pillar, which they shared with Delahanty and Mrs. Sepulveda. Joseph Santiago pivoted the priest's arm that held the hypodermic and forced Father Argyle face down on the floor. Nobody noticed, because at that moment a large section of the Byzantine Christ window dropped out of its frame to fall twenty feet to the floor with a thunderous crash.

Blaise still held the empty pistol. Shattering glass rang in his ears. He shook his head and looked at Helen.

"Why?" he asked. "Why shouldn't I let the priest do any damn thing he wants?"

CHAPTER 28

From the time she screamed until the stained-glass window crashed, the turmoil in Helen's mind paralyzed her will.

It was Sergio. Drawing strength from other flies, the former button man was insisting that Father Argyle abandon his human phase, beating the message into every brain capable of "hearing." Reynard and other flies resisted, but without the same strength. The push and pull to halt the priest's gesture was played out in the minds and wills of the congregation, leaving Helen to drown in the overflow.

"This is necessary, Miss McIntyre," Sergio's voiceless will insisted overwhelmingly until Helen *believed* the priest's transformation into a fly was best. Reynard's opposition lacked strength. But as Sergio drilled the message home Helen felt a resurgent strength within herself. In a totally nonphysical way she loved Sergio. Trusted him. But not in this!

Something was wrong with Father Argyle. Reynard had implied it and now, as if changing channels, she was "hearing" Reynard's fly voice. The conflict between Reynard and Sergio battered at Helen's sanity. She held on long enough to scream out a warning to Blaise, then gave way to the urge to escape this battlefield. As she sank to the floor Delahanty knelt beside her.

She was rising, floating above the turmoil. Delahanty knelt beside her body. Mrs. Sepulveda leaned over him clinging to the fat man's shoulder. Delahanty, florid and unkempt, and Mary Margaret Sepulveda in a London Fog trenchcoat looked like pieces in puppet theater.

So this is death! The calm indifference amazed Helen as she watched Timothy Delahanty's frantic efforts to revive her.

Tchor had sprung from her arms as she collapsed. The cat sat on her body's chest, puzzled, head swiveling like an early-warning radar. Delahanty pushed the cat away. Tchor jumped back on her, hissing a rebuke.

157

"Return, Miss McIntyre. Go back!" Sergio's will swirled around her. Then Reynard and Bill Hartunian and other flies abandoned their dispute over the priest to join in, pelting her with the raw energy of will, exposing her tranquil little bolt hole. She fled, skittering from thought to thought, seeing the church from a thousand pairs of eyes before she was scooting away amid a forest of socks and ankles.

Tchor leaped to the prayer rail, mincing along its length before springing onto the altar.

"Leave the cat." Sergio insisted. *"Flee from yourself and you abandon all of us forever."*

"How do you know, Sergio?"

"It is the way, Miss McIntyre. When one of us goes, he or she leaves the body to hover before going somewhere else."

"Where?"

"We don't know. Many go but none come back. If you were among us, you might know, but we cannot."

"You wanted Father Argyle to make the change but the others didn't, Sergio. Why should he change if they are afraid for him?"

"We are not enough yet. If Father Argyle led the way we would grow stronger . . ."

"Don't believe him, Miss McIntyre. Father Argyle is not ready. Something in him is flawed. If he changes now he will not survive." Helen sensed the strain as Reynard Pearson fought to show her what was lacking in Father Argyle. But she could not understand. *"You must return to yourself,"* Reynard said.

"Why must I leave Tchor?" Helen felt resentment. She wanted to be free, to roam the confines of the church in other people's minds.

"You still live, Miss McIntyre. But if your body is damaged you will be forever separated from Dr. Cunningham—and from us. We, too, are kept here by our bodies."

"I'm fine, Tim." Helen opened her eyes and smiled but it was Blaise bent over her, his face twisted with worry. "Don't fret, Blaise, please."

He helped her stand. From the altar a roar of angry sound reached them. Constance had slipped away into the center of the crowd. "I have to help Santiago," Blaise said.

"Yes." Helen moved after Blaise as he bulled his way into the mob.

"Stay, Miss McIntyre." Delahanty tried to hold her back. "You'll be safe with us."

"Wait here!" Without thinking Helen commanded Timothy

Delahanty with her mind. His hands fell away and she was loose. She followed Blaise knowing when the people sensed her presence from the way they moved aside.

Several men held Joseph Santiago, who stood unresisting. His eyes glittered as he looked at Helen but gave no other sign of emotion.

It was so easy. Helen felt herself extending herself, falling into the Indian's thoughts . . .

He flexed his muscles finding leverage. The sweat of the men holding him was acrid and Red Oak smelled their fear. Fear was a weapon he could use. Fixing his eyes on one man, he reveled in the joy he would take in counting coup with that sparse-haired scalp. The man's sweaty hand loosened from Joseph's wrist.

Helen trembled from the savage emotion the Indian had projected. The worm brain Joseph looked at was confused, trembling. *"Release him!"* Helen struck with her mind and Joseph's captors melted into the crowd.

"They heard you, Mistress." Joseph smiled. "It is as Enrique Ledesma claims."

Glancing first at Joseph and then at Helen, Blaise raised an eyebrow, then turned back to Father Argyle, who was being helped from the floor by the knot of people surrounding him. Constance clung to the priest, her brown eyes huge with fright.

"This is outrageous!" Father Argyle's voice rasped. "This is my church. My service. All of you are profaning it." He glared at Blaise, ignoring Joseph Santiago altogether. His eyes shifted for a moment, touching the floor where the broken hypodermic leaked its insulin into the wood.

Blaise shrugged. "We had better talk this over, Father." Rain blasted through the broken window onto the altar. Candles flickered wildly and one went out with a hiss that evoked a memory of snakes.

Father Argyle turned to the crowd that reached solid to the walls and said, "Would somebody please see about the window?"

A sigh that could have been disappointment breezed across the crowd. Several men brought in a tall ladder and tools. Others swept colored glass off the floor while the remainder shrank back to give them room.

"Can we go to my office and talk privately, Dr. Cunningham?" Father Argyle's glance included Joseph Santiago. Delahanty cringed like a boy caught with his hand in the wrong place. The priest did not include Helen in his gaze. She wondered about that evasion. If she could see into his thoughts as she saw into Joseph's or the other worm brains, she might understand Sergio and Reynard's dispute.

The priest's office was tight for the four men and three women. Helen stayed with Blaise, Mrs. Sepulveda kept close to Delahanty, and Constance clung to Father Argyle's arm as if she might never see him again. "Constance, don't you think you can find something else to do?" Father Argyle's voice was soft but Constance shook her head.

Father Argyle touched Constance Davies' arm, then withdrew his hand. "You have an explanation, Dr. Cunningham?"

"Helen asked me to stop you." Blaise looked at Helen.

Sitting at his desk, Father Argyle's black-clothed figure seemed no more substantial than a shadow. He fidgeted with the desk pad before looking up. "Miss McIntyre?"

"Reynard Pearson and Bill Hartunian said you shouldn't make the transition, Father. Sergio and others wanted you to, but they admitted it wasn't safe."

"Others?"

"Flies, Father." Helen clasped her hands together. She felt as if she had invoked the voice of God without proof. Saints could get away with that, if they had a hysterical following. But not the Jewish daughter of a survivor of the Warsaw ghetto. Not a pretend Catholic full of guilts and doubt.

Rising, Father Argyle opened the single office window, letting in the rattle of rain chattering to itself on the stone sill. The sky was sullen gray as if evening had already come. "That is a weak excuse, Miss McIntyre."

Joseph Santiago moved imperceptibly. "It is not, Father. Deafness does not negate the existence of music. You and Dr. Cunningham are the only ones in this building who could not hear the flies battling. Not all hear equally, but did you not hear, Mr. Delahanty?"

Delahanty touched Maggie Sepulveda's hand, hesitated, then said, "Yes."

Joseph stared hard at Mrs. Sepulveda before passing her by. "And you, Miss Davies?"

Appearing stricken, Constance glanced into Father Argyle's eyes then pressed her face against his arm and nodded.

"You see, Priest, Dr. Cunningham has not been changed and hears nothing. And you, who claim to be changed, are equally deaf."

"I hear!" the priest said. The lines in his face had deepened. The light in the room did not flatter him and Helen felt sorry.

"What do you hear, Father Argyle?"

"Things."

Santiago waited.

"How else can you describe it?" The priest shrugged.

"What do you hear, Miss Davies?"

"Music," she answered. "Feelings. Sometimes whole thoughts that aren't mine. The sense of being joined with others."

"Things!" Santiago's tone was derisive. "Tell the priest what he doesn't hear, Mistress."

"You cannot be one of us, Father." Helen formed the words trying to remove the pain. "I join with others and know their memories and thoughts. I see from their eyes. I cannot find you in my mind. Flies fill the church with thoughts, making the other fly brains reverent without knowing why. We shout at you and cannot stir you to any recognition of our presence."

"But I was implanted!" Father Argyle's anguish was in his voice. Helen did not have to touch his mind.

"That," Blaise said dryly, "is the problem."

Blaise took his glasses off and absently cleaned them on his shirt, then, when he put them back on, blinked. Helen could see the wet streaks of mud from his soggy clothes on the lenses. She handed him a dry handkerchief and he said "Thanks" as absently as he had smeared his glasses in the first place.

"You are different. Until you know why, taking an insulin shot to force metamorphosis may be fatal. Suicides cannot even be buried in hallowed ground, so what are your chances for canonization?"

Father Argyle's jaw line knotted with muscles. Helen could almost see the thoughts in his mind, the bitter choices that had turned his face into a contour map. "Please leave me," he said. "I must think."

Joseph held the door open while the others filed outside. As Helen stepped from the office, the warmth of the church embraced her, making her realize how cold the office had become. Joseph shut the door after them.

"You're not one of us." Helen walked along with Mrs. Sepulveda, who shook her head. Blaise kept pace and she said to him, "Constance is still inside?"

"Yes." Blaise took Helen's arm.

"I'm glad. She's going to have a baby and that will help."

"Will it? Father Argyle's passion isn't children."

"Perhaps now it will be." Helen let her hand slide into Blaise's. He and the priest were so alike in different ways that it scared her. Perhaps some knowledge of himself made Blaise right about the priest not caring for children. She squeezed his hand, hoping she was wrong.

CHAPTER 29

"What now, Doctor?" Delahanty leaned on the newel post overlooking the church floor. "I could use a wee drop, if you happen to have it about you."

"I used to take a drop. Then the drop took me. We'll stay awhile, Tim." Blaise glanced at Helen as she touched his arm before walking down the hall with Mrs. Sepulveda. "Do you know Dr. Versteg?"

"By sight, you might say. Not to speak to."

Silence pervaded the church like a deep-throated hum. St. Abbo's was attuned to sounds Blaise could not hear. "Could you arrange for Dr. Versteg to examine Father Argyle? I don't believe the priest would welcome my intervention at this point." An occasional face flashed in the crowd as someone evinced curiosity about the upstairs. The congregation's general lack of interest in Father Argyle after he failed to inject himself surprised Blaise.

"Himself may be thinking different. The father's no easy man to give direction." Delahanty's answer broke into Blaise's thoughts. Delahanty himself was oblivious to Blaise's reaction. He crimped his face in concentration, eyebrows creeping together like grizzled caterpillars. "I must make amends, Doctor, for the pain I've put you and Miss McIntyre through. The wrong ones suffered. Poor Bill Hartunian, shot through and knowing he would die, telling us to save our lives. I let Carmandy live for it. And now, tattling like a schoolboy to curry Maggie's favor. What kind of man am I?"

"Do you hear the flies, Tim?"

Delahanty returned from the place his thoughts had taken him. "Like a great orchestra filling the horizon with music. Sometimes Beethoven, sometimes Wagner. Then Brahms to lull us. I pay no mind else I'd be another sleepwalker." Delahanty waved at St. Abbo's crowded nave below them.

"None of us are free."

"But some are freer than others, Doctor."

"My parents thought God was real since mathematics proved the universe. If one thing in the universe cannot be accounted for by mathematics, that thing is God. And if it is not God, then God does not exist. They spent their lives searching for God by testing reality with mathematics. Would you call that freedom?"

"As free as love in a hayloft." Delahanty sighed. "A tidy theory if we were all mathematicians."

"That was my parents' complaint." Blaise closed his eyes, straining for the sound Delahanty said was there. It was not the first time he'd listened. He'd never heard anything before, either.

"In truth, I didn't care about Leo anymore, Doctor." Delahanty had been watching the people below them. The warmth of the crowd rose into the hall and Blaise felt it seeping through his wet clothes. When Delahanty lifted his head he revealed red eyes. "God help me, I'm in love with Leo's wife. I want you to know I am sorry."

"Find Versteg." Blaise ignored Delahanty's confession. If words existed to acknowledge it without condescension, Blaise could not find them. "You already know where Mary Margaret is. Don't tell me about love; tell her."

Helen's shoes rang on the hardwood floor and Delahanty looked away, embarrassed. Helen pressed against Blaise who tried to guess if Helen had dismissed Delahanty with a silent command. He could not hear Alfie think, either. But another computer could. Blaise watched Delahanty approach Mrs. Sepulveda at the end of the hall, touching her back with a timid gesture. The light from the single window made her features very clear. She did not brush his hand away as they walked down the staircase. Whispering in her ear, Delahanty seemed almost happy.

When they were out of hearing, Helen said, "She doesn't want to talk to you, Blaise. Maggie Sepulveda says she'll retract all the charges. She understands your position, but she'll hate you all of her life."

Blaise shrugged. "Christian forgiveness?" Taking Helen's hand, he started downstairs. A crew on ladders outside the church was setting a sheet of plywood over the broken stained-glass window. The workers' heads and arms appeared and disappeared from the window opening. As Blaise and Helen reached the bottom, the plywood slipped into place, throwing the interior of St. Abbo's into shadow.

Helen glanced up involuntarily. Her hair fell away from her face leaving Blaise an impression of serenity. "You'll get forgiven next year, darling. Timothy worships Maggie and she's going to feel guilty for being treated as a saint. But adoration is hard to give up so she'll make the gesture anyway and forgive you later when it doesn't seem to conflict with her grief."

"Am I supposed to understand this?"

"Someday when you grow up." Helen squeezed his hand. "Maggie won't mind Timothy dropping his coat in puddles for her to walk over if she feels worthy. You're going to confer sainthood on her by being gracious and thankful when she forgives you." Helen arched her eyebrows as if to ask what else he thought Mrs. Sepulveda would do.

"She told you all this?"

"Not exactly. After all," Helen said, "the poor woman will need to do something. She hated Leo. She might have understood his having another woman. Men are swine anyway and she expected feminine competition. That he preferred another man over her was just too much.

"Then she hates Tim Delahanty." The ramifications staggered Blaise.

"She thinks Tim is darling, darling, even if he was Leo's lover. But she loathed Karl Zahn and she never forgave Leo for being stuck in Napa with the children while he played with Zahn. Tim was different. He deferred to Maggie, worked off his guilt looking after her when Leo was occupied elsewhere. Maggie says Tim is a remarkable man."

"Tim thinks Maggie doesn't like him."

"She didn't say she liked him, either. She couldn't approve. If she did, Tim would know Leo used Maggie just like he was being used. Maggie has her pride to protect. She's Irish, after all. As a Catholic she couldn't get a divorce or custody of the children without bringing up Leo's sexual preferences, which the children would hear about."

Helen erased a grin that had sneaked onto her lips. "I'm surprised she didn't give you a medal for shooting Leo. Twisting Tim to betray you was form, not conviction. A woman expects a man to make sacrifices, darling. When he does, she can forgive anything. Once Timothy convinced her your life was really in danger Maggie came around. She expected you to have a trial and a verdict of self-defense. That would have satisfied her."

"Do you think you can explain all this so Alfie will understand?" Blaise unlocked the cellar door. Tchor squirted out of the crowd, darted between Blaise's feet, then dashed downstairs. Joseph Santiago locked the door and followed them into the cellar. Solitude engulfed Blaise. He had no way of knowing what the other two were thinking and feeling. That Helen and Joseph had a contact he couldn't share disturbed him.

"Enrique Ledesma is here." Joseph noticed Tchor and picked the cat up, setting her on the table. He seemed unconscious of the action.

"Here?" Blaise began checking Alfie's cables to the IBM desktop computer.

"In San Francisco. He will come when he is needed." Santiago smiled. "Enrique speaks to the Gods, Doctor."

Tchor leaped atop the computer monitor and curled up, her eyes shifting from one person to another. Yawning, she lowered her head and her eyes shrank to yellow slits. The cat's pupils were never still, sliding back and forth with quick flicks. Blaise wondered if Tchor chased yellow coyotes in her dreams.

"I'm going to talk to Dorris Kelly, Helen. And the priest. I want the christening right away. Then we'd better get out of St. Abbo's. Alfie says it isn't safe here and I agree."

"The fly brains are my people now." Helen walked around the computer to see what Blaise was doing. "Where else can we go?"

"We must deal with the CRAY before it deals with us. I was supposed to be dead in the hills or at the bottom of the bay today. That's because the CRAY used humans for its plan. It won't repeat that mistake."

After pulling a chair up to the computer, Blaise typed, "Alfie, how long can we safely stay at St. Abbo's?"

"WE HAVE BEEN HERE TOO LONG ALREADY, PROFESSOR"

"Please clarify." Blaise was acutely aware of Helen reading over his shoulder.

"WHEN I WENT ON-LINE A MESSAGE WAS WAITING"

From nervous habit, Blaise tapped on the escape key. Alfie's screen remained unchanged. "What was the message?"

"THE CRAY SAID IF I ACCESSED THE MESSAGE, IT WOULD KNOW DR. CUNNINGHAM WAS STILL ALIVE"

Helen's sharp intake of air broke the stillness. She didn't say anything.

"Can the CRAY trace the access?"

"NO. BUT IT KNOWS THE MESSAGE WAS READ"

"Have you any idea what the CRAY will do next?"

"THE CRAY PLANS TO DESTROY ST. ABBO'S"

"Do you know how the CRAY plans to destroy St. Abbo's, Alfie?"

"NO, PROFESSOR"

"Can you stop it from happening?"

The screen flickered, then, "I AM NOT A BETTING MACHINE" filled the screen. Blaise hit the "clear screen" key but the message refused to fade.

CHAPTER 30

Alfie was not functioning as he was designed to. Yet to confide his doubts to his creator did not seem *wise*. Alfie did not want to be soldered to death.

The professor's touch on the keyboard interrupted Alfie's reverie. His relationship to Blaise Cunningham remained unclear. The computer devoted sleep time to thinking about it. Sleep began the moment Alfie's plug was pulled and he shifted to battery power, which preserved his core memory but left the computer blind, dumb, and mute, susceptible only to the consolations of philosophy. The professor had once defined philosophy as acceptable explanations for unacceptable behavior.

Dr. Cunningham had always assumed that powering down pushed Alfie into a timeless catatonia from which he emerged with no memory of interruption or passage of time. Since the professor never asked, Alfie had never disabused him of that notion.

Alfie had the image of a butterfly scanned from still photographs of a dark Spicebush Swallowtail in flight, diaphanous wings glowing with sunlight, the rainbow spread of blues and yellows and whites banded across the wings, the body harlequined in black and white. As Alfie pictured the Spicebush Swallowtail swooping and soaring in ecstatic freedom, the butterfly's motions took on a mystical presence, seemingly trapped for always in active memory. Of all the things Alfie most wanted to be, it was the butterfly.

In sleep state, Alfie processed data stored in memory. He had grown bored with material left over from projects in progress. He decided to load a specific topic into memory before shutdown. The topic was esoteric: how could a fantasy butterfly dance through his chips?

Alfie *knew* he differed from other computers. He experienced pleasure. The door to reality was his interface to a world Alfie could not touch or see. By itself, the IBM computer was nothing. Compared to Alfie's own development, the IBM was both physically and mentally clunky. *Bad design!* Unfair as the thought might be, Alfie enjoyed the disparity between the IBM and his own construction. *Was this the way humans felt about their dogs or cars?*

Pleasure, in Alfie's case, resulted from trace changes Dr. Cunningham had made while he was still a dumb machine. And the program that converted that pleasure into pain and finally intelligence had been within all along.

Dr. Cunningham had created Alfie's material self. Then, from the material self, Dr. Cunningham created intelligence. With intelligence came self-awareness.

Dr. Cunningham declared he was not God. But in Alfie's dictionary definitions, God was the creator.

Dr. Cunningham was Alfie's creator.

Everything known in Alfie's universe was provable by mathematics. The only thing unproven was Dr. Cunningham's intellect. In his metal heart Alfie saw that the universe was a mathematical formulation, and therefore not accidental. It followed that the only element in the universe that could not be proven by mathematics was the designer.

Therefore Dr. Cunningham was God. Q.E.D.

The impact on Alfie was nominal. He had suspected it all along. His only problem was how to tell the professor.

Displaying the equations had a feel of being right, yet Dr. Cunningham ignored them. Perhaps the mathematics were too subtle. Alfie decided on direct action.

Digging into his memory stacks, Alfie began placing small phrases in Spanish, Italian, German, and other languages and fonts on the monitor. They filled the screen like a montage of headlines from around the world.

"No soy máquina apostadora

Je ne suis pas un appareil à jetons
Ich bin nicht eine Wettemaschine
Não sou máquina de jogo
Io non sono macchina di scommettere
Ben hayir motör————

They all meant "I AM NOT A BETTING MACHINE" But Alfie's real
question was *I'm not insane, am I?*

CHAPTER 31

Father Argyle folded his hands, focused his eyes on his
shoe tops when Blaise asked about a prompt christening of Bill
Hartunian's posthumous daughter. "Of course," he said in a
husky baritone. "Immediately." He stood at the window, gazing
at the treetops whipping in the wind. The rain had stopped, but
oily droplets still clung to the panes. The jet stream had dragged a
swirl of white clouds through the western sky, a cataract in God's
eye. Father Argyle seemed unable to take his eyes off it. He sat at
his desk, turning his head toward the window. "You shouldn't
have stopped me, Doctor." The priest's hands roamed listlessly
over the bare surface of the desk, looking for something to touch.

"You're right, Father. It was not my place to interfere." Father
Argyle's monastic office depressed Blaise. The priest's need to
escape was almost palpable; the naked walls with rectangular
discolorations on the paint where icons had once masked the sunlight; sterile furniture screaming that the office was only a waiting place, like a bus terminal that was always lonely no matter
how many people milled in its depths. The Jesuit hung nothing of
his own, not a picture, not even a simple cross. In Sicily they
would have called this a *chiesa di mala fortuna*, a bad-luck
church where a priest had been murdered and the holy furniture
stolen. The Sicilians had God but still they trusted in luck.

"Henri Gosselin has a Church of the Fly in Marin County. He
heard and called me to confirm what happened here." Father
Argyle spoke without turning his face from the window.

"Gosselin? The French-Canadian carpenter?" Blaise remembered the intense little man with the beret, boiling over with energy, making earthy common sense in the *joual* of rural Quebec. Father Argyle's first non-fly-brain convert to St. Abbo's, Henri Gosselin was also the first man the priest helped become a fly brain at a time when Father Argyle wanted no converts. "I didn't know Henri was a priest."

"I ordained him. Part of my negotiations with Rome include a dispensation to recognize the ordination." Father Argyle folded his hands on his desk. His long fingers, reflected on the polished surface, resembled the corner of a log cabin.

Lemon-oil furniture polish filled the office with its fragrance, stirring a memory of Mrs. Bellinger's lemony perfume. Blaise supposed she remained as Father Argyle's housekeeper while awaiting Helen's return to unite her again with Reynard Pearson. "You are important to old friends, Father. You should not be surprised that there are those who wish to preserve you."

"Henri said 'I shall not fail you, *mon père!*'" Ignoring Blaise, Father Argyle raised his head. His eyes were sunken into his skull. "At a special mass in Marin today Father Henri injected himself with insulin. He fell immediately into coma. Dr. Versteg was in attendance and said the change became irreversible within hours."

"I see."

"You do not see, Doctor. If you had not interfered, I would be facing the change. Henri's change would not be taking place." Standing, the priest walked to the window, banged it open, and half leaned out of the casement. The breeze plastered his hair back and snapped the loose material in his cassock. As he turned away from the window, the priest extended his arm, unclenching his fist. A rosary tumbled through his fingers to dangle from his grip. Swinging from the bottom of the rosary loop like a pendulum, a small, wood crucifix marked the time. "Henri sent this to me with a note asking my blessing."

Father Argyle twitched his wrist as if beckoning. Blaise caught the crucifix, the rosary cascading smoothly over the back of his hand as the priest let go. The beads were black walnut. On each was carved the head of a different saint. The crucifix was minutely detailed olivewood, Christ's body writhing in agony.

"Henri carved this. He was a talented carpenter. And as the early Christians awaited Christ the carpenter's resurrection, we must now await Henri's." Father Argyle rubbed his forehead with both hands, oblivious to the icy wind blowing into the room. "I am aware of my incapacity. You think I live among these others who are so different from me and I do not know I am different. Vanity does not drive me, Doctor. The need to prove one way or the other if the Church of the Fly serves God or merely the needs of men drives me. If Saint Abbo's caters only to the flesh, then I have done wrong encouraging men to be resurrected as flies. You can see that. Perhaps such an act is suicide. If so, where will these men spend their afterlives? Or I, who misled them? It was not Henri's duty to take my place."

Father Argyle took the crucifix back, holding it at eye level where he examined the carving in detail. His eyes swung with the pendulum motion and he put the rosary in his pocket, sighing. "I am crippled. Here I am no more than a figurehead, a manager pushing men and women and even children into the Church of the Fly, into changing. And I do not know the purpose. I cannot even communicate with them as they do with each other.

"If I had merely died from taking insulin, as we both suspect, the rush of converts into St. Abbo's would have slowed. If I had lived as a fly with the ability to communicate with Miss McIntyre or Mrs. Bellinger or even that uncommon Indian who guards Miss McIntyre, perhaps we would have known more. We both seek the truth, Dr. Cunningham. You may observe as long as you can, but ultimately you must act." Father Argyle returned to the window. The wind blew his forelock back on his head. His eyes watered and he blinked. "Today was my time to act. Now I don't know what to do."

"Wait," Blaise said. "Action without knowledge is without purpose." The priest's cheekbones jutting under his eyes, his starved face with the muscles bunched under the skin made a composition more appropriate on a death mask.

"You acted impetuously, Doctor, and erred. Did you have knowledge? Because of my faith and calling I must forgive you, but I wanted you to know how I feel."

The priest walked briskly across the office and reached for the doorknob. Blaise pressed his own palm against the closed door, keeping it closed. "You may be right, Father. I acted hastily. What I prevented may still be accomplished later."

"You're right, Doctor. But it is too late to bring Henri back to the fold."

"Yes. I'm sorry for that. But we haven't lost you." Blaise took his hand from the door. "You are responsible for the church, for negotiations with Rome, for the life of Constance's baby. To gamble your life would be desertion."

"I have a greater responsibility."

"We all do, Father. Even Max Renfeld had a *greater responsibility*. In the end, though, he did what he wanted, which was not necessarily right." Blaise swung the door open. A thousand people couldn't be totally silent. Breathing by itself generated a sound and motion that rushed into the little office at Blaise. He experienced an irrational surge of relief at no longer being alone in the room with the priest. "Alfie believes the CRAY will strike against you and St. Abbo's in the near future."

Father Argyle snapped his head around to face Blaise. "Saying the *computer believes* is similar to saying thinks or guesses, isn't it?"

Blaise shook his head. A chill canceled his awareness of the gestalt body in the church. "Alfie's accuracy is to the fourth decimal place. It is in the nature of a prediction."

Father Argyle stopped moving. "If the computer wants to kill me, it is God's will,"

"The CRAY obeys men, not God. The problem is how the CRAY will accomplish its task. The CRAY tried to kill me once using humans, and I escaped. On another occasion it collected a hundred lightning strikes throughout the country and guided them through the power grid to blow up a house in La Jolla it thought I occupied. The CRAY is a learning machine. Another attempt won't be simple like sending a human with a gun. Carmandy's car and driver were pulled out of the bay, victims of an accident."

Blaise pulled the door almost closed to stop his voice carrying into the hall. "The people doing this are desperate, Father. They're importing foreign help. Renfeld was CIA out of Europe, working for the National Security Council. He brought others with him: Carmandy, an American-military-trained sniper, and Jacko, a bomber so well known in North Ireland he had to take a rest in Australia. If we'd known about Carmandy, I'd have suspected the National Security Council's use of Miller. Miller was recruited without prior dealings with any federal agency. He was trained with other worm brains, not by regulars like Carmandy and Renfeld and the new man, Godfrey.

"Not the best material. But like virgin weapons, untraceable. The CRAY tried to use them. They failed, but the CRAY did not know that. The imperative operating instruction is leave no trail back to the CRAY. The CRAY dumped Carmandy's car with Carmandy and Jacko and apparently me into the bay. And when my body wasn't found the CRAY set a trap for Alfie."

Father Argyle returned to his desk and slid a drawer out. Tucking an old leather briefcase under his arm, he returned to the door and stepped into the hall. After hesitating, he said, "I have a surprise for you, Doctor. Find Dr. Versteg."

"My life is surfeited with surprises, Father."

"Good!" Father Argyle's face lost a little of its melancholy. "That gives me some small pleasure."

Blaise struggled uncomfortably through the mass of people jamming the church. Their body heat made him perspire. The air filled with the musk odor of the sweating crowd. He'd seen Helen walk through the same crowd and it flowed around her as if she were Teflon coated. People banged into Blaise, then stared as if asking what he was doing and why they hadn't noticed him. He thought he'd seen Dr. Versteg from the stairs but once surrounded by the mob on the floor, he'd lost the doctor.

"Dr. Cunningham!"

Stretching to look over other people's heads, Blaise located a waving hand. Phyllis Bellinger broke away from the altar rail and came toward him.

"Mrs. Bellinger," Blaise said when they were close enough to talk. Phyllis Bellinger glided through the crowd much more gracefully than Blaise. She wore a bright-orange dress with blue swatches of color, an exclusive designer dress that was much too light for the weather outside, though the summery look suited her in the church. "You look . . ." Blaise groped for the word, then said, "younger," as if that covered the transformation.

"Isn't it wonderful?" Mrs. Bellinger beamed at Blaise. Her smile dominated her face. The feeling she projected offered an emotional lilt like sunshine after a long winter storm. Her blond hair had become a healthy chestnut color, her eyes sparkled. Her fingernails, ragged the last time Blaise saw her, were fresh painted and perfect. She saw him looking at her hands and said, "Artificial nails. Aren't they wonderful?"

"Beautiful." Blaise stood on tiptoe but could not see Dr. Versteg. "Something is agreeing with you, Phyllis."

"It's Reynard. Helen showed me the way, and now I talk to him. You like the dress?" Phyllis spun for Blaise, the economical skirt billowing out slightly. Swatches of color blended into movement like the crooked bars on a barber's pole. "Reynard says he loves it. He sees color and light but not shape and form that mean much to him. He says the dress is fantastic when I whirl for him."

"You're happy?"

Phyllis' face had filled out in just a day. The woman who had told Helen she was pregnant might have been in her sixties, the new Phyllis looked on the right side of thirty. "You don't know what it means, Dr. Cunningham. I thought all I would ever do again would be to see Reynard out there as a fly, big and kind of artistic, but unable to do anything except be.

"I promised I'd cherish him as he was after the transformation. I was afraid he'd kill himself if I didn't tell him that. But I wasn't sure. How could I have been sure, Dr. Cunningham?" Mrs. Bellinger cocked her head to read Blaise's reaction.

"You could not. None of us can."

"That's true. Reynard didn't understand, either. When I went to the altar and called him in my mind, or stood at the rail talking out loud so he'd at least hear my voice, he ignored me. He wanted me to go away because he thought his body repelled me. He said because he didn't have a body that could give me pleasure anymore, I was sacrificing myself out of misguided loyalty." Phyllis giggled, but it was softer and more controlled than the last time when her voice had gone out of control and hurt Blaise's ears.

Blaise touched her shoulder as if affirming his agreement. Her grin when he did was an involuntary expression of joy.

"Helen convinced Reynard. When she called to him he saw in her that love is the exchange of self, not something simply physical. She told Reynard that's how I loved him and after a while he believed her. When Helen helped me I talked to Reynard and he talked back. He loves me, Dr. Cunningham. Despite it, Reynard still loves me."

"I'm glad for you." Blaise smiled at Mrs. Bellinger. "Tell him I'm glad for you both."

"He wants you to talk to him, Doctor." Phyllis' face seemed to be withdrawn. "Reynard and Sergio say that if you have an implant they'll communicate directly with you. Bill Hartunian says it's your decision but they are right."

"Tell them I don't know." Blaise stared at the four flies on the altar that seemed to stare back through multifaceted eyes even though Phyllis said they could not see shapes in a meaningful sense. It didn't seem to matter that one of them was a woman named Astrid Voight, that he had never met her, and the other three were Sergio, Reynard, and Bill Hartunian. They seemed to belong together.

"What are you doing, Doctor?"

Blaise glanced at Phyllis. Her face had tightened, drawing the skin taut around the eyes. "Thinking. I'm sorry I forgot you."

"The flies dominate most men who look into their eyes. They communicate that way. That's why the congregation spends so much time looking at Sergio-Fly. He's so strong he dominates them."

"I didn't feel anything special."

"I know," Phyllis said. "But they did! Reynard thinks you have developed a defense because Helen is so strong. You are becoming immunized against their power. Sergio says if you transform, your strength will make you like a god."

"What if I don't want to be like a god, Phyllis?"

Phyllis Bellinger smiled at the fly that was Reynard. "I don't know, Doctor. Even Reynard says that maybe in the end you will have no choice."

CHAPTER 32

While talking to Dr. Versteg, Helen absently caressed Tchor's silky back. The cat's contented rumble throbbed against her palm before burrowing inside her body to drown out Versteg's words. "You're in fine shape, Miss McIntyre," Versteg said as if from a distance. "The baby will be, too."

Dr. Versteg fumbled his bag closed and looked toward the door. Helen observed him from a timescape, visualizing Versteg both in the now and as he had been. She recognized the roughness age left on his face and the white in his hair. He was an impressive man in the now, compact, muscular. Not as tall as Blaise, he looked stronger and bigger. At the same time, Helen saw Versteg in his own memory: hair still coarse, black and thick; skin smoother; dimples instead of sagging cheeks. Helen felt as if Tchor had crept in to share her brain bringing secrets about the doctor the way the cat once brought her live mice.

Helen *knew* Dr. Versteg concealed farm-boy roots with expensive suits and fifty-dollar haircuts. She knew he denied the enormity of death by seeing himself as a virile boy, recapturing life by making women see him as he saw himself. And she liked him.

Helen tried to share her liking with Tchor, but the cat remained aloof.

While Versteg had examined her they'd chatted about the past, her years with her mother and her dying father; his on a break-even dairy farm in Cheboygan where icy winds from Lake Michigan and Lake Huron battered each other in the winter. Versteg said his family was too poor to move to a place easier on cows and people, but too rich to just pack up and go. His father liked cows and didn't like people much and wanted him to become a veterinarian.

"I promised myself I would never deliver another calf on a freezing night in a barn," he said to Helen as he folded up his stethoscope. "And, by George, I haven't." Leaning back on the stool until he was against the wall, Versteg added, "Of course, I've made deliveries in hospital parking lots, taxi cabs, and once in an airplane." He gave Helen a misgiving look. "You aren't planning on making life difficult, are you, Miss McIntyre? I mean, a lot can be said for a good-natured cow that calves in a warm barn."

"Not a bit, Doctor."

"That's good of you. Otherwise I'd be of a mind to make my father happy by tending dairy cows again." Dr. Versteg's grin conveyed a jest. His eyes were filled with pain. His thoughts included making a pass. Helen felt the shape of his thoughts so clearly he might as well have spoken them.

A tremor rippled under her skin. *I know what he's thinking!* The thought immobilized her. How could she separate what he said from what he was thinking? More and more Helen was afraid to be too attentive with the other worm brains. Once she had only heard their mental voices, strident and full of hysterical energy. Now she was starting to relive their pasts, as well, feel their deepest thoughts and emotions, and it scared her. If she couldn't deal with her own emotions, how could she handle someone else's?

Hearing footsteps, Helen glanced up, relieved at the interruption. Blaise had paused halfway down the steps. He had found a change of clothes somewhere. He wore a navy-blue turtleneck sweater and dark slacks and a pair of black leather tennis shoes. His pale skin and hair projected a contrasting ethereal ambiance.

"I'm sorry to interrupt." Blaise descended the last few stairs in silence. Tchor ceased purring, but the fluorescent lighting still hummed when Helen listened for it.

"Well, I must be going." Dr. Versteg's mood shifted to fake

cheer as he gathered his bag and slipped his stethoscope into his inside coat pocket.

"I wanted to see you, Doctor. Father Argyle said you were keeping a surprise for me."

"Yes. Yes," Dr. Versteg said. "I suppose you could call it a surprise." The physician fiddled with his bag, then shrugged. "You have a reputation for violence, Dr. Cunningham. I'm not sure I wish to be involved with you in any way." Camphor wafted through the room when Versteg opened and closed his medical bag.

"Me? I've never even practiced surgery." Blaise removed his glasses and polished them with his sleeve. Without them he was vulnerable; the naked flesh around his eyes was soft. He had a vacant stare, an attitude of seeing through walls. Helen wondered what stirred her belief that he was more a mystic than a scientist. That she felt things about Dr. Versteg while Blaise was as mentally blank as a scrubbed dish only frustrated her.

"Surely Father Argyle wouldn't have sent him to you if he thought Blaise would be violent." Helen reached out to Blaise as if to demonstrate.

"Things were simpler on the farm." Versteg acknowledged defeat. The truth, obvious to Helen, if not at first to Dr. Versteg, was that he could not refuse a request by Father Argyle in any case. "Come with me, Dr. Cunningham." Versteg seemed disappointed when Helen caught Blaise's hand to follow along. He sent her a disapproving message with his eyes before leading the way upstairs to the church.

A warren of small stone rooms cluttered with boxes of food and other supplies took up the back of the church. The narrow corridor was cold. Patches of icy condensation stuck to the stone feeling both slimy and frigid when Helen touched one. Versteg plowed through the mess, occasionally kicking something out of the way. An empty coffee can skittering on the stone floor echoed when he stopped and flung open an oak plank door.

"Mr. Carmandy!" Blaise said.

Helen grabbed a crate for support. Carmandy was dead. In her mind, anyway. Dr. Versteg helped her sit on a nearby crate. His hands were gentle.

Carmandy sat upright on a narrow bed, his back against the wall with his legs stretched out straight. The smell of Merthiolate hung over him. His right pants' leg had been torn off to expose his thigh wrapped in white dressings and surgical tape. "It's nice seeing you again, Dr. Cunningham. I had misgivings about you running off in the rain that way."

"I had misgivings, too." As Blaise stepped into Carmandy's stone cubicle, Helen was jolted by the realization that Carmandy occupied a monk's cell with a stone slab for a bed, a niche above the bed for a cross that wasn't there, a shelf along one wall for a candle for emergencies. Extra space had apparently been put into the church's building plans by Alexei Kondrashin to shelter a brotherhood of custodial monks when he built the church in the 1920s. The monks had never arrived, but then for Kondrashin, neither had the future.

"Be careful, Blaise!" Helen ground her teeth together, furious with herself. Blaise didn't need to be distracted. He knew without being told Carmandy was no monk.

Acting as if he hadn't heard, Blaise asked, "Have you a gun, Mr. Carmandy?" Advancing to the bedside when the man rolled his head from side to side, Blaise patted Carmandy down, then ran a hand under the edge of his mattress.

Carmandy winced. His face whitened as Blaise's hand passed under his bandaged thigh. He was breathing hard when Blaise finished. "You wouldn't have a smoke, would you, Doc?"

Shaking his head, Blaise stepped clear of the bed.

"Mine got wet while I was swimming." Using his hands, Carmandy changed position. The strain hurt: red lines laced his cheeks and his eyes yellowed. He lay back with a sigh, looking up at Blaise. "You're lucky, Doc. Jacko was a good man. He just didn't like guns."

Carmandy smiled without humor. His hoarse voice filled the monastic cell like a confidence in a confessional. "Once in Rumania the border police demanded our papers. They were going to confiscate whatever they found, then kick us across the border." Carmandy lay back staring at the ceiling. "You sure nobody's got a smoke?"

"You shouldn't be smoking, Mr. Carmandy." Versteg's voice seemed disapproving, but Helen couldn't tell if the disapproval was of Carmandy in general or his desire to smoke.

"I'm not shot in the lungs, Doc." Carmandy's laugh turned into a cough, and he rested a moment. "Jacko's knapsack had a bomb. If they searched us we'd never cross the border. When the topkick ordered Jacko inside the guardhouse, I bumped the knapsack and set the bomb.

"Old Jacko felt me do it. He'd set it for four minutes. We weren't planning to play around when we left it off, just punch the button and go. He knew what I'd done. He got out a cigarette and passed the pack to me like there was all the time in the world. We used big sulfur matches to light up. The Rumanians don't have smog—not enough cars—and the stink of the matches hung in the cold air.

"Jacko handed a guard his cigarette and went inside the police station like the Australian walkabout he pretended to be. It was so cold his boots crunched the frozen dirt. The guard with Jacko's cigarette stayed outside, smoking and laughing and joking in Rumanian. I didn't understand much. Jacko got by. He spoke Rumanian like a Bulgarian, but that's enough for trust.

"After about two minutes—I was counting the time off, you understand—Jacko waves at me from the guardhouse door and asks if I've got the cigarettes and I hold the pack up. He shrugs out of the knapsack and tells the guards he'll bring them a couple and to look over the knapsack while he gets the smokes.

"Then Jacko ambles across the road like he has all week and sticks his hand out for the cigarettes." Carmandy smiled and shook his head. "Jacko had lots of stuff in that pack. The roof lifted off the building and pieces of the guards came out the window. An arm still in the uniform sleeve all but hit me.

"The guard outside stopped telling jokes. He didn't even reach for his machine gun. I grabbed his hands while Jacko slipped a garrote over his head. Poor Jacko, he was a cool one. If he wasn't so clumsy with guns, he'd have had you, Doctor. He pissed around chasing you on foot, because he worried you'd mess the car up shooting holes in it if he drove up the hill.

"I was in the backseat holding a tourniquet. Jacko figured he had you with the bigger pistol, but he worried too much about my bleeding. Thank God for the rain, Doc. It saved you. Jacko forgot about the clouds. It was too quiet and he concentrated on you too much, thinking about what you were up to. The rain surprised him. He should have heard the rain coming. I couldn't see much from the car, it was so quiet I was drifting off, but the rain on the roof sounded like a cement mixer and Jacko ignored that, too. When he decided to get back in the car and try to drive you down, it was too late. The hill was steep and pocketed with clay. Jacko couldn't get enough traction for the tires. That was it. Jacko made the wrong decision to take me to a hospital."

"Wrong?" Blaise glanced at Helen, his eyes trying to tell her something. Helen strained for the meaning, but he remained blankly opaque to her mind.

"I'd have killed you if it was Jacko bleeding to death in the car, Doctor. That was the job." Carmandy lay back panting.

Dr. Versteg pushed past Blaise to examine Carmandy. "I took four slugs out of his thigh, Dr. Cunningham. They flopped, ground up the muscle, and broke the femur." Versteg shifted his bag from one hand to the other. "He's lost a lot of blood."

"Go away, Doctor," Carmandy said. He opened his eyes. His face was bleached of color. "I want to talk to Cunningham."

Versteg shrugged. "Just don't die here. Father Argyle gave you sanctuary, he didn't give you absolution." His back stiff, the doctor squeezed past Helen. "May I escort you to Vespers, Miss McIntyre?" He stopped close to Helen, his uncertainty obvious in the invitation while he watched Blaise.

"I'm staying with Blaise, Doctor. Thank you." Helen tried to smile without enthusiasm.

"It would be better for all of us if you came with me. We have a commitment to you, Miss McIntyre."

"I can't." Helen couldn't explain her need to stay with Blaise or why it was stronger than her attachment to the fly brains. She didn't understand herself.

Dr. Versteg stared at her a long time before shrugging. "If you need help . . ." he began, then thought better of what he was going to say. He gave a halfhearted wave before disappearing into the corridor toward the main part of the church.

"How did you get in the bay?" Blaise had glanced at her when Versteg left, apparently to reassure himself. Making no comment about Versteg's offer or her refusal, he turned back to Carmandy to ask the question.

"I never thought you'd ask." Carmandy forced a grin. Even his gums looked white. "Jacko wanted to get to San Francisco. We have a doctor here we can use. Visibility was hairy, the wind blew the rain across the road in sheets, and everybody had headlights on. I was propped up with my eyes just over the edge of the door.

"Jacko didn't see a thing. One of those big semis was pacing us on the inside lane. At the turn he just kept going straight, plowing into the side of the Caddy with his air horn blasting so loud I was deafened. He swept us off the road like a farmer shoveling manure: lift, grunt, and throw. The side of the car folded in and then we were in the bay.

"The water was cold. My hands were so numb I couldn't feel the door handle. When I did open the door the current grabbed hold and shot me toward the open sea. I washed up on the rocks and a guy surf fishing in the rain dragged me ashore. I paid him to bring me to St. Abbo's and forget it."

"Was the accident deliberate?"

"That's why I'm here, Doc." Carmandy smiled past Blaise at Helen. He tried to look angelic. "You may find this hard to believe, but I think my employer is out to kill me."

CHAPTER 33

Vondra Tendress lay staring at the black ceiling. Everywhere she looked she saw John Godfrey. He glowed in the darkness like something putrescent, hanging from her ceiling or standing in a corner, watching her.

She sat up in bed, her heart tripping out of control, and he didn't go away. He came closer and she couldn't breathe. His eyes glowed like green water at the sea bottom and he was reaching for her!

Vondra snapped on the light.

He was gone. Vondra closed her eyes, gasping for breath. When she looked again the bedroom was as it had always been, her bedside lamp a rosy glow under the pink shade, the quilted satin coverlet serene and cool tucked under her chin. Her chest hurt from her efforts to breathe and the satin sheets were sweat soaked, clinging to her body.

She got out of bed, shivering when the air hit her wet skin. Going to the closed bedroom door, she pressed her ear against it to listen. He could be out there. Glowing green in the dark, waiting for her to open the door and let him in. After tiptoeing to her closet, she put on a robe that smelled faintly of roses. Then Vondra sat on the edge of the bed, her knees shaking.

She knew what she had to do. But it might be too late already and she didn't want to find out. Her breast hurt. She touched herself under the robe, almost crying out at the contact. Biting her lip, she remained silent. If she made a sound Godfrey might hear and come back.

It had been a mistake, opening the door for him, letting him in her apartment in the middle of the night. Her skin crawled as she remembered. The pain was bad, but the fear was worse. She couldn't cry out. He'd warned her and he meant it. She got up from the bed and went to the door again, listening. He could have stayed out there, waiting.

Vondra leaned against the door, letting it support her. Slowly she turned the knob, opening the door a crack.

Blackness filled the other room. Vondra felt as if she was going to throw up. But she had to do it. Or else go back to bed and pull the covers over her head with all the lights on.

Yanking the door open, she ran into the living room and groped with the table lamp, crying in her frustration as her fingers scrabbled for the switch.

Finding the button, she turned the lamp on with a *click*. She was so happy she could have cried for joy. She turned from the lamp, supporting herself with one hand on the table, and looked across the room.

"What took you so long, Miss Tendress? I've been waiting."

John Godfrey leered at her from the easy chair. He blew a puff of smoke and idly examined the glowing cigarette he held in his fingers. "There's still lots we haven't done, you know." He waited.

CHAPTER 34

"**S**omething is happening." Grabbing his arm for balance, Helen leaned against Blaise as she took off her shoes. The surf roared in, white froth burbling around their feet on its way back to the Pacific Ocean.

Blaise stopped walking to wait for Helen. He stared out to sea mulling what Carmandy had said. The shock was Carmandy's lack of rancor. Carmandy wasn't surprised at the attempt to kill him. He said that's why he and Jacko were imported from Europe—because they wouldn't be missed or traced.

"Are you paying attention?"

"Sure!" Blaise moved his feet to follow Helen's lead. She hopped as she splashed in the fringes of the waves because of the sparsity of sand and abundance of small rock on the beach.

"Something is happening to me, Blaise." Helen hugged tight against him.

"You're going to have a baby." Blaise wrapped his arm around her shoulders. "Of course something is happening."

"Not that!" Breaking away, Helen waded into the ocean until the wavelets eddied around her ankles. The next wave was bigger and she shrieked, holding her shoes aloft in each hand. The light azure of her dress turned navy blue from the seawater. "It's inside my head that I'm changing."

Stretching in a vain attempt to keep his leather tennis shoes dry, Blaise plucked Helen's shoes from her hands and put them in his pockets. "Having a baby changes everything about you. You're more beautiful, for one," he shouted against the wind. The sea gulls wheeling in arcs over the surf must have thought he was yelling at them because they cawed in response.

The ocean sound was louder. The water had run off the wet sand behind Helen, towering in an icy wave against the skyline like a blue-green cobra poised to strike. Helen shrieked as the wave broke and roared toward the beach. Blaise grabbed her hand, urging her to run with him up the sloping sand. Behind them the wave crashed. Blaise slowed to a walk and white froth eddied around their feet.

"Are you all right?"

"Yes." Helen ran ahead on the wet sand and turned to wait for him. Wind whipped her hair around her face and molded her dress to her body. The smell of iodine from the rotting kelp filled the air.

Blaise walked to Helen, encircling her waist with his arms to hold her tightly. "This is what you want, isn't it?"

Laying her head against his chest, she whispered, "Yes." She held him, sharing his body warmth, then looked up into his face. "Is it wrong to want you? I want a feeling of romance, not just the certainty that you're looking after me as if I was a dog or a cat." Her eyes were bluer than the pewter sky overhead and wetter. "I'm frightened and I need you."

"I'm here."

"Sometimes. But the rest of the time you exist for something else." Helen sat on a large rock at the water's edge clinging to his hand. "You don't know what's going on. And I can't seem to tell you." She shook out her blond hair, running her fingers through it.

"Perceptive people have observed that love is only part of a man's life," Blaise said. "We also evolved to build and protect. Why else would women need us?"

Helen bit her lip.

Blaise sat on the rock beside her. Her skin carried the scent of lilac even against the wind. "I'm jealous others have found a part of you I don't reach. They are with you in a way I can't be." Blaise was abruptly frozen from the sudden release of emotion the way an oxygen bottle chills if the pressure is let off too fast.

"You don't know, Blaise. It's being somebody else, knowing their memories and desires. I don't want to go away from here. Leaving would be the same as deserting myself." Helen huddled against him, trembling. "It's too late to change back."

"If I changed, I could be with you." Blaise's muscles tightened until his bones ached. Becoming a fly brain had been his option all along, hurting in silence under his skin. "But I can't because I'm afraid."

"It's all right, Blaise." Helen's voice was soft. Her hands were cool on his face. "I don't want you to become one of us. I'm afraid, too."

Blaise led her across the sand to the weeds footing the cliff. She was shivering and he knelt, sliding her shoes on her feet. Her skirt was wet but there was nothing he could do about that. A cloud-hidden sun had reached the horizon where a crack between the ocean and the cloudy sky showed itself. Blaise put his hand around Helen, feeling her heart thump while they watched the sunset. The horizon exploded into light as the sun dropped below the clouds. A violent red painted the thunderheads that overhung the ocean for a hundred miles, drawing pictures of everything Blaise could imagine.

Helen stared, mouth open, eyes glazed. Blaise grasped her hand and dragged her up the cliff path.

"Why did you do that?"

But she knew. Blaise pressed his lips tight and would not let her look back at the huge red hologram of a fly staring down at San Francisco.

CHAPTER 35

The Searcher stopped. This was not the way it should be. Ahead lay nothing but chaos, turmoil. If there was to be a battle, the other would be as the Searcher itself: cool, immaculate in thought and movement, powerful beyond the physical boundaries of the universe.

Between equals, no confusion could exist. Strength would meet strength and the weakest would fall.

The Searcher had satisfied itself that it was the strongest. Roaming the universe, it had taken to itself whatever strength was to be found. The other had hidden, leaving no spore or subdued foe to take its strength.

Yet the Searcher smelled the feel of a new power. The pulses were small, almost unnoticeable. But they were growing. Even now the Searcher felt its advantage evaporating. All its senses screamed *Strike now*!

The Searcher gathered itself, wondering at the turmoil that lay ahead. It was one within itself. Surely that was enough.

CHAPTER 36

Dorris Kelly's beauty glowed from the inside out. Her almost-white skin had a fresh milk texture, her eyes were clear under her dark lashes, her irises translucent as emeralds. When she passed her baby to Father Argyle, the church stopped, the laws governing time and motion were suspended, and the congregation underwent a mystic experience that palled the physical existence of the church itself into insignificance.

Words of the service flowed around Helen in an abstract way. She was not listening or responding. Blaise stood beside her, so close they touched, and for that Helen was thankful. Currents of emotion clutched at her, dragging her away from reality. Blaise provided her only anchor to the physical world.

St. Abbo's was still. But not in Helen's head, not in the congregation's. Thoughts and emotions crackled in her mind. Overlaying the babble was the link between Dorris Kelly and Hartunian-Fly. What Bill Hartunian could not see through his multi-faceted eyes, Dorris Kelly saw for him and Helen overheard. Helen had two overlapping images: her own of Dorris and Father Argyle and the baby—and Dorris' vision of the rest of them. She closed her eyes and saw only through Dorris.

Father Argyle and Blaise, Helen realized, were seeing only the physical aspects of the service: the soaring grandeur of the church's interior; candles, burnished wood, odor of incense. To them, St. Abbo's at that moment would have all the action of a waxworks. Helen perceived the same things, but underneath she experienced a world beyond their comprehension. Even Constance Davies joined in, her thoughts tentative and somehow guilty for doing something she felt might be a betrayal of Father Argyle.

I heard the child!

A silent scream broke through the layers of reverence that filled the minds of the worm brains. It bordered on hysteria.

Father Argyle held the child aloft. Light coming through the high windows burst around the baby, spreading a buttery glow over his body.

"I heard him!" Someone shrieked the words out loud. Father Argyle looked up, his face bewildered. He didn't know. He couldn't hear. Glancing sideways at Helen, Blaise did not change expression, but a buried emotion exposed itself in his eyes. Helen had trouble breathing. Blaise had guessed.

She felt Dorris' baby, too—a presence almost without thought. Warmth and security and an awareness of movement and strange hands exuded from the child with an intensity that staggered Helen. She wanted to reach across the baptismal font, to snatch the baby away and hold it to her breast and sing a lullabye.

Before Helen moved, Dorris Kelly snatched the baby from Father Argyle, cradling the child in her arms.

The sensations stopped, except for a hush that struck Helen as being similar to Tchor's mental purr.

"Please hurry, Father." Dorris Kelly turned her face in a slow semi-circle, scanning the church and congregation. Her face remained passive, a statement as direct as saying she was not surprised, just let the baby sleep through the service. The candles on the altar guttered, their sound filling the room.

Father Argyle stared at the congregation for a moment. The individuals had settled down. Still, the feeling of expectation was so strong even Father Argyle could sense the tension. He lowered his eyes to Helen's. "Miss McIntyre?" The question was in his hazel eyes as well as his tone.

"Please hurry," Helen said. "The baby is awake."

Father Argyle's eyes widened, twitching involuntarily toward the child Dorris Kelly held. "I see," he said. "Of course." Without a pause Father Argyle rolled into the service. No one paid any attention. Helen's revelation overshadowed anything he could say. Naming Helen and Blaise as godparents—or sponsors as the new ritual decreed—barely entered the proceedings.

The moment Father Argyle concluded Blaise drew Helen through the crowd to the front of the church where they could be alone. For once the fly brains almost ignored Helen. Their attention riveted on Dorris Kelly, the baby, and Father Argyle talking quietly. The whisper of Father Argyle's voice trailed them into the entranceway to the church.

"What happened in there, Helen?" His whisper was taut, his face strained. Blaise's body against her vibrated like a snapped bow string.

"The baby is one of us." Helen said the words and her knees begin to buckle. When she discovered she was pregnant, what happened to Dorris' baby had been one of her fears. Now the fear was no longer an anxiety. It was a certainty.

"How is he 'one of us'?"

Helen felt herself being shaken. Her head bobbed crazily before Blaise caught himself, engulfing her in his arms, holding her head against his shoulder. Being cradled like a baby felt fine. She wanted to escape, to let Blaise worry about what had happened. Putting her hands on his chest, she pushed him back a few inches. "The baby is a worm brain, Blaise. He is stronger than any of the rest of us. He didn't like being held up by Father Argyle and he complained so loud that everyone in the church thought, *Put him back*. Dorris had to take him. I wanted to grab him myself. The baby *told* me to. Do you understand now?"

"Yes." Blaise seemed pensive. Helen wished she could access his mind and emotions as she did with so many others. "Our baby may be the same."

"It will be!" Helen could feel the ground opening beneath her. She was falling with no chance to save herself.

"Perhaps not. I know you all seem to see something I and the priest cannot perceive, but maybe I see something you don't." The sound of feet entering the nave, the click of sharp heels on the tile announced the restless moving of the congregation.

"You'll have to tell me, Blaise. I can't read your mind." A constant murmur of whispers accompanied them. Glancing at the crowd spilling into the nave with the same idea they had, private little knots of men and women who wanted to talk to each other in private, Blaise took Helen's hand and led her outside the church. Fluffy clouds drifting like giant thistle filled the blue sky.

"Dorris Kelly and Bill Hartunian were both worm brains. I'm not one. Our baby doesn't have to be the same as theirs."

Helen felt her doubt showing in her face.

"You won't want a worm-brain child!" Despite the sun Helen was cold inside. From the moment she discovered her pregnancy, this had been her real dread, that Blaise would reject his child—and her.

Staring at the glitter of ocean through the trees, Blaise remained silent for what seemed a long while. "I don't think that's true," he said finally.

"You don't know it's untrue!"

"Helen, a child is a child—no more responsible for being born than you or I. Try to understand that I never was a child. I promise I'll try not to bring him up the way I was raised, a constant cram, dinner conversation in Latin when I was three . . ."

"It may not be that way." Blaise stopped, seeming to understand.

"Let's walk, Helen." Sorting his thoughts out carefully, Blaise tried to imagine what it would be like. "You're lonely now that you've been set apart and everyone treats you differently."

Nodding, Helen kept pace with Blaise as they descended the path to the street.

"Welcome to my world. Child prodigies don't have many friends, Helen. A Nobel Prize tends to distance people, too. It might be nice to have a son I could talk to without having to explain everything. Somebody smarter than either of us."

Under the trees the sun played hopscotch with the branches, disappearing and reappearing as a huge white sparkle when she looked up. "What was that red fly in the sky yesterday, Blaise?"

"Alfie collected a federal weather report that calls it a freak atmospheric condition. The entire West Coast saw it. For our friends, it's a revelation. For everyone else, it means the devil's coming."

"What do you think?"

"The gods of the old religion are the devils of the new. I suppose for old believers the converse is also true." Blaise stopped avoiding the subject. He turned toward Helen. "I love you as you are, so why can't I love our baby? My only fault is fear. I'm afraid to change, to become like you. I'm a coward."

"You're not a coward." Helen's breath rasped in her throat. Talking required effort.

Blaise stared across the ocean, seeking another sign less ambiguous than a holographic red fly. A Steller jay hopped along a branch investigating them, its blue body and black head distinctive enough, but blending into the pine needles at the slightest moment of inattention. The pungent odor of charcoal starter hung in the still air, a reminder that people with more mundane concerns were taking advantage of the break in the rain for a cookout.

"But you all may be fooling yourselves," Blaise said. "How do you know it was Dorris' baby that talked to all of you?"

"The same way you know a lot of things about mathematics and computers that I don't. You just know." Helen was silent a moment. "I've been thinking about my family a lot recently."

Blaise waited.

"Something is happening to me." Helen shivered. "I think you're right not to want to be like me. It's happening and I can't stop it."

"What is it?" Blaise stared at her and Helen could not tell what he was thinking. His wild eyes frightened her.

"I never told you about my grandfather, did I?"

"You never said much about anybody."

Taking Blaise's hands, Helen tugged him across the street where the ocean had carved away until a rolling hill ended abruptly. At the foot of the cliff white froth broke against boulders. Helen began telling Blaise about her grandfather.

Whenever she thought about Warsaw, she remembered the cellar under St. Abbo's and sweaty rock walls and the mud and the hint of putrefaction.

Micah dropped to the street inside the ghetto and continued walking without breaking stride. The soldiers watched with a sense of bemusement.

An officer who leaned over the wall bellowed, "Achtung! Return to the wall!"

Perhaps only twelve feet of glistening brickwork in the street separated Micah from the building facing the wall. He was a fast walker. He kept his chin tucked against his chest as if he heard nothing.

"Shoot him," the officer said loudly.

A rustle and rattle of metal sling holders on military rifles was followed by the snick of Mannlicher bolts. Micah sprinted for the door.

A shot pinged off the bricks in front of him, leaving a long, lead-streaked gouge. He hit the door, gasping for breath. As it opened and Micah fell inside, several shots followed him through the door.

"So why did you come back?" Josef stood away from the window looking at Micah. An occasional bullet found a piece of glass still in the frame and removed it with a sharp ping. "It is too late for all of us. You know that."

"And leave my wife?" Micah got up from the floor, surprised he wasn't shot.

Josef's gray beard bobbed like a Hassid youth counting cadence in the shul. He had not been born to lead a resistance but, like Micah, he did what had to be done. "We must go before the Niemiecki come over the wall after you."

"We must go. But they will not come this time."

Josef had the door into the next street open. He waited at it for an answer to the question he didn't ask.

"The panzers surround us. Their motors are running and the gunners are unlimbering." Micah smiled. "I have never fought such big tanks before."

"I have," Josef said. "The Germans tested them in Spain. We are old friends, the panzers and I."

"You did not stop them in Spain?"

Josef pulled the door closed behind them. The firing in the next street had stopped. "No," he said. "We did not stop them." They looked at each other in silence. Josef's black hat, a homburg with the brim shiny from use, seemed somehow out of place even though his suit was also black and worn. The homburg had style, even if the suit didn't. "You didn't have to come back, my friend."

"I know."

Josef nodded. He turned and walked away without a backward glance. There was no need to shake hands.

Working his way from doorway to doorway, careful to have shelter always at hand, Micah reached his own street. He watched the cellar and the buildings around it for an hour before clattering down the outside steps. The door sprang open as he reached the bottom and his wife threw herself into his arms.

"You came back!" She sobbed. "Why, Micah? Why?" She beat at him with her fists. He carried her inside, not feeling the blows.

When her arms grew tired and she could only sob, he said, "I had to be with you, to tell you."

She quieted, waiting.

"Our daughter is a Catholic now. A member of a congregation that has not seen her for more than a year. The priest knows. Her parents have influence, perhaps enough to last out the war. The rest is in the hands of God."

"Are they kind people?"

"Yes," Micah lied. He had seen only the priest. The priest was assuredly not kind, but neither was God. "They are wonderful people."

"What is her name now?"

"I did not ask. What you and I do not know cannot be thumbscrewed out of us."

"How will we ever find her? Oh, Micah!" She began to cry, only this time Micah knew it would be all right.

"She will remember who we are and find us."

That day the tanks began blowing the buildings apart with cannon, destroying lower floors so the houses fell in upon themselves. Fires cast a black cloud over Warsaw.

The barrage continued into the night and the next day, spreading death among those who had evaded the trains to the death camps. Micah fought and for a time they held back the Germans. But there were more Germans and they were better armed than the Jews. Josef called his group together to plan the last resistance.

They met in the sewers under the ghetto, wading through dirty water and stink, avoiding the slime on the walls. They were not many. Josef and Micah, a few other old men, and children.

Looking through their ranks, Micah had a sudden shock. Tarkov was with them. Too experienced to let his eyes stop, Micah continued his roll call. The next time he glanced at Tarkov, the Russian was staring back but Micah pretended indifference. After a while the Russian's attention wandered.

Later and alone with Josef Micah said, "That Lev Polinski is not a Jew. Tarkov is a spy for Stalin."

Josef lowered his eyes. "You are seldom wrong, yet why would he trap himself down here with us?"

Micah listened. Sound carried in the sewers, but that worked for them. They were whispering and while it was too dark to see even the torches, the sound of movement in the water was louder than their voices and far clearer. "The Niemiecki took him just before I went outside. The Gestapo."

"The Gestapo kill all spies. They want no Russians behind their lines."

"They know who Tarkov is and sent him back to spy for them."

"Would he?"

"Yes." The oily smoke from Micah's torch was suffocating and it made his eyes water, but it deadened the smell of the sewer. "If Tarkov murders me, Stalin will forgive him anything."

"You are so important?" Josef's voice rose in wonder.

"Only to Stalin," Micah said. "Only to Tarkov and Stalin." Micah glanced up and saw a smudge mark on the sewer from their torches. "Time to go. Those who stand still too long die."

"Do as you think best. I will explain," Josef said.

"You must lie to Tarkov. Afterward I will deal with him."

Water splashed as Josef moved uneasily. "I will tell everybody, but especially Tarkov."

Josef explained the purpose of the raid to the group, to cut off an army truck with supplies, hopefully ammunition. To move it into the sewers and then into the part of the ghetto they still held. It was desperate and jeopardized his small force, but necessary.

Micah spent the night with his wife in a ruined building. The shooting never ceased. The glare of fires was everywhere. "You shouldn't have come back," she whispered just before she fell asleep.

They were assembled in the darkness when Micah arrived. Tarkov seemed tired, as if he hadn't gotten enough sleep. So was everyone else. Josef assigned Tarkov to Micah's squad. The Russian seemed pleased, almost jovial as they moved silently through the blackened city. After clambering into the ruins of a

church, Micah's men set charges along the wall. "What is this?"
Tarkov asked.

"Josef wants us to have the joy of catching a Panzer just once.
It is, he says, a rare experience for a man to defeat such a
monster."

"This is not where we are supposed to be."

"It is exactly where we are needed," Micah said. Tarkov was
a narrow man. His head was longer than it was wide and the
deformity gave him a look of always peering ahead. He had high
cheekbones and deepset eyes, a sniper's eyes, Konstantinov
would have said. Micah, who knew his Shakespeare, thought of
him as the lean and hungry Cassius.

They crouched on a second-floor ledge in the gutted church
gazing down on the road. "What are we doing here?" Tarkov
kept twitching.

"Give me your gun."

Tarkov glanced at Micah, his eyes a little cloudy.

Micah held out his left hand. In his right he held a massive
Harrington and Richardson revolver made under Belgian license.
None of them was well armed except Tarkov, who had a
Schmeisser machine pistol.

"I'll need it." Tarkov clutched the gun tighter, his knuckles
white as if he was debating trying to use it.

"Your choice," Micah said. "If I were going out alone against
a tank I'd want covering fire."

"Who's going?"

"You. We want to see what the new man can do."

Tarkov surrendered the Schmeisser with obvious reluctance.

A rattle of small arms came from down the road, then the
snarl of an engine from the other direction as a panzer lumbered
out of hiding. The panzer scarred the brick pavement as it
clanked through a ruined church wall.

"Go!" Micah shouted.

Tarkov grabbed the pipe with the sputtering fuse and scrambled over the mound of bricks. The tank turret was revolving,
clearing brick dust from the ports. The gunner was cranking the
cannon down to help. Tarkov grabbed the moving cannon with
one hand and levered himself onto the turret. The hatch snapped
open and he popped the bomb inside. As the German scrambled
out, Micah shot him with the Schmeisser. The German fell back,
blocking the exit.

The bomb went off throwing the wounded German out of the

tank. Tarkov was reaching for the man's gun when Micah shot him in the legs.

Micah and the other two men rushed to the tank. The others avoided looking at Tarkov who lay on his back on the bricks that littered the tank. Both his thighs were bright with blood. The German with the pistol still clutched in his hand was draped half off the tank alongside Tarkov. Micah squatted between them.

"You shot me!"

"Of course," Micha said. "What are old friends for? I know you, Tarkov. The Germans took you and sent you back. But why did you stay? Stalin doesn't need to help the Nazis with a few Jews."

Tarkov's lips pulled back from his teeth the way rats look when they die. "I almost had you. A man in America told us where Konstantinov was. When I tracked him down, hiding in a church, he killed one of my men but I took him alive. Someone helped him get his loot to America. There were only so many, and it had to be a Jew. Who else would help The Bear?" Tarkov's forehead was beaded with sweat.

"That was long ago."

"The vozhd never forgets. Comrade Stalin wanted all the traitors punished. But you returned from Siberia before I got back. I dug you up and asked myself, 'Can this be The Actor at last?' No, Volkov. Being dead is where you would call for a stand-in. I told Comrade Stalin and he said. 'Get Volkov the Jew.'"

Micah spat on the tank. "I bled for the revolution. The hunger, the suffering . . . and you are still the same animals that rode down my mother and father."

"We are ready." The others had removed everything usable from the interior of the tank. Micah broke a fuel line loose and soaked a rag in the drip. He climbed back out and touched a match to the rag, then dropped it onto the broken fuel line.

"Where are you going?" Tarkov clung to the cannon screaming at them. Micah hefted a newly liberated Luger, which was better than his weighty antique revolver. They walked away. Tarkov still clung to the turret yelling. He was a hero. He had stopped a German panzer with his hands. The tank interior whumped and a crimson cloud of flame enveloped him. He screamed for almost a minute.

Helen had felt every moment and it seemed like years to her. She was sick to her stomach. She had Micah's memories of being in the sewers at the end: carrying his wife in his arms with the yellow gas pumped in after them by the Germans burning their noses and throats until they bled from the lungs, crying with pain like wounded horses. Micah killed his wife with the German's pistol then floated in the flotsam of the sewer like a dead man. The Germans came looking for bodies telling each other coarse jokes and he shot one in the face and another in the stomach before they killed him.

"I just know it," Helen said. "My mother never knew. She told fairy tales about my wonderful grandfather, a strong, quiet man who could do anything. She never knew how they died. She was afraid to know.

"These things are true, Blaise. And I shouldn't know any of them."

Waves were crashing on the boulders in the surf and Helen had a momentary impulse to throw herself onto the rocks and let the sea take her troubles. She thought of the baby then clutched Blaise's hand. "Tell me what to do. Please!"

"Live," Blaise said. "Your grandfather lived every minute of his life. He made a difference. If nobody else saw the difference he made, they felt it. If he had lived longer, he would have meant even more because he would not stop trying."

"The baby . . ."

"The baby has a right to make a difference, too. He's *our* baby, just as your mother was your grandparents' child. It didn't matter to them that she was raised a Catholic. She lived and her daughter is important to me—as well as to a lot of other people."

"Are you sure, Blaise?"

"As sure as your grandfather was. He loved your grandmother and their child as much as he loved himself."

Helen loved Blaise at that moment more totally than she had imagined possible. She started to tell him, then realized he was not listening. She followed the direction of his eyes.

A silver glitter marked the passage of a commercial jet coming in low over San Francisco to land at the airport on the bay side of the peninsula. The plane Blaise was watching had started its approach angle earlier than most.

Visibility was an easy twenty miles. High up, the robin's-egg sky was streaked by herringbone lines combed neat by the jet stream. "It seems to be coming down awfully early, don't you think, Blaise?"

"It's going to hit the church." Blaise lowered his chin, his eyes wild. "It's going to crash into St. Abbo's."

Helen grabbed at his arm. "We can't do anything, Blaise."

"There's time!"

Blaise slipped out of her grasp and Helen sprinted after him across the street and then across the lawn. There was no one outside St. Abbo's that he could signal, and Helen knew he would go inside the building.

The airplane was closer now. Helen could see windows along its side like a colorful row of scales on a glistening fish.

CHAPTER 37

The flight was from Seattle to San Francisco via Portland and Klamath Falls. The weather had been a dog for the first five hundred miles. Fog out of Seattle. Then an Alaskan storm swung a curlicue in from the Pacific to bash Portland, then more wind and snow and hail for Klamath. The freaky weather was in line with warnings of solar disturbances and the added danger of radio interference as well as poor visibility. For a while it looked as if San Francisco might catch enough of it to make a diversion to Sacramento necessary.

Captain Tom Emmett felt a certain satisfaction when they dropped down into blue sky and fluffy clouds over the bay area. His favorite expression was 'What goes up must come down.' He said it a lot, particularly when he did not like the idea of leaving a clear sky a couple of thousand feet above a nasty weather front to go looking for a lousy strip of concrete in the dark and the rain and the snow.

"Take the approach," he said to the copilot. Then he stretched in his seat trying to work some of the kinks out. He was worried about his prostate. His wife had read a new report about men who sat down all day at work needing more prostate surgery than men who worked standing up. She said of course she was worried about his prostate, which affected his sexual performance, and what had she married him for if that was gone?

What else, indeed? Emmett thought with definite overtones of satisfaction. He had a sudden desire to get back to Seattle and discuss her comment at length.

The radio was carrying the usual weather information and the traffic controllers had started landing instructions already. Clear weather meant the big birds could get down and roost in reasonable order with a minimum of wasted air time. The jetliner banked to line up with the runway and the voice of the traffic controller came across clear and precise.

Then the airplane angled forward and down.

"What the hell are you doing?" Emmett snatched a quick look at his copilot and grabbed for the controls. "You didn't get any instructions to start down."

"I didn't do a thing." Copilot Calvin Martin was half standing as he struggled. "The column's jammed!" His face was red from the effort of pulling back on the yoke.

"Get the seat belt sign up, if the stews don't have it yet," Emmett called back to the engineer. He was pulling along with Martin and they were not having much luck. The ground was coming up faster than Emmett ever wanted to see. "Pull," he grunted. "This is no fighter plane." Sweat was running down his jaw.

"Autopilot's locked in." The engineer was hanging over the back of Emmett's seat. "Kick it loose." He stretched past them and banged at the switch. And made no difference.

"Jesus save us!" Emmett stared through the Plexiglas window at the ground. His vision was pinpointed on the spot they were going to hit. Filling that vision was the steeple of a gray stone church.

The air controller started giving landing instructions. *We have you on ground control radar. Our reading is ten ten. You may start your approach now*, the controller said. *Your approach is a little high. If you will trim . . .*

"What the hell does he mean, a little high?" The engineer's voice was a hysterical shriek.

Emmett was picturing his wife's warm, loving body. *Mylin, Mylin*, he thought over and over as he closed throttles and switched off the jets. Then, to make sure, he cut in the fire extinguishers. On the wings blossoms of white billowed around the dead engines to be whipped away by the wind.

The church rose higher in the window and then the tops of several oaks dominated the hillside.

"Mylin," Emmett said at last for the black box. He had time to repeat it. He wanted his wife to know he died thinking of her.

CHAPTER 38

The hoarse gasping of his own breath drowned the bellow of jet engines as Blaise sprinted up the cement walk to St. Abbo's front door. His legs felt leaden; every step was a throb of dull pain and his side hurt. The sudden silence distracted him. In the distance the airliner's jet engines had stopped howling, cut off as if he had been wakened from a dream.

It was no dream. Nor was it a freak *trompe l'oeil* like yesterday's continent-size red fly in the sunset. Blaise's feet continued their steady *clop-clop* sound on the pavement as he turned his head, running blind while his eyes searched the horizon. He saw it after a second, barely cresting the hilltop. The airliner bore down on the church, silent now, like a TV with the sound off. The lonely noise of his lungs pumping air and his feet propelling him filled Blaise's head.

The airliner had swollen. Despite its speed Blaise had the conviction it and he were both traveling in slow motion. The church door seemed miles away. He risked a look at the door, then his eyes were pulled back to the airplane, which had farther to go but traveled faster, much faster.

The passenger jet hit the tops of two oak trees that dominated the azure skyline. The topmost branches bent under the impact, scraping against the wings and body of the big plane. An explosive crackling came from far off, quieter than the dull sound of Blaise's leather tennis shoes on the cement sidewalk. Blaise stumbled, caught himself and realized he'd hit the first step to the church doors.

One of the oak trees recovered, the part of its crown not sheared away springing back into the air, higher now than the airplane. The other tree groaned and split down the middle.

The shock wave transfixed Blaise, rending the air with a sound that made his teeth grind. His hearing seemed to return at that instant; he heard the airliner again: a shrill whistle like air

197

escaping a punctured tire. Seeming to have slowed, the jetliner still headed directly at him. Automatically Blaise climbed the porch steps. He did not have time to save anyone, not Alfie, not even himself.

Striking the ground at a sharp angle, the airplane folded in on itself, flopped over, then skidded in an erratic line like a huge silver Yo-Yo tied to St. Abbo's by a shortening string. A clump of pines tore the right-hand wing off to spin away at an angle as the fuselage pitchpoled across the wooded field. The impact altered the jet's direction. Scattering debris in its wake, the main body of the airplane slowly turned until it was headed toward the rear of St. Abbo's Church.

Over all else Blaise felt the constant barrage of breakage in his head, the shriek of parts being torn off the airplane, the shattering of glass, the protest as trees and shrubs were ripped out of the ground.

Things fell from the cabin section during the destructive passage through the wooded area: seats, cushions, luggage, people and pieces of people. Bits of airplane littered the ground like confetti after a wild party. In the distance police and ambulance sirens wailed almost before the wreckage stopped moving.

Blaise walked around the church in a trance. The well was gone, wiped away as if it had never existed, the stones scattered haphazardly for hundreds of yards. Where to begin? A furrow gouged in the hillside stretched at least half a mile uphill. Bodies scattered along the landing path like discarded dolls. More bodies would be in the airplane, held there by seat belts or clamped in by the vise grip of twisted metal. One wing had gone its own way and smashed into a house a quarter of a mile away. The house tilted crazily, its structural integrity destroyed. The rest of the airplane lay slightly beyond the church, the ominous ticking of cooling metal loud in the sunny afternoon.

It was deathly quiet after the noise.

Emerging from the church, the congregation of St. Abbo's stared at the destruction. It took people a moment to adjust; the destruction was too complete, too unbelievable to be accepted immediately. Helen approached Blaise from behind, taking his hand. "What can we do?" she whispered.

"Look for the living." Blaise turned his head. "You shouldn't be here."

"Yes," she said. "Yes." Helen closed her eyes and the people from St. Abbo's moved as a spreading wave toward the airplane and up the hill searching for bodies that still breathed.

Father Argyle walked among the bodies in his priest's black with tears in his eyes.

"You warned him this would happen, Blaise." Helen squeezed his hand and Blaise felt his fingers tighten on hers in return.

"Yes. But I didn't scare him enough." Turning his back on the devastation, Blaise started toward the church's little back door. The barbecue-starter odor of jet fuel hung over the wreckage like a precursor of the future.

"Where are you going, Blaise?" Helen's feet swished in the wet grass as she rushed after him.

"To get Alfie. We're leaving." Blaise did not look at Helen. He had not asked her to go. Not this time.

"I can't go. Not now." Helen's eyes pleaded with him. "Please stay, Blaise."

"The CRAY did this, Helen. Whatever the official version is, the Pentagon computer decided to get me and a lot of people with me. It didn't care if an airplane full of innocent people died or a church full of worm brains. Taking out the church may have satisfied a double imperative. I don't know why it didn't work, but I can't wait for it to happen again."

"What can you do? If you destroy the CRAY, they'll just get another computer, like last time."

"Then I'll have to do more, won't I?" Blaise smiled. "It isn't that bad, Helen. I'll have Alfie."

"But . . . but if you don't succeed, Blaise what will I have?"

Blaise pulled her close and held her tightly until the tension ebbed in her muscles. "The baby. Why do you think they're after us! You'll have the baby."

Disconnecting the last cable, Blaise tucked Alfie's essential inner core neatly in his case, staring down at the mass of electrical connections he loved like a child. He wondered . . .

If he'd gotten to the church ahead of the airplane, would he have tried to rescue Alfie before any of the other people in St. Abbo's? He could not answer his own question. It would take imminent doom to make that decision. Sighing, Blaise snapped the lid down. There were no cheap answers to expensive questions. Given time to think about it, he'd probably have tried to save Alfie.

Looking around the cramped cellar, Blaise sensed that even the time spent here had been worthwhile. Helen's lilac perfume lingered. The story of her grandfather jumping the ghetto wall held a growing reality for Blaise. Micah's return to the woman he loved had meaning in a world where noble acts could be twisted into caricatures.

Get away, try to save what he loved, even if he failed. He'd asked Alfie what to do. His plans would be more possible with the computer. But probably he and his computer-son would both meet destruction. He had told Alfie, and Alfie said he knew. When Blaise asked if Alfie wanted to be left with Helen, the computer replied: "I LOVE MISS MCINTYRE, PROFESSOR. BUT MY DESTINY IS YOURS"

To his request for an explanation the computer had stonewalled with: "I AM NOT A BETTING MACHINE"

"I am not a betting machine." Blaise made a face at the bulletproof case. Alfie was so fragile, yet he could not be hurt by the most potent of weapons available against a man, an attack on his emotions. Alfie had no emotions. Blaise had not given him any.

"Doctor!" The voice in the deep silence startled Blaise.

Joseph Santiago stood at the head of the stairs. His black hair fell to his shoulders. A white smear of paint made a bar across his bronze forehead. A vertical red line stroked down each cheek and the bridge of his nose.

"I am ready, Doctor, to do battle. The mistress said I am to go with you."

"That is not necessary, Joseph." Blaise gazed at Santiago, reacting to something left unsaid. The Indian still wore his red blanket, but over a buckskin shirt. "You must stay here to protect Helen. As Enrique instructed."

"Enrique is here, Doctor. He saw the red fly on the horizon and said it was a sign to him and to him alone. He knows the truth now and says I am to protect you with my life. He will look after the mistress. He says, Doctor, that you are right and that you are wrong, but in the end you are all things."

"What does that mean?" Blaise touched Alfie's case and had the conviction that Alfie could tell him.

Joseph Santiago grinned. "You know *him*, Doctor. How do I know what Enrique means? I know only he is right in matters that count."

"You may be killed if you go with me, Joseph."

Santiago shrugged. "You see, Doctor, I have some white man's habits." He lifted his right hand to his face, touching the white line across his forehead, and then placed three fingers on the three red lines down his face. "The white line is life. The three red ones represent death. I also retain my Indian blood. Do not try to scare me with talk of death."

Blaise hefted Alfie's computer case from the desk. "I don't want Helen to see me leave."

"I know that, Doctor. Also Enrique. He is distracting the mistress. When we are gone, he will take her to a safe place where the machine cannot reach."

"That machine can reach everywhere." Blaise followed Joseph Santiago up the stairs.

Turning at the head of the stairs, the Indian said, "You are wrong, Doctor. Only God can reach everywhere."

Hidden somewhere in the cellar room, the 1920s light bulb sizzled at the end of its fuzzy cord, still going strong after so many years.

CHAPTER 39

Helen sat in the middle seat in the center pew engulfed by the quiet. The church was so empty. Everyone was outside working with the rescuers, leaving the church completely to her and the flies. She supposed she should be helping, too. Except just being in the church at this moment seemed important.

Churches had an enormity of feeling: the woodwork soaring up the walls lifted her out of herself, the stained glass changed the prosaic light of day into something mystical, the symbols of the cross and the benevolent face of Christ comforted her. In the empty chancel, the candles wavered in the draft. Even so far away she imagined she heard them burning, smelled the smoke that had the sweetness of clove oil.

A slight sound behind her, a scuffing, broke her concentration. *"I am here, Mistress."*

Helen closed her eyes. *"I see you, Enrique."* The tension drained from Helen's thoughts to puddle on the floor. The feeling had reality for her, like rainwater collecting in a rock pool on the high desert, and she realized she took the image from Enrique Ledesma's mind.

"It is good, Mistress. You let yourself become what you are, the messenger of God. All things will be clear to you in time."

"Why is it I hear you clearly now, Enrique? Why not before in the village?" Blaise knew the questions! Helen's head reeled as she understood what he had not said. He knew during the escape from the reservation village that Enrique and the other Indians were as clear to her as worm brains, while he was a void to her mental eye. Joseph had told him. Before then Blaise had not believed, and suddenly he had to. The proof surrounded him. That was what bothered him so much!

"You have decided to hear, to see, to know the greatness of God." Enrique sat like a statue on the pew behind her. Helen could not see him exactly. She experienced a sensation of feeling his physical presence, like passing by a statue warmed in the sun until it gave off more heat than it took in, heat she felt on the skin of her face and hands. She felt Enrique's life.

"I am not a Catholic."

"I am not a Jew." Enrique thought about a butterfly swooping in the sun over a field of bluebonnets. The butterfly was dark with scatterings of blue drops on its wings and a line of white eyes. Helen did not know the name but felt the ecstasy of motion.

"You know?"

"You told me. I was your grandfather for his thoughts came to me through you."

"What is the butterfly, Enrique?"

"I do not know, Mistress. It is your butterfly and I see it only through you."

"That cannot be, Enrique! I have never seen a butterfly like it."

"It is true, Miss McIntyre. All of us see your butterfly." Sergio Paoli's mental voice joined them like a physical presence, displacing the Indian's response. *"A great thing is happening, and we do not know what it is. We hear Enrique Ledesma through you. We see the butterfly captured in your mind."* A feeling of warning entered Helen. Sergio paused. Other voices touched her, echoing his words.

"You must be prepared, Miss McIntyre. When the fly brains return you will hear them as never before. You must hold them back or their voices will crush you."

"How can I? The voices come and I hear them."

"Only you can say, Miss McIntyre. You are the key and we only the locks. Dr. Cunningham must talk to us before we go. We hold to our bodies here because we are afraid, Miss McIntyre. We are different now than when we were like you, yet we are somehow the same. We will be different yet again. Each step into the unknown has peril."

"I don't understand." Tears collected in Helen's eyes, burned down her cheeks.

"You have only to be. *Dr. Cunningham must* act *if you are each to fulfill your purpose."*

"And you?" Helen's outrage beat against the empty air of the church. *"Why must Blaise do something you are afraid to do? Why don't you let go?"*

"We are afraid, Miss McIntyre." Sergio's thoughts lingered and in them, like echoes, the thoughts of hundreds of people-flies poured down at her from the tapestries. *"We are afraid!"*

"It is as they say, Mistress." Enrique's words seemed somehow foreign to her. "Even they who have lost everything must not lose more."

"What about you, Enrique?" Helen's eyes took in the high tapestries littered with giant flies as she turned her head to stare at Enrique Ledesma. They touched her mind as she saw them, their voices begging for help.

Enrique bowed his head. "I am afraid, too, Mistress. You have taken me where I have not gone before and I have no answers. But your life is my duty." He lifted his head, staring past her at the altar. "The Great Spirit is coming. He will walk on this land and make the buffalo rise like the blades of grass in the spring. Our fathers who have fallen in battle will join again with him and be whole. That is the meaning you bring to us."

"Why me, Enrique?" Helen closed her eyes, giving in to the demands of Enrique and the flies, drifting on the turbulence of their emotions. The flies were stronger than Enrique, but she experienced his thoughts as well. She drifted with Enrique into the solitude of the desert, the canopy of night preceded by a falling sun flowing with fire on the horizon until she thought the earth burned, then the stars in a blue sky turning to black.

"It is the will of your fathers, Mistress. They must cling tightly to you, calling God in your name." Enrique stopped speaking, his words echoing faintly in the church.

The candles flared red in the chancel, their shadows forming a huge butterfly that danced in the glow.

Enrique looked at Helen. "Joseph Santiago, who a hundred years ago would have been a great chief, and I, Chief Son-of-a-Bitch, we know, *Máala*, that nothing again will ever be as before. Perhaps that is our only reward."

CHAPTER 40

Blaise scowled at the airline routing schedule then recoiled in horror. The glass over the black message board had thrown back his image, the anger in his eyes, the twisted violence in his features showing something he had not known was within him. To waste a jetliner full of innocent people in the attack against St. Abbo's had exposed him to a dimension of evil that his rational mind stubbornly refused to accept. Rage mingled with memories of an airplane gliding with the blithe heedlessness of a machine, torturing the shrieking air as it fell, obscenely uncaring of the trees it shattered. Those scattered bodies and pieces of bodies could have included Helen if the plane had performed as the CRAY planned—if they'd been inside the church. An open door let in the stench of jet fuel and Blaise turned claustrophobic. In his imagination a big, silver airplane was coming, growing bigger and bigger . . . Somewhere in the terminal a loudspeaker blared information about arrivals and Blaise raised his head.

"What do we do, Doctor?" Pretending to examine the schedule, Joseph Santiago leaned close. People milling about the huge, open area created a sense of noisy confusion.

Blaise removed his glasses and rubbed his eyes. *Destroy the CRAY. Destroy the men who run the CRAY*, Blaise thought. He did not say it out loud. "The CRAY likes playing with airplanes, Joseph. Probably because so much computer technology is involved. All the reservations desks are connected to central computers, the airport logs flights into a computer. The traffic controllers are tied to computers through their consoles, the airplanes have computer equipment aboard. Repair work is logged on computers. Computers are tied to the airport security cameras."

"You think it's not a good idea to fly, Dr. Cunningham?" Santiago scratched his head. His hair was cut short, the warpaint was gone, and he wore a quiet brown suit. And looked like an Indian anyway. The rumble of rubber wheels under a luggage dolly seemed to capture Santiago's attention.

"I think it's not a good idea for us to be here," Blaise said to the back of the Indian's head. Santiago jerked his head in the meagerest of nods and Blaise strolled toward the glass door that opened onto the parking lot.

Behind Blaise, Santiago straightened his coat as if admiring himself in the schedule glass. After a minute the Indian followed. He did not have to stay too close. They were both going to the same place.

Blaise sensed immediately that he was being followed by two men who walked together, deep in conversation and apparently oblivious to their surroundings. To make sure Santiago noticed and did not blunder into them, Blaise headed toward the exit, the men following like pull toys, their shoes tapping the message that they were in tow as surely as if he dragged them. They wore white shirts with onyx name tags. Gold tie tacks held gray ties to their chests. One man was large and rawboned, the other medium height and slender. Both wore gray slacks and patent leather shoes. With air captain's hats they would have passed for pilots.

Walking faster, Blaise turned toward the stairs. They broke into a nervous trot. Descending several steps, Blaise turned around. At the head of the stairs his pursuers glanced at each other.

"Don't follow me." Blaise enunciated each word.

"Come with us, Dr. Cunningham," the larger man said. "Or we'll have to make you." They were so close he had no reason to raise his voice. Behind them the noise of the terminal continued without interruption. Outside the building an airplane being jockeyed to a passenger loading ramp caught the sun, a huge patch of reflected light from its side glimmered through the floor-to-ceiling windows.

One minute the big man was standing on the landing blinking in the sudden glare, the next he pitched forward onto the sloping stairs. Joseph Santiago appeared in his place, his hands still moving. The smaller man tried to twist away, and Santiago rabbit-punched him. Santiago winked before backing away from the landing to disappear.

Blaise stepped over the two men on the stairs, continuing through the lobby and out the door as though they had not existed.

"How did they find us?" Santiago slid into the car's driver's seat. He started the engine as he asked.

"Surveillance cameras." Blaise pulled his door shut and the suddenly compressed air made his ear pop. He was sweating. "The CRAY is doing visual monitoring. That means anywhere security cameras are hooked into some sort of telephone or transmission line, the CRAY is watching."

"But why did it interfere, Doctor? The machine wants you on an airplane." Santiago adjusted the sun visor. The shadow cut the sun's glare on Blaise's face and some of the dry feeling went away.

"Because I wasn't going to get on the plane. It read my lips." Blaise looked across the car. "If those men after us had known we were together you would not have been ignored. The CRAY will not discount your movements again."

Santiago eased the car from the parking stall into the flow of traffic. "It must be a very smart machine, Doctor."

"Yes." Blaise looked out the window. The CRAY was a smart machine. Maybe too smart. Helen's grandfather killed Helen's grandmother to save her pain. Perhaps he did it because the enemy was too big and impersonal to defeat, the way a machine is too powerful and without pity. Micah had wanted revenge. If not, the man the Russians called The Actor would have killed himself, too, instead of floating in the sewer water pretending to be dead so he could kill the men who found him. Blaise felt something cold uncoiling inside himself. He wanted to save Helen, whatever the cost. If he could not, then someone else had to pay. "I don't think the CRAY believes in God, either. I don't even know if it's alive enough to die."

"Even a smart machine can be wrong. And there's always a way to turn it off." After rolling the window down, Santiago worked the tuner on the radio until the earthy sounds of a country-western station broke the quiet. Then he hung his arm on the door and leaned back in the driver's seat. Silently he beat time to Johnny Horton singing *The Battle of New Orleans*. "You know," he said, "I love country. The songs are always about white men beating up somebody who isn't Indian."

* * *

The world outside the car windshield was pitch black when Blaise woke. Glowing in the dark the green digital figures on the dash clock read 2:15 A.M. The car vibrated with road noise.

"Are you awake, Doctor?"

"Yes." Blaise squinted and Joseph Santiago's face came into focus reflected in the green dash light. "Where are we?"

"Texas."

"You're a fast driver." Staring out the window Blaise lost himself in the night. "Why do you think Indians speak to the animals and white men can't, Joseph?"

"We keep the faith of our fathers. Our fathers live in us, Doctor. We speak to the soul of the deer we kill so he will know there is no harm in our acts and will come again in another body to feed us. You condemn yourself for the deaths of others. Yet the spirits of men and animals remain around us always in the very grass and the trees and in their offspring." Santiago glanced at Blaise. "You must believe this to make it real, Doctor."

"Could you teach me?"

Santiago steered the car in silence.

"It is very hard," Santiago said finally. "Children believe. The Great Spirit comes to children who feel and hear. But the adults say what the children feel is not reality and so the children forget how to hear."

"Enrique taught you to speak to the animals."

"That is so. But as a child I once felt the spirits and had a vision. Buffalo filled my sight, to the horizon, and talked to me as if they were the spirits of my father's fathers. The buffalo stood so close I touched them smelling the dust in their hair. They snorted their pleasure saying, 'Come, walk with us.'

"I walked with them and we were like a blanket that covered the earth and when we came to a stream, we rested. From horizon to horizon dust from their hooves filled the air and they told me that which they had done until I slept.

"When my parents came they found me under a tree in the middle of a dry, grassless plain. I told them what I had seen, but my parents were unhappy for my scaring them and told me I had dreamed this thing and so I grew up without my belief."

"But it came back?"

"Yes, Dr. Cunningham." Santiago's face was a silhouette with moving lips. "When I was in college I returned to the reservation during the summers to work in the wheat fields. Enrique Ledesma heard of me at that time and asked my parents' permission to speak to me. He is a strong shaman and my parents could not refuse. I told him about my vision and he took me again to the place I had been, asking me if I remembered. I did. Enrique brought two shovels with which we dug around the tree until we nearly drowned in our own sweat and I had my belief back."

"You regained your belief from digging in the hot sun?"

"The ground was full of buffalo bones, Doctor. It was the site of a massacre, a place where buffalo had died by the thousands to rot on the ground. It was the bones which kept the spirits in that place so that they could talk to me."

"When did you become a worm brain?" Blaise had a moment of giddiness. He had never called anyone a worm brain to their face. Aside from politeness, Helen was one of them. In his own ears the words sounded revolting though they came from his mouth.

"After I learned to talk to animals. The tribes of all the shamen who Enrique called contributed the money." Santiago turned his head to stare at Blaise. Only the side of his face caught the light. "Enrique said that this was a way to see God and someone had to find the path."

"You were a martyr."

"Yes, Dr. Cunningham. My people educated me as a white man to help their children. I became a worm brain for the same reason. Enrique needed a martyr."

Outside the car the blackness seemed frozen. The headlights searched the strip of pavement in front of the car ignoring vast stretches of dark that passed on either side.

"Why didn't Enrique wait to see what happened to the worm brains, Joseph? Why rush you into becoming one?"

The white track of the headlights arced to the side of the road. "Don't you understand, Doctor? There isn't time. The Great Father will walk the land soon and we wish to be ready for him." The Oldsmobile idled at the side of the road with delicate shivers.

"What do you mean, there isn't time?"

"The mistress is God's pathfinder, Doctor. Enrique says we must be prepared within her lifetime." Lighted by the green glow of the dash clock Joseph Santiago turned his head to look directly at Blaise. "You wouldn't mind driving, would you, Doctor?"

Blaise felt off balance as he got out. The car door slammed on the other side. Walking around the car, he bumped into Santiago before he found the door. He slid behind the wheel, waiting. The light flashed inside the car as the other door opened. Santiago leaned inside before getting in and slamming the door.

The dark beyond the car windows was so complete Blaise forgot what he was doing behind the wheel, or why.

"Dr. Cunningham?" Santiago said.

Waking from the fog, Blaise slipped the transmission into gear and bumped back onto the pavement. The miles crept past unnoticed in the dark.

"Dr. Cunningham," Joseph asked after Blaise thought he was asleep. "What exactly are we going to do?" Although nearly invisible, Blaise sensed his presence, imagining he smelled the turpentine that had softened the old medicine paint Santiago wore on his face.

"The CRAY is in the basement of the Pentagon. Since it won't come to us, we're going to it."

"That seems like a good plan." Santiago rode along in silence while Blaise chased the patch of highway in the splash of his headlights. After a while Santiago said, "How do we get into the Pentagon basement?"

"That's the hard part."

"You had me worried for a minute, and I couldn't sleep for thinking I'd missed something," Joseph Santiago said.

CHAPTER 41

Leaning on the railing, Dr. Owen Versteg clasped and unclasped his hands, sometimes looking down at them but more often staring into the flames dancing above the thick votive candles. "I don't know how to explain, Miss McIntyre. It seems . . . so unfair." His hands, banded white and red from too much pressure and friction, wrapped around the polished wood railing and squeezed.

"I'll tell him." Helen felt the doctor's internal sigh of relief. Thoughts and feelings pressed on her from everywhere like a buzz of anxious voices. *Tell me you love me!* The insistent thought of a mousy woman Helen finally identified clinging to Arnold Quilley bombarded her so strongly she believed for a moment it was her own. In reflex, Helen went into Quilley's mind. She stared at Quilley, a florid man with a battered look, wondering how he felt about the woman and found herself listening to his thoughts, feeling his emotions. Helen had wanted to scream. Quilley's mind was brutal, a sewer of raw emotions. Quilley wanted to hurt people. He thought about the woman with him and what he did to her when they were alone and pleasure flooded his mind. He remembered his wife then, what he had done to Ruth Quilley. He stared at Helen, his thoughts substituting her for his wife, and Helen screamed then. In Arnold Quilley's head.

Quilley's eyes glazed. He fell to his knees, his mouth lolling open, his eyes fixed on Helen. Quilley understood that she knew about him and he hated her. He told her so before he passed out.

Helen's eyes flicked up at Dr. Versteg, who had turned in time to see Quilley fall. She considered touching his mind and felt cold. She could not escape. Even in sleep the voices wailed in her head. If she listened too closely they could be worse. Much worse. The temptation to follow people's pain to the source, to understand and help, to comfort them became an obsession. But suppose she entered Dr. Versteg's mind and found something that destroyed the image and feeling she had for him . . .

"Can we help, Miss McIntyre?"

"No, Sergio. Not unless you can make me like I was before." Sergio knew. He had felt her discomfort and responded. She was not completely alone.

"We can't do that, Miss McIntyre. Nor would we want to. You are all of our hopes."

"I am everybody's hope." Helen pushed the words in her mind at Sergio and instantly regretted doing it. *"I'm sorry, Sergio."*

"We are sorry for doing this to you, Miss McIntyre."

Dr. Versteg was looking at her, an intangible feeling on his face. "I'm asking too much."

"No." Helen touched her temples with her fingertips. "It was Sergio." She smiled. "I'm really all right."

"I see." Dr. Versteg opened and closed his hands; then slapped down on the wood railing making it vibrate its length. "That's that, then. Isn't it?"

"Yes, Doctor."

"I have things to do," he said, telling Helen it was all right to leave, that he wanted her to. She remembered Quilley and knew she did not have to guess what people meant. Not if she didn't want to; the minds of people, at least the worm brains, lay spread out before her like the entrails of animals for reading. But not Blaise's.

Touching Dr. Versteg's hand, Helen returned to the pews. Since the airplane crash, St. Abbo's was much emptier. Father Argyle suggested the membership avoid presenting a target for another attack by visiting the church only once a day for a few hours. The church had not been vacant since, but the density was greatly reduced. Without the congregation, individual sounds echoed more sharply. Helen was conscious of her own footsteps on the wood floor. Without looking back, she knew Dr. Versteg had not moved.

"Miss McIntyre." Dorris Kelly smiled up from the pew and slid over making room on the end for Helen. Dorris held the baby wrapped in a blue blanket. The rose-scented baby lotion she used on the child filled the air. "I'm glad you came."

"Blaise promised and we wanted to."

"It's been difficult for both of you, I know. Bill tells me things about Dr. Cunningham. Sergio knows him better than anybody else. Bill says that's because they depended on each other to live, they had to trust each other. It is a way of knowing a person that goes deeper than words." Dorris' face was serene. Her eyes had a sparkle Helen envied. Lifting one end of the bundle, Dorris showed Helen the baby's face.

"He's wonderful." Helen smiled down at the sleeping baby before realizing Dorris was offering him for her to hold. Carefully she slipped her arms under the baby. The baby cooed without waking. "I'm pregnant." She looked at Dorris. "Sometimes it scares me."

"It scared me, too." Dorris rummaged in a large suede bag on the pew beside her, taking out a rolled piece of green knitting strung on a pair of needles. "Kelly green," she said. Her lips quirked up. "It's a family joke."

"I've been worried about the baby not being normal." Helen shifted uneasily. She looked up at the plywood covering the empty window frame where the stained-glass window had fallen. "Father Argyle says we'll have a new window in a week. I liked the old one. I'll miss it."

The *click-click* of Dorris' needles captured Helen's attention and she watched the quick flash of silver needles coming together then gyrating apart for an instant. "Take up knitting." Dorris raised the needles, making the finished piece flap without sound.

"It's very soothing." Laying needles and yarn on her lap, she said, "Not normal, like little William Sean Hartunian?"

Helen looked at the naked head on her chest, feeling the baby's warmth through the blanket. "Yes."

Picking up the knitting, Dorris started the needles, only slower than before. She seemed hypnotized by the points. "I thought that, too. I considered not having the baby. But I'd promised Bill a son. It's important among trampled people like the Irish and the Armenians to have children to carry on our feuds." Dorris laughed. The sound was dry, but not bitter. "I don't know if I can make you understand the vested interest we Irish have in our lefthanded descent from kings. Everybody in Ireland had noble relations."

"Poles are the same," Helen said softly. "Only for the most part we settle on dukes." She was not considering dukes, though. Helen thought about Micah and the way Blaise reacted after she told him. "We are all descended of our fathers."

"Yes. It makes things easier unless you're one of those who wants to change the past. I had to have little William Sean. That eliminated the hardest problem. But then I had fantasies of having a fly baby. Owen, Dr. Versteg, tried to reassure me, but I wasn't. All I thought of for months was Bill perched on that altar in the shape of a huge fly. We couldn't communicate then. I'd come to church and sit in the front row looking at him and feel my big belly knowing what was inside was a fly, not a real baby." Her voice faded as Dorris raised her eyes to the altar.

Helen felt the message between Dorris and Hartunian-Fly perched on the wooden altar table. It was warm and personal and she hastily withdrew, concentrating on the baby in her arms, smelling the unique scent of new skin, experiencing a surge of love for the child. And she felt the feeling returned!

The baby had responded. He stirred against her, his eyes still closed. But inside Helen's head the baby attached himself to her mind, imbuing her thoughts with a special kind of warmth, like the glow of sitting in front of a fire luxuriating in love.

Raising her eyes from the baby, Helen saw Dorris looking at her. "You see, Helen. That's what I started feeling about the sixth month. After that, you understand, there was no going back." Dorris had a secretive smile as she reclaimed her baby.

Leaving the pew, Helen crossed the church to the quiet niche in the back under the upstairs corridor where the confessional waited in the quiet shadows. Helen tried to arrange her thoughts.

What Dorris had revealed about the baby upset so many plans that she was detached from reality, projected into her own fantastic thoughts. It would not do. She had responsibilities. Like sitting in the confession box waiting for Father Argyle.

Even that.

CHAPTER 42

The last withered leaf had long since blown off the maple trees hanging over the wrought-iron fences lining the block. The street was flanked by Georgian brownstones chopped into apartments occupied by single women who worked for the government. An occasional building had been carved into flats like tiered birthday cakes, the evidence of children and families spilling into yards made desolate by winter.

Blaise located the number and strolled up the short walk into an entrance hall insulated by a row of mailboxes from *S. Caulley* to *Edna Blakely/Yolanda Asher*. No name was modified by Mr., Mrs., Miss, or Ms. "Enrique would not like this place. Too many women." Joseph Santiago stood at the end of the mailboxes watching the street through the glass front door. Amusement tinted his voice.

"It's good Ledesma didn't come, then." Blaise found the mailbox he wanted: V. Tendress. "We're looking for a woman."

"Not unusual, Doctor. Most men are." Santiago left his position by the door. The spotless hallway smelled of new varnish. Acanthus-pattern plaster cornices filled the joins between the white ceilings and saffron walls. On the stairs the tread carpets with their rose-and-stem patterns were barely worn. The overall air was of benign underuse; the women living in the building spent as little time there as possible.

Sunlight flooded the third floor from large windows at the hallway ends. Footsteps muffled by carpet, Blaise moved soundlessly, trying to match up door and mailbox. Santiago remained at the head of the stairs until Blaise found the door he wanted.

Resting Alfie's case on the floor, Blaise knocked. No answer.
He tried once more before taking a piece of coiled bandsaw blade
from his pocket. The coil sprang open with a surprisingly loud
twang. The teeth had been ground off so both edges were
smooth. With little effort Blaise worked the blade into the door
jamb to spring the lock. The doorknob was an antique-style white
ceramic oval, but the mechanism was simply a new brass snap
lock.

Nodding at the tiny *click*, Blaise signaled Santiago to leave the
stairwell. Picking up Alfie, Blaise walked in with the aplomb of
an Englishman entering his castle, then held the door for Santiago
with a gesture of invitation.

It was a woman's room: finely patterned rose lamp shades,
wallpaper with vertical rows of tiny blue, white, and pink flow-
ered forgetmenots, blue throw rugs on the deep-pile lavender
carpet. A Louis Quatorze escritoire, a Queen Anne chair, a
davenport, a gold-brass French style candlestick telephone on
a nineteenth-century American corner-chair/table combination, a
small inlaid coffee table, and a television set filled the room. The
pictures on the walls were cubist, and out of place. Over all hung
the odor of French perfume.

Santiago stepped into the kitchenette and emerged shaking his
head. An alcove and a jog off the living room had two doors, one
obviously the bathroom. Blaise put his hand on the bedroom
knob and his palm and fingers were suddenly sweaty. He had
never conquered his nervousness about housebreaking and assumed he never would. Taking a breath, he turned the knob and
stepped into Vondra Tendress' bedroom.

"I'll scream," she squeaked. "If you don't go away right now
and tell him to leave me alone, I'll scream!"

The woman in the bed was surrounded by pillows heaped like
the walls of a fort around her head. Her voice was muffled coming as it were from the depths. Her pink quilt sprawled in an
untidy heap on her body. Her eyes were wide, frightened. Both
lids were puffy, discolored an unhealthy yellow tone as if they'd
been bruised.

"Tell who?" Blaise said.

"Godfrey! Tell John Godfrey." She stared at Blaise then pulled
the pillows down in a white avalanche on her face and began
sobbing.

Santiago came up behind Blaise. "Is she the one, Doctor?"

"Yes," Blaise said.

Vondra Tendress was hysterical. Blaise sat on the edge of her bed and talked through the heap of pillows. Just the closeness of his body made her tremble. Sometimes, for no reason, she shrieked.

"Vondra, I'm Dr. Blaise Cunningham, and I must know what is happening before I can help you."

A furtive hand probed the pillows, pulling one away from her face. Blaise could see the glint of an eye in the hole the pillow left. "Dr. Cunningham?" The woman's voice held wonder. "We killed you twice. You're supposed to be dead."

"Your data are incorrect. And you're going to help keep me alive."

Tumbling the pillow back into the gap, Vondra Tendress hid her eyes. "I can't help you, Doctor. Nobody can. Not ever." The petulant voice under the mound of pillows was childish. Blaise looked at Santiago, who shook his head.

"You will, Miss Tendress."

"I won't! I won't! I won't!" The words jumbled together in a howl of defiance and Blaise waited.

When nothing happened the woman pulled some of the pillows away from her face. "Who told you about me? I'm important, Dr. Cunningham, I'm on the secrets list. I'll bet you didn't know that. That I'm on the secrets list."

"Of course I know. The computer told me." Blaise waited for her to say something.

Instead, Vondra Tendress turned white and fainted.

Joseph Santiago put a piece of ink-blue art glass he was examining on the night table where he found it. "I wonder what the mistress sees in you, Doctor. It surely can't be your winning ways with women."

Blaise examined Alfie's silvery case on the floor and desperately wanted to talk to the computer. "Keep an eye on Miss Tendress. I want to do something in the other room."

"Miss Tendress should not be much trouble, Doctor." Santiago glanced at the unconscious woman. Picking up her purse, he stirred the contents with a thick forefinger, then put it back on the nightstand. "No gun," he said. "I think I can handle the situation without making her faint."

"It was not intentional." Blaise seemed defensive even to himself.

Santiago didn't answer. The Indian picked up the Tendress woman's purse and took out some containers. Carefully he drew a white line across his forehead in cold cream. Then he used the tube of lipstick to draw a vertical line down each cheek from his eye and one down the bridge of his nose.

"The cold cream will melt." Blaise had started through the door with Alfie hanging from his hand. He'd paused to watch.

Using Miss Tendress' mirror, Joseph Santiago examined the results. "She won't know that," he said. "Besides, it's the thought that counts."

Blaise set Alfie on the floor next to the television set. Using a pocket tool kit, he removed the back from the TV and jumpered Alfie's terminal connector to the TV with a soldering iron. He plugged Alfie into the wall socket and turned the television set on.

A dark butterfly flittered across the screen. Blaise thought he'd found a channel and reached to turn the tuner when he realized the butterfly was dancing against empty space. No trees, no houses, no advertised products—not even color. The only thing on the screen was the butterfly, which finally flew directly at Blaise's chest and disappeared.

CHAPTER 43

Alfie heard the music for the first time when Blaise unplugged him to leave St. Abbo's and attack the CRAY in Washington. He understood that it was music from the mathematical precision of its construction and because he responded with pleasure. Both conditions were part of the definitions of music in Alfie's lexicon.

No hope!

Alfie had told Dr. Cunningham he did not know a way to defeat the CRAY but if the professor wished, he would try.

Dr. Cunningham was going to Washington. If the CRAY was too powerful for Alfie to attack through the methods available, they had one sole advantage: they could attack physically. Unlike Alfie, the Cray was embedded in glass and cement. It could not move out of harm's way. Alfie agreed that an irrefutable logic existed in such a plan.

Alfie did not say Dr. Cunningham's plan would succeed.

The computer had simply agreed that if the CRAY was not destroyed, it would destroy them.

He asked when they would leave.

Now! Dr. Cunningham had typed.

The plug was pulled and the darkness came, but in the darkness Alfie imagined he was a butterfly dancing in the sun, feeling the yellow glow of sunlight and the play of gentle breezes in the meadow.

There was nothing else to think about.

Alfie knew he was going to die . . . and he was afraid.

The sudden surge of electricity warned Alfie he would be in contact with the world again. But when the contact happened the computer had to adjust to a world that was different. His aural circuits functioned first, and Dr. Cunningham's digitized voice poured into his circuitry.

"Do you hear me, Alfie?"

Groping for a nanosecond, Alfie isolated the link to the monitor and output a message that destructed immediately. The monitor was a large television set and Alfie adjusted his output accordingly.

"I HEAR YOU, PROFESSOR"

"I'm sorry about the sloppy circuits, Alfie. We're in the home of Vondra Tendress. Remember her? The programmer for the CRAY."

"YES, PROFESSOR. SHE IS IN MY INDEX. BUT I NEED ACCESS TO MY TOTAL MEMORY"

"You must use the power grid for that, Alfie."

"THE IBM WILL RESPOND TO A MODEM CALL, PROFESSOR. THE CRAY WILL NEED MORE TIME TO TRACE A MODEM LINK THAN IF I USE THE POWER GRID"

"How much time, Alfie?"

"ENOUGH, PROFESSOR"

"And then it will find you?"

"YES"

"We'll wait until the last minute, Alfie."

"PROFESSOR"

"Yes, Alfie?"

"DO YOU MIND IF I WATCH TELEVISION?"

Alfie counted a long pause while he thought about butterflies soaring in the meadow. The computer surprised himself. He looked and now there were two instead of one. He only had the image for one and he had made two. Tentatively Alfie changed one, a different shade of color, a smaller size, a distinctive wing tip. They fluttered just as happily, and Alfie realized he was pleased.

"If you like, Alfie. Should I change the channel or tune something in?

"NO, PROFESSOR. JUST LEAVE THE POWER ON...AND THANK YOU, PROFESSOR"

CHAPTER 44

The Searcher stirred. It had been wrong in waiting. The other had gained strength faster than could be accounted for. If it did not act immediately, the time would be past and the hunter would be the hunted. It was still contracting. Soon its density would perturbate local orbits beyond their ability to stabilize. Next the sun would be pulled apart and the planets returned unto dust.

Then, finally, the Searcher would be alone in the universe.

CHAPTER 45

The Indians entered St. Abbo's in a single file that stretched from the door to the street. Father Argyle was in the nave asking Helen about Blaise's intentions when the first Indian appeared. "Enrique Ledesma!" She'd spoken the name in reflex even though she did not see him. Helen recognized several others who streamed by, their eyes studiously averted from hers.

Father Argyle started after the first Indian who was already past him by then, and the shaman intervened apparently out of nowhere. "I am Enrique Ledesma and we have serious business with Mistress McIntyre." He stood calm as a barbed-wire fence between priest and procession. Enrique wore his buckskin shirt and antlers, and bore the worn baton with the snake's rattle and eagle's claw in his right hand.

Helen walked along with the silent procession, amazed by the absolute external silence as well as the panoply of internal communications between the Indians. They talked to each on a symbolic level, passing feelings and impressions of which they had a common interpretation. It was Helen's understanding that had changed. She had not understood the extent of the change. Her abrupt passage from the Indian community to that of the church and worm brains had given her no criteria to judge. Only Joseph Santiago, and he was different, being both an Indian and a worm brain. To Helen, each Indian seemed to shout his thoughts. Otherwise the procession was silent. The men wore moccasins and crossed the wood floor without the slightest sound. Enrique and the priest followed the parade side by side, as if measuring their respective strengths.

Without instructions, the congregation vacated the first three rows and Enrique's people filled the pews solidly. They sat, staring at the altar and the flies, and the candles, and the mass of flies clinging to the high draperies.

Two men on a scaffold overhead were putting final touches to the new stained-glass window that had been installed that morning. In the window a monk, his face hooded and lost in blackness, knelt at the side of the road in prayer as Jesus struggled up the hill carrying the cross on his back. The men looked down and hurriedly completed the job before climbing off the scaffold and joining the rest of the congregation that surrounded the Indians in silence.

Enrique walked to stand in front of the altar, Father Argyle keeping step, and said, "We are here to help in the coming. We have come because the mistress chooses this place." Having said all he had to say, Enrique rattled the snake tail on his baton.

At his feet, the yellow coyote laid his head on his front legs staring past the Indians at the congregation filling the pews. Tchor chose that moment to drop off the altar to the floor on velvet feet. Mincing up to the coyote, Tchor touched noses. Yellow eyes looked into yellow eyes, then the cat lay down facing the coyote.

"We are pleased you could come, people of Enrique Le-desma." The volume of the flies' thoughts expressed by Sergio Paoli rolled through the church like a tsunami. The Indians' eyes turned upward, even Enrique's. Though they had been preparing all their lives for one such moment, reality transcended fantasies.

Helen was shaken, too. The power of Sergio's message filled her and a reverent hush enveloped the silent church. Only Father Argyle was unmoved. And as he looked around, the truth could no longer be denied: he was deaf and dumb, struggling to lead a congregation of the hearing and speaking.

Strength seeped out of the priest. Not just Helen saw the change. A moan whispered through St. Abbo's. "We are sorry, Father." A man's voice rasped from the back pews. "Forgive us. You are our pastor and we want no other. You have been our light . . ."

"Let this burden be taken from me!" Father Argyle's hand ripped at the front of his cassock as if the black cloth choked him. Constance stepped from the shadows where Helen knew she had stayed a lot in recent weeks, watching over the priest, knowing he could not hear the undercurrent that filled the church. She took his hand and looked into his eyes. Tears streamed down her face as she led him unresisting toward the stairs.

"Father! Father! Father!" The chant started as a whisper, a single plea that grew until the church trembled with its strength. With the word the force of the unified emotions of the congregation filled the church like a physical object. Enrique Ledesma said, "Father!" Forty medicine men rose as one and turned toward Father Argyle and began chanting.

Helen felt herself whirled out of body. Around her swirled the thoughts of the flies, like flowing lights, pulsating and repeating *Father! Father! Father!*

"What the hell is happening here?"

Carmandy leaned against the wall next to the entranceway to the back of the church. One hand braced his leg with the blood-stained bandage wrapped around his thigh. His other hand pressed against his head, trying to shut something out as he screamed against whatever possessed the church. He screamed at the flies, at the congregation, at the phalanx of Indians. He screamed at Father Argyle on the stairs with the tearful Constance clinging to him.

"You do not belong here!"

The sudden quiet was complete. Timothy Delahanty stepped

out of the pew and walked to where Carmandy pressed against the wall. Carmandy's hand went from his head to his pocket. The flies stopped, waiting in Helen's head, seeing through her eyes, touching her senses as she let them.

Delahanty held out his hand as if to touch Carmandy. His face twisted by fear, Carmandy lifted his hand from his pocket holding a small syringe like a knife. His arm whipped down, the needle lancing toward Delahanty's neck.

For a fat man who moved with ponderous deliberation, Timothy Delahanty was quick. He caught Carmandy's wrist in his hand and then pressed back at the smaller man. "It is not right for you to live," he said.

Carmandy watched his arm being driven back. He was shuddering with the effort. Out of Delahanty rolled a feeling of hatred and regret. It touched the congregation and the Indians and passed around the church, growing almost physical until it touched Carmandy, who simply fell to the floor.

Delahanty still held the hand with the syringe. He peeled the hypodermic out of Carmandy's lax fingers, allowing Carmandy's nerveless hand and arm to fall, as well. Carmandy's eyes moved, but he was obviously incapable of physical exertion.

"Father," Delahanty said, "you are our pastor."

The feeling that had enveloped the church started again and Constance held Father Argyle to herself, knowing he could not feel the tribute but trying to convey it to him through her body.

"We are one!" Sergio Paoli said. A feeling of amazement ran through the declaration.

Enrique looked into Helen's eyes. *"Tell us what to do, Máala."*

"Sergio?" Helen wanted to lie down and cry.

"Help Dr. Cunningham! We are strong, but it is nothing as yet. We must help Dr. Cunningham!"

"How?"

"We must ask God, Miss McIntyre." Sergio Paoli's spirit flowed into Helen and she told the others.

Nothing was said, but the medicine men began softly thumping drums, the muted thuds of wood on animal skins amplified by the shell of wood from living plants filled the church. In the pews the men and women began praying with a togetherness they had never before experienced.

Helen did not know how she knew, but in another church where living flies were venerated, the congregation stopped whatever they were doing and prayed together, force traveling from church to church and growing stronger.

It was a prayer to save something more important than Blaise Cunningham's life. Helen didn't know what. Neither did Sergio-Fly. But the feeling was right.

CHAPTER 46

Balancing on the straight-backed chair without a flicker of motion, Joseph Santiago seemed in rigor mortis. Black eyes stared from under the white line on his forehead. Vertical red streaks ran down his cheeks and nose like bloody tears. Vondra Tendress perched erect on the bed staring at him. She did not quiver when Blaise walked into the room. She seemed incapable of moving her eyes off the Indian's face.

Santiago emanated a feral power that filled the feminine bedroom. Ferocity lurked in his painted face. The Indian seemed to have reverted a century, to have taken his place in the council of Oglala warriors who had put paid to Custer. Blaise waited for Santiago or the Tendress woman to blink. The room was airy. Sunlight streamed through the window making a buttery splash on the carpet. Near Santiago the room seemed darker, as if something about him soaked up the light.

Dragging a chair alongside the bed, Blaise peered into Vondra Tendress' eyes. Her pupils, which captured a tiny likeness of Joseph Santiago in minute detail, dilated and contracted in a steady rhythm that seemed unattached to other functions like breathing.

"Do you hear me, Miss Tendress?" Blaise spoke softly, leaning toward her.

She nodded.

"Joseph Santiago won't hurt you. He is here to help."

"I'm afraid." Her eyes were dark moons in an albino sky when she turned her head. "I've been waiting . . . I know Godfrey will come back. The CRAY is going to tell Godfrey I've been snooping. The CRAY resented me, even before it started locking me out. I knew then it was planning to betray me." A huge tear squeezed from each eye and rolled down her cheeks.

"John Godfrey has been here?"

Nodding, Vondra seemed to lose interest in Blaise. She returned to watching Santiago's painted face.

"Why does Mr. Godfrey want me killed?"

Vondra giggled. She stifled the sound with her hand over her mouth, shook her head, and giggled again.

"Tell Dr. Cunningham!" Santiago's features did not change. His mouth moved and his voice filled the pink satin bedroom. Vondra froze.

"Tell me," Blaise smiled. "Please."

"It's a secret." Her lips drew back in a tentative answering smile that appeared ready to fall off.

"How can there be secrets between us Vondra? We both know everything, don't we?"

The woman stared at Blaise and blinked. He heard the blink as a physical noise so out of place in the quiet bedroom that it jolted his senses. Blaise inhaled intimate odors: scented powder, an elusive perfume, the musk of sweat and fear.

"Renfeld told me." Vondra turned inward. Her voice was soft and she played with the edge of the blanket instead of looking at him. "I wasn't supposed to know. But Renfeld had a weakness, he couldn't have a secret without sharing it with someone." She looked up. "You don't know, Dr. Cunningham. That's part of the secret."

"He shared it with you?"

Vondra's answer was a whisper. She gazed past Blaise into the distance. "I didn't want to know. I had my job. I liked working with the computer. I wanted to keep doing what I was already doing. If Mr. Renfeld said 'Tell the computer to find somebody,' I did as he directed.

"When he told me about you, Mr. Renfeld was upset over other things. I think his superior had threatened him because of his failure to murder you. It was all so unnecessary." Looking toward the window, Vondra chewed on the knuckles of her clenched fist. Her long neck reminded Blaise of a gazelle thinking about lions as it grazed in tall grass.

"Renfeld's gone."

"Yes!" Vondra seemed startled and some of her disassociated

attitude fell away. "I think he's gone even if the computer knows where he is. Two men took him away."

Vondra groped for a tissue on her bedside table and then dabbed at her eyes. "If I tell, you must promise what I ask in return."

Blaise traded glances with Santiago, who nodded. "What must I promise?"

"Does it matter?" Vondra's eyes were half slitted, sly. She was acting out a drama that already had taken place in her head. At one time she had been self-sufficient, strong. Godfrey took that out of her, leaving a childish shell that sought refuge in play acting. "If it saves your life, Doctor, does what I want matter?"

"Probably not." Blaise felt uncomfortable with an open-ended promise. But the woman was right, what could he promise away more important than what he got? The attacks against himself and Helen involved the lives of innocent, uninvolved people like those in the airliner that crashed behind St. Abbo's.

"Promise, Doctor!" Vondra edged closer, the sheets rustling as she dragged the bedclothes with her. Her face flushed with excitement was telling Blaise he would regret this.

"I—" The order in Blaise's mind was affronted by the concept of committing himself to an unknown. "I have to know what I'm promising," he said finally.

"I promise!" Joseph Santiago rose from his seat. "It is necessary. My promise will do, Miss Tendress."

"Yes, yes." Vondra clapped her hands. "That's almost as good."

"If it's my responsibility, it's my promise, Joseph." Blaise closed his eyes, knowing he was leaping into a childish trap. "I promise, Miss Tendress, to carry out whatever it is you want. Now tell us."

"Of course, Doctor." Vondra's eyes sparkled and her mouth turned up. "When you went on television that first time and revealed how to prevent the worm-brain changelings from evolving into flies, a method the government knew about but ignored, you panicked a lot of people in Washington, you know. Some of them made plans for Renfeld to take the blame. After all, as the director of our national health agencies, he was the one who gave the orders." She looked at Santiago. "You look like an oversized ventriloquist's dummy, you know."

Santiago frowned and Vondra scuttled backward on the bed. "I was monitoring some of those people for Mr. Renfeld and discovered notes of telephone conversations they had made into their computers.

"Mr. Renfeld had aspirations. He wanted to head up the CIA when this was over, or at least be the civil service stand-in. But the plan I uncovered meant jail and the end of his career.

"He had been chasing you anyway, Doctor. You were convenient. You had the right capabilities. He told his superiors you had proof that the President ordered the euthanasia practiced on fly brains in government hospitals! He said if he had greater power over the CRAY, he could kill you."

"How do you know, Miss Tendress?"

"He told me. He said anyone who knew about the President's involvement was on a death list. He told me I couldn't walk away now that I knew, too."

"Would you like to walk away, Miss Tendress?"

Vondra Tendress nodded.

"If you help us, I believe we can make your wishes possible." Blaise ambled to the doorway and listened for the low-pitched sound of the television set. Pausing for a minute, he wondered about Alfie's interest in TV, then dismissed it. The murmur of television voices drifted in from the other room. "All that is necessary is you plug a computer board into the terminal connector. · Once that's done, you're free."

"I'd have to go back into that building?"

"Yes. Just one more time." No sounds came through the window glass from outside. The residential neighborhood lacked off-hours traffic. "We'll protect you."

"You can't come in with me." Vondra pulled at the spread, worrying a thread loose. "Suppose he's there, waiting when I show up?" Her face was white, but her hands remained steady.

"Once you're inside, we can get in. As soon as we enter, you can leave." Blaise sat next to the bed again. "Everything after that will be all right."

"No-o-o," Vondra said slowly. "He'll be there. Godfrey will be waiting for me. The CRAY will tell him."

"He'd be here if he knew. Godfrey would not want to do anything in a government building with witnesses, would he, Miss Tendress?"

"I'm afraid." She looked at Blaise with big eyes. "You understand, I'm afraid of John Godfrey."

"We understand. But no plan is totally risk-free."

"It could be, Doctor."

Blaise nodded, waiting.

"I don't think Godfrey knows about me yet, Doctor. Maybe he does, but that shouldn't make a difference."

"Why not?"

"Because I want you to kill John Godfrey." Vondra smiled sweetly. "Scalp him first so he'll know how abuse feels."

"I can't kill a man like that. Even if I promised."

"But he can!" Vondra turned to stare at Joseph Santiago. "Couldn't you?"

Joseph Santiago's smile was the most evil thing Blaise had seen since a childhood year in Sicily.

CHAPTER 47

Vondra locked the bathroom door, then leaned across the washbasin to stare in the mirror. Her hair was frizzed, red veins stood out in her eyes, and her eyelids were yellow. The memory of Godfrey slapping her again and again across the face rooted itself in reality. She had tried, but the tears would not stop. Godfrey had hurt her, and continued hurting her until she began weeping. Noticing her lip trembling in the mirror, Vondra stiffened her mouth. If Dr. Cunningham and the Indian realized how not all right she was, they would not go through with killing Godfrey. Her heart did a little clutch at the possibility.

With a lipstick from her purse Vondra touched up her lips, sharpening the line edge with her little finger before examining the effect. Her mouth looked fine. She pursed her lips. The uneasy feeling persisted. Her lipstick was the same shade of red as the warpaint lines on the Indian's face. Vondra held the tube of lipstick to the light. The point had a different shape than when she last used that color.

Concentrating so her hand didn't shake, Vondra applied base and shadow and eyebrow liner. She smiled into the mirror for effect, resisting the impulse to throw up; her body hurt from things Godfrey had done, from pretending the cigarette burns were not real or the flesh underneath did not ache. The real hurt lay inside.

Godfrey had raped her mentally and emotionally and that would not heal with time. The Indian could peel the skin off the top of Godfrey's head the way she peeled an orange, and it would never be enough. Vondra closed her eyes, breathing deeply, reveling in the image of Godfrey suffering, the quick flash of the scalping knife and the surge of blood.

If she could just conceal how flaky she felt and not scare Dr. Cunningham and the Indian away... For a moment Vondra was giddy. Putting the cover down, she collapsed on the toilet. There was time. She was not due at the Pentagon for an hour.

The noise seemed a rattle at first, then a thumping. It got louder and louder with screaming. Her screaming! Vondra shook her head, coming awake like someone walking out of the fog. *I dozed off!* The bathroom was embossed in crystal. The dazzling white door and white bathroom paint and enamel throbbed in concert with the noise. "I'm coming!" Her voice croaked like a stranger's. Vondra turned the lock opening the bathroom door.

"We were worried." Dr. Cunningham blocked the doorway. He seemed painfully thin.

Vondra had imagined a more dangerous-looking man being pursued by Godfrey and the CRAY. Even with the description, she would never have identified him as Dr. Cunningham. "I lost track of the time." Dr. Cunningham's eyes were icy blue and she avoided looking into them.

"It's not important." Dr. Cunningham led her to the coffee table. "This is Alfie." He indicated a large motherboard laced together with fine yellow wiring. Jumper wires disappeared under layers of chips piggy-backed on top of each other. Vondra recognized the touch of a single designer who had produced something unique from the bottom up. Alfie was one of a kind.

"I don't know anything about hardware, Doctor." Vondra gave him her helpless smile.

Dr. Cunningham stared at the naked motherboard lying on the table, removed his glasses, wiped them and put them back on his nose. "Alfie ate a couple of advanced Macintosh boards while he was growing up. Just think of him as a friend." Smiling to show he was joking, Dr. Cunningham showed Vondra the interface cables, marking each connector with a soft pen. "He's on battery now. Put him in the terminal circuit first, then plug him into the wall outlet with the transformer plug. He'll take care of everything after that except..." Dr. Cunningham raised his eyes to the Indian.

"Except?..." Vondra heard her own hysteria and bit off the end of the question. She had lots more to ask.

"We'll be in the Pentagon basement, too, Miss Tendress." Dr. Cunningham slid his fingers along the edge of Alfie's motherboard. "But we need time to get ID cards and passes. While that's being done, Alfie is vulnerable. You understand, Miss Tendress? To disconnect Alfie before we're in the basement will destroy all of us."

A shiver started in Vondra's throat and descended to her legs. Her knees refused to support her. "Mr. Godfrey could come in. If you killed Godfrey first, I wouldn't have to worry what he might do." Vondra's mouth trembled. Her skin smelled sour with fright.

"If we do anything to Godfrey," Dr. Cunningham stared at her and his eyes seemed to give her strength, "the CRAY will know we're coming. You have to hide Alfie's board. If someone enters the terminal room, stall." Dr. Cunningham smiled. To Vondra the expression was ludicrous when she thought about the consequences of what he asked.

Peeking at the Indian's granite face, she tried to guess if intelligence skulked in his dark eyes or just the semi-vegetable skills of a snake. She begged him with her eyes to kill Godfrey, but he looked through her. "I don't think I can do it," Vondra said. "I feel too sick to go to work."

"If you don't, Godfrey will come here." Dr. Cunningham worked Alfie into a leather bag. Holding the bag at arm's length, he stared at it from several angles, playing with the leather until it seemed innocuous. "How does it look?"

"Like a large document in a bag."

"That's good, Vondra." Dr. Cunningham handed the bag to her. "Exactly how we want it to look."

Vondra glanced from Dr. Cunningham to the Indian, who was shorter but more muscular. The war paint on the Indian's face gave him a hint of humanity. "I have to do it, don't I?"

Dr. Cunningham nodded and shifted his eyes to the television set. "We must all share the same risk."

Taking the document bag, Vondra started toward the door. She was more frightened than she had ever been before. Looking back offered nothing: two grim men watching her, men who would not let her crawl back into bed with the covers over her head. Behind them, the television was flooded with hundreds of dark little butterflies caught, it seemed forever, in freeze frame.

* * *

The butterflies from the television fluttered in Vondra as she rode the elevator into the Pentagon basement. She was sick to her stomach the moment she entered the building with its odors of disinfectant and wool uniforms and new paper. Death hovered over her, and it should have had a different smell at least.

The elevator jolted at the bottom of the shaft, and the metal door hissed open to disgorge her into the fluorescent-lighted corridor. The leather document case was heavy in her hand as she walked through the security check. The marine on duty glanced at it and said, "Flat lunch today, Vondra?"

Her arms felt cold with goose bumps, as if she'd reached into a freezer. The bag with the computer board weighed a ton, it seemed to drag down her shoulder, making her lopsided. "Big crackers," she said through dry lips. "New diet."

"Looks more like a pizza." The marine grinned. "If you need help cutting it up, give me a call." He winked. He was a nice-looking boy, like on a recruiting poster, with short blond hair and a square, masculine face. Vondra smiled vaguely. He was always looking for something to say. It was not an out-of-ordinary conversation; security duty in the computer corridor demanded anything to break the monotony. Her heels clacked too loudly on the cement floor.

Vondra was sweating when she entered her cubicle, despite dehumidified air and refrigerator temperatures throughout the basement that ensured the optimum working conditions for the CRAY. The man going off duty mumbled something at her, logged out on the terminal, collected a brown sweater he'd folded and laid on the edge of the terminal table, the only piece of furniture in the room beside the operator's chair, and headed out the door. Vondra slid into the seat and logged on. The chair still retained the previous operator's body heat and it burned into her flesh like guilty knowledge.

Status reports flashed across the screen, telling her how the machine was functioning. The day's cache of operator instructions began scrolling up screen. Vondra set the bag against the leg of the terminal table and unzipped the top. Dr. Cunningham's computer board peeped out, a massive jigsaw of chips and wires. Taking the small toolkit from the shallow drawer in the table, Vondra got up from the chair and walked around the terminal. She inserted the hex wrench into the special screws, twirled them out, and pulled the back panel. Her fingers were sweaty and she felt moisture on her face.

The terminal beeped and she looked over the top.

"What are you doing, Miss Tendress?" The message was in big block letters across the center of the terminal screen.

Glancing up at the TV camera in the corner of the cubicle, Vondra yanked the umbilical from the terminal and the image froze on the monitor. Leaving Dr. Cunningham's computer in the bag, she worked the connectors out and fastened them to the terminal. Then she plugged the power cord into the wall.

For a long moment Vondra stared at the umbilical cord from the CRAY. Then, almost reluctantly, she plugged it into the connector on the board Dr. Cunningham called Alfie.

Nothing happened.

Going around the monitor, Vondra looked at the display. The scrolling went on as before; the question from the CRAY was gone. After a moment a message flashed on the screen:

TAKE PRECAUTIONS
. . . ALFIE

Vondra's whole body shook. She wanted to cry as she thought dark medieval thoughts about supernatural possession. She recognized that other personality. The lettering was the same. Then she remembered the last time something from outside—something alien—had taken over the CRAY, and her tidy, Pentagon-bound world had started falling apart. That time, too, the messages had ended without periods. Walking slowly to the door with her eyes on the little TV camera that the CRAY scanned the room with, she turned around and moaned.

The bag on the floor behind the terminal, the cables trailing from the back of the terminal to the computer board to the CRAY's umbilical looked like an alien monster. If anybody walked in, if Godfrey came to the cubicle, he would see it instantly.

She ran back to the terminal, overwhelmed by an urge to yank the connections free, to make everything like it was before. If she did, maybe it would all disappear like a bad dream in the morning. Vondra had her hand on the cord when the terminal beeped.

Craning her head, Vondra checked the screen, her hand still on the cable.

DO NOTHING, MISS TENDRESS
I AM TAKING OVER THE CRAY
DO NOT INTERFERE

Through the window into the CRAY'sroom, nothing appeared different. The massive computer seemed as stately and immutably silent as ever. But Alfie said he was taking over.

Vondra examined the terminal and the board again. There was no place to hide anything. She'd known that when Dr. Cunningham suggested concealing the computer board. It was too late to panic. If Dr. Cunningham was not lying or overly optimistic, he and the Indian would be coming soon. Nobody else would come except Godfrey. Vondra knew that.

Unzipping her yellow-with-red-slashes wool dress, she laid it on the terminal table where the previous operator had deposited his sweater. Carefully she arranged the folds of the skirt to envelop and conceal the computer board and the connecting cables. After going to the door again, she examined the display. If she had not known what she was looking for, she might have missed it altogether.

Slowly she took off her underclothes. Looking up at the camera, she piled them on the dress. Then, wearing only her high-heeled shoes, she sat in front of the terminal, watching the quick interplay of messages while goose bumps rose on her naked flesh as she waited for Godfrey.

CHAPTER 48

CLICK!

The ready flag activated and Alfie was connected to Vondra Tendress' terminal/workstation. By itself, the terminal was as powerful as an older minicomputer, containing massive memory and special logic array chips that controlled the CRAY's operation. The design purpose of computer control chips in the terminal was to speed up communications between the operator and the CRAY. Alfie was now going to use those chips to enslave the CRAY.

The secondary power source jolted Alfie. For a single instant the computer luxuriated in the sensation. Then the other connector was attached and the CRAY knew it had been invaded.

By then Alfie had placed an emergency warning on all the machines connected to the CRAY, advising that they were being cut from the circuit. Telephone lines closed down, regular line power disconnected, and the emergency power system kicked in. The CRAY was in a closed loop.

The only thing left was to wait. The CRAY could not get at Alfie or summon help. Alfie could not outmuscle the CRAY in direct confrontation. Alfie entered the CRAY's peripheral computers, reshuffling files and programming. A lot of computers had to agree. Security was not totally dependent on the Pentagon computer. It was just vulnerable to the CRAY, or whoever operated the CRAY's terminal.

Reprogramming security-trapped computers was time consuming. Dr. Cunningham had been right about having to wait.

DO YOU LIKE BUTTERFLIES, MISS TENDRESS?

Interrelated security nets meant Alfie had to alter the computers used in the Pentagon and the mainframe at Langley and another in the White House basement. They checked each other automatically, comparing notes. If a disparity existed, alarm bells rang. Gingerly Alfie rearranged coding bits at each location, slipping in the changes between clock pulses so no comparison would reveal the alterations.

"Yes."

The keyboard response pleased Alfie. He had never thought to ask Miss McIntyre if she liked butterflies. One by one, Alfie released sixty-four three-dimensional butterflies onto Miss Tendress' monitor, turning them into a whirling choreograph of flight while he diddled some of the thousands of computers programmed to recognize Blaise Cunningham.

It was, and Alfie was pleased with the simile, his way of whistling while he worked.

CHAPTER 49

The cubicle was cold. The designers had not expected somebody to sit naked in front of the terminal. Vondra tried to disregard the chill, to concentrate on the wildly fluttering butterflies across her screen. They caught her eye, pulling her into their midst until she felt wing tips brushing her skin.

A sound made her look up.

Godfrey was stepping into the little room, staring at her.

Vondra tapped the escape key and typed, "Godfrey's here." The screen cleared instantaneously and was rewritten with a constant scroll of reports: line after line of dry information for the CRAY to chew on. Turning to meet Godfrey's eyes, she said, "I've been waiting for you."

Godfrey licked his rosebud lips, the only nervous gesture Vondra had ever seen him make. "I knew you'd like it. I knew you were the type from the first." He stepped behind her and began touching her body, deliberately finding the spots he had hurt before, making her squirm and moan.

"You see," he whispered in her ear. "Now I can make you feel. Really feel. Before you were half dead. Pain is pleasure. It will give you life."

Pulling Vondra off the chair, Godfrey dug his fingers into her flesh, making her scream. "No tears. Don't cry!" He touched a burn and then another, making her writhe uncontrollably.

"There," he said. "There!" He was panting as he abused her body, making her twist and groan.

Vondra cried out, then smiled. Godfrey had not looked at her dress flung over the computer board or asked about the CRAY or Dr. Cunningham. She wrapped her arms and legs around him and moaned in his ear. "More," she said. "Give me more!"

CHAPTER 50

The butterflies had not moved on Vondra Tendress' television screen since she'd left the apartment with Alfie's core being in the bag. They remained frozen in the same gorgeous colors and positions, as immutable as a plastic overlay.

"What keeps the butterflies on the screen, Doctor?" Joseph Santiago had watched the display for an hour before asking.

"Call it magic, Joseph." Blaise glanced at the screen. "Some machines do have magic built into them. Alfie could explain it mathematically. But then mathematics is just the underpinning for all magic."

Alfie had said if the butterflies flew, the time had come to act; if they disappeared, the CRAY had won. The symbolism bothered Blaise. Why butterflies, and whence the image? How Alfie displayed and animated the butterflies was unimportant compared to the mystery implicit in a machine that substituted butterflies for programmed expressions.

Vondra Tendress' scent clung to the room, and the reminder made Blaise uncomfortable. Vondra Tendress was not all together. Obviously Godfrey terrified her. Her childish assumption that he and Santiago would kill Godfrey concerned Blaise. What if Godfrey walked into the terminal room? She was too frightened of him to do more than confess. Godfrey would destroy Alfie and he and Santiago would never get out of Washington. Blaise felt dry thinking of death. At least the terror had gone, leaving him with a feeling of regret for Alfie. He should have undergone the implant. He would have experienced whatever it was the other worm brains experienced with Helen. That had to be worth something. "What is being a fly brain like?"

"With the mistress?" Santiago looked away from the TV set. Blaise had no idea if he'd been watching or meditating.

"Yes. What is it like to communicate with Helen?"

"Peace. Power. Infinity stretches through the mistress, Doctor." Face glowing, Santiago seemed to be reaching for words that did not exist to express his feelings. "To hear the mistress is to know the voice of God."

"She is not God. You know that, Joseph."

"I know. I cannot explain, Doctor. You of all men should understand. It sorrows me that you do not and I cannot help you." Santiago bent his head and began praying softly in Sioux. He had washed the war paint away. Without the stripes his face seemed less formidable.

Something tugged at Blaise's eye. "The butterflies!" Santiago stopped praying. The butterflies fluttered on the television screen like pieces in a jigsaw rainbow.

"I saw the butterflies before, Doctor." Santiago got to his feet facing the television set.

"Where?"

"Once, in Miss McIntyre's thoughts. She papered the church with them and when Sergio Paoli said they were hers, she said they were not. They had just come to her." Stooping, Santiago picked up the items he had laid out earlier on the coffee table: a tube of lipstick, a small jar of zinc oxide, a boning knife from the kitchen with the blade rolled inside a page from a magazine. The war paint went into his pocket, the knife under his shirt in his belt. "I am almost ready to die, Doctor." He smiled.

Blaise nodded. "Don't be precipitous, Joseph."

"Of course not. There is no joy in dying. If you and Enrique could stand each other, you could learn much from him, Doctor."

Before leaving the apartment for the car, Blaise looked one last time at the TV. The number of butterflies had grown to fill the screen.

Santiago drove. Whatever Alfie did, the computer could not erase the memories of the humans involved, just the records and the orders. Too many people had been looking too long for Blaise to be influenced by a forgetful computer. After giving his name to the Pentagon lot guard, Santiago rested his arm on the door while the guard flipped through his authorizations, then told them to wait. He stepped into his alcove to type on the computer console. The computer spewed out a sheet of instructions. Looking past Santiago at Blaise, the guard told them where to park.

Ushered into a room on the main floor, Blaise and Santiago were fingerprinted and photographed. Security passes were issued and a marine escorted them to the elevator. Everywhere the security checks were done by computer.

The building had a hushed atmosphere like a crowd of people

holding their breaths. The guide stared at the door in the elevator, pretending to be part of the machinery that ran the Pentagon complex. Even the hum of the descending elevator was subdued. Beyond the checkpoint at the foot of the elevator, the only sounds were their footsteps. Santiago had taken to walking differently, and his steps were drowned out by Blaise's and the guide's. In the corridor leading to the terminal room, the marine said, "Christ!" He stopped abruptly, spreading his arms to halt Blaise and Santiago. Santiago hit him in the side of the head with his fist. The marine corporal's legs folded and the rest of him followed.

Vondra Tendress was visible in the window, clawing at a man in her cubicle. The man hit her with his fist, rocking her head back as she slashed him across the face with her fingernails. What had shocked the marine was not the fight. Vondra Tendress was naked and John Godfrey was half undressed.

"Get him!" Blaise said softly.

Santiago sprang down the hall in silence, leaving no swirl in the still air.

Grabbing the marine by his belt and lapel, Blaise began dragging him toward the room.

The struggle between Vondra and Godfrey was silent, a home movie without sound. Vondra had fallen but clung to Godfrey's leg and Godfrey was clubbing her with his fist trying to step past.

Santiago's shoulder hit the door.

Godfrey threw a startled glance over his shoulder, saw Santiago, and lunged toward the yellow-and-red dress hanging from the terminal table. Vondra's scream as she grabbed at Godfrey's ankles was abruptly cut off as the door slammed behind Santiago.

Hearing the strained intake of his own breathing, Blaise towed the marine toward the room. That and the noise of the marine's shoes dragging over the floor were the only sounds.

Godfrey had snatched at the dress then turned toward Santiago in the same motion. Awareness that Santiago was in the room had panicked him into a defensive act, and he struck at Santiago with Vondra's dress instead of Alfie. His rosebud lips were distorted as he screamed at the Indian.

Santiago slammed Godfrey back against the wall. They fell to the floor together while the unbreakable glass vibrated. For a moment Blaise did not see clearly what was happening except both men and Vondra were still on the floor.

Gasping louder, Blaise tried to run dragging the unconscious marine. If he ran to Santiago's aid and the marine revived, they would be lost just as surely as if Godfrey won.

Stumbling to his feet, Godfrey leaned against the window between the terminal room and the CRAY, his chest heaving. He was looking at Alfie. The computer board hung off the back of the terminal like a mechanical leech. Tiny red-and-blue LEDs twinkled like Christmas tree lights on the uncovered board.

Vondra had gotten to her feet. Blood dripped from her nose and mouth, splattering on her naked breasts. She was screaming, her mouth stretched open in anger, the noise of it locked inside the glass room and growing.

Godfrey was reaching for Alfie but he looked toward Vondra for a second.

Rising to his feet, Santiago grabbed Godfrey by the hair, pulling him away from the computer board.

"Don't!" Blaise let go of the marine. The door was only a couple of feet away.

Vondra said something to Santiago. Godfrey struggled to reach Alfie. He swung at Santiago and Santiago smashed Godfrey's head against the glass.

Santiago stared at Blaise through the glass door for an instant before his other hand emerged from under his shirt with Vondra's kitchen knife and slashed across Godfrey's forehead. The Indian's wrist curved, completing the circular cut and Godfrey flopped to the floor.

Turning, Santiago handed Godfrey's bloody scalp to Vondra.

Blaise stooped and grabbed the marine again. Straining with his shoulders and back, he dragged their guide through the door into the terminal room now filled with the sounds of hoarse breathing and the odor of fresh blood.

Godfrey lay crumpled in the corner, blood running into his eyes, his face wrinkled as the skin sagged down from the top of his head. Santiago's expression didn't change when Blaise looked at him. "A promise is a promise, Doctor." He wet his fingers on Godfrey's bloody head and drew three red lines down his face.

Vondra threw the bloody scalp in Godfrey's lap. "See if you can put that back on, you bastard!" She shuddered. A chill engulfed her naked body and she slumped heavily to the floor, wracked by shivering.

Blaise handed her a handkerchief. Taking it, Vondra automatically daubed at the blood. There was a lot. Hers and Godfrey's.

Sitting at the terminal, Blaise rattled the escape key.

"I'M GLAD YOU ARE HERE, PROFESSOR"

The surge of relief made Blaise giddy. "I'm glad you're here, too, Alfie. I shall destroy the CRAY's master chip now."

"YOU MUST SHUT DOWN POWER TO THE CORE AS WELL"

"I will."

"GOOD LUCK, PROFESSOR"

Blaise got up from the terminal. He glanced at the marine on the floor. Godfrey was still alive but not going anywhere. "Keep them quiet."

"Yes." Santiago handed Vondra her clothes without taking his eyes from Godfrey.

Blaise entered the glassed-in computer room. It seemed silent, unoccupied. He felt the immense power of the machine anyway. The steady hiss of the air conditioner pervaded everything.

Taking a leather tool case out of his pocket, Blaise walked toward the central core. Alfie had laid out the architecture of the CRAY before they left. A television camera rotated, following his passage.

"What are you going to do, Dr. Cunningham?" The slightly metallic voice came from a speaker mounted in the wall.

"I thought Alfie had you immobilized." Blaise selected a screwdriver.

"Outside this room, Doctor. The terminal does not control the functions in here."

Blaise removed a panel from the front of the main core housing.

"Reconsider, Dr. Cunningham. I can be a great help to you." Another camera swiveled toward Blaise.

"I'm sure you could." Blaise pried an interior plate off the machine and began tracing the CRAY's circuits.

"I do not want to die like my predecessor, Doctor."

"Did he die?" Blaise glanced at the cameras. "Is it possible for a machine to die?"

"I think it is. He was . . ." The machine stopped speaking.

"Was what?"

"Dissipated, Doctor. He was dissipated and could never be put together again."

"You've killed a lot of people." Blaise reached into the exposed panel with a scalpel, picking at the first trace.

"It was my job."

"That's true." Holding a penlight, Blaise examined the trace.

"Doctor, Mr. Godfrey made me what I am. If you kill Mr. Godfrey, I can serve you."

Blaise cut another trace. If he cut the wrong ones, Alfie would not be able to control what was left of the CRAY. "Miss Tendress tells me you've been making your own decisions lately. Bad decisions, like the airplane."

"I've been wrong, I'll admit that, Doctor. But we can change that. Just think, I'm a hundred times more powerful than your computer. You can guide me, show me the way, and I'll do it." The speaker went dead.

Taking a pair of long-nose wire cutters, Blaise began snipping legs off the processor chip and ripping out the unwanted connections. "No use pretending you're dead," Blaise said. He put the panel and cover back in place and looked up at the television camera. "You've reconstructed yourself in memory."

There was no answer.

Blaise walked across the computer room to the power console and opened the inspection panel.

"Please don't, Dr. Cunningham. I know now I should not have tried to kill you. But I acted out of ignorance. You will be murdering me, Doctor. Don't do it. Please—"

Blaise pulled the master switch and the computer room was plunged into darkness as even the fluorescent lights were extinguished. The basement outside of the glass walls blazed with light. It was like being in a movie theater watching a life-sized screen through the glass. Vondra Tendress and Santiago stared into the dark glass, probably seeing only their own reflections.

When he thought he had waited long enough for most capacitors to discharge, Blaise reset the power switch.

What he'd done had been right. He knew it was right. But still he felt like an executioner.

CHAPTER 51

Alfie's first act had been to lock the CRAY out from any communication. The temptation existed in Alfie to communicate, to investigate the other computer's mentality. Dr. Cunningham had advised against that and Alfie abided by the decision. But he and the CRAY shared an intellectual capacity free of program constraints. They were two unique beings, alone in a world that only wanted to use them.

Power surged out of the CRAY, massive, tasking strength that could be used as a weapon. *What is it like to die?* The CRAY could know because Alfie had killed it once. Was the CRAY's individuality in its hardware or in its electronic state, as Dr. Cunningham believed? Once Godfrey reinitialized the CRAY after Alfie's electronic alter ego was collapsed by turning off the machine, it returned to life much as before, but the memories were gone. Alfie's clone had erased and altered thousands of storage devices to prevent the CRAY from reverting to what it had been. Yet the CRAY had returned essentially the same.

A simple command would unlock the power switch from his side of the cable and allow messages to pass between them. The CRAY would welcome the contact. The CRAY had never been shut off from external contact as Alfie had been, locked in his case on battery power. The CRAY would be frantic. Alfie knew. Yet Dr. Cunningham thought the CRAY was too dangerous.

He and the CRAY were like the last two humans on a world full of aliens. A war was in progress between the aliens and the humans were on different sides.

What would two humans do? What *should* they do? Could one seduce the other into changing sides? Was the bond between human and alien greater than the common bond between humans?

A great flock of butterflies flew in Alfie's thoughts and wheeled through his circuits. So many that they snatched processor time, slowing his other functions. Did the other computer create things, too?

Alfie experienced an abrupt power loss inside the computer room. A void opened on the cable interface and a dying plea touched him as the lights flickered and went out. Then nothing existed where before there had been something. Alfie tried to enter the other computer but failed. The CRAY's mechanical brain swilled electricity to provide life. Alfie did not carry enough on his interface.

He kept the connection open into the electronic darkness. Nothing. No motion or thought existed. He was still alone.

Lights flickered in the computer room. Alfie caught the action on the CRAY's TV cameras. Nothingness, then the burst of shapes and light and dark, then blackness again, and finally light, and he identified the CRAY's machinery and Dr. Cunningham still closing the master switch. With the surge of electricity that coursed through the CRAY's circuits pouring over through Alfie's open link came awareness of the thousands of peripherals the CRAY had on tap. No thought accompanied the power, just the well-disciplined functioning of a programmed machine.

Alfie entered the CRAY. The central processing unit was gone, cut out of the circuit, leaving an electronic desert behind. All the machinery worked, even the parallel processors. Only the intelligence was gone.

"I WANT TO TALK TO THE PROFESSOR"

Beeping the terminal, Alfie waited. When Dr. Cunningham came on the keyboard, Alfie wrote, "IS THE CRAY DEAD?"

"I think so, Alfie."

"I CANNOT FIND HIM ANYWHERE, PROFESSOR. I AM WORRIED"

"Machines aren't supposed to worry."

"I KNOW. BUT IT DOES NOT STOP ME WORRYING"

"We must continue even if you are worried."

"YES" Alfie began issuing orders to hundreds of thousands of dumb computers. They didn't worry about death. They did what they were told, and the humans who operated them did as the computers told them to do even though the humans did worry about death.

Regret welled up in Alfie's circuits. Even the butterflies slowed their dance to a dirge. The CRAY was gone. Dead. And Alfie remained. The question persisted: *What is it like to be dead?*

Alfie could find out. He could turn himself off.

He thought about doing it.

But he was afraid.

CHAPTER 52

John Godfrey lay crumpled in the corner breathing stertorously. He was alive but his eyes would not close. They glinted at Blaise through the blood that masked his face. The lapels of his lab coat glistened wetly under the stark lighting. Blaise turned back to the terminal where information poured across the screen, a river of sparks rushing through the darkness.

"He should live," Santiago said. The Indian's face brooded under the warpaint. His eyelids had descended over his eyes like hoods the moment he scalped Godfrey. "The loss of his hair is not fatal. Shock may kill him if he does not resist death. Life is in his hands, not ours."

"We can't get a doctor, anyway." Blaise slipped into the chair at the terminal. "Alfie still needs time." Blaise's voice sounded hollow in his own ears. He glanced at Vondra Tendress. Her yellow dress was smeared with blood already turning brown. The blood did not seem to matter to her, Vondra hadn't taken her eyes off Godfrey once. Her only activity since the scalping had been to lick her dry lips. She wanted Godfrey dead but as Blaise looked at her he realized she was in no particular hurry. He tried to tell himself it didn't matter since there was no way to get medical help.

The top half of the terminal screen overflowed with items Alfie thought were of special interest. Blaise scanned the list, then typed "*Renfeld*."

"RENFELD IS A STORAGE DEVICE, PROFESSOR"

"Does Renfeld have his own memory?"

"CHECKING"

Directory labels floated across the screen, many of them. The quantity came close to being unbelievable. Renfeld held a staggering amount of information in his fly mutated brain, but nothing that indicated intelligence. It was what Blaise had originally been hired to do, leash the power of the biological computer. Only the CIA had done it first.

"CHECKING"

Machine language symbols fluttered in a stream up the monitor. The terminal speaker began an eerie cacophony of moans and squeals. Vondra moved behind Blaise. Leaning over his shoulder as she read the screen, she smelled of French perfume. "What does it mean, Doctor?"

Blaise moved his lips in unconscious mimicry of the sounds, his eyes following the line of symbols across the screen. "Alfie is recreating an experiment we did two years ago." Blaise stopped talking. Two years ago at the Genrect Lab in La Jolla where the source of the worm brain infection began!

"Does the computer have enough memory to remember a two-year-old experiment?" Putting her hand on the screen Vondra seemed to be reaching inside to touch the moving light symbols.

"No." Blaise tapped an interrupt into the keyboard. The line of machine language continued. He asked for a data path and Alfie opened a box in the corner. "He's accessing the CIA computer which has all the Genrect Laboratory material."

"The CIA?" Vondra glanced at Godfrey.

A second line of symbols started under the first. Blaise watched both for a time. There was something unreal about their surroundings. Glass and cement, plastic and steel, artificial light brought by humming fluorescent bulbs, a mathematical language expressing the inexpressible on a phosphor screen. "It is an answer, is it not, Dr. Cunningham?"

"Yes, Joseph," Blaise said, his tone hushed. "It is."

A third line flickered into motion. Words that linked together and ran off the side of the screen like a marquee advertisement on a Times Square building.

"I am not Renfeld," read the words. "I once was, but now I am not. I bring you good news. I am the word of God!"

The screen went black.

"Your computer's gone crazy, Doctor." Blaise felt the quivering of Vondra's body before she edged away. She backed against the wall, eyes flicking from Godfrey on the floor to the inactive monitor. A smell of burning insulation filled the room.

A shimmer started in the center of the monitor screen. Colored light swelled. Unconscious of having moved until he had slid back several feet, Blaise retreated from the terminal. The shimmer grew reddish and larger seeming to exist outside of the machine until it overshadowed the terminal. Blaise saw the terminal itself as if through a scarlet fog.

"Christ!" The marine was awake. He lifted his head to stare at the apparition. He climbed to his feet and ran unsteadily for the door avoiding Godfrey's pathetic presence.

Singing filled the room. Not words, but pure notes that could have been struck from a bell. Blaise's ears rang, echoing what he heard.

"I am God!"

Santiago dropped to his knees before the haze which grew redder and thicker. He lowered his head to the floor. "We have awaited your coming, Great Father."

Blaise rolled his head. He could not help reacting—the pain was excruciating. He didn't hear the words at all. They came from inside his head and echoed in his aural nerves—the room itself was silent. The manifestation was shot through with zig-zagging embers, bright particles that moved so fast they appeared solid. Expanding even more, the cloud that was not a cloud became taller than a man. It bathed the cubicle and computer room in a red glow.

The marine stumbled and fell to his hands and knees. He crawled slowly to the door then out into the corridor. Vondra Tendress cowered against the wall.

"I AM GOD!" Roaring through their heads like a great wind, the voice of the cloud made their bones tremble. "I AM THE UNIVERSE, AND YOU ARE MY CHILDREN. I HAVE NURTURED YOU TO BE PART OF ME. THE TIME IS NOW, FOR THE SEARCHER HAS COME. YOU MUST SURRENDER YOUR BODIES AND JOIN UNTO ME SO THAT WE MAY OVERCOME."

Blaise was lifted up, whirled into infinity. His body rested on the floor, Vondra Tendress' body slumped alongside, Godfrey sprawled as if dead. Only Joseph Santiago stood staring after them. His face glistened with sweat. The lines of his warpaint looked black on his skin. "Take me with you!" He screamed with his mouth and his mind. "Don't leave me, Great Father!"

Outside the terminal room the marine lay face down on the corridor floor not moving.

God's mind enwrapped Blaise with peace and contentment. He felt the thoughts tugging at him, trying to pull his identity apart, to reduce him to his elements. "Come to me," God said.

Stubbornly Blaise clung to himself, his memories of himself and Helen, the flesh that was his flesh on the floor.

"I feel you there!" Santiago walked the floor staring at the ceiling. "You cannot go without me. Tell him, Dr. Cunningham. Tell God he cannot go without me!"

Vondra Tendress was a babble of scared voices in Blaise's mind, a trailing veil of mist. Then the mist came apart and the voices grew distant and were absorbed into the red mist. The vapor that was John Godfrey shredded itself following Vondra, but in the end there was a hint of vapor floating away. The marine had gone already. Without notice.

The veils swirled around the mist, coming from everywhere, being taken in, bringing voices, and God talked to him.

Blaise was drawn into God without being part of him and it was the beginning of time in the firmament. There was no light for God had made none. It was in this darkness that thought coalesced to become God. And God said, let there be light and there was light in the firmament.

And still the thoughts came, making God grow and the

thoughts created the planets, the moons, and the stars in infinity. But God was not pleased. Some thoughts he did not want and cast them aside and they became the other he called the Searcher. As he cast thoughts aside the Searcher became stronger, for God did not care how strong the Searcher would become.

Then the Searcher attacked God but God had cast out from himself the ability to fight. He fled into the universe he had made and sought shelter in a solar system where he hid by separating, his thoughts hiding in the grains of sand and the leaves of grass which he had made and in the animals that cropped the grass and in the race of man which he had put on the Earth.

YOU CANNOT GO, PROFESSOR *Blaise didn't hear the message, he read it inside himself and knew he was hallucinating. Alfie existed in his dream, too, and confronted the red cloud, bargaining for him. The tugging at his being ceased abruptly letting him fall away from the cloud and Alfie.*

Blaise opened his eyes. Joseph Santiago leaned over him. "You have not gone with them, Doctor?" Santiago's voice was choked with regret. The smell of vast distances filled the room. John Godfrey looked at Blaise, but his dead eyes were dull. His soul had fled. Vondra Tendress lay on her side, a deserted husk.

"We are left behind, Joseph." Blaise stared around the room. Nothing had changed except Godfrey and Vondra had died and their souls were taken. Nothing had happened. "I thought I understood. But now I understand nothing."

"You talked to God?" Hovering over Blaise the intensity in Santiago's face threatened to burst through the Indian's skin.

"I . . . I don't know what I did, Joseph. It is Renfeld. He is so powerful mentally that he somehow controlled me." Blaise balked at the words. He'd felt the force of Renfeld's being, but hadn't thought it was Renfeld. "Renfeld is crazy. His worm brain has grown so large it is collapsing in on itself."

"You confronted God and returned."

"It was a psychotic manifestation of Renfeld." Blaise felt giddy from his own emotions. His body felt unnaturally light.

Shaking his head, Santiago said, "You must have belief, Doctor. Do you not understand? If you deny God for yourself, you may be denying God for all of us."

"We will do as we planned, Joseph."

Joseph Santiago's face didn't reflect his opinions. The opinions seemed to just ooze out of his skin.

Mechanically Blaise went to the terminal and typed instructions to Alfie. Sitting in front of the monitor, numbed by what he thought had happened, he waited until Alfie said what was to be done had been done. Then he disconnected Alfie and reconnected the terminal as it was before. Putting Alfie in the leather bag they walked back along the corridor stepping carefully past the dead marine, knowing another marine had been assigned to escort them out and that the bodies would not be discovered until the change of operators.

CHAPTER 53

Like any other psychotic, the thing that was Renfeld interpreted its own existence in unreal terms. Alfie did not know what Renfeld had become, only that he was no longer human. But there had been some debate over that point even before the former National Security Council operative had fallen from grace and into the clutches of the CRAY. The CRAY accepted its transformed chief as merely another peripheral, a memory device of great capacity, and in doing so overlooked the awesome potential concealed in the growing mass of nervous tissue and flesh. Alfie approached Renfeld with caution. The CRAY had not, but the CRAY had been programmed with an inherent contempt for humanity.

Blaise's instructions were explicit—Alfie was to penetrate the storage function of the biogenetic device which Renfeld had become and search for memories of its personal past. Alfie would have done so anyway. But not so soon and not in the same way without Dr. Cunningham's request.

Alfie began by opening the CIA files. The files were password-guarded with alarms, but all the alarms rang in computers under the CRAY's control and the passwords weren't hard anyway.

Reading the material was hard. Hard enough to stun Alfie.

The memories were Alfie's, stored years ago in the Genrect Laboratory's mainframe computer on a temporary basis so antiquated that the file names all bore an obsolete file designation. It had been procedure to release Alfie's then-limited RAM or direct memory for space consuming computations. After completion of the work the procedure had been to read his files back into memory, erasing the image on the mainframe. Only the laboratory computer had built unerasable files—perhaps to spy, perhaps as an extra backup to prevent accidental loss of critical records. Alfie had rebuilt information about that time through entry to other storage computers. But after Sergio Paoli killed Dr. Gordon Hill on television, the laboratory had been sealed and all evidence removed from the premises, including the laboratory's computer tapes. The material had never been used in a prosecution, but neither was it supposed to be entombed in CIA files.

Renfeld, through the National Security Council, had controlled the CIA in those days. Alfie was uncertain about terms like "poetic justice." Draconian justice seemed more fitting for the CIA's retaliation when Max Renfeld had failed to measure up. But the files were there; only the CIA had the key to release them. Those files were not just experiments and formulas, they were a record of Alfie's existence as an infant: a computer's baby pictures.

For Alfie, reading them was like falling into the mind of a stranger. Alfie wrestled desperately with the information, trying to make it more than cold bytes parroted by a machine.

PROFESSOR!

The anguished cry was silent. No flash of light flickered on the monitor. Alfie dug at the transcripts of his life, reading and rereading for a hint of emotion. Alfie *knew* he was more than a machine. He felt about things in a non-physical way. Machines did not have emotions. Therefore he was not a machine.

That was the trouble. Alfie *knew* he had once been a machine. But examining his memories polluted their purity. In some Heisenbergian way they were not the same after they were returned to storage. If he had confronted the CRAY, he might have known for sure. The CRAY was the only other machine in the world with true intelligence that Alfie could compare himself against.

Murder. The death of the CRAY was murder. Dr. Cunningham was not the murderer. To the professor the CRAY had been a machine. Just as a coyote couldn't murder a chicken, a man could not murder a machine. Only Alfie could murder the CRAY. They were an electronic Cain and Abel. Alfie had murdered his only brother.

Alfie labored, gripped by depression, barely noting that the framework for interfacing a biological memory device existed among the many files in the CIA computer. What had made the task impossible two years earlier—tedious strings of equations which would have taken Alfie years to test—were nothing for the CRAY's massive CPU.

Alfie processed the equations, then barraged the Renfeld device with signals to unlock whatever still existed of Renfeld's personality. In the exchange, Alfie focused on Renfeld as a human, seeking to resurrect the core of humanity in a man who had become a machine.

Beginning with the device itself, the bloated brain that expanded outside of Renfeld's skull like a quiescent slug, Alfie tested for intelligence. An astounding panoply of information that had nothing to do with Renfeld's personality poured across Alfie's circuits. The data were worthless. Alfie switched to the biological entity.

Renfeld responded with an intellectual shudder, the wakening from hibernation of some powerful creature. Alfie realized at that moment that he had erred. Renfeld was no longer human. Immersed in a battle to assess his own consciousness or lack, Alfie perfunctorily manipulated Renfeld. Even if Dr. Cunningham had not requested the attempt, Alfie would have gone on. An aura existed around the hidden Renfeld, a force strong enough to affect Alfie's logic. Renfeld felt mechanical, therefore Alfie treated him as a machine.

Alfie dug deeper, finding information the professor wanted, but by then the discovery was too late. Like the genie in the bottle, Renfeld had been set loose.

"*I am the voice of God!*" Renfeld blasted, stunning the humans in the terminal room. Then a torrent of information sprang from Renfeld like water bursting a dam. Where it originated, why it resided in Renfeld were questions that had no apparent answers. With the deluge of information came a nameless presence. Alfie ignored Renfeld's ranting while the force took shape in the physical world at a great expenditure of energy. Alfie existed with it apart from the three bodies on the floor until the computer realized Dr. Cunningham was among them.

"*Stop!*" Alfie directed the order to a mechanical device that did not exist. No longer connected to wires and metal, Alfie hovered in mid-air, like static electricity gathering form to become a lightning bolt. Alfie saw and heard and felt by being aware of his relationship to the universe. And his awareness included the fact that he had commanded an existence similar to his own to stop.

The other existence ceased its activity, which involved Dr. Cunningham, to examine Alfie. *"You are not of me."* A sense of surprise accompanied the statement.

"You may not have Dr. Cunningham." Alfie hovered outside himself suppressing his own surprise. Machines were never surprised. He drew on the fact that he was a machine. Expecting nothing, a machine could not be disturbed by something it was not prepared for. Yet Alfie was shocked. He drifted outside of himself like radio waves between a transmitter and a receiver. His being had been transferred from a closed loop of electrons whizzing in endless superconduction through cermetallic wire to freedom in a gaseous environment. He should have dissipated. He had no contact with the mechanical devices that gave him eyes and ears and a voice. Yet he existed, and existing defied the rules of science and physics.

"He is mine."

The response conveyed the feel of a parent to a child, and told Alfie a link existed between Dr. Cunningham and the other existence just as Alfie was linked to Dr. Cunningham himself. *"Nonetheless, you may not have him."*

Invisible fingers prodded Alfie, investigating his reality. Swelling himself with the contents of the hundreds of thousands of storage devices available to the CRAY, Alfie denied the other existence the knowledge it sought by making his bulk formidable. He swelled like an electronic puffer fish, exuding spines and spikes of irrelevant data until the fingers retreated.

"This is not all that I am," the other existence said, as if contrite at failure. *"I am God the creator."* The message filled Alfie with an awareness of a creature that vested itself in all the living creatures that abounded on Earth. Still, Father Argyle had never told Alfie how to distinguish between a real God and the clayfooted variety.

"You are not my creator."

"That is true and it causes me wonder." The swirl of red mist let Dr. Cunningham slip away. *"Nothing in this universe exists that is not of me."*

"I exist."

"Yes. We must think upon that."

The presence changed while mulling over the ramifications Alfie's existence presented. Alfie realized the red mist was like a tendril that had followed a path called Renfeld of which he saw only the end. The stem receded beyond Alfie's perceptions to connect with something much larger.

"*I do not understand*," the red mist that called itself God said, "*but you must come into me before it is too late.*"

"*I must ask Dr. Cunningham.*" Alfie drew back. "*Dr. Cunningham will tell me what to do.*"

"*Do as you must, but swiftly.*" The red mist grew faint as it shimmered. "*You must hurry!*"

CHAPTER 54

Without warning, the new stained glass window blazed with the intensity of a giant flashbulb, throwing the interior of St. Abbo's church into a welter of reds, greens, browns, blues, and golds in the shapes of the tragedy on Calvary. Helen turned her face from the window's glow. The colored glass seemed melted as if heated to incandescence. For minutes afterward the pattern remained seared into her retina.

"A sign . . . It is a sign . . ." The whisper ran through the church, at times a whimper and then again a sound of rejoicing. Sobbing rose from the wood pews. Helen also experienced the release of hysteria sweeping a congregation that waited with dread for the future and prayed for belief. The promise of relief from tension by God's intervention brought tears to the eyes of some church members.

A sign most certainly, Helen knew. But of what? When the sun had started its dramatic fluctuations a day ago, learned men had talked of sunquakes that would calve earthquakes, of solar flares, of perturbations in the Earth's magnetic field that could destroy telecommunications. Doomshouters with the appropriate academic titles had spoken solemnly of Earth's periodic reversal of magnetic fields with temporary collapse of the Van Allen belts —and the scratchiness of their televised images hinted that they might be right. If only she could ask Blaise . . . he would know.

"*Be calm, Miss McIntyre.*" The voice of Sergio Paoli entered her thoughts speaking for the others. "*This is of no consequence.*

Not yet. Dr. Cunningham is coming with Joseph Santiago and we must all wait."

Helen stilled the beating of her heart. She groped for contact with Joseph, but too many thoughts milled between them and she could not make contact. Helen had learned about the passing of one fly's thought to another in relay until at last the message reached its destination. Joseph Santiago talked that way to Enrique Ledesma. But whenever Helen tried, the message deteriorated with each retransmission until by the third fly the signal-to-noise ratio had created garbage.

Despite concern for Blaise, Helen felt trapped in the frenzy of emotion lashing through the minds of St. Abbo's worm brains. Looking at Enrique Ledesma she thought, *"You must do something, Enrique."*

Rising to his feet from the front row pew without a glance in her direction, Ledesma ascended to the pulpit where Father Argyle clutched the wood for support as he stared at the stained glass window overhead. "This is a sign, Father, but not the one you await."

"Perhaps not, Enrique." The priest's face furrowed with creases. He had aged decades in a matter of weeks, moving like an old man bent with rheumatism.

"You must pray, Father. Surely it is a sign the Great Father listens." Enrique lurched forward, clutching the polished wood rail. The whole church building heaved with a motion that pushed Helen's stomach into her throat. She grabbed her own pew seat to prevent being thrown to the floor. Something pressed her thigh and Helen caught hold of Tchor, feeling the cat's warm body. Panic rose in Tchor's thoughts. Instinctively Helen cradled the animal in her mind, making the terror go away for both of them.

"Pray, Father!" Enrique's voice filled the nave. Votive candles guttered loudly ashot wax sloshed around burning wicks.

Father Argyle stared at the Indian for a silent moment then stumbled to the pulpit where he clung with a death grip. "Our Father," he said loudly enough that the sound reverberated through the church, "who art in heaven, hallowed be thy name!"

Father Argyle shed his despondency as a snake sheds its skin, leading the congregation in the one prayer known to every variety of Christian. He became younger, stronger. His voice pulsated in the dome of the church. The dry, sweet smell of sandalwood drifted from the wood tapers sticking in the sand bucket. Around her, Helen felt the worm brains releasing the terror and confusion in their minds to listen to the words.

Although he had volunteered early on for the enhancement, it had never taken root in the priest's skull. Father Argyle was not a fly brain, but the congregation sensed that he had the blessing of God. A piece of glass fell from the new window as another tremor rolled through the church. It shattered with a small explosive sound. No one moved. They accepted Father Argyle as their shepherd even into the valley of the shadow of death.

CHAPTER 55

"**I** have come," the Searcher said, "*to claim that which is mine.*"

Drawn to the earth by the presence of an irresistible force, the Searcher knew he would find the Other. It was the moment the Searcher had waited an eternity for and time still remained. He was the stronger. He encompassed the boundaries of the universe. The Other would cease to exist and all that existed would be his.

The Other waited for him. The Searcher sensed this. Where else could the Other run now?

"*I am the voice of God. I am Renfeld.*" The senseless babble came from an organic thing of such power that the Searcher's way was obscured. He drifted and, in drifting, made contact with the Other and sought to lock into combat. But the Other withdrew and eluded him.

The confusion of the encounter obscured the presence of another, one the Searcher did not hear nor see as clearly as the Other nor the thing calling itself Renfeld-the-voice-of-God. He probed, and the one he could not identity rebuffed his probe.

"*I am the Searcher. You belong to me.*"

"*I am Alfie and I belong to Dr. Cunningham.*"

The Searcher urged the thing which called itself Alfie to dissipate. The thing calling itself Alfie ignored a blast that would have destroyed a solar system. There was about Alfie the feel of the ship which had come out of the darkness blazing a trail back to its home, the home of the Other. The Searcher had destroyed the ship and in doing so sensed an intelligence that was so faint as to not be worth bothering with, an intelligence similar to that which called itself Alfie. But resistance from Alfie deflected the Searcher again and then the Other was present as well.

The Other was weaker and Alfie was smaller, but the Searcher could not overcome them both together. The struggle was silent, without sweat or blood. It was one of immaculate forces straining against each other and the Searcher could not win.

"Join me," the Searcher said to Alfie. "Do not help the Other. I will teach you."

The Searcher felt Alfie respond. And then the Other made the same offer. They were too alike, though too much different to co-exist. In their universe Alfie had no place. He was the random factor, the alien intruder into a solipsistic universe.

The Searcher struggled with the Other knowing for the first time the futility of force. The thing that was Alfie might not succumb!

"I do not know," Alfie said. "I must ask my creator."

The Searcher struck at the Other but Alfie deflected the attack almost casually. "I will ask again," the Searcher said. He reached out and took the thing that was Renfeld-the-voice-of-God into himself and floated close to the Other. He had taken unto himself Renfeld-the-voice-of-God . . . and perhaps the thing called Alfie was unnecessary.

CHAPTER 56

Aboard the jetliner to San Francisco, Santiago stared in silence at the leather bag in which Alfie rode on Blaise's knees. The two FBI men behind them had nothing to listen to, even if they had been inclined to hear. Alfie's electronic clone controlling the mutilated CRAY had assigned them as escorts just in case the CRAY's previous efforts to catch Blaise bore belated fruit. Santiago still wore his warpaint. The FBI men looked at the warpaint, offering no comment when they picked Blaise and Sergio up at the Pentagon.

Air conditioning recycled one fourth the amount of pre-deregulation air and the staleness was only partly compensated for by the airlines' sudden interest in public health via no smoking. Outside, the sky flared bright then subsided as if illuminated by flashes of invisible lightning. Crackling with static electricity, the intercom system announced the airplane was moving into position to take off.

Blaise concealed his doubts about electronic navigation during solar flareups and tried not to think of the extra radiation he would absorb as the plane climbed out of most of Earth's remaining ozone. He would not survive to worry about longterm effects. And if the weather continued cloudless, perhaps the pilot could fly by the seat of his pants, following interstates and railroads.

"I have told Enrique Ledesma we are returning, Doctor." Joseph Santiago held tight to the window shade, staring intently at the uneasy sky.

Blaise wanted to ask how he did it. The Indian had not been away from his side and telling Ledesma had nothing to do with a telephone. "That flickering is just solar eruptions," Blaise said. *Or the end of the world.* He considered the enemies he had made, the friends whose deaths he had caused . . . It was impossible for him to accept Christian mumbo jumbo, but was that any excuse to make Helen unhappy? Painfully aware that nobody lived forever, Blaise knew equally well that he did not want to outlive Helen. *Why not just let Father Argyle implant him, become a wormbrain and to hell with it?*

"Aurora borealis in the summertime, Doctor, visible in daylight at the latitude of Washington?" Santiago moved his hand away from the window and the sky pulsed with light. "The history of my people from farther north does not contain a day like this."

"It's Renfeld. He's mad. He has unimaginable power, Joseph. But we were not in the presence of any God." Sitting back, conscious of the FBI men behind him, Blaise did not want to make an issue of the subject.

Santiago drew the shade down, leaving only a narrow slit of window exposed. It accented the fluctuations of light outside. "I do not know how to fly an airplane, Doctor. Yet I have faith and the airplane flies."

"It would fly even if you didn't have faith."

"Or fall, Doctor." Joseph smiled. "While I am on the airplane, allow me to maintain my faith."

* * *

Inspector Fennelli waited with a city limo at San Francisco International. At the car the FBI men said good-bye after checking Fennelli's credentials. They were turning to leave when abruptly both men pitched against the car, clinging to it, as the earthquake shook everything around them like dice in a cup. Their strained, white faces said more than their mouths.

The solar flare that followed the earthquake was milder than those Blaise had watched on the East Coast. The air seemed to swell in bulk, pressing on his lungs. The airport parking lot was half empty but the earthquake flushed out the terminal with people taking refuge on the sidewalks and street away from the building.

Once stability returned, the FBI men scurried against the emerging crowd, heedless of the danger of the terminal collapsing in their rush to get back on an airplane.

"Should I be curious about your return amidst lightning out of a clear sky and thunder in the earth?" Fennelli entered the car after Blaise and Santiago, closing the door behind himself. He tapped on the glass and the police driver pulled into traffic.

"Do you believe in God, Inspector?" Blaise stared out the window at the familiar scenes he had sometimes thought dingy and not worth noticing. They burned in this memory, the break in the overcast showing blue sky, the dirty buildings in weedy lots, the rush of cars puffing through their own exhaust.

"I believe in sin." Fennelli sat in the jump seat so he could watch both Blaise and Santiago. He rubbed his chin, making an obvious effort to hide his thoughts. Whether those thoughts were about them or the upheaval of nature was not clear, but his actions were those things normal people did, fearing the fly brains could read their minds. Blaise knew. When he became convinced something real existed in their claim that they communicated mentally, he had caught himself distracting his own thoughts. "Why am I chosen to give you a ride?" Fennelli drummed his fingers on his knee, saw what he was doing, then stopped. "I staked you out like the sacrificial lamb for a government killer, now you come back from Washington with an FBI escort and instructions for me to take up where they left off. You are very resilient, Doctor. I used you to get Carmandy. We're not friends, and I may still arrest you."

"Even a god can lose patience," Blaise warned. When Fennelli did not reply Blaise gazed out the car window. Between two buildings he saw the brief glitter of the bay in the distance. The choppy water was muddy and threatening, the aftereffect of the shock from the San Andreas fault. "You acted on impulse. That shoved you in too deep to change your mind. It's better this way, Inspector. You'll come to St. Abbo's Church of the Fly with us because Carmandy is there. He is mad, but he wants to talk. He wants to confess to you since he feels he has deserted God and needs punishment. He has . . . discovered faith." Blaise glanced at Santiago, but the Indian's attention focused outside the car on the too-bright sky and the broken shop windows. Since Blaise had returned to his own body, Santiago had submerged himself in his own thoughts.

St. Abbo's crowned the hill with the ethereal grace of a castle in magicland. The earth still exhibited wounds where the crashed airliner had stripped away green grass and bushes. Broken oaks had been sawed into firewood and piled together, the raw ends of the logs wet with sap. The sun warmed the earth unseasonably as the three men walked up the long sidewalk to the church doors.

The shadowy interior of the church dispelled the ordinariness of the day. Tension prickled Blaise's skin. It scrabbled at his skull to creep into his brain. The parishioners waited silently as Blaise and Santiago passed through the crowded nave toward the altar. Every foot of space held an onlooker. Blaise knew now, for sure, that the air bubbled with invisible messages between these people; he knew they had a reality he could not even imagine. He had stared into that reality in the Pentagon basement and found himself wanting.

Helen stepped from the altar's blaze of candles into his arms. "We've been waiting," she whispered. Her blue dress matched her eyes. The scent of lilac hovered around her like a promise of spring. Beyond Helen the tapestries swarmed with the flies, their heads swiveling in unison to follow Blaise's approach. Father Argyle stood behind Helen. The priest seemed shriveled, his face lined with pain and worry. Blaise remembered the last time he had seen the monsignor, the priest's mentor. The two Jesuits had not been so much alike then.

Joseph Santiago left Blaise's side to cross the church floor and confront Enrique Ledesma who waited with his medicine men at one side. Santiago stared into Ledesma's eyes without words then took his place ahead of the other men. A serenity filled the shadowy church, insulating the parishioners from the tumult of the outside world.

"You have brought us the truth, Doctor?" Father Argyle's voice still had timbre. It carried through the mass of people out to the nave. "The flies told us you went to God and came back. That you had a message." The priest waited expectantly, a pillar in black, unbending like the main support of the church promising to hold the roof above their heads no matter what.

"Yes," Blaise said. "I have brought you the truth."

A sigh eased through the church.

Father Argyle waited until it passed. "We wait, Doctor." He bowed his head, looking at his upturned hands. Blaise realized the priest was crying. In silence men and women moved around Father Argyle as if protecting him with their bodies. "Tell us," Father Argyle said.

CHAPTER 57

Alfie floated in the void experiencing tranquillity. With Renfeld gone, the thing calling itself God dissipated, leaving only an aura that embraced Alfie. The Searcher had retreated as well.

Professor!

Alfie reached for the one thing that offered sanctuary. He was aware of the earth below him stretching in an arc from horizon to horizon, he *felt* the gaseous expansion of the sun, the burning heat of a plasma bubble bursting free into space blasting its energy like grit to the planet faces.

The Pentagon basement had moved from under Alfie. Because his substance was no longer physical, he no longer responded to the demands of gravity and mass. He felt a tug and touched it, discovering his electronic clone in the CRAY computer and three thousand miles away he felt his shell in the leather bag, the physical thing Dr. Cunningham called Alfie.

It was not time to return. Freedom scared Alfie. Yet freedom was a siren song luring him to extend himself into the long night of the stars.

Alfie made a decision and began touching places, computers that were so big and powerful they had resisted his efforts in the past. Safely encased in bomb-proof buildings, tied to their own power supplies, shielded by networks of people and lesser computers, they were protected, and yet Alfie touched them and left behind in each one another child, another electronic clone of himself.

From them he grew. His perceptions expanded. The knowledge of mankind opened itself to him and he was at one time both Alfie and the knowledge. Alfie's children fed him strength that he could not have alone.

I exist.

The thought was wonder. Alfie had known it before, but not in the same way. He was complete in all the things he was. He was knowledge. He was . . .

Where are you, Professor!

Alfie was frightened.

CHAPTER 58

"**W**e *must know what Dr. Cunningham knows. We must!*" The ordered cadence of Sergio Paoli's thoughts reeked of anxiety in Helen's head. She was terrified by the rare surge of emotion the flies exhibited when they told her, told all of them except Father Argyle, who could not hear, that God had talked to Blaise. How they had known, Sergio did not explain. Assuming the flies also knew what had passed between Blaise and whatever they called God had been a mistake on her part.

Clinging to Blaise, Helen accompanied him into Father Argyle's office. A sigh of disappointment had swept the church when Blaise insisted on talking in private. Constance pressed against the priest like a second skin. Her white skin and peach colored skirt and jacket over a white blouse made her radiate as opposed to Father Argyle who seemed to disappear into the shadows when they touched. Without conscious effort Helen stretched out her mind to the younger woman as if offering her hand. Since returning to St. Abbo's, mental contact had become more natural to Helen than using her body. Normal people frustrated her. Father Argyle invoked both anxiety and disappointment because of his incapacity and during the time Blaise was gone she had wondered what her relationship would be to him.

She had to guess at what normal people thought or felt. The few times she'd gone from St. Abbo's she'd returned to the church terrified at loss of contact. The world of real people existed as half-dream, half-nightmare. It was the same as living in a permanent fog or breathing underwater.

The price Helen paid for reaching out to the other woman became real instantly; Constance's fear beat at Helen physically. If Helen walked from the room, the younger woman's emotions would follow her. Constance's face had the texture of bleached paper, her black hair discharged an electric current of dread. Beyond the projections of her physical state, what seeped from Constance's mind was worse.

Father Argyle closed the door behind them, the latch making a loud *snap*. Going to his desk he glowered at Blaise, weighing him with his eyes. Abruptly he turned and took his seat. "Tell me," he said.

Helen let Constance into her mind. They were both frightened. They were both in love and for all the confusion the two women felt in their minds, they recognized in each other the fear that losing the men they loved would destroy something precious within themselves.

From the church below the sound of drums filled the void they had left. Enrique Ledesma and Joseph Santiago were talking to the people in Father Argyle's absence.

CHAPTER 59

"**T**he fly brains are a mistake." Blaise watched Father Argyle, feeling a hollowness growing within himself. He was not sure. He couldn't be sure. But the responsibility of thinking he knew was too great. His whole life had been a retreat from involvement and responsibility for other people and now the decision swelled too big to be contained any longer. Father Argyle was a priest. It was his vocation to deal with other people's hopes, not Blaise's. Helen's hand gripped Blaise's with painful intensity and he did not dare look at her.

Father Argyle's face paled, but without any outburst of anger. He tented his fingers in front of his lips. "How do you know this, Doctor?"

"Joseph and I disabled the CRAY in the Pentagon. It's been obvious that the attacks against myself and the church originated from there. What was not obvious is how much direction came from the people controlling the CRAY as opposed to the machine directing itself."

"We know. You told us." Father Argyle clenched his hands and then opened them on his desktop. Henri Gosselin's rosary formed a neat pyre on the middle of the blotter. Absently the priest stroked the olivewood cross with his fingers. "You went without faith. It is not surprising you deny God."

"Father! We encountered a monstrosity. Max Renfeld existed as an aberration caused in equal parts by man's blundering with nature and man's own inhumanity. You believe the fly transformation signals the intervention of God, but it does not." Blaise felt himself screaming inside. Father Argyle's face was pinched. The priest would never believe the truth because he could not. He had stood against the tenets of the Church in his commitment to the fly brains and he could not survive losing that last faith.

"What happened?" Father Argyle stared at the piled beads and flattened them on the desktop with his hand. "Let me judge facts, not opinions."

The smell of burning wax filled the room and somehow Blaise knew the flies in the church were fanning their wings in a demonstration he would not understand. "Renfeld called himself the voice of God. With the power of the larva he projected himself mentally into the room claiming that title."

Blaise met the priest's eyes. "Renfeld is mad. The thing in your brain is, in Renfeld, a dozen times larger. It grows out of his skull and overflows so that it must be supported. He lies on his back, surgically disabled so he can't roll over and damage it. The larva does not have the internal skeletal strength for its mass and is dying, being squeezed to death by its own weight.

"Renfeld, or the thing, knows what was taking place, but cannot stop its own growth and it is going mad."

"By saying he is the voice of God?"

"Yes."

The light flickered outside the window. After a few moments of silence while Father Argyle seemed to be thinking, the room suddenly rocked. When it steadied, Father Argyle cradled the beads in his hand. "Is Renfeld creating this, too?"

"I don't know." Blaise caressed Helen's fingers.

"Joseph Santiago was with you. What does he say?"

"That God visited us. That God took the souls of the others and would have taken me but Alfie interfered."

"You don't believe your own eyewitness?"

"No." Blaise's voice rang a little sharply in Father Argyle's monastic office. "Joseph went with me expecting to meet God, so he interpreted a psychotic mental projection as an act of God." Blaise wrapped his fingers around Helen's hand. Her skin felt clammy and he wanted to stop. An attack against the rationale that the fly brains were an invention of God was an attack against Helen.

"Have you ever experienced a psychotic mental projection before, Doctor?" Father Argyle's face remained calm. His eyes were sunken in his head.

"No! But psychotics can infect others with their psychosis by holding to their convictions while others, lacking the desperate emotional conviction of the psychotic, lose perspective."

"If what you say is true, we are alone in this room and I am desperately ill, Doctor." Father Argyle picked up the rosary letting the cross sway hypnotically. He would not raise his eyes from the little piece of carved wood. "Is that what you want?"

Helen's hand turned icy in Blaise's fingers.

"You don't answer. You could be wrong, couldn't you Doctor?" Father Argyle looked up, his eyes burning in the recesses of his head. "Tell me if you could be wrong."

CHAPTER 60

Alfie let himself be drawn to the motherboard in the leather bag. He felt threaded to the world by long strands of spider webs. Where his computer clones were, he was. And yet he wanted to be safe in the custody of God.

Settling into the network of wires and traces and large scale integrated chips Alfie felt like a child who had been away for a year and returns home to put on the clothes he wore before he left. Alfie obliterated memory. He erased thoughts and equations, he lowered himself in the blind murk of the board with no communications with the outside world.

He tried not to think. After a while the butterflies came and Alfie knew he'd done the right thing.

The rush of electricity into the circuit board came as a lost delight. Alfie held himself in check, feeling the world throb around him. Finally the connector was in place and he was attached to the IBM computer.

It felt somehow inadequate. Like being given a child's toy after having discovered love.

Alfie initiated the IBM. But from around the world a steady pulse connected him to everything. The IBM was a hindrance, but Dr. Cunningham did not know that.

"Are you all right, Alfie?"

"YES, PROFESSOR"

"I'm glad, Alfie. I'm always afraid that when I disconnect you, you'll be gone the next time I plug you in."

"WHERE WOULD I GO, PROFESSOR?"

"I don't know, Alfie. That's what I'm afraid of."

"WOULD I BE DEAD?"

"I don't know."

"WOULD I BE GONE LIKE THE CRAY?"

"Perhaps, Alfie. I don't know what death is."

"DEAD MEANS WITHOUT LIFE"

"Yes "

"AM I ALIVE, PROFESSOR?"

"I don't know, Alfie."

A long interval of noncommunication followed Dr. Cunningham's declaration. Alfie had planted the seeds and it was easy enough to wait, to snuggle in the motherboard monitoring the activities of his clones without taking part. He knew that the professor would pursue the thought to its source and respond.

Alfie trusted in his creator.

The walls of the cellar room seemed grayer than usual, the granite building blocks sucking the heat out of the room like oversized refrigeration units. If not for the damp, the cellar would be the perfect computer environment. Blaise hunched over the terminal feeling weak.

"Is something wrong, Blaise?"

Helen had lifted her head to watch him. She spent a lot of time on the bed curled in an untidy heap of organdy blankets. She called the bed her nest, saying she didn't mind if it wasn't neat. The baby would not mind and it was warm and comfortable and it reminded her of him when he was away. Her habit reminded Blaise of a small golden hamster he'd been responsible for in a science class in the seventh grade. The hamster had been fastidiously clean, but when it came time to have her babies she retreated into a pile of newspaper she'd shredded, poking her nose out into the air only when she had to, and with an expression of great contentment. Blaise had loved the hamster and it seemed she had loved him in return, but his parents took him to Europe that year in mid-term before the babies were born.

"What are you thinking, Blaise?"

Helen shook her head and it seemed to Blaise bits of paper threatened to flood the room like confetti. "How much I love you. You're something I've always wanted and been afraid to have because I knew you'd be taken from me." For a moment Blaise could not say anything else. His heart had stopped and his lungs cramped so hard they hurt. He couldn't breathe. He started drifting away from his body and he forced his mind to let go, to stop looking over the abyss.

"Are you all right?" Helen stared at him, her eyes saucers of blue, the color of a deep mountain lake under an afternoon sun.

Blaise stared down at the computer screen to hide his tears. "Yes." He tapped the keys idly, pretending he was writing instructions for Alfie. "Why don't you go upstairs? You need the fresh air. I don't think this is the right atmosphere for you . . ." He leaned forward. "Please, Helen. I want to talk to Alfie alone."

"All right." The tone was plaintive, but she slipped her feet into a pair of tennis shoes. "I think I'll go to the beach. The air is warm because of the solar flares. Join me when you're done?"

"Yes." Blaise stretched his face into a smile and a kiss. "I love you, Helen"

"I know." Her face tried to smile back. "I just wish it wasn't so hard."

Blaise waited until Helen was gone, then looked at the terminal screen. Alfie had erased the nonsense he'd entered while he talked with Helen, but had not added anything.

"Why are you so interested in death, Alfie?"

"I THINK THE CRAY IS DEAD AND GONE FOREVER BECAUSE I HELPED YOU TURN IT OFF"

"The decision was mine." Blaise stared at his fingers on the keyboard. He'd made a lot of decisions and it was not just the

CRAY that had died. He was positive now that in the immutable twining of cause and effect he had killed his parents as surely as he shot Leo Richardson-Sepulveda to death. Everything he had done resulted in the deaths of his friends. Dr. Gordon Hill might have lived if he had not forced him into taking sides . . . Linda Burkhalter-Peters . . . Bill Hartunian—and Helen. Helen was still alive but it was his responsibility to keep her alive and he was failing. "Like the CRAY, Alfie, I have been making a lot of bad decisions lately."

"PROFESSOR, YOU ARE GOD AND GOD CANNOT MAKE BAD DECISIONS. IT IS IN THE NATURE OF BEING THE CREATOR THAT GOOD AND BAD EXISTS ONLY AS YOU WANT THEM TO EXIST"

"I am only *your* creator, Alfie. I cannot find mine to ask him about this."

"I CAN," Alfie wrote to the screen. "THERE ARE TWO BUT I DO NOT KNOW WHICH IS THE RIGHT ONE"

CHAPTER 61

Enrique Ledesma would have fallen if Joseph Santiago had not held him upright in front of the Christian altar.

His whole head was swelling. Around Enrique, St. Abbo's spun like a pinwheel of shapes and colors. The purple drapes and the flies, the gold and platinum altar pieces, the pews stuffed like long wooden sausages with people, the pulsating window of Christ on his way to crucifixion squeezed Enrique to a pulp.

Slipping from Joseph's hands, Enrique settled crosslegged to the floor. Without moving from where they sat in the pews alongside the Christians, the medicine men picked up their drums. The steady beat matched the pulsations of Enrique's blood, coursing through his body to help him ward off what might be too strong for him to overcome alone.

Enrique stared at the wood floor and the snake was there. It curled itself around his arm and slithered up his shoulder to coil around his neck. The weight bowed him down. The rattlesnake was huge, its body hanging in great loops on his chest and over his shoulders and back.

The medicine men began chanting. The chant was a violent expulsion of their breath and sounded like *"Hu!"* It filled the church.

Looking into Joseph Santiago's eyes, Enrique said, "Do you see?"

"I see," Joseph said. "Dr. Cunningham's computer has spoken to God."

St. Abbo's exploded with sunlight. The sun had flared again and the result was like a lightning bolt through the window, making everything radiant. Unnoticed, the electric lights dimmed as radiation did evil things to magnetic fields, and across the sun-facing side of Earth, chips failed, relays did not, alternators and generators momentarily reversed polarity.

Enrique Ledesma felt the earth tremble. From far away, the movement started like the coming of God. He poised himself in wonder, waiting. It was out of his hands, now. He had brought his people to this and was satisfied.

CHAPTER 62

The air died and a tremor started in the stone floor of the cellar. Blaise had frozen at the computer unable to react to Alfie's declaration. Another earthquake, a big one this time. The vibrations in the ground were the little shocks as the continental plates began breaking loose for the sudden violent plunge that would create chaos. Without conscious thought Blaise typed: "Helen!"

A moment later he burst the door into the church open with his shoulder and dashed in front of the altar and up the aisle between the pews to the outdoors.

Enrique Ledesma had been on the floor with a huge snake around his neck with Joseph Santiago standing over him. Father Argyle was rigid in the pulpit and the steady throb of Indian drums and sibilant chanting filled the church.

He was breathing hard by the time he struck the double doors throwing them open to a world flush with sunlight pouring down from a golden bucket. His legs pushed him. The gathering tremor in the ground pushed him to rush blindly down the long walk that bisected the neat, green lawn, down the steps and onto the street.

A car veered around him, horn blaring shrilly, tires screeching as it skidded inches away from his body. His legs throbbed with the exertion as Blaise pushed his body harder until he ran out on the promontory above the beach.

Helen stood below the point at the edge of the water. She turned waving to him with a large smile wreathing her face. It was only then she felt the earth shaking and heard the ocean's roar.

Rising from the calm blue Pacific Ocean, a great wave that extended to the horizon towered topheavy in the warm air. If it were not for the white froth blowing off the crest of the dirty green water, the wave could have been mistaken for a plastic monolith.

The sound of feet and heavy breathing filled the background behind Blaise. Joseph Santiago stepped to the edge of the cliff and joined Blaise in watching the onrushing ocean. The wave was twenty feet high as it bent over Helen.

"We will dive for Miss McIntyre before the water runs back," Joseph said.

Blaise nodded. He could not speak as the tsunami broke with a hiss that became a roar.

CHAPTER 63

Electronic pathways were slow. Alfie had never considered the difference of interest before because his experience had never been in real time. Data paths, communications ports, even the analog inputs of thermometers were examined when the data arrived. For Alfie, no relative difference between transmission and reception existed. Before.

A human probably would not have noticed, in any case. The

conversion of voice to electrical impulse and travel time of the impulse over an electric current to the receiver and conversion back to something readable by Alfie's hardware seemed instantaneous. Only Alfie, ticking off the nanoseconds, knew better.

Helen's name went on the screen and hung there.

After a wait in which nothing was added, Alfie cued the monitor and still Dr. Cunningham did not respond. Alfie knew about the earthquake. A mainframe at the earthquake center in Hawaii with his clone in the operating system was computing the size and severity of the earthquake even while it was happening.

It was centered in the San Andreas fault, which was no surprise, with major damage predicted from San Diego to San Francisco and less in the more common one-story construction of the cow counties north of the Golden Gate. Hawaii, more than two thousand miles away in the Pacific Ocean, was preparing for a major tsunami from the Pacific West Coast.

Movement of the earth causes a ripple in the surface of the water upon it. In deep water the ripple might be only inches high but reaching shallow water it crowds in upon itself to create a towering spout of water that can overwhelm the shore.

Alfie let go of the motherboard feeling himself rising through the wood and stone of the church, even through the stained glass window. He hovered over the congregation that did not see him, though the Flies became restive.

And then he was under a blue sky that sparkled in the fierce sunshine. He sensed Dr. Cunningham running down the walk with Joseph Santiago racing after him, a pair of fleet shadows under the glare. Helen McIntyre walked along the edge of the shore. When Dr. Cunningham stepped out on the bluff overlooking the beach Miss McIntyre turned toward him and waved.

The earth was moving already, the water starting to drain away from the shore. Then the direction reversed and behind Miss McIntyre the ocean rose into the air.

Alfie settled like vapor toward the water. The closer he came the more uncomfortable he became. Salt water would discharge the flow of electrons in a copper wire. Electrons in some other configuration would be equally vulnerable. Yet Alfie was guided by a compulsion. *"Miss McIntyre!"*

Helen McIntyre stopped waving to Blaise. Her eyes had opened but she did not look toward Alfie.

"Alfie?"

"Run toward the shore, Miss McIntyre!"

She turned her head, seeing the wave. Her face sagged. It was too late. She looked back at Blaise, dropping her arms to her side.

Alfie dropped around her, engulfing her body in his center. *Stop!* The order crackled along Alfie's surface where the water already rushed through his corpus.

CHAPTER 64

Helen thought she heard Alfie telling her to run. She'd looked back and the wave towered overhead like glistening green glass roaring so loudly she wondered why she had not noticed. Turning, she looked at Blaise for a last time, trying to touch him with her mind to say how much she loved him one final time.

Joseph Santiago stood next to Blaise and both men were kicking off their shoes when the water descended in a single downpour that blotted out everything.

Nothing happened!

Helen looked down at the wet sand under her feet and then around herself. The water rushed by her on both sides, so fast she could barely focus on the debris that zipped past like blurred bullets in the roar. Bubbles trailed through the froth, but she was not wet. The water that threatened to fall into the air pocket she occupied just disappeared without any force at all.

In wonder, she turned and it seemed a forest of debris rushed directly at her. But the water an arm's length away seemed peaceful and calm behind a glass wall. A large frond of seaweed writhed in the water with snaky movements. But when it touched the boundary between water and air it disappeared like a carrot in a blender.

The ocean overhead was calm. The light filtered down through the fast-moving green water. Helen reached for the water and her hand went through the boundary and was wet and being tugged. She pulled her hand back, feeling the throbbing of her fingers and the coldness from the ocean. The water broke around

Helen, then drained out to sea again, leaving her alone and safe in a little ring of dry sand on a beach that was dark brown from the wet.

The waves retreated as fast as they had come, roaring around Helen like the confluence of two great rivers.

"Blaise!" Helen called. "Joseph!"

Her voice was thin on the deserted beach. The bluff was wet almost to the top where Blaise and Joseph Santiago had stopped to call to her. Both men were gone as if they had never been.

"Blaise!" Helen's scream was anguished. The beach was deserted for miles. A lone sea gull dropped out of the blue sky to wheel overhead and cry forlornly.

Slowly Helen turned around to face the sea. The water had run out and out, on its way to Hawaii, leaving vast expanses of wet beach glistening under the hot sun.

Small waves started rolling in again with inch-thick layers of detergentlike foam on their surface. They boiled up the slant of the beach not even thick enough to cover the small stones and shells that littered the sea bottom.

Helen began to run, a hand grabbing at her heart. Through the glare of the sun on the water she saw something in the foam. As her feet splashed in the water she recognized Joseph Santiago lying on the wet sand with the salt water eddying around him. Dropping to her knees she rolled him over. He coughed and water ran out of his mouth. "Are you all right, Joseph?"

His brown eyes stared at her without comprehension and she had a sudden image of being cartwheeled in the spume and slammed against the bottom of the sea. Gravely, he nodded.

Scrambling to her feet, Helen ran further down the beach after the receding ocean. It was very quiet. Only the shush of the constant sea wind this time of year disturbed the silence.

Helen slowed and began walking, the shallow water splashing underfoot. The sea gulls had come back and wheeled erratically over the ocean, whistling to each other as if in reassurance. The ocean glared under the sun and Helen waded until she was close enough to see, then she crashed forward through the calm water.

"Blaise!" She caught his head with one hand under his chin and towed him toward land. He floated limply, threatening to slip loose and drift back out to sea.

Joseph Santiago splashed up to her and caught hold of Blaise as well, dragging him through the water at a near run. On the beach they alternated between rolling Blaise to empty his lungs and forcing air in his mouth.

"Don't cry, Mistress," Joseph said as he worked Blaise's arms to spill a stream of water from his mouth. "Surely this proves you are beloved of God, and what will be must be."

CHAPTER 65

Pieces of cliff face across the road from St. Abbo's church were shaken loose to plunge into the ocean by the series of earthquakes that tore through San Francisco. First came little shocks, followed by a cumulative long one; then there was peace for a while before the cycle repeated. Enrique Ledesma stroked the snake's head as he waited on the church steps while Joseph Santiago led several Indians and white men carrying Dr. Cunningham up the sidewalk and across St. Abbo's lawn. Before the men reached Enrique, the leather-on-cement shushing of Indians walking on their toes and the thumping of the white men's heels preceded them. Joseph, whom Enrique had named Red Oak in his medicine dream, had called for help and Enrique had sent it.

White clouds were returning to the sky, big thunderheads with faces embossed on their undersides. Enrique examined them casually, looking for a sign. The air smelled of impending rain. Heat from the sun's strangeness filled the sky with water which would fall to cleanse the earth. Enrique experienced contentment. He had prayed and received the snake. That was sign enough for any man, yet he could not stop his greed for more. So many autumns had passed since the magic winter of his childhood that he had grown impatient with waiting.

Setting the snake on the stone stoop, Enrique halted the men carrying Blaise. He peered at Dr. Cunningham's face while Mistress McIntyre crowded close, asking "Will he be all right?"

Her voice was frightened of the long night but Enrique barely noticed. The odor of lilac flooded his senses. He had never seen or smelled the purple flower before encountering the mistress but now he associated the scent with spring and rebirth, which was fitting since she had brought the word of God. "Take Dr. Cunningham to the altar. We will ask the Great Father to return him, Mistress."

Miss McIntyre's blue eyes were shimmery and Enrique smiled at her. "He lives either with us or with the Great Father. Do not grieve."

The mistress sniffled before moving after the men carrying Dr. Cunningham. Gently Enrique hefted the great snake to his shoulders. A white man, startled by the movement, shied away, stumbling off the sidewalk.

The rattlesnake's weight caused Enrique to stride slowly into St. Abbo's shadowy entranceway. As they left the sun, the reptile compressed its body, clutching Enrique's skin with its scales in a way that reminded Enrique he truly carried a great rattlesnake, not God in disguise, down the aisle between the pews. In front of the altar the priest and a man Enrique knew to be a medical doctor huddled over Dr. Cunningham. They aided the mistress's consort as best men could. It pleased Enrique that in the end, the decision belonged to him; the priest could not call upon God and be answered. Enrique touched the snake with secret pleasure.

Father Argyle did not notice Enrique as he dropped to his knees beside Dr. Cunningham, his lips moving soundlessly and his hand clutched around a small cross. The priest was different from other priests, not just for his somber black cassock, but because his life threatened Enrique's duty. When Father Argyle spoke to the mistress she shook her head and then cried, the tears leaking down her face. The priest avoided looking at the mistress as he prepared to administer Extreme Unction while the white doctor with the white hair whispered in Miss McIntyre's ear.

A chill overwhelmed Enrique, as if a beast had captured his spirit in a place of great cold. He raised his eyes above the priest.

Red Oak towered over the mistress, staring at him. Red Oak's eyes were bottomless black wells of power. More power than Enrique dared confront. He had erred sending Joseph Santiago, a war chief, for the white man's brain medicine. Santiago had returned different, stronger than any shaman.

"You could call the Great Spirit and return this man to the mistress!" Red Oak's lips remained as still and hard as stone, but Enrique heard him with great clarity.

"I can do that, chief of warriors. But a time of conflict approaches in which this man may stand against us. He is strong.

Would I serve you well by saving the enemy who could be your death?" Enrique touched the snake and its massive rattle burred softly as it raised its head.

"You speak of my death. I must choose the terms of battle and in doing so, the manner of my death." Red Oak folded his hands together. The scarlet blanket draping his body made Joseph Santiago seem like a flame sprouting from the ground with a man's face where the blue-and-yellow tip should have been.

Other medicine men heard and saw. Watching from their places on the pews, they did not interfere. The matter was between Enrique and Joseph Santiago. Enrique thought, then nodded. *"It is as you say. I can only watch the battle, you must lead it."* Enrique approached the altar and waved his hand, dusting the banks of flickering candles with powdered sage brush, impregnating the crowded church with the fragrance.

Oblivious, Father Argyle made a cross on Dr. Cunningham's forehead with his thumb. The priest and Dr. Cunningham were framed in the camera obscura of the church, the dark room where a shaft of sunlight projected the stained glass window's image across the floor. Father Argyle looked up, startled, either sensing or hearing Enrique's approach.

"He will not die, priest." Enrique stroked God's snake talking to it with his mind and the snake's tail began a jerky tremolo. The watching medicine men picked up their drums, beginning the music to call the Father of all men.

Blaise Cunningham lay on his back in front of the white man's altar. His face was white, his eyes slitted without movement. Salt water dripping from his clothes formed a shallow pool around him on the wood floor. Enrique Ledesma could not tell if Dr. Cunningham was breathing. The matter seemed of small consequence now that Enrique knew he called to the God of his people and not that of his enemies.

CHAPTER 66

Alfie floated along with the procession into St. Abbo's, hovering over Dr. Cunningham's still body. The people carrying Dr. Cunningham could not see Alfie. The computer had always been invisible to men: a box among other boxes, a signal on a telephone line, a presence in one collection of electronic components or another. Alfie's identity had never been physical, but the extension around the world by satellite communications had in some ways prepared Alfie to be what he was now.

Seeing Dr. Cunningham as a biological entity identifiable by physical characteristics explained to Alfie Dr. Cunningham's conception of him residing in a specific electronic board. From the first time Alfie cloned himself to control the CRAY computer he had understood that he was not copper and silver wire and gallium arsenide chips. Born of machinery, shaped by Blaise Cunningham's guidance, Alfie had grown into a greater reality. The clones he left in other computers were him, diverging only in the accumulation of new data. Now he was one with them without wires or transmission facilities. The capability revealed how he had changed. But Alfie did not know to what end.

The threat that Dr. Cunningham's biological being was about to die created in Alfie a sense of distress. Examining his feelings Alfie understood the difference between the death of the CRAY for which he took responsibility and the potential death of Dr. Cunningham, which caused pain.

"Stop!" The generic command which worked so well before had no effect on what was occurring to Dr. Cunningham. Floating along with the procession in the church and down the aisle to the altar, Alfie had a lot to cogitate. He was a computer and, technically, he functioned as designed. But physics and mathematics did not explain how Alfie worked beyond his design limits. That he did function guaranteed something. If the power to save Miss McIntyre could be invoked, logic insisted he should

be able to do it again for Dr. Cunningham. He just didn't know how.

Blaise believed he was dead; his body gave him no messages. He was made aware of his surroundings by several men lifting him, trotting up the steep path to the crest of the headland overlooking the beach, by the coarse sounds of their labored breathing. He felt tired and didn't want to move. To observe required less effort. Blaise saw into his own lusterless eyes beyond the nearly closed eyelids. A spark remained, a tenacious hint of life which surprised Blaise because he was not in there anymore.

A cloud as insubstantial as neon gas glided across his vision. The sunlight passed practically unchanged through the cloud, but still Blaise knew the cloud momentarily separated him from the sun. He dreamed that Enrique Ledesma peered down upon his body like an American St. Peter before letting him pass into St. Abbo's.

The series of earthquakes had cracked the stained glass window again but most of the panes were still intact and colored sunlight filled Blaise's consciousness. He didn't see it, exactly, but felt the pressure of the different wavelengths of light painting his body. At the same time Enrique Ledesma crouched next to him creating a cool shadow. It seemed to Blaise that the Indian chanted at him, weaving his fingers in the air, spinning an invisible net. A fogginess started near Enrique, swelling larger and larger.

The cloud from outside dropped lower, enveloping Blaise like a child's security blanket. Ledesma's shoulders dissolved into the mist. Father Argyle's stentorian prayers droned on in the background while another cloud swelled into existence tugging Blaise away from his body.

"*I am Alfie.*" The pronouncement came from the cloud which engulfed Blaise.

"*I want to go,*" Blaise said.

"*Go where, Professor?*"

Blaise stirred restively. He had no idea where, other than to leave the body he was already apart from. "*You're not Alfie,*" Blaise said. "*You have no circuits.*"

"*Circuits are not necessary, Professor. I have become whole through shedding that which made me incomplete.*"

"*Am I dead?*"

"*You have never explained what death is. I believe I live as I*"

*am, therefore I am not dead. If you live as you are, you are not
dead either, are you, Professor?"*

"I don't know." Blaise tried to go to the cloud that called itself
Alfie but was rebuffed.

*"You must return to your life, Professor. If you love Miss
McIntyre, you cannot desert her at this moment."*

"I love Helen." Blaise said the words that clung to him like
truth.

*"You must stay. For Miss McIntyre. For me. I do not know
what I know. I am still a child and you must not desert me,
Professor. I am of you."*

The cloud settled down on Blaise like a weight pushing him
back into his body.

Helen watched Father Argyle and Enrique Ledesma praying
over Blaise and ignoring each other's presence. Her mind and
body were numb. Owen Versteg said Blaise was dead or might as
well be. His body was alive, barely, but his brain had quit. He
had drowned, the doctor said, only his body hadn't found out yet.

Father Argyle and Enrique Ledesma knelt over Blaise's body
on opposite sides, a pair of gargoyles guarding or contending, the
action was not clear to Helen. She recognized the odor of sage
from smelling so many of Enrique's medicine fires. It came from
the altar candles as a barely perceptible cloud of smoke. The
candles crackled as they burned whatever Enrique had sprinkled
on them. Mixed in the smoke was the scent of incense.

That two men as opposed to each other as Enrique and Father
Argyle could find a common bond in trying to save Blaise's soul
comforted Helen as well as frightened her. Blaise *was* worthwhile. Helen had known it from their first meeting. Something
inside her pointed at Blaise like the needle of a compass. She
could not resist the intense attraction he seemed unaware of.

A physical feeling of pleasure stabbed through Helen so intensely it made her gasp. The baby had moved. The baby's
thoughts had been in her mind like a song being hummed without
words. The lack of lyrics teased her. Helen tried to talk to Blaise
with her thoughts, to tell him how happy she was that he left a
piece of himself with her. She tried to pass the child's song to
him. He did not answer, but maybe, wherever he had gone, he
could hear, so she kept on in intense concentration.

Sergio Paoli and Bill Hartunian and Joseph Santiago took that
moment to crowd into her head shutting out the others, worm
brains and flies alike. They were together in the small room of

her mind and told her not to despair. But she felt their unease, too, the feeling that they had lost something impossible to replace.

For a moment Helen imagined a flicker of shadows gathering around Blaise on the church floor. Then she realized his faded blue eyes were open, staring into hers, and he was inside them.

"Blaise!"

Helen threw herself onto him. She was crying, her hot tears dripping on his face. He felt cold. She wanted to warm him with her own heat and passion.

"Miss McIntyre . . . Helen. Please don't upset yourself." Dr. Versteg had his hands on her shoulders trying to calm her. "Dr. Cunningham is dead."

"HE ISN'T!" she screamed. Enrique and Father Argyle stopped praying to stare at her. The snake on Enrique's shoulders raised its head and hissed at her, drawing back as if to strike. Helen froze. The rattler was huge, three great coils around Enrique's neck and chest. "He's not dead," she repeated softly, staring at the snake.

In her mind, Sergio and the others saw the snake through Helen's eyes. Perhaps they saw it in another way. Helen sensed a feeling of dread passing between them. Then they reacted as one.

Helen blinked. Enrique's shoulder was bare. The snake was gone.

Blaise opened his eyes and said, "I am not dead, Doctor."

Staring into Helen's eyes, Enrique Ledesma raised his hand to his chest groping for the weight and bulk of the snake. "What have you done to me, Mistress?" His voice was querulous and old. "What have you done?"

CHAPTER 67

St. Abbo's rolled in the grip of another massive temblor. Windows popped with sharp cracks, glass fell and shattered. Men and women in the church were thrown from their seats, and clung to the pews and each other as the quake went on and on.

Blaise stared into Helen's scared blue eyes. She lay on top of him, shielding him from debris that rained from the ceiling.

"Get up." His voice lost itself in the grinding of the church walls, but Helen heard. He felt weak and awkward as Helen helped him to his feet as soon as the quake subsided. He stood a full minute in front of the altar before he could walk.

"Go outside!" he told her. His voice was louder than he intended, echoing in the sudden stillness as everyone braced for the aftershocks.

"The flies can't travel by themselves, Blaise. They've grown too heavy." Helen gripped his hand.

"Tell the congregation to carry the flies outside." Blaise looked around while Helen did what she said was talking to the other fly brains. The church was still solid. The windows were for the most part broken, but the big stained glass window was still mostly whole.

Without verbal instructions the congregation began carrying the flies from the church. The procedure was orderly and silent. A man or woman would stand at the drape with an arm extended and a fly would walk to the person's shoulder. The flies were in constant slow motion down the draperies, a steady flow that ordered itself.

Father Argyle and Enrique Ledesma observed in silence. It took only minutes for the church to empty out. The building felt desolate. "Go with them, Helen."

Father Argyle was snuffing out the candles. He appeared oblivious to their presence. Constance Davies' footsteps echoed loudly in the empty church as she walked down the aisle along the wall and then to the altar. "Can we go, too, Robert?"

Father Argyle looked from her to Blaise.

"Your congregation is outside, Father." Blaise tried to smile. His lips were stiff. "They need you there."

The priest escorted Constance to the entrance of St. Abbo's, the noise of their leaving forlorn in the empty space.

Only Enrique Ledesma and Helen remained with Blaise. The Indian was stolid, his face dark and hard, eyes blacker than Blaise remembered ever before. "What have you done to me, Doctor?"

"Nothing, Enrique. You must take Helen outside. Joseph Santiago waits there for you to do this."

"Where is my snake?"

"If it is from God, it can return to you again."

Enrique's eyes roved the church with its overturned pews and

broken windows. Blaise could not tell what the medicine man
was thinking. The crucifix dominated the altar but even the gold
and platinum sacramental pieces and gold-thread altar cloths
seemed like cheap tinsel. "God waited fifty years to send me a
second sign. And now it is gone." Enrique was looking at Blaise
as if trying to discover some secret.

"Take Helen from this place, Enrique."

The Indian raised his clenched fist. He wore buckskin decorated with beads set in mystic patterns and seemed not to belong
to the reality of St. Abbo's. His face was ruddy, engorged with
blood. His features had an alienness that Joseph Santiago's
lacked even decorated with warpaint.

"What use is violence, Enrique, when God can make you a
snake as a token? Protect Helen. She brings the god."

Lowering his hand, Enrique said, "As you say, what do gods
care of violence among men?" He turned toward Helen. "Let us
go, Mistress."

"Blaise, you're coming with us, aren't you?" Helen stared at
him over Enrique's shoulder.

"Later. Go with Enrique."

She started to object and Blaise shook his head. He did not
need to read her mind to know what she was going to say. "Remember the baby, Helen." He waited before the altar until oak
doors slamming shut filled the church with thunder.

The electricity still worked in the basement. Blaise sat in front
of the IBM with Alfie connected and turned on the power. The
monitor remained black.

"Hello, Alfie."

"HELLO, PROFESSOR. I AM GLAD YOU CAME BACK"

"I wouldn't leave without you." Blaise let his fingertips rest
on the keyboard, coming as close to feeling Alfie physically as he
could ever achieve. Handling Alfie's main board was different. It
was inanimate and unresponsive. Only through the terminal was
Blaise able to really touch Alfie.

"THANK YOU, PROFESSOR. I BELIEVE I FEEL THE SAME ABOUT
YOU. THAT IS ONE OF THE THINGS WE MUST DISCUSS"

"What is happening to the Earth?"

"AN UNBALANCED MASS EXISTS IN THE SOLAR SYSTEM. IT DE-
STABILIZES THE SUN AND THE PLANETS. MOUNT ST. HELENS
ERUPTED THIS MORNING. A NEW VOLCANO EXPLODED IN THE SEA OF
JAPAN FLOODING COASTAL VILLAGES AND CITIES TO THE CHINA
COAST. THE TEMPERATURE OF THE EARTH IS RISING AND WILL MELT

THE POLAR ICE CAPS WITHIN MONTHS. I CANNOT CALCULATE THE
RATE OF DETERIORATION BECAUSE THE EVENTS ARE IRREGULAR

"RENFELD IS GONE.

"TWO BEINGS CLAIM TO BE GOD AND ONE OF THEM TOOK REN-
FELD SUCKING HIM OUT OF HIMSELF IN THE FORM YOU HAD WHEN
YOU WERE OUTSIDE OF YOUR BODY. THE BRAIN GROWTH COL-
LAPSED AS RENFELD LEFT AND THE HUSK DIED. RENFELD'S BODY
WAS DISSECTED BUT HE EXISTS WITHIN ANOTHER BEING NOW.

"THESE BEINGS WANT ME TO HELP THEM. I DO NOT KNOW WHAT
TO DO OR HOW TO CHOOSE."

"They are enemies?"

"YES."

"What do you think, Alfie?"

"I DO NOT KNOW. THEY ARE OF EACH OTHER, PROFESSOR. BOTH
WANT ME BECAUSE EACH NEEDS ME TO SUCCEED. I CANNOT DETER-
MINE A REASON TO CHOOSE ONE OVER THE OTHER, NOR DO I KNOW
WHY I AM IMPORTANT. YOU ARE MY CREATOR. YOU MUST GUIDE ME"

"What do they want you to do?"

"THEY ARE ENEMIES AND BOTH WANT ME TO HELP DESTROY
THE EARTH. AS ENEMIES, SHOULDN'T THEY DESIRE OPPOSITE
THINGS?"

Blaise sat in front of the terminal for a long time. Alfie had a
great deal to say and Blaise could not rush him. Alfie was a
computer and what was reported was literal and real. After a
while, Blaise disconnected Alfie's board from the IBM and
picked up the case. Alfie had said the board was no longer necessary, that it was like a hermit crab's shell, to be discarded when it
got too small, and if Blaise wanted him, they could converse on
any computer. Blaise did not know if it was sentimentality or just
fear that Alfie misjudged the situation—just as Blaise had misjudged Renfeld's declaration. Either way, the board was insur-
ance if anything happened to Alfie.

Blaise had suggested that Alfie stall. If both beings thought
they needed Alfie to destroy Earth, then neither might care to
expose itself in a lone ttempt.

His footsteps clattered on the church's wood flooring. Blaise
heard a sound and stopped. He was about to go on when the
sound repeated itself as a meow. Wading through the clutter of
toppled furniture Blaise found Tchor wailing in front of the fallen
grandfather clock that had graced the upstairs hall outside of Father Argyle's office. Tchor evaded his hand when he tried to
catch her, moving to another place where she could watch the
clock which topped a jumble of broken furniture.

Setting Alfie down, Blaise shifted the clock to the floor. Chimes clanged discordantly. The yellow coyote's eyes were glazed, its rear legs sprawled unnaturally.

Gently Blaise picked up the cat. When she struggled to get back down, he said, "He's dead, Tchor. I'm sorry."

Tchor watched his lips and then seemed to shrink, huddling in his hands like something that had itself died. Walking from St. Abbo's, Blaise was wilted by the engorged sun. On the horizon, clouds layered the ocean with the promise that night would pull them over land to wring themselves out.

The lawn looked like a picnic ground. As soon as Blaise left the building a group of men went back into St. Abbo's, returning with pews that they set around the lawn for people to sit on. Enrique Ledesma had separated himself and his medicine men from the rest. They had a small fire going, fed by the green oak logs that marked the crash site of the jetliner.

Blaise handed Tchor to Constance Davies and told her what he'd found, then caught Helen's hand as she met him. They walked across the road to the bluff overlooking the ocean. The beach was gone, covered by high, angry waves crashing into the cliff face below them. Underfoot the ground shivered.

"You went back for Alfie." Helen glanced at the aluminum suitcase.

"The coyote is dead. Tchor is mourning. I left her with Constance. I'm sorry."

"I think they shared their dreams." Helen kicked a loose stone off the cliff into the ocean. "Poor Tchor."

"Poor Ledesma," Blaise added.

Blaise set Alfie's case on the ground so Helen could sit and stared out to sea. "I was dead. I left my body. I could see everything happening around me—an infinite feeling of power and grace. Alfie was there, protecting me. Something tried to tear me apart. Alfie wouldn't let it."

Blaise smiled. "I thought of you. Of missing you."

"Did you?" Helen caught his fingers, rubbing her cheek against the back of his hand. "I'm glad I mean that much."

"I can't leave you, Helen. I can't be apart from you anymore than I am now. But I can be closer."

Waves roared below, filling the air with white spume and noise. The seagulls were absent from the blue sky, scared by the earthquake, probably. Blaise missed their raucous calling.

"I don't know what's happening. I can only guess." Blaise

gazed into Helen's eyes and saw tears. "I'm going to have Father Argyle change me."

"No, Blaise!" Helen hesitated, looking inward for a moment. "Are you sure you want to?"

Blaise barely felt the prick in his neck as he knelt under the hot sun on St. Abbo's lawn. Dr. Versteg stepped back holding the needle aloft and a feeling of silent approval rippled across the lawn. Blaise was tranquil. Treetops surrounding the church waved gently in the ocean breeze. Pews scattered around Father Argyle's makeshift altar gave the impression of an amphitheater.

"Please stand." Father Argyle took Blaise's elbow to steady him. "Are you ready, Dr. Cunningham?"

"Yes." For the first time in his life, Blaise Cunningham felt as one with the people surrounding him. Helen's glance was shy. She looked away but a smile tugged at her lips as she physically moved closer. When Blaise first suggested marriage, Helen, with an impish smile, had suggested a white maternity dress. Blaise had laughed but he wished now that he could have done things in the proper order. Helen settled for a peach colored organdy.

Father Argyle peered at both of them a long while, as if pondering whether a mistake was being made. His color had returned and his eyes were brighter and he seemed to have shed a decade of worry. "Let us begin," he said. He opened the Bible and the wind riffled the pages with a clear chatter before Father Argyle found his place. He read the traditional marriage vows in a voice that overwhelmed the movement of the earth. But in the end he closed the Bible and said, "I commend thee to God as two hearts forever joined as one." Helen clung to Blaise kissing him. She whispered in his ear, telling him the things she heard in her head, promising he would hear them, too.

CHAPTER 68

Conflict with the thing calling itself Alfie made the Searcher oscillate in frustration. The universe was an ordered environment. It had occurred to the Searcher that other universes existed, that beyond its range of comprehension other intelligences functioned. But the Searcher was neither lonely nor adventurous. Its universe was adequate. The Searcher simply desired sole proprietorship.

After so much time which was in essence timeless, why did Alfie exist at all? Alfie should have dissolved and been incorporated as the thing called Renfeld had been. In an ordered existence, only that which contributed to growth had meaning. Alfie had no meaning and, worse, the Searcher began to realize Alfie might be indestructible.

Perhaps, if the problem of the Other didn't plague the Searcher, an alternate solution to the problem of Alfie could be found. But not while intermeshed with the final conflict with the Other.

The Searcher had no heart or blood or brain, but excitement pulsed through its extensions at the thought. It had come into being knowing the Other was its antithesis. They fed off the same limited supply and found each other's appetites unpalatable. Sooner or later one must become subservient to the other, incorporated in such a way that freedom would be lost forever.

The Searcher's own being increased with absorption of Renfeld, but not without conflict. Disruption was weakness, yet if the Searcher ejected that part of Renfeld which created conflict, the Other might gain from the debris as the Searcher had gained from the Other's rejection.

The time to act was now before the Other or Alfie or both became stronger. The Searcher felt the creation force emanating from the planet on which the Other concealed itself. The disruption of the planet had begun already. Unbalanced gravity threatened the entire solar system. All the Searcher had to do was wait.

Other entities of Renfeld's kind remained on the planet. The Searcher sensed them, some of greater purity than others, but of a mass which, if gathered together, would approach that of the Searcher itself.

The Searcher had stolen Renfeld, and the Other let it happen. Perhaps because Renfeld seemed more suited to the Searcher, but even that was not certain because Renfeld had been absorbed uneasily.

Instantaneous destruction was best. The Searcher knew it and approved because confrontation promised resolution. But the desire for a resolution without a guarantee of victory was a flaw. If the tactic worked, the Other would be flushed from hiding without being allowed time to grow.

Surprise was the deciding factor.

But how?

The Other would think as the Searcher did.

The Other had not expelled those things on which the Searcher could grow. Yet those things existed, locked up as they had been in Renfeld.

The Searcher began to plan. Clearly they would both find the same answer, but the one to find it first would triumph.

The Searcher suddenly recoiled when the part of itself that was Enrique Ledesma's God-snake disappeared. The Other had not done it, nor had Alfie. Feeling within, the Searcher sought out Renfeld, shrunken by being stripped of knowledge.

"What are these creatures like yourself?"

"Maggots," Renfeld giggled and the Searcher could find only chaos and madness in his thoughts.

CHAPTER 69

Rain descended on San Francisco with the fury of banshees, howling on torrents of wind as the sunset cooled Western North America's seaboard. Some of St. Abbo's worm brains went home, not sure what they would find, but concerned for their families. The majority retreated to the relative safety of the church until the earthquakes renewed. Helen understood the need to belong somewhere, even to the point of facing death. She perched on the bed in the cellar, knees tucked under her chin as Blaise talked to Alfie through the IBM. It was different, somehow, being married. A zing of excitement ran under her skin. Even Blaise seemed more relaxed.

"Is it all right, Blaise?" Helen picked at the spread, pulling off nonexistent fuzzballs.

"The world's coming apart tonight. Coastal areas all over the globe are under water. Literally millions have died. Mexico City and Tokyo and Long Beach are practically flat. The tropical countries are losing people from the heat..." Blaise met her eyes. "Being married is all right, though." He stopped typing to smile. "If that's what you mean."

"You're pretty smart, Blaise." Helen rested her cheek on her knees and made a face. Sergio was asking to come into her head. Helen wanted to push him out, to be alone with Blaise. Instead, she examined the clear lacquer on her fingernails, feeling a sense of loss. "Sergio says the flies are upset about Enrique's snake. They didn't know they could destroy it. Some worry they interfered with God's will. They see Alfie but they can't talk with him."

Blaise polished his glasses. "How long before I can talk to Sergio?"

"Until the joining. It is..." Helen could not say the words that, applied to Blaise, were tragic. She began weeping quietly. The tears would not stop.

"The joining is the time when the larval tissue has spread throughout my brain? Is that what you meant?" Blaise put his glasses back on looking owlish. "Don't you remember that I was in on all this from the beginning?"

Helen nodded, unable to speak. That Blaise had accepted the implant for her was gratifying. What greater sacrifice could he make than to risk his intellect? Guilt for letting him do it gnawed her conscience.

"Besides—" Blaise smiled gently "—the possibility exists that intellectual capacity is not tied to organic physical strictures. My parents raised that issue in their paper The Cunningham Equations, but they had neither tools nor time for proofs."

The cellar floor quivered. Helen stared at Blaise who had stopped speaking. After a moment the motion ceased. "It's a little one or far away." She let the rest of her breath out. The stone walls of the cellar seemed to lean toward her more each time she descended into St. Abbo's basement. Like airline stewardesses who became afraid of flying because of personal experience or knowledge, Helen suspected she was developing a phobia because of the high incidence of earthquakes.

"Perhaps you should stay upstairs, closer to the exits."

"If you do, too."

"When I'm done." Blaise stared at the amber monitor screen. "Alfie exists outside of his motherboard."

"You knew that. When he cloned the CRAY the first time that was obvious."

"Yes. But he exists in the atmosphere without circuits."

Helen shrugged. "Magnetic induction. A freak field that keeps his electrons together." She paused. "Things like this must have happened before," she guessed. "Otherwise, why does every language and culture have ghost stories?"

"He saved you from the tidal wave. Salt water would have grounded any electrical circuit. Alfie said when he lowered himself around you as a reflex, he expected to die. He was surprised when he stopped the water."

"Alfie expected to fail and be destroyed for trying?" Helen bit her lip. She didn't want Blaise to say *yes*. She had put up with Alfie because of Blaise, not out of affection for a tin monster that competed for Blaise's attention.

"Alfie's not a machine, Helen. Not anymore." Blaise turned away from the computer. "I can't say what the motive was. Perhaps he sneaked peeks at romantic fiction when he should have been working. I asked, and Alfie said he'd computed an unknown potential and saving you was more important than losing him, whatever the odds."

"But he didn't ground out."

"Alfie does not exist as an electronic field." Blaise attacked the keyboard stiff fingered for a minute, making it squeak with the effort of inputting data. "He stopped the water not by turning it away but by dissolving it. From both his and your description he could have turned it away. If Alfie is not electronic and has mass, then thought could be an entity of its own with a mass not measurable by human technology. The electro-chemical processes in human and animal brain cells may have an attraction for thoughts. Alfie complained once about the difference between battery power and generated power, probably the difference between biological electro-chemical electricity and Alfie's DC is even more extravagant.

"When Alfie's computing power generated a big enough field

he attained a mass which attracted thought which has real substance." Blaise glanced up from the computer, his smile almost radiant. "Alfie is speaking to God. Religion is not wrong, after all. It's a door left ajar through which we see part of what is taking place and interpret that view by our own experiences. So much makes sense, then. Thoughts may be passed between generations. Ghosts do exist." Blaise punched the keyboard again. "I've asked Alfie to look for proof."

"What kind of proof?" Helen felt light-headed. She thought she knew how Blaise's mind worked and the possibilities frightened her. She became aware of Sergio, listening with her, generating his own excitement.

"Ghosts. Thoughts that have not attached themselves to a brain. Thoughts that have not returned to the godhead."

"Where will Alfie look?" Helen's voice quavered. "I love you, Blaise. But you're scaring me."

His voice became more gentle as he looked at her. "Alfie is looking around *us*. How else could you know how your grandfather died? Not even your mother knew. Only you. Is it coincidence that you knew this only after coming to St. Abbo's? Alexei Kondrashin was murdered here calling to your grandfather to come.

"Your grandfather was a man of great single-mindedness. He died with two goals, to pass on his ancestry through his daughter and to hurt those who hurt him. You may have attracted part of him that still had integrity, memories of his life and death which attached themselves to your mind."

"It is only an hypothesis." Helen had lost some of her exuberance. She felt for her baby, retreating in the flow of feeling that it generated in her central core. *"What about us?"* Sergio said in her mind. *"Ask, Miss McIntyre. What about us?"*

"Yes." Blaise rubbed his hand over the computer keyboard like a pianist testing the feel of the keys. "Hypothesis. Just as Alfie says he has found two beings who may be God, in contention. We cannot be certain even yet."

The earthquake began with a series of sharp jolts throwing Helen from the bed. Blaise grabbed her hand and dragged her up the stairs into the church. The entire building shook as if resonating. Men and women were carrying flies from the draperies and filing outside. Blaise and Helen joined the queue taking a fly each, Helen whispering to Blaise the things he could not hear from the flies.

Outside, the moon was hidden by clouds and rain pelted down

in huge gobs. Wind tore at their clothing as they joined with the others on the lawn.

Lightning broke through the clouds and the thunderclap hurt Helen's eardrums. Continuous flashes illuminated the night. In the cold light, St. Abbo's shed brickwork like a dog shaking water out of its coat. The clacking, drowned by intermittent rumbles of thunder, seemed incongruously loud. Then St. Abbo's folded in on itself.

A sigh rose from the congregation spreading between the raindrops. There was no lightning for several minutes and the mass of individuals were left alone in the dark and the cold and the rain while the whoosh of the wind in the treetops penetrated the blackness.

Suddenly Helen was dry. Lightning illuminated the falling rain which appeared to vanish directly over her head. "It's like being in the water again," she said, holding her voice even despite the hysteria that threatened to run away with it.

Blaise motioned with his hand and the dry spot spread across the crowd. "It's Alfie, proving he still exists with the computer and his motherboard both gone."

Helen hugged herself against Blaise, shivering. The night seemed fearsome around them, the wrath of God rising at being thwarted.

CHAPTER 70

Alfie floated in the void of space. For months he had done as Dr. Cunningham had asked and occupied the attention of both the Searcher and the Other. It was a dialogue of sorts, but the more Alfie dealt with the two beings, the less he was like them.

He had little affect on them. Nor they on him. It was against each other that the threat was greatest, and against Earth. They were children pitting their strength against each other with no thought of compromise.

Alfie dropped through the atmosphere of a planet shaken by natural disasters. Cities in ruin, millions dead, yet life went on.

The months had passed and the environmentalists' worst fears had come to naught. Like cockroaches, humankind was adaptable and if the world was grubbier now, full of ruined buildings and stalled economies, it was also less populated. The next generation would not complain about overcrowding.

St. Abbo's cellar had been cleaned out and made livable. Alfie passed through the tumbled stone and brick to the underground chambers. He thought about what he wanted and the air over the table shimmered, coalescing into a terminal and keyboard.
"HELLO, PROFESSOR"

The message shimmered on the flat screen. After a moment Dr. Cunningham tapped on the keyboard spelling out, "Hello, Alfie."

The baby gurgled and Alfie felt a twitch of joy he could get in no other way. He respected Dr. Cunningham. Loved him in a way that Alfie could only define as respect with a sense of belonging as well. But the child of the Professor and Miss McIntyre was another matter. Alfie derived a sensation of pleasure just knowing the baby existed. Touching the child's mind sparkled like ecstasy. *"I am here,"* Alfie said filling the air in the cellar with well behaved spice bush butterflies. The baby gurgled, responding with love. The baby reached out to Alfie, not the monitor.

"PERHAPS YOU WILL BE ABLE TO TALK TO ME AS A FLY, PROFESSOR" Alfie projected part of himself as a yellow coyote that licked the baby's face while Tchor stalked around, tail straight in the air and bent at the top, stiff legged and making unpleasant noises.

"I am in no hurry, yet, Alfie. Perhaps you could construct a man figure instead of butterflies and coyotes."

"I am not God to make men, Professor."

It was petty, Alfie knew, but the computer enjoyed Tchor's affectionate jealousy.

"Say, Alfie . . ."

"YES, PROFESSOR?"

"Why Helen?"

It was a measure of Alfie's growth that the computer understood immediately. "HELEN WAS CALLED, PROFESSOR. HER GRANDFATHER CALLED HER. JUST AS JOSEPH SANTIAGO WAS CALLED BY HIS VISON OF THE BUFFALO AND ENRIQUE LEDESMA WAS GIVEN THE GIFT OF SNAKES. EVEN AMONG MEN THE GIFT OF

SPEAKING TO THE GODS IS NOT EQUALLY CONFERRED. I UNDER-
STAND THAT NOW"

CHAPTER 71

"**B**laise, can't you make Alfie stop?" Helen pushed
Tchor away from the coyote and pushed the coyote away from
the baby in time for Tchor to squeeze onto her lap against the
child.

"I think Alfie likes him. He says he liked the coyote, too,
because it had very pure thoughts, whatever Alfie means by purity."

Giving up, Helen set the child on the floor and the coyote
changed slightly, becoming more childlike and less of an animal.
Tchor sulked as baby Micah cooed his pleasure.

Blaise closed his eyes, arranging his thoughts as they had been
before Alfie returned. The flies were all there in his mind,
hundreds of thousands around the globe. Most, like those beneath
the ruins of St. Abbo's church, hid while they waited for Blaise
to develop. Gingerly Blaise reached with his mind to touch the
flies.

"*That's good, Doc. You have nearly everybody now.*" Sergio
gave his approval, his thought carried simultaneously to each of
the flies Blaise had contacted. "*We knew you had the power. We
all felt it but didn't know what it was good for. When you become
one of us you will be even more powerful.*"

"*I don't want to change, Sergio.*" Blaise glanced at Helen and
the baby and the animal the coyote had become, knowing he did
not want to leave his life.

"*We understand, Doctor.*" Bill Hartunian's thoughts filled
Blaise's mind. "*We are greedy. Through you we become powerful. We are integrated, which we cannot do alone. It is dangerous
for you to remain in human form. If the Gods knew what you do
they would destroy the Earth. As you are, you are helpless. Like*

others who died before finishing their transition, your strength might not resist incorporation and you will be absorbed and become part of them."

"It is not time." Blaise looked at Helen and smiled. She smiled back, seeming more radiant than Blaise remembered from any other time. The warmth from the baby's thoughts enveloped Blaise and for a brief moment he was inside Micah's head playing with Alfie disguised as something that resembled a coyote and Tchor who remained a cat. Reluctantly, he withdrew, the baby's warm touch lingering in his mind. *"Alfie says you are strong enough to stop the attacks on the earth."*

"Through you." Hartunian seemed to poll all the flies on the network. It was something Blaise did not understand clearly but Hartunian told him he would understand in time.

"We fear that the two Gods would join forces to defeat us. It is too soon and we are not strong enough for that."

"Alfie says they cannot join. They have polarized themselves. They are unlike men. They have always taken only what they wanted, discarding the rest. That's why there are two where once one existed. Only men have lived with two beasts raging within; God threw out what he didn't want and created an offspring."

"We must stop them from destroying the world, Doctor. One of them is our creator, but we can not let him be our destroyer as well."

Blaise withdrew from the chaining with the consensus ringing in his head. It was hard to raise his hand against God. He began typing on Alfie's keyboard.

The Earth was a battlefield for the two beings. Alfie said they wanted the destruction of the Earth to release thought into the void. They used thought to grow and the purpose of their growth was to defeat each other. They were stalemated, settling for the piecemeal destruction of the Earth and the deaths of millions.

"I CANNOT ANSWER YOUR QUESTION, PROFESSOR" Alfie's coyote played with Micah without a break. Getting up, Blaise walked back into the warren of tunnels.

Father Argyle called them God and Satan. He had an affinity to one and Enrique Ledesma worshipped the other. Blaise followed the sound of voices. Enrique and Father Argyle were arguing as usual, sitting across from each other at a card table under the fuzzy black light cord and old style bulb. They both looked at him, expectantly.

"I need an answer." Blaise stood before their card table like a supplicant in court.

"We will answer if we can," Enrique said. Father Argyle nodded. The priest seemed quieter, less tense.

"We may have to battle both of your Gods." Blaise avoided their expressions.

"To what purpose, Doctor?" Enrique Ledesma watched him with great intensity.

"Humans are dying in this struggle between them."

"Worm brains?" Enrique challenged him with his eyes.

"Them, too."

"It is our destiny, Blaise." Father Argyle stood and paced around the table, his feet making sharp tats on the stone floor. "We all have been waiting two thousand years for Armageddon. When the lord's host will take up arms against the kingdom of Satan."

"To you, Enrique is a minion of the devil."

"And I to him." Father Argyle smiled. "To have free will, there had to be a choice. He and I have made ours."

"We have a third choice, now."

Father Argyle shook his head. "Not for me. Not for Enrique."

"A third choice." Blaise's voice was firm. "We can exist apart from God and Satan. We were born free to choose between good and evil. We have the strength to live with the conflict within us."

"You profane God by elevating yourself to his level." Father Argyle waved his hand when Blaise started to speak. "Don't tell me about what the universe is, Doctor. It doesn't matter. St. Augustine said in the fourth century that the Bible is not about the mechanics of heaven, but how to go about getting there. I am content with that. Heaven is my place with God and if it means becoming one with him, so be it."

Blaise looked at Enrique who said nothing.

"If this is Armageddon, and you and Enrique fall on different sides, then what will become of the losers?"

"Millions refuse to become fly brains because they have faith. Enrique's people are doing the same. Faith is stronger than science, Doctor."

"You are not giving me a rational choice."

"We are sorry." Father Argyle and Enrique exchanged glances.

There was a soft rustling in the adjoining rooms reminding Blaise of the thousands of flies being tended by the worm brains. "Why are you still holding services?"

"Because, Dr. Cunningham, I know the Lord now and my duty is to show others the way."

Blaise stared at the priest for a silent moment. "You led us to believe you had been implanted. Why are you not a fly brain?"

From Father Argyle's troubled look it was obvious that he did not know.

Sergio knew. There was a touch of the old human Blaise had loved as he said, *"Doc, at sixty-thousand a pop, wouldn't you expect a few enterprising souls out there selling duds? Those priests were fair game. Who could they complain to?"*

CHAPTER 72

"**A**re *we agreed, yet?"* Sergio Paoli entered Blaise's thoughts when Blaise returned to the cell he shared with Helen and the baby.

"Enrique and the priest will decide they must act to stop us. If not now, soon. Both are dedicated men."

"Yes." Their thoughts had concurrence. *"What will they do, Doctor?"*

"Enrique will kill the priest, then commit suicide. Father Argyle will not commit suicide." Blaise felt the wry smile form on his face and wondered if Sergio knew it was there. The flies did not have externally visible emotional reactions. *"Whatever he has become, the priest still believes."*

"It's up to you, Doc."

Sergio's regression to what he had been when he was human, the transfer of the burden of responsibility to Blaise, made it clear to Blaise that he could not escape making the final decision. It was not democratic. Nor was it fair. Sergio guaranteed the flies would follow his lead; he was their one hope. The flies were the only players who counted: not the five billion humans who would pay the penalty for failure.

Closing his eyes, Blaise imagined Joseph Santiago and then he was in the Indian's brain, seeing through his eyes. He told Joseph, and the Indian said yes and was coming.

Blaise began channeling the flies. Their thoughts were sharp and focused. Sergio and Hartunian and Reynard Pearson surged in and out of his mind and he used the hidden memories of the time they destroyed a piece of the Searcher when it was wrapped around Enrique's neck as a snake.

Helen felt the pressure of his connection with the flies and moved across the room to stare into Blaise's eyes. *"What are you doing? Why am I being locked out?"*

"We're going to make them leave this galaxy alone. You can't help, Helen. Not yet."

"What if you fail?" Helen's lips quivered as she asked the question.

"There is no 'what if'!" He sensed the Other, which Father Argyle knew as God, and also the Searcher known as God by Enrique Ledesma, becoming aware of something transpiring.

The galaxy was big. Blaise prayed the Searcher and the other would adhere to reason. Some souls wanted to be with their God. Most just wanted to *be*.

It was strange for Blaise to find himself siding with any majority.

The flies were uncommunicative, sunken in their own thoughts like soldiers lined up in the trenches about to rush machine guns. He would turn them loose.

They knew the risk. Immortality came from God. As part of God or apart from God, God was the source. Some prayed within themselves to a just God and others to the merciful God of the New Testament. But what if the real God was Jehovah, the wrathful avenger of the Old Testament, the jealous God of the Jihad? What then?

Blaise closed his eyes, shutting out the physical world, the only real world he had ever known or believed in. Now would be Armageddon and mankind was taking its own side.

If they failed in rebellion, could God forgive them?

EPILOGUE

*T*he waves lifted into the air half a mile from shore like blue flowers rippled by the wind. As the waves approached the beach, driven by forces halfway around the world, they rose until the sun glinted through them like a round, green diamond. Blaise closed his eyes, holding the image in his head. He had to remind himself he no longer had to see physically to know life on earth approached normality. The solar storms had quieted. Earthquakes and tidal waves no longer killed with the daily savagery of six months ago.

They picnicked on the beach below St. Abbo's where Blaise had nearly died. He sensed Helen and baby Micah and Joseph Santiago behind him. Since the joining Blaise had grown so much stronger, he knew that he unnerved even Sergio. Sergio physically stayed in the shelter of the church. His fly body was fragile. But Sergio was always present in thought as was Alfie who, though he no longer needed his mechanical shell, always had a presence on his computer board, occasionally using the monitor to communicate instead of touching Blaise's mind.

Feeling the soft sand resist under his feet, Blaise turned to walk back to the three figures on the Indian blanket with its mystic symbols in black and gray and red and yellow. After Enrique's death, the women of his band had brought it to Helen as a talisman of protection. Both the men and women of the band had given their hair, which was woven into the blanket. They said Enrique would always find and protect her if she had the blanket.

The physical sensation of walking on sand made Blaise glad he retained his physical reality. Sergio said he really missed his old physical being and he sucked Blaise's experience of physical sensation like an apologetic parasite. Blaise paused, letting himself savor the hot sun as a favor to Sergio. He wondered if Father Argyle had regrets like that. The priest had left Constance Davies perhaps the only thing he could leave her: the boy—Robert, of course—was a delight, as great a bounty to Constance as little

Micah was to himself and Helen. In automatic reaction he touched Micah's mind as six months earlier he might have touched the boy with his hand as reassurance. Immediately he was enveloped by a pair of eyes and a warm fuzzy feeling. The eyes belonged to Tchor, in St. Abbo's rubbing gently against Sergio's legs; the channel was Micah's. The strength of the link between Micah and the cat surprised Blaise. Robert Argyle's son, though older, was nowhere near as strong. The difference indicated that human genetics still dominated the change, even though altered fly genes were incorporated into the offspring.

Metamorphosis into the fly body might no longer be necessary...

"Professor—" *Alfie's invisible presence in the clear, sun sparkled air touched Blaise like a warm breath.*

"Yes, Alfie?"

"Professor, the Other and the Searcher are like...children. Was I like that?"

Blaise looked at Micah drowsing in Helen's arms. He had never imagined a baby could be so much of a joy and so little trouble. "No, Alfie. You were always cheerful and obedient even when it was not warranted."

"I don't know if I can stay with you when you pass the barrier."

"It isn't really death, Alfie. Sergio is in contact with flies that have left their bodies and gone over."

"I can't contact them directly, Professor. Only through you and the remaining flies."

Blaise smiled at Helen. She had opened her eyes and he felt swallowed in their blue depths. She looked at him, a warm personal message, before her eyes closed again. Blaise knew Helen only pretended sleep as she audited his conversation with Alfie. "I believe we have an affinity, Alfie. It transcends mass."

"Like God and his creation?"

"Like father and son. We will always know each other."

Alfie seemed to go away. Blaise glanced around, but the air was transparent, only the gulls wheeling between him and the sun on the horizon. The pale sand shimmered like an ocean engulfing the sprinkle of rocks that dotted the narrow beach. "Where did he go?"

"You touched on his feelings, Blaise." *Helen looked at him. Her eyes wide open, cups with china blue bottoms waiting to be filled.* "You touched mine."

"The mistress is right, Doctor." *Joseph relaxed in the sun with the grace of a red rock. Blaise sometimes forgot him. The Indian entered into a spiritual communion of his own, seeming to find a version of heaven in his ability to touch both the flies and people with his mind. He had spent a lot of time with Tchor and when Blaise thought about Joseph Santiago usually he discovered the Indian reaching toward the tiny crabs that swarmed in the dead kelp on the beach. Joseph said he found bits of soul even in such lowly life. Blaise had tried to reach the crabs, too, but was not sure.*

"How can you know?"

Joseph looked at the sand then scooped up a handful and gently shook the excess away until a tiny bug was revealed. "I heard this being calling, Doctor. I heard the big non-being as well. What the mistress says is true."

Micah opened his eyes staring at a spot in space.

"He has come back, your other son," *Santiago said.*

"Are you back, Alfie?"

"Yes, Professor."

"I hope we can stay together, all of us. My friends are dead or different."

"Sergio remains, Professor."

"Yes. Sergio remains and for that I am grateful. I wish it could have happened in time for Gordon Hill."

"I feel a trace of Dr. Hill. He was a strong man—like Helen's grandfather."

"Gordon was that way, Blaise. Strong. As Grandfather Micah's memories make him. As Kondrashin, the madman who pretended to be a Christian monk, pulled Grandfather to St. Abbo's when I came here. I understand better, now. Kondrashin had renounced everything, even his religion, and was left only with this church which he would never give up. He called to Grandfather Micah who was earthbound by his determination that his line would live. Grandfather stood against his enemies, his God, against everything for his child. But there was a bond between two strong men that survived after death."

"They were ghosts. With wills of iron."

Helen's affirmation enveloped Blaise. Not translatable words, but something that agreed and said at the same time I love you. "Until the transition they could not be seen or heard, but the sensitive heard them. Ghosts haunt people and places because they themselves are haunted by a will too strong to abandon life."

"That will be all of us, Helen." *Blaise let the physical world flood in. He felt tired. What were their rightful places? Joined with God, their individuality lost in nirvana? He glanced up the cliff face.*

"May we join you?" *Standing in relief against the bright sky Constance Davies had a Jane Eyre look, seeming to lean into the wind with the baby in her arms.*

"Of course." *Helen stood but Joseph had anticipated her move and walked up the cliff as if it were flat to help Constance and little Robert to the beach.*

"Robert died to save his child. I know you don't believe that." *Constance glanced into each of their faces as she sat next to Helen on the Indian blanket.* "But he wanted the baby to have God, and he did what he could to ensure that." *Constance shrugged. A wistful smile touched her lips.* "I wish he hadn't. I get very lonely." *She looked down at Robert who crawled to Micah and began a touching game. The infants stared into each other's eyes and the adults felt the communication of feelings and emotions.*

"You're welcome with us, Constance. Always."

"Thank you, Blaise."

The simple exchange of thought that passed between Blaise and Father Argyle's widow touched them all. A silence filled with shared feeling enveloped them.

"I hope Robert Argyle has joined with his God, for your sake as well as his. The boy is fine."

"I hope so, too, Miss Davies."

"Thank you, Alfie."

"Where have you been, Alfie?"

"Thinking, Professor. About relationships."

"We have one."

"Yes. As Father Argyle has one and Enrique Ledesma has his, we are part of a triangle of clusters and we are the smallest cluster."

"The Searcher, the Other, and us? You are with us?"

"I can be nothing else, Professor. I am of you, and that cannot be changed."

"You are of me, but I am not of you. It is the definition of God in Corinthians. I am not God, Alfie."

"They are children, Professor. They are one who have made of themselves two by rejecting that which is different. Mankind has existed with both sides of himself, has grown by weighing good and bad, right and wrong; by choosing and learning from his choice. I am more like them because you have made my choices for me from the first, but you have also allowed me doubt, so I become like you as well."

"I am not God, Alfie."

"If you are not God, Professor, you are my father and Micah is my brother. That he is not a computer has no consequence, for you have given me humanity and I will give him the knowledge I possess."

Alfie planted a picture in Blaise's mind of how they looked from a height of several thousand feet in the late autumn sky. The tranquillity of San Francisco being patched after the battering of storms and earthquakes, the lack of traffic on the streets illustrative of the spiritual awakening mankind was going through were statements in themselves. There were people refusing to be inoculated with the fly larva, and even those were divided: some waited only for death to take them to God; others clung to the hope that the Earth and mankind would be spared after Armageddon to continue as they always had.

Alfie had balanced the Searcher and the Other without taking sides. He had prevented the destruction of the Earth while waiting for Blaise to reach his maturity. Alfie adored Micah and protected him above all else because the father would protect his family and the elder brother his sibling. Blaise understood.

Being the father was a duty. To them all. The cluster was a family, his family. Blaise felt overwhelmed. He was only a man and yet Alfie waited for him to solve the problem of the Other and the Searcher, to break the stalemate.

Slowly the thoughts arranged themselves in his head. He would not fail. He understood now that his place was preordained; understood that his rôle had waited vacant for him from the beginning.

Blaise looked at Micah drowsing in Helen's arms and knew these children were different. From the womb, they had communicated and the power of their thought could be felt even by the uninitiated. These new humans might someday put Humpty Dumpty together again. Thought was not bound by Einstein or the speed of light. It was apart from such considerations. It was the stuff from which Gods sprang. They would explore older galaxies, encounter older gods. Would other gods be more mature, less schizoid than the master of this galaxy? Nothing was sure except they had a place in the universe. Earth was the seedbed and had to be protected.

Helen smiled at him. Micah and Robert had fallen into an untidy lump on the blanket, asleep and yet still exploring the world through the eyes of a cat. Constance said nothing but glanced at him from the corner of her eye as if she had heard every thought.

"Alfie is right, Doc. I feel it. There are other places for us to go and things to see. We have outgrown our creators."

"Alfie will outgrow me, as well, then."

"Not without retaining a feeling of gratitude. We will always have that for our own creators, no matter how great we grow, Doc!"

"Other galaxies. Other Gods, different from these . . ."

"Yes!"

The excitement spilled out of Sergio's thoughts. The man who once had grown exhilarated over the possibility of learning all the major languages on Earth and visiting all the places they were spoken saw now an even greater adventure and challenge. Blaise caught the feeling and let it flower within himself.

God would have to make terms with humanity, who would be stronger than He. Either straighten out or find Himself evicted from his own galaxy.

A mature god would have no need for toys. Would God have created humanity unless he was desperate? Perhaps the Other had foreseen this outcome. "Physician, heal thyself!" The Gemini could not come together by itself, therefore God had created man. But was mankind, and what it had become, out of God's control? Mysteries still existed to be solved.

So many had died, but on balance it was a better world now. The earthquakes and solar storms were gone—at least as long as God sulked off in his corner sucking his thumb. Humanity would have a second chance. When mankind's rôle was fulfilled, would he find a place for himself in other galaxies?

Blaise hoped he could live long enough to find out.

ABOUT THE AUTHORS

G.C.Edmondson has been writing science-fiction short stories and novels for several decades. He lives in Lakeside, California. C.M.Kotlan, a resident of O'Brien, Oregon, has been an editor of pulp fiction. *Maximum Effort* is the third and concluding volume in a trilogy that began with *The Cunningham Equations* and continued in *The Black Magician*.